OUTSTANDING PR
AND H

Heni
An Indie Next

"A story of strength and reconciliation and change."
—*The Sunday Oregonian*

"Lamb delivers grace, humor and forgiveness . . . positively
irresistible."
—*Publishers Weekly*

"If you loved *Terms of Endearment*, the *Ya Ya Sisterhood*,
and *Steel Magnolias*, you will love *Henry's Sisters*.
Cathy Lamb just keeps getting better and better."
—*The Three Tomatoes Book Club*

The Last Time I Was Me

"Charming."
—*Publishers Weekly*

Julia's Chocolates

"*Julia's Chocolates* is wise, tender, and very funny. In
Julia Bennett, Cathy Lamb has created a deeply wonderful
character, brave and true! I loved this beguiling novel about
love, friendship, and the enchantment of really
good chocolate."
—Luanne Rice, *New York Times* bestselling author

"In *Julia's Chocolates*, Cathy Lamb has created a passel of
characters so weirdly wonderful that you want to hang out
with them all day just to see what they'll do next. It's a ride
that's both hilarious and poignant, and all the while you
cling to the edge of the pickup truck because you'll want to
make sure you stay in for the whole trip."
—Amy Wallen, author of *Moonpies and Movie Stars*

Books by Cathy Lamb

JULIA'S CHOCOLATES

THE LAST TIME I WAS ME

HENRY'S SISTERS

SUCH A PRETTY FACE

Published by Kensington Publishing Corporation

JULIA'S CHOCOLATES

CATHY LAMB

KENSINGTON BOOKS
http://www.kensingtonbooks.com

KENSINGTON BOOKS are published by

Kensington Publishing Corp.
119 West 40th Street
New York, NY 10018

Copyright © 2007 by Cathy Lamb

All rights reserved. No part of this book may be reproduced in any form or by any means without the prior written consent of the Publisher, excepting brief quotes used in reviews.

If you purchased this book without a cover you should be aware that this book is stolen property. It was reported as "unsold and destroyed" to the Publisher and neither the Author nor the Publisher has received any payment for this "stripped book."

All Kensington titles, imprints, and distributed lines are available at special quantity discounts for bulk purchases for sales promotion, premiums, fund-raising, educational, or institutional use.

Special book excerpts or customized printings can also be created to fit specific needs. For details, write or phone the office of the Kensington Special Sales Manager: Attn.: Special Sales Department. Kensington Publishing Corp., 119 West 40th Street, New York, NY 10018. Phone: 1-800-221-2647.

Kensington and the K logo Reg. U.S. Pat. & TM Off.

ISBN-13: 978-0-7582-5563-1
ISBN-10: 0-7582-5563-2

First Kensington Books Trade Paperback Printing: May 2007
First Kensington Books Mass-Market Paperback Printing: April 2010

10 9 8 7 6 5 4 3 2 1

Printed in the United States of America

For my parents:

Bette Jean (Thornburgh) Straight
1941–2002
and
James Stewart Straight

🍃 1 🍃

I left my wedding dress hanging in a tree somewhere in North Dakota.

I don't know why that particular tree appealed to me. Perhaps it was because it looked as if it had given up and died years ago and was still standing because it didn't know what else to do. It was all by itself, the branches gnarled and rough, like the top of someone's knuckles I knew.

I didn't even bother to pull over as there were no other cars on that dusty two-lane road, which was surely an example of what hell looked like: You came from nowhere; you're going nowhere. And here is your only decoration: a dead tree. Enjoy your punishment.

The radio died, and the silence rattled through my brain. I flipped up the trunk and was soon covered with the white fluff and lace and flounce of what was my wedding dress. I had hated it from the start, but he had loved it.

Loved it because it was high-collared and demure and innocent. Lord, I looked like a stuffed white cake when I put it on.

The sun beat down on my head as I stumbled to the tree and peered through the branches to the blue sky tunneling down at me in triangular rays. The labyrinth of branches formed a maze that had no exit. If you were a bug that couldn't fly, you'd be stuck. You'd keep crawling and crawling, desperate to find your way out, but you never would. You'd gasp your last tortured breath in a state of utter confusion and frustration, and that would be that.

Yes, another representation of hell.

The first time I heaved the dress up in the air, it landed right back on my head. And the second time, and the third, which simply increased my fury. I couldn't even get rid of my own wedding dress.

My breath caught in my throat, my heart suddenly started to race, and it felt like the air had been sucked right out of the universe, a sensation I had become more and more familiar with in the last six months. I was operating under the sneaking suspicion that I had some dreadful disease, but I was too scared to find out what it was, and too busy convincing myself I wasn't suicidal to address something as pesky as that.

My arms were weakened from my Herculean efforts and the fact that I could hardly breathe and my freezing-cold hands started to shake. I thought the dress was going to suffocate me, the silk cloying, clinging to my face. I finally gave up and lay facedown in the dirt. Someone, years down the road, would stop their car and lift up the pile of white fluff and find my skeleton. That is, if the buzzards didn't gnaw away at me first. Were there buzzards in North Dakota?

Fear of the buzzards, not of death, made me roll over. I shoved the dress aside and screamed at it, using all the creative swear words I knew. *Yes*, I thought, my body shaking, *I am losing my mind.*

Correction: mind already gone.

Sweat poured off my body as I slammed my dress repeatedly into the ground, maybe to punish it for not getting caught in one of the branches. Maybe to punish it for even existing. I finally slung the dress around my neck like a noose and started climbing the dead tree, sweat droplets teetering off my eyelashes.

The bark peeled and crumbled, but I managed to get up a few feet, and then I gave the white monstrosity a final toss. It hooked on a tiny branch sticking out like a witch's finger. The oversized bodice twisted and turned; the long train, now sporting famous North Dakota dirt, hung toward the parched earth like a snake.

I tried to catch my breath, my heart hammering on high speed as tears scalded my cheeks, no doubt trekking through lines of dirt.

I could still hear the dressmaker. "Why *on earth* do you want such a high neckline?" she had asked, her voice sharp. "With a chest like that, my dear, you should show it off, not cover up!"

I had looked at my big bosoms in her fancy workroom, mirrors all around. They heaved up and down under the white silk as if they wanted to run. The bosoms were as big as my buttocks, I knew, but at least the skirt would cover those.

Robert Stanfield III had been clear. "Make sure you get a wide skirt. I don't want you in one of those slinky dresses that'll show every curve. You don't have the body for that, Turtle."

He always called me Turtle. Or Possum. Or Ferret Eyes. If he was mad he called me Cannonball Butt.

Although I can understand the size of my butt—that came from chocolate-eating binges—I had never understood my bosoms. They had sprouted out, starting in fifth grade and had kept growing and growing. By eighth grade I had begged my mother for breast-reduction surgery. She was actually all for it, but that was because all of her boyfriends kept staring at me. Or touching. Or worse.

The doctor, of course, was appalled and said no. And here

I was, thirty-four years old, with these heaving melons still on me. Note to self: One, get money. Two, get rid of the melons.

But the seamstress couldn't let go of them. "It's your wedding day!" she snapped, her graying hair electrified. "Why do you want to hide yourself?"

I hemmed and hawed standing there, drowning in material so heavy I could hardly walk, and said something really sickening about loving old-fashioned dresses, but I could tell she didn't believe me.

She stuck three pins in her mouth, her huge eyes gaping at me behind her pink-framed glasses. "Humph," she said. "Humph. Well! I've met your fiancé." Her tone was accusatory. As if he were a criminal.

"Yes, well, then, you know his family is a very old Boston family, and they have a certain way." I tried to sound confident, slightly superior. Robert's mother was brilliant at that. Brilliant at making people feel like slugs.

"Very old, *snobby* family," the dressmaker muttered. "And that mother! Talk about a woman with a stick up her butt!" She tried to say that last part quietly, but I heard her. "Well, fine, dear. That's the way you want it, then?"

Again, she pierced me with those sharp owl eyes, and I couldn't move, caught like a trapped mouse who knew she would soon be eaten, one bite at a time.

She dropped her hands. "You're sure?" The words came out muffled through all those pins. "*Very* sure?"

"Yes, of course." And inside me, that's when the real screaming started. Long, high-pitched, raw. It had been quieter for months before then—smothered—but, sometimes I could almost hear my insides crying. I had ignored it. I had a fiancé, finally, and I was keeping him.

I had dug my way out of trailer life and scrambled through school while working full time and battling recurring nightmares of my childhood. I had a decent job in an art museum. People actually thought—and this was the hilarious part—that I was normal. The rancid smell of poverty and low-class living had become but a whiff around me.

I tried to be proud of that.

At that point, the day the dressmaker fitted me, the wedding was exactly two weeks away. Exactly two weeks later I was on the fly.

I bent again to the cracked earth and caught up a handful of dirt, heaving it straight up at the dress, sputtering when some of it landed back on my head.

I spit on the ground, wiping the tears off my face with my dirty hands, flinching when I pressed my left eye too hard, the skin still swollen. Damn. That had been the last straw. I was not going to walk down the aisle with a swollen, purple, bloodied eye.

Then everyone would know how desperate I was.

I whipped around on my heel to the car, then floored the accelerator, the old engine creaking in protest. My wedding dress flapped its good-bye like a ghost. Sickening.

Goodbye, dress, I thought, wiping another flood of tears away. *I'm broke. I'm scared shitless. Inhaling is often difficult for me because of my Dread Disease. But I have no use for you, other than as a decoration on a dead tree in hell.*

I was now headed for the home of my Aunt Lydia in Oregon. Everyone else in our cracked family (cousins and aunts and uncles) thinks she's crazy, which means that she is the only sane one in the bunch.

Robert would come after me, but it would take him a while to find me, as my mother had run off again last week—with her latest boyfriend, to Minnesota—and would not be able to give him Aunt Lydia's address. I almost laughed. Robert would feel so inconvenienced.

But he would come. Burning with fury and humiliation, he would come to eke out some sick, twisted punishment.

My hands shook. I gripped the steering wheel tighter.

* * *

Aunt Lydia is my mother's older half sister. Although my mother decided to marry no less than five times, and have only one (unplanned) child, my aunt has never married or had children. She lives on a farm outside the small town of Golden, Oregon, in a rambling hundred-year-old farmhouse.

When I was a child, Lydia would pay for my plane ticket to come and see her during the summer for six weeks. It was the highlight of my life, a pocket of peace next to my mother's rages and her boyfriends' wandering hands and bunched fists.

Two years ago, before I met Robert, I visited Aunt Lydia. When I arrived she was standing in front of her home, hands on her hips, with that determined look on her face.

When I got close, she engulfed me in a huge hug, then another, and another. "The house is depressed, Julia!" she bellowed, which is the way she always talks. She never speaks at a normal volume; it's always at full speed, full blast. Her long gray hair floated about her face in the light breeze. "It's anxious. On edge. Sad. It needs cheering up!"

My suitcases were piled around me, and I was still clutching a gift to her, a large yellow piggy bank shaped like a pig. I knew she would love it.

"This house should be pink!" She jabbed a finger in the air. "Like a camellia. Like a vagina!"

That week we painted the house pink, like a camellia and a vagina, and the shutters white. "The door to this house must be black," Aunt Lydia announced, her loud voice chasing birds from the tree. "It will ward off evil spirits, disease, and seedy men, and we certainly don't need any of that, now, do we, darlin'?"

"No, Aunt Lydia," I replied, nudging my glasses back up my nose. At the time I hadn't had a date in four years, so even a seedy man might be interesting to me, but I did not say that aloud. My last date had asked me, in a sneaky sort of way, if I had any family money to speak of. When I said I didn't, he excused himself to the bathroom, and I had picked up the check and left when it was clear he was gone for good.

We painted the front door black.

During my visit, people would come to a screeching halt in front of Aunt Lydia's house, as usual. Not because it looked like a pink marshmallow, burned in the center, and not just because she has eight toilets in her front yard.

But let me tell you about the toilets. Two toilets are tucked under a fir tree, two are by the front porch, and the rest are scattered about on the grass. All of them are white, and during every season of the year Aunt Lydia fills them with flowers. Geraniums in the summer, mums in the fall, pansies in the winter, and petunias in the spring. The flowers burst out of those toilets like you wouldn't believe, spilling over the sides.

She also built, with her farmer friend Stash, a huge, arched wooden bridge smack in the middle of her green lawn. The floor of the bridge is painted with black and white checks, and the rails are purple, blue, green, yellow, orange, and red. Yes, just like a rainbow.

But I think it's what is under the trellises that has drivers screeching to a halt. Four trellises, to be exact, lined up like sentinels in the front yard, which are all covered with climbing, blooming roses during the summer. The roses pile one on top of another, dripping down the sides and over the top in soft pink, deep red, and virginal white. And underneath each of the trellises sits a giant concrete pig. Yes, a pig. Each about five feet tall. Aunt Lydia loves pigs. Around the neck of each pig she has hung a sign with the pig's name. Little Dick. Peter Harris. Micah. Stash.

These are the names of men who have made her mad for one reason or another. Little Dick refers to my mother's first husband and my father. His real name was Richard and he decided to leave when I was three.

It is my earliest memory. I am running down the street as fast as I can, crying, wetting my pants, the urine hot as it streams down my legs. My father is tearing down the street on his motorcycle after fighting again with my mother. The plate she threw at him cracked above his head on the wall, missing him by about an inch.

The dish was the last straw, I guess.

Within a week, another man was spending the night in our home. Soon he was Daddy Kevin. Followed by Daddy Fred. Daddy Cuzz. Daddy Max. Daddy Spike, and numerous other daddies. I have not seen my father since then, although I have heard that he was invited to be a guest in the Louisiana State Penitentiary.

The pig named Peter Harris is named after Peter Harris. He is a snobby bank teller in town who refused to take a four-dollar service charge off Aunt Lydia's bank account and then explained the situation to her in a loud and slow voice as if she were a confused and dottery old woman. For her revenge, she simply asked her friend Janice, a concrete artist, to make her another giant pig and then hung the Peter Harris sign around his neck.

When the pigs were featured in a local newspaper, Peter Harris was plenty embarrassed and came out to the farm in his prissy bank suit and told Aunt Lydia to take down the sign.

"I . . . CAN'T . . . DO . . . THAT!" she said, nice and slow, at full volume, as he had done to her. "THE PIG LIKES HIS NAME AND WON'T ALLOW ME TO CHANGE IT."

When Peter started to argue with her, she said, "YOU OBVIOUSLY DON'T UNDERSTAND THE SITUATION. DO YOU HAVE A RELATIVE WHO COULD EXPLAIN THIS TO YOU?"

He kept arguing, stupid man, and even reached for the sign around the five-foot-tall pig's neck, but Aunt Lydia said again, "THERE ARE A LOT OF PEOPLE IN LINE TODAY. PLEASE, MOVE ALONG."

Peter Harris got a little more peeved then and told Lydia he was going to sue her from this side of Wednesday to the next. His anger didn't faze Aunt Lydia.

He was only about three feet away from her when she yelled, "I'LL BE RIGHT BACK," and went inside and grabbed not one, but two rifles, and came out shooting. Peter Harris left. He went straight to the sheriff, but as the sheriff is one of Stash and Aunt Lydia's best friends, he walked Peter Harris to the bar and bought him a few stiff ones, and that was that.

The pig named Micah was named after a skinny, gangly cousin of hers who had a penchant for Jack Daniels and loose women. He was a belligerent drunk who never worked but always had time to pester Aunt Lydia for money. One night when he'd been at the local bar too long, he accidentally crashed his car into her front porch. As she had just painted the front porch yellow with orange railings, that was the last straw.

Lydia dragged his body out of that beater, his head lolling to the side, and stripped him naked. Next she drew a short red negligee over his unconscious head, then hauled him into her own truck. She dumped him off in the middle of a field right behind the town.

The gossip in town over gangly Micah in the red negligee didn't subside for two weeks, and the little girls who found him and ran and got their mothers will never forget the sight. Micah woke up surrounded by giggling women and rough and tough farmers and townspeople who looked at him with disgust and pointed their guns at his personal jewels.

"We don't need your type here, Micah," Old Daniel said, who owned the gasoline station and had regular poker games in the back room.

"You're disgustin'," said Stace Grammar, who worked in a factory and had biceps the size of tree stumps. "Get out of this town. Next thing you know, you and your boyfriend will be demanding equal rights." He shot off his gun six inches over Micah's head. "Take it to the city, boy!"

Micah turned and ran as fast as he could through town to Aunt Lydia's, his bottom jiggling out the back of that red negligee. He ignored people's hoots, hollers, and another gunshot, revved up his truck, and zoomed out of town.

We have never seen Micah again.

Stash is the only man in town who can ever beat Aunt Lydia at poker—that's why a pig has been named after him. No one will play with Aunt Lydia anymore unless she agrees to play for pennies only, except Stash.

Aunt Lydia says he cheats. Stash is a grizzled man with a white beard and a bald head who's built like an ox. His eyes are always laughing, and every time he's come over when I've been there, he brings me fruit or candy and gives Aunt Lydia a plant or a new herb for her windowsill. Twice now he's brought her perfume.

One time during my visit, he brought her a little box with something silky inside. Aunt Lydia shoved it back in the box real quick, tied the ribbon up tight, and threw it at his head. I've never seen Stash laugh so hard. He left the box on the dining room table.

Stash owns hundreds of acres of farmland, all of it surrounding Lydia's five acres. He has a company called Oregon's Natural Products, and he sells his goods all over the nation. He has farmhands and "business hands," as he likes to call them, who help him run "The Biz."

I remembered that Aunt Lydia pretended to get angry every time he came over. "Would you quit staring at me, Stash?" she'd snap, and he would laugh. "Can't look away from a beacon of light," he'd always say. Then he would settle back in a chair and watch my Aunt Lydia as she puttered around the kitchen or talked to her plants.

Whenever Stash could, he'd run his fingers through her thick, graying hair or hug her slender body to his. Now and then she'd allow it, but most of the time she slapped his hands away and told him to behave because there was a child in the house. The last time this happened, I was thirty-two.

He always kissed her right on the lips before he left and then told her what he was going to do. "I'm gonna plow your back acres tomorrow, Lydia Jean," or, "I'm sending the guys out to harvest your corn on Thursday," or, "If you make some more of that jam, I'll sell it for you at the Saturday market."

"Stay off of my land," Aunt Lydia always yelled as the screen door slammed behind him. I could tell she didn't mean it, because she had to try hard to hide her smile. Stash always left with one of Lydia's jars of jelly or fresh-baked bread.

I don't really know why Aunt Lydia has named a pig after Stash except that she really does take her poker seriously and is not a good sport about losing.

But the pigs do gather a lot of attention from anyone driving by her farm. "No sense having a boring front yard," Aunt Lydia has told me on several occasions during our talks. "Life is too short for boredom, and pigs are never boring."

Aunt Lydia also has a real, live pig she calls Melissa Lynn and a multitude of parakeets and lovebirds she lets out of their cages twice a day so they can stretch their wings in the house. Remarkably, they will usually agree to go back into the cages.

She cleans her gun every day after target shooting, loves to do crafts of any type, and grows a little pot in her basement. "For my colitis," she tells me, although she hasn't been to a doctor in decades.

Aunt Lydia, I reflected, was the one stable person in my life, and within about three days, driving almost straight through, I would arrive at her home. I wiped the tears from my face, tears I had no idea had sprung from my eyes, and floored the accelerator, even as fear gnawed at the insides of my stomach like giant claws.

No need to worry about the size of my butt anymore.

Robert was gone, and I had no use for men. None. I wiped my eyes again. Stupid men. Stupid and mean and beastly and selfish. With all the men running the world it is a damn miracle we have not blown ourselves to smithereens. Yet.

The wind whipped around my head, and on impulse, I ripped the rubber band out of my brownish-blondish curls and let them whip around my face for the first time in two years. Robert had had no use for "wild-looking women."

Sweating, dirty, and exhausted, I knew the only cure: chocolate. I drove with my knees and peered through the red bag on the passenger seat, grabbing a Baggie full of chocolate squares I had made myself. The first bit of chocolate hit my tongue like a slice of heaven. The second had my tears drying up. The third had me laughing, in a pathetic sort of way, about my hapless wedding dress.

I dropped two chocolates into my mouth. I had failed in almost every aspect of my life, I thought in a burst of disgusting self-pity, but the one thing I was good at was melting in my mouth right at that moment. I knew chocolate. And, Lord, no one *anywhere* made chocolate as good as I did.

Golden reminded me a bit of the tree where my wedding dress was probably still flapping. It had at one time been a thriving little town, but the logging boom was over, the endangered species had won, and many of the residents had moved on. There was one rather long Main Street, lined by the requisite trees; spring flowers hung from the lampposts. The flowers were the only things that looked alive.

Several of the shops were simply gaping black holes of businesses that had come and gone. But there was a corner drugstore with a broken sign that read S MS DRU STORE.

There was also a movie theater, a cozy-looking coffee shop with red tablecloths, a grocery, an auto repair shop, a hardware store, and several other stores one would expect to see. There were people out on the streets—coming home, I thought, from one of the town's two restaurants or a board meeting at school.

I suddenly felt my heart lighten a bit. I didn't feel like I was going to vomit in fear, the way I did when I was packing up my suitcases in Boston over a week ago, leaving my tight white heels behind.

"For God's sake, Possum, your feet are huge!" I could still hear the sneer in Robert's voice a month ago. "Shit, bitch, don't look at me like that! I'm just stating a fact. You always take things so personally."

He had picked up my foot and then shoved it off his lap as if he couldn't bear to have it touching him for a moment longer.

And still, I tried to appease him, briefly wondering if I could get my feet surgically shortened. But Robert had wanted me. Me—with my frizzy curls and large butt and a family history that could make your blood curdle in your veins and a past I couldn't share for fear of the revulsion I'd see on people's faces. I wanted out of my past before it became my present, and Robert offered me a new type of life, light years from apartments with rats the size of possums and cockroaches that knew no fear.

He had been so charming, so possessive at first, wanting to spend all his time with me, sweeping me off my very big feet. He wanted to know where I was all the time, who I had talked to at the art museum, had any men talked to me? Who?

He had discouraged me from going out with any friends. Not that I had a lot. Okay, I had only two women friends, but he soon thought I shouldn't see them anymore and I had caved in and agreed.

At first I was almost sickeningly dizzy with delight. Robert wanted me all to himself! He loved me! That was why he didn't want other people in my life.

But then I had started to irritate him, and I felt his scorn like a sledgehammer. He would upset me, I would cry, he would pin me down on the bed and badger me until I sobbed, but then he would so sweetly apologize, blaming his bad behavior on a fight with his high-profile father or the checker at the supermarket.

Later Robert sometimes lost his cool and sometimes cracked me in the face with his palm or shoved me against the wall, or leaned me over a chair and stripped off my pants even though I protested. Well . . . later he would beg me to come back to him, to forgive him, and I did.

And soon I had my ring. I had slept with him, and come hell or high water, I was going to get married. I was going to leave my wasted mother and jailbird father behind. I was going to be proper and respected in a proper and respected family.

Even though Robert's violent behavior escalated and scared the living shit out of me more and more as time went on.

I shook my head, blowing thoughts out of my mind, and rolled down my window, the mountain air cool. I inhaled the familiar scent of pine trees as I paused at the town's one and only stoplight. I thought I could hear the river rushing by, although I knew that was unlikely because it was too far out of town.

After running my fingers through my hair, I switched on the overhead light and stared in the rearview mirror. Yep. Looking lovely again. My eyes were swollen, my face a lovely shade of death, my lips puffy and chapped.

Gorgeous. No wonder the men were breaking down my door. I ate more chocolate.

I turned right, went past a few other small businesses, and then through a tiny neighborhood where big wheels and bikes were scattered in the front lawns. Taking a turn into the country, I drove about two miles straight out, then took a left at the mailbox with a giant wooden pig attached to the top with his tongue hanging out.

Like I said earlier, you can't miss Aunt Lydia's house, and

when I turned into the gravel drive and saw the giant pigs, the toilets, and the rainbow bridge, all freshly painted, just like I remembered from years ago, I parked the car, bent my head against the steering wheel, and cried.

And that's how Aunt Lydia found me.

✥ 2 ✥

"**M**en are pricks!" Lydia whacked a wooden spoon against the giant pan, the strawberries melting into a thick goo that would turn out to be the most delicious jam you have ever tasted in your life. I remember drinking the jam right from the jar as a child.

It was Aunt Lydia who had turned me on to cooking and, particularly, baking chocolate desserts and cookies when I was a kid. We had spent hundreds of hours right here among her plants and books and birds. It was the happiest time of my life.

"Big pricks. Little pricks. They all are"—she slammed the wooden spoon against the rim of the pot for the umpteenth time—"pricks!"

I sipped the herbal tea she had thrust at me the instant I arrived. It was laced with a good deal of rum, so I figured I would have at least three or four teas tonight. Maybe five. I took a shuddery breath. The wood stove she'd settled me by in the kitchen was blowing out heat like a fire-breathing dragon.

"But!" Aunt Lydia declared, her green eyes flashing, her thick gray hair dancing around her face as if all the energy packed into her was flying through the follicles. "I am so glad you didn't marry the King Prick, Robert."

I ignored the stab of pain that shot right through my heart. "You never even met him." Why was I defending him? Geez. I am a sick, wimpy woman. And my eye had looked like hard purple and green vomit today, too.

"I knew by the way you talked, by what you *didn't* say. By how I could never call you at your apartment because he would tell you to get off the phone." Her eyes flew open so I saw all the white. "I didn't want to spend any time with King Prick. Do you think I should have Janice make me another pig and name him King Prick?"

I opened and closed my mouth. A giant pig named after my ex-fiancé. There was some appeal.

"No!" Lydia shouted, arguing aloud with herself as she stomped her tiny foot. "I won't. I don't want any piece of him near my property. Oh, Good Lord." She sorted through the cabinets above her head. "I am ALMOST out of cinnamon! I can't BELIEVE it!" This last part she yelled so loud the multitude of birds in three giant cages went crazy.

"I'll go get you some cinnamon—"

"No! Heavens, no, Julia. I'll get some tomorrow. But I JUST CAN'T BELIEVE IT!"

This is classic Lydia. The smallest problems leave her totally exasperated, even furious. Astounded. And yet, the big problems, the terrible things in her life that had happened, like losing her father and brother as a child in a car accident and being stuck in that car with two dead people for hours while the police dismantled the car, she rarely talked about, and when she did it was with strength and courage and acceptance.

And she never talked about being raped by a stranger when she was twenty-five. That was about five years after she had a miscarriage and a drunk doctor slipped with the knife and made Aunt Lydia forever infertile, and then her husband left her. My mother had told me about that.

Aunt Lydia's phone rang again, but she didn't answer it. In the other room I could hear her birds singing to each other.

"Cinnamon. Well, I don't need it for the jam. But I was going to make cinnamon rolls for the girls tonight. It's Psychic Night, and we're having it here, I did tell you, didn't I?"

"Psychic Night?" I choked a bit on my tea, but I could feel the rum floating through my body, and it felt like a river of pure warmth. Or maybe that was the wood stove that was so hot my back felt as if it were on fire.

She pushed her gray hair out of her eyes and peered at me. "We're discussing the power of breasts."

My mug dropped onto the table. "The power of what?"

"The power of our BREASTS!" Aunt Lydia held two fingers in the air, then pointed at her own breasts. "You know what they are! Your mother and I and *you*"—she glared with indignant accusation at my chest—"all have the same big boobs. *And there's power there*. We have to rein it in and use it for our own benefit."

"Absolutely," I muttered. "I need to rein in my Breast Power."

"That's right! Rein in your Breast Power!" Lydia rolled the words in her mouth. "Brrreeeassstt power! Perfect! We'll call it Breast Power Psychic Night. Every week we have a new title. I'm so glad you're here, honey. Here, come and stir the jam for me."

I brought my big breasts with me as I got up obediently and started stirring, watching the strawberries getting smaller and smaller, the color a brilliant burgundy and soft red. It fascinated me, and I couldn't look away as Lydia picked up the phone and called her friends.

I heard her talk to a Katie, a Caroline, and a Lara. It was only on the last phone call that I really listened in.

"No, no, don't bring a thing, Lara," Lydia tossed a dish towel from one hand to another like a ball juggler. "I'm making The Brownies. I ran out of cinnamon! Can you BELIEVE IT? No cinnamon!" She tsked herself deep in her throat. "So a little pot would be okay? Right, just enough to take the edge off of life, that's a good way of putting it, dear.

And good luck with that infernal Bible study. Oh, for God's sakes, you know as sure as hell I don't want to go to anything like that! You know what happened the last time. . . . I don't care if Linda still talks about it, she needed to hear that God doesn't like self-righteous, sanctimonious prisses who tell everyone they're going to burn in hell!"

Aunt Lydia listened again, then laughed. "Oh, heckles! Tell them to pray for my poor soul and that I'm hoping to get saved by next Tuesday at eight o'clock, right before I out-drink Stash before our next poker game. See you tonight, love."

"Who was that?" I finally looked up from my stirring and took another sip of tea. Aunt Lydia tipped a bit more rum into my cup.

"That was the minister's wife, Lara Keene. Dear girl. She'll be here tonight."

I stopped stirring, my jaw falling open. If there had been a fly in that room, it could have flown straight in, making several circles around my molars. *The minister's wife is coming to Breast Power Psychic Night?*"

"Of course! Lara is a splendid person. Very religious. Very kind and holy." Aunt Lydia tightened her lips. "I had to agree to only put a bit of pot in the brownies, though. Lord knows, after Bible study with that group of Bible-thumping losers, she's going to need more than a bit of pot!"

"I can't—"

"What is it?" Aunt Lydia, in a whirl as usual, started dumping the ingredients for brownies all over the huge wooden farm table that sat in the middle of the kitchen. Windows surrounding the room and two sets of French doors brought in the spring sunshine in golden columns, their rays settling on the ingredients as if in blessing.

"I'm surprised, that's all, that a minister's wife would be coming."

"Well, she is. She comes every week. She needs a break from the preaching and screeching and likes to hang out with people who don't use Jesus as a weapon to make others feel inferior. God. One time she dragged me to one of those Bible studies, and I swear all those women wanted to do was stand around and see who could say, 'I've been blessed . . . I've been praying . . . the Lord has been good to me . . . it's His will . . .' the most number of times. It was pathetic. I'm positive God is sick to shit of them."

"Do . . . do other people in the town know that Lara comes to the Psychic Night meetings?" Sheesh. A minister's wife at a meeting like this? In a small town?

"Heck, no. Are you kidding?" Aunt Lydia started melting chocolate. She's good at her chocolate desserts, but not as good as me, although she is better at every other type of dessert. "Four people know. Me, you, Katie, and Caroline. And all of us took an oath over a bottle of brandy and a cigar and swore to keep it secret. Lara needs a place where she can be herself without someone talking about all the souls in Golden who will not be saved and will be thrown into hell to burn there forever like hot dogs on a stick."

I contemplated burning in hell forever like a hot dog on a stick. The rum wound its way down my body. "So, what do you do in these meetings?"

"Caroline is psychic, like I told you, and she tells us what's going to happen to us, which makes it an official Psychic Night. Caroline only charges the women of this town a few dollars to do their readings." Aunt Lydia, a true business-woman, shook her head. "Although she did it for Mrs. Guzman for homemade tequila and for Dr. Tims for some of his salsa. Come to think of it, she also does readings for Terri, the post-mistress, in exchange for Terri's pies, which I think are terrible, and she does readings for Chad Whitmore, whose wife died. He takes care of their four kids and works. In exchange he gives her bacon every year from one of their pigs.

"I have no idea how that woman makes it. She owns a tiny little home, about the size of a dollhouse, not far from here, and drives a car I swear will break down any second.

Stash has had to go and get her on three different occasions."
Aunt Lydia froze for a minute. "I should tell Caroline to
paint her door black to ward off diseases and seedy men. I
can't BELIEVE I forgot to tell her that. Next time she goes
to the city I'll whip on over there and paint it for her. She'll
appreciate that."

I imagined a woman leaving her home with a maroon-
colored door and coming home to a black door. "She makes
a living as a psychic?" I imagined tea leaves and cards and a
woman whose face looked as if it had been shoved through a
strainer, the wrinkles hardened and grooved on her cheeks.
A cigarette would burn aimlessly, and I'd reach to share one
short drag, then stop myself. No more smoking. I had
smoked for a year, then quit. And the lust for nicotine could
still turn my head.

"I wouldn't call it a living, my dear Julia. She ekes out a
life. Barely, I think. She sells her vegetables and fruits at the
farmer's market, and she also bakes bread. Delicious bread.
Bread that can almost bring you to orgasm, it's so good. I
told her to call it Orgasmic Bread, but she didn't think that
would work. She does the readings on the side. I have never
met anyone as frugal as Caroline. Oh, she's generous with a
capital G, but if you gave her a piece of sackcloth, she would
whip out her sewing machine and make the most beautiful
curtains out of it you've ever seen."

I started to chuckle, and Aunt Lydia narrowed her eyes,
but I could see a smile tugging at those full lips of hers.
Sixty-three years old and her mouth was one that many a
starlet had paid thousands and thousands of dollars to
achieve.

"You don't believe she's a real psychic, do you?" Aunt
Lydia put her hands on her hips, as if ready to draw her guns.

I didn't roll my eyes and prided myself on that. I was back
to staring at the reds swirling hotly in the pan.

"I'm telling you, Julia, that woman has been right on the
button so many times—for all of us. And she doesn't charge for

her services on Psychic Night. We try to pay her, but she won't take a dime, so all of us, just to keep her going, drop off eggs and cookies and dinners." Lydia shook her head back and forth like a bowling ball gone crazy. "She's a proud one, though. Proud as a stallion who can flip all the cowboys off his back.

"And it's her upside-down pineapple pound cake and her carrot bread with cream cheese frosting that brings in the most money every year at the church's auction. Every year. Sweetest woman you ever did want to meet, that's dear Caroline. Doesn't open up and tell us much about herself, but she is as straight and honest as my cornstalks."

"I'll look forward to meeting her." Unexpectedly, my eyes filled with tears. "Thanks for letting me come, Aunt Lydia."

"You're welcome. You'll love Psychic Night." She had misinterpreted what I said. She walked over and gave me a big hug, smelling like vanilla and lavender and chocolate, and I buried my face in her shoulder. "Don't cry, love! You've escaped a life prison sentence with King Prick. Prison! You might as well have worn a shirt that said 'Inmate' on the back. 'Inmate of King Prick'! Aren't you happy you're not an inmate?"

"I am," I cried. "I am." I ached. My face hurt. I'm fat. No one would marry me. Robert had wanted to, but as I couldn't see letting my face become his punching bag for forty years, I'd bolted. Finally. And I didn't regret it, did I? I wanted a husband, but not that much. Right?

I pulled away from Lydia, sniffling. She went back to her brownies, extolling the virtues of feminine freedom from men, how they and they alone were responsible for the turmoil of our hormones. Then she made up a song about men with little penises.

My stomach gnawed again at my insides as if anxiety were eating it alive, and my heart suddenly started to palpitate, seemingly bent on cruising me right into a coronary.

I coughed, coughed again, knowing what was coming. The Dread Disease was back. I instantly felt as if I couldn't drag enough air into my deflated lungs. My hands froze into little clenched blocks of ice while at the same time my body trembled as if a giant hand were shaking it.

I closed my eyes in defeat, knowing I could easier stop a speeding train with my ample buttocks than stop this. Death was after my sorry hide, I knew it. I had some horrible, currently unnamed disease that would torture me for months, probably devour my insides until they collapsed into their own wormholes, and then I'd die. That was why my heart often raced as if I'd been running a marathon and why I would feel cold, then burning hot, and my hands shook like leaves on speed and I couldn't breathe.

I listened to Aunt Lydia's penis song half-heartedly, trying to hide the fact that, at least to me, the air had been siphoned from the room, every last molecule of it. I rode the "wave of fear," as I'd dubbed it, the best I could. The air was already gone, and then a familiar feeling of overwhelming panic flooded my body. This happened because my body knew it was dying, I surmised.

I clenched my teeth together and tried to breathe through my nose as dizziness struck. I was going crazy. Losing my mind. Hello, sanitarium!

And then, after what seemed like hours, my heartbeat started to slow, the air whooshed back into the room, and my body stopped trembling. It was replaced by a familiar bone-racking exhaustion, but it was better than suffocating—much better.

I have so come to appreciate air these last months. Air, glorious air.

I pushed my frizzy curls off my damp forehead with a shaky hand, desperate to get my mind away from my imminent death and on to another subject. I inhaled, ragged and low. "What are we doing at Breast Power Psychic Night, then?" I choked out, amazed that Aunt Lydia hadn't noticed that I was temporarily dying, though I prided myself on my ability to hide this peculiar aspect of my life from others.

"Why, we're going to be talking about our breasts. What else did you think we were going to do?" She blinked at me, her huge eyes round and curious as she used both hands to crack six eggs at once with great force against the rim of a pan. "Breasts have a lot to say, Julia! You simply have to listen to them."

I looked at my breasts, still heaving. They had nothing to say, I surmised. They were simply happy they weren't attached to a corpse.

Breast Power Psychic Night had begun in Aunt Lydia's living room. The lights were turned down low, windows opened to let in the freshness of a spring evening in the mountains. The furniture might be old, but it was plush and worn and plentiful. A red couch and two purple loveseats were covered with pillows Aunt Lydia had embroidered and two quilts she had sewn. Stacks of books competed for space with herbs growing in huge trays, a forest of plants, and an abundance of vanilla-scented candles.

A huge wreath decorated with dried roses, purple and sage-colored ribbons, raffia, pinecones, and tiny birdhouses hung on the fireplace hearth. As much as my Aunt Lydia likes her guns and her chickens, she loves a good craft project. Martha Stewart would love her.

"We're here to find the power within our breasts," Aunt Lydia semi-shouted, cupping her boobs, her tie-dyed T-shirt bunching up under her hands. "Men have objectified us long enough, judged us by the size of our breasts. Our worth summed up with a look at our top half."

The darkened room flickered with candlelight, alighting on each of the women's faces as Lydia led the group. I laced my fingers together, almost surprised I wasn't having another coronary.

Here I was, sitting on an overstuffed pillow, in the dark, on the floor, about to flip off my shirt in front of three women I didn't know, and I felt perfectly calm. As if I disrobed and swung my boobs around and about all the time in front of people.

"It's so nice to meet you," Katie Margold said quietly over the candlelight when Aunt Lydia made a quick trip to the bathroom to expel "the earth's yellow poisons" from her bladder.

Katie's brown eyes were soft, like chocolate, but they looked tired, defeated. They skirted about as if she were waiting for me to quickly move on and talk to someone else more interesting. But then she examined my cheek and my eye, both still a lovely shade of purple with puke-green thrown in. Her lips pursed, though not in judgment.

"It's nice to meet you, too," I said. "I love your hair. It's so bouncy. It reminds me of mermaid hair."

Oh, I am strange, I thought instantly, my shoulders slumping. I was searching for something to say, and there it was.

Tall, no makeup, and heavy, Katie wore an old green T-shirt with a couple of stains and baggy blue jeans. But her hair was her crowning glory. A reddish auburn color, it tumbled in deep waves down her back, clean and shiny. She could have been in one of those shampoo ads.

But I felt like an idiot. The poor woman probably thought I was gay. I wasn't gay, but neither did I particularly like men at this point in my life.

"Oh! Well, I . . ." it was hard to tell in the darkened room, but I think Katie blushed a little, then looked enormously pleased, and huge tears formed in her eyes, giant, perfectly shaped tears. If eyes had to breathe for us, she would have drowned.

I stumbled about for something else to say. Good Lord. I'd been invited to Breast Power Psychic Night, and already I had one of the women in tears. I was a classless, chubby, socially inept cow, who often couldn't breathe and who was going to be chased down by an obsessive fiancé at any moment.

Katie wiped the tears away with her fingers. "Thank you." She sighed, the sigh a little shaky.

The thank-you was so heartfelt, I felt hot tears spring to my own eyes. "You're welcome. I've always wanted red hair, long hair. I always thought . . . I saw this mermaid in a book with long red hair once, and I never forgot it. Compared to a mop of dirty-blond curls, well—"

"I remember a mermaid just like that, too—the Little Mermaid." Her brown eyes pooled again. "I can't believe I'm crying about a mermaid!"

I couldn't believe she cried about mermaids, either. "What a loon," I said, shaking my head, and Katie laughed.

But I knew I didn't really think she was a loon. About a month ago, I had stood in line at the library and cried because it was so wonderful I could check out books without paying for them. I didn't have any money that day because I had taken Robert out to an expensive meal the night before, which he had complained about being tasteless, and I thought to myself, "I love Thomas Jefferson." And then I had cried, right there in line.

Katie and I were two of a pathetic kind.

To her left sat the psychic, Caroline Harper, and there was not a woman on the planet who looked less like a psychic than she. Petite and willowy, wearing a loose flowered skirt and a black tank top, she looked more like a model for tiny women. High cheekbones plunged to a full mouth, her murky, sea-green eyes slanting in her face.

The only remarkable thing was the constant twitching of her right eye, which she now and then raised a hand to rub, to hold, as if willing the twitch away. When she'd walked into the house, I'd instantly reached up to tuck my wayward curls behind my ears, feeling like a mammoth, worm-eating buffalo as I towered over her. One wrong step and I'd crush the woman.

Caroline was the frugal one. The woman who lived off pennies and made the best pineapple upside-down cake ever.

The one who sold produce at the farmer's market each week and did readings on the side and barely made it month to month with the help of her neighbors, those who dropped off eggs and meals and were then treated the next day to one of Caroline's perfect baked goods.

Caroline smiled at me over the candlelight, her smile huge, her teeth large and brilliant white, her eyes crinkling just a bit in the corners. I judged her to be about five years older than myself.

She peered into my eyes, bruised and otherwise, and I waited for her to recognize the quaking, ridiculous woman with a yucky past and a strange disease that I am. She would foresee my future and turn pale and sickly-looking.

But she didn't. In fact, she just kept smiling at me. Cheerful-like. Open. For some reason she reminded me of Cheerios.

"Welcome to Golden." Caroline's eye kept winking, but the rest of her face was peaceful, tranquil. "Did Lydia tell you that she calls this Psychic Night each week?"

I nodded my assent, kneading the edge of my blue sweater in my lap, hoping it would hide my hips. Had I gotten even fatter since tiny Caroline walked through the door?

"Lydia!" she laughed, as Aunt Lydia walked back into the room, her bladder apparently having expelled all poisonous yellow liquids from her body. Caroline's laughter bubbled right there at the surface, even as that eye kept twitching. Twitch. Twitch.

"Well, it is, Caroline! I always call it Psychic Night. After each session, you do our readings for us." Lydia then glared at her. "I did not like my reading last week, Car-o-line. Not at all."

"But I was right, wasn't I?" Caroline laughed, pushing her long brown hair away from her finely carved face. She looked like a queen, not a near-poverty stricken neighbor living off her backyard's vegetables.

"You planned it with Stash," Lydia declared, hands on hips.

"I did nothing of the sort. I merely told you that I saw a bit of red in your reading. Soft red for love. For passion. It was all around you, Lydia. Red, red, red." Caroline smiled, and two dimples flashed in her cheeks.

"And then Stash brought me this!" Lydia stood with righteous anger and opened a drawer of a nearby armoire and yanked out a red negligee with black furry trim.

I tried not to laugh.

"He is a bad-mannered old fool. Comes by, parks his tractor in front of my house, hands me the box, forces a kiss on me, and drives off. I'm going to get another pig and name him Stash Two, that I am."

Aunt Lydia dropped onto the floor with me and Katie and Caroline, fluffing out the negligee. "Stash thinks that because he owns all the land surrounding my place that he can do what he wants. Really! As if I'd get in something like that!"

"Be glad you get negligees."

The words, soft, with a tinge of bitterness, dropped from Katie's lips like tiny ballistic missiles. When we turned to look at her, she covered her mouth with both hands. "Oh dear. Dear, dear. I didn't mean to sound so pitiful. Of course, my husband and I are past that stage, and look at me. I'd hardly fit in one, anyhow!" She laughed, hollow and embarrassed.

Lydia tossed the negligee over her shoulder, and it landed in a silky pile on the floor. "I am glad we're having Breast Power Psychic Night tonight! A negligee is really a gift to the man. To the man!" She leaned over and shook Katie's shoulders, the flame from the candle only inches away from her swinging gray braids. I reached out and lifted them away before her hair turned into a flaming mass, but Aunt Lydia hardly noticed.

"Do you think women, *real women*, want to be dressed up like hooker dolls? Lace isn't comfortable. It itches my crotch. It causes me to break out in an emotional rash! These negligees go straight up your butt, and no woman should be showing the backs of her thighs to any man when she's passed the age of sixteen. See? This is what men do to us! They make us feel like sexual objects who are there to please them, listen to them, cater to them!"

"Right," said Katie. Her brown eyes darted to the negligee, and I saw her swallow hard. "We don't need that. It's ridiculous, really. We're not toys. It's ridiculous that women would want to wear them in the first place."

"Of course it is!" We all looked at our fearless leader with more than a little fear as she raised both fists in the air. "They drive up in tractors, toss us lingerie that we're supposed to model for them, making us feel downright cheap, with our breasts yanked to our throats, then we're to tickle their teensies, and they drive off! Leaving our breasts spiritually unawakened. Dead!"

"Amen to that. Dead breasts, I mean." The door slammed as another woman walked in, dropping three bottles of wine on the kitchen counter, then expertly opening each one of them. I could only assume it was Lara Keene, the minister's wife.

Lara grabbed five huge goblets from the cupboards. The goblets were in the shapes of ogres. She filled each ogre goblet to the top. "Praise be to God that I did not kill Mrs. Ellensby."

Praise be to God that she didn't kill Mrs. Ellensby?

Lara distributed the wine to all of us, with a nod and a perfunctory smile in my direction. "She called me over, supposedly to study the Bible, then left the room 'for a wee minute' to spend $5,489 online at Pottery Avenue. Then, in the midst of my reading Psalms to her, at her request, she informed me that she sees no reason to have a fund-raiser for a new roof for the church even though there's an enormous hole over the preschoolers' classroom."

Lara imitated the woman's voice by pitching hers at the highest level, then pinching her throat and waggling it back and forth. "'We don't need another roof. We need to pray to God and ask Him what He feels we need. God will provide what needs to be provided. That's His will, and I know that God will say that the church is fine. I know how God works! People have no money in this town!'" Lara's voice rose several octaves, shrill like a fish wife's. "'We're scraping by, Lara. Really. You young ministers. You need everything. You want everything. Im-med-i-ately.'"

Lara settled herself to my left and took a very long drink of wine. The ogre goblet was half empty when she finally put it down. "I told her that it was difficult for the children to concentrate on their Bible verses when there was water trickling down a wall, and she said, 'I am going to pray for you, Mrs. Keene. Pray that you will grow with the Lord and not against Him. Suffering is what makes us better people. Suffering is what makes us sacrifice for others. Jesus suffered for us, and we must suffer for Him, and those young children need to learn at an early age that not everything in life is perfect. Now, let's hurry up and pray. I need to get my manicure.'"

"Damn." Lara slumped into the circle beside us. "Damn and damnation."

The silence was complete as all of us women, preparing for Breast Power Psychic Night, contemplated damn and damnation.

After several quiet minutes, Lydia spoke up, "Lara, this is my niece, Julia."

Lara and I shook hands. "A pleasure," I said. "What did she buy?"

"Sorry?" Lara looked confused.

"The woman who talks to God. Who knows what He wants. Perhaps God told her what to buy at Pottery Avenue?"

Lara smiled, then sagged. "Well. He told her to buy three different sets of dishes, a chair, tablecloths, a new set of pans . . . I listened to her arguing with the saleswoman about the bill. 'No' to the roof for the preschoolers, but 'yes' to a set of striped picnic basket plates for $535."

Lara's blond hair was ripped up tight into a bun. Bright blue eyes summed me up pretty quickly. I knew that she was taller than me, but almost as thin as the twitchy-eyed but beautiful psychic.

She was wearing proper beige pants. Proper, boring flat shoes. A dull blue blouse that was buttoned straight up. A medium-sized gold cross hung around her neck.

"Nice black eye," she observed. "Who did that to you?"

I was not surprised by her bluntness. "My ex-fiancé. Fine family. Fine old, respected Bostonian family," I muttered. "Fine, proper, respected men dot the family, and they all take fine, old potshots at their wives. Apparently they don't beat up on their girlfriends—no, scratch that. Those scandals are covered up. Who wants to argue with a fine, old respected family, especially when they imply that the woman, the hittee in question is clearly an addict and a slut and after the family money by filing frivolous lawsuits."

"Ah, I see. Don't worry. They'll slip right into hell when they die. If there's one thing I know, it's that wife beaters and child abusers go straight on down. Forgiveness does not extend to those who hurt the innocent with no remorse." Lara took another long sip of her wine, then tiredly ripped the rubber band out of her hair, letting her blond locks fall about her shoulders.

She undid the top few buttons of her sweater and the stiffly starched white blouse, twisting her neck around from right to left as if the shirt had been strangling her.

The transformation was astounding. Lara had gone from looking like, well, like a proper, devout *minister's wife*, to looking like a college student who sat around with friends and drank every night.

Lara raised her glass to me, her mouth trembling. "You're lucky you left. You would have had to be prim and proper

your whole life, and you would have to smother exactly who
you are as a woman. Forever. You would have to do what
everyone expected you to do, be who everyone expected you
to be."

She drank again, and I saw a pulse leap in her temple as
she watched the flame dance on the candle.

"And if you deviated from the course even a little bit,
people would look at you with shock and disgust, and your
mother-in-law would suggest to your husband that you
needed counseling and more Bible readings. You, as a person, would be gone. Squashed down like a bug. All because
of a mistake you made years ago, when you were young and
in love and desperate to please your father but even more
desperate to escape from him."

"Eat this." Lydia handed her a brownie. "Here. Have two."

"Is there?" I heard hope in Lara's voice as she took a bite.

"Just a bit. As requested."

Lara ate the brownie, interspersed with long gulps of
wine, her eyes closed tight. She shook her head. "I'm sorry,
what is your name again?"

I told her.

"Julia. Julia. Julia." She rolled the name around in her
mouth, as if tasting it. "That is a lovely, lovely name. And
you escaped. *You escaped*!"

"Quiet, ladies, quiet!" Aunt Lydia commanded, taking a
deep breath, the candlelight flickering against the soft curves
of her face. After Lara's "escape" comment we had all taken
a detour away from awakening our breasts. The conversation
had flown as we all discussed our own quick escapes. I did
not mention Robert. "Reach into your inner souls, into your
breasts. Do it now. Come on, now, dive into the rhythm of
your body, harness your inner beat, and don't be shy."

Perhaps it was the wine, but I didn't feel a shy bone in my

body as I whisked off my shirt, then my bra. I almost sighed with relief as my boobs were released from their bondage. Wearing a bra with boobs this size can make you feel like you're wearing giant blobs of hot metal secured to your chest with duct tape.

I took a deep breath and looked at my boobs as instructed. They were huge, but at least the nipples still looked straight ahead, like they should. Go, nipples!

I studiously avoided looking at the other women's breasts, giving them privacy as I heard bras unhook and shirts come off. The candles flickered again.

"Now, look at one another," Aunt Lydia insisted.

Oh, sheesh. I didn't want to look. I resisted, but could feel other eyes on me, so I lifted my head. What the heck. The first breasts my eyes landed on were Lydia's. Big, like mine. Sagging a bit, but I have to say she looked great.

Caroline's were small and pretty. I wondered if, being a psychic, she could see into the future and see what her breasts would look like in fifty years.

Lara had a fairly large chest. She certainly covered up well. I could hate her for having such perfect boobs, but she was swigging another long drink of wine, and I knew why she was drinking, so I decided not to hate her. I wouldn't have been able to stand being a minister's wife, either.

Katie's boobs were even bigger than mine.

She must have been thinking the same thing. "I have wanted to get rid of these things since I was a kid," she said quietly.

"Me too. God might as well have attached mammoth watermelons to my chest."

Katie stifled a giggle.

"Ladies, we are one, under the Sisterhood of Women. The Sisterhood of Breasts," Lydia said, her voice low and hypnotic as she clasped her hands in front of her as if in prayer. "No breasts are better than others, just different." I would have to disagree with her on that, but I kept my mouthola shut. "Now, ladies, close your eyes. Hold your breasts. Feel the soul inside of them, the core of your womanhood."

The core of my womanhood was tattered and tired, I thought. Did I even have a core anymore?

"There is courage in our breasts," Aunt Lydia said, her voice rising. "There is fortitude. There is passion. But we must keep them free of all evil forces, men included. We must offer them freedom."

Freedom for my breasts? If they were any more free at the moment, they would pop off my chest and do a jig. I grabbed them anyhow. They felt like they always feel. Heavy. Very, very heavy. I wondered for the eightieth time how much they weighed. A hundred pounds each?

"The evil of this world surrounds us, surrounds our nipples," Aunt Lydia intoned. "We must sensitize our nipples to the dangers, to respond to their cries for help!"

My nipples were probably crying out to be attached to less weight.

"Do not hate your breasts, ladies! Do not diminish them! Your inner soul tells you to love them. Love them! Love them! Love them!"

We were quiet. I closed my eyes, thought about the Mammoth Melons attached to my chest and tried to love them, love them, *love them*.

"I have reached into my inner soul, into my boobs," Lara cried, "and I think I need more wine." She grabbed another bottle. "And a new life."

"But, Lara," said the psychic, her eye twitching in quick succession, clearly not focusing on her perky breasts. "What about Jerry? He loves you and you—"

"He loves who he thinks I am, who he wants me to be!" Lara cried. "And I'm not that person. I can't be that person anymore. *I just can't.*"

I rubbed my fingers over my injured eye. Yep. Still

swollen. Still painful, although dulled by the wine. "What kind of a person is that?"

"What?"

"You say you can't be the type of person that Jerry wants. What kind of a person is that?"

"It's a nothing person," she said bitterly. "A nothing person."

A Nothing Person. Yes. I knew a person like that. A Nothing Person. I grabbed the mirror, looked at the underside of my bulging breast. There did not seem to be any power there at all. Only a large curve that pointed more or less up. I closed my eyes. At least the underside of my breast didn't curve downward like a ski slope yet.

Still, I knew a nothing breast on top of a nothing person when I saw it. I lifted my head just enough to let a bit more wine slide down my throat. For a moment I wondered if I'd run far enough for Robert to leave me alone.

No, I told myself. That was impossible. He hated to lose. He would come.

"I don't want to help run a church any more," Lara said, her voice ragged. "I don't."

The silence was deep, heavy. It covered the five of us like an invisible black wool blanket.

"Well, then!" Aunt Lydia declared, putting both hands under her boobs and giving them a lift. "Grab those boobies! What do they tell you to do?"

Even in the darkness I could see Lara roll her eyes, but she cupped both her breasts, studying the nipples as if they would suddenly sprout mouths and tell her exactly what she wanted to know. "They're telling me to do what I want to do."

"Good!" Aunt Lydia stood up, at least a dozen braids swinging over her naked breasts, the candlelight flashing against her skin. Sixty-three years old. I got teary-eyed looking at her. She was fabulous. Must be all the target shooting and jam making and brownies with pot and the tea she drank that was laced with rum.

"Your breasts, ladies, *will talk to you*. They'll offer sage advice, help to corral in your courage, steer you on your womanly course. They are, after all, closest to your heart. So. Tell us, Lara, what do you want to do? What have your breasts communicated to you?"

"That's simple." Lara dropped her breasts, her eyes flashing in anger, her mouth twisting. "They can't stand being a minister's wife any longer. They can't stand the lid that is tightly nailed down onto the box. They want out. Completely out. They want to be free. Very free. Completely free." She took another swig of wine, her blond hair falling about her shoulders.

"Well, then! Your breasts are offering you truth! Wisdom! Share more, share!" Lydia's eyes opened wide, awaiting the official announcement.

"They want me to leave here and become an artist," Lara said quietly. "In New York."

And then she burst into tears, burying her face in her hands, the cross dangling between her knees until she reached up and broke it right off the chain.

3

Sometimes life is better when you're woozy. Very woozy. My shirt and bra were still off, discarded somewhere behind the couch, the candles flickering between me and the four other women.

We were still examining our boobs, trying to understand their psychology. Well, all of us except for Lara, who was on her sixth brownie and fourth glass of wine and laughing hysterically on the couch as she mimicked the voices of various people in her church's congregation.

At one point she stopped, yanked her boobs up so she could see them well, and said to me, "Still young. Still happy-looking. What happened to *me*?" She kept laughing, the sound getting more high-pitched as the evening went on.

I glanced down at the Mammoth Melons. I had always felt completely detached from my breasts, as if they were another appendage, an appendage that I didn't need and didn't want. 35 DD. And they had been that big and bouncy since eighth grade. I almost needed a harness to rein the things in.

The women in our family line for as far back as we could remember had all had huge boobs. Huge, protruding breasts. We'd all tried to hide them. Even in old family portraits the women are sitting ever so slightly hunched, their shoulders pulled inward, as if they couldn't stand for future generations to know what lived on their chests.

Yes, we all tried to hide our top halves, except for my mother, who wore them like a giant come-and-get-me banner.

And it had worked. Many husbands. Many boyfriends.

My whole childhood was filled with Creeps Who Liked Large Breasts. Even on children. I groaned as an avalanche of memories started to cave in on me, black and dirty and horrifying, and I fought them off, knowing how they bended what little sanity I felt I had left.

Robert had liked my breasts, but really nothing else. He had played with them, squeezing them until I'd cried out, pushing them together, then back out. Massaging them as one might massage bread.

"Come on, baby," he would whisper, "arch your back for me." He'd push me onto his king-sized bed in his bachelor pad, insist I strip, then make me pose in various positions.

At first I had liked it. "You look hot, baby. Open your mouth. Oh, yeah." I thought it was kind of sexy. I had only been with one man before Robert, a hurried and somewhat drunken affair, and that a man like Robert wanted to be with me at all, that he was willing to risk seeing me naked, well, that in itself was sexy.

He'd straddle me and play with my boobs with his hands, his mouth, then he'd flip me over and do the same thing. It was as if my breasts were the only thing about me he really liked. He rarely kissed me at all, even less so on the lips, and the second after we'd finished having sex—and he'd never noticed that I'd never orgasmed—we were out of bed, and he would start in on his complaints and demands . . .

"We're going to my mother's tomorrow night. . . . I know your cooking class is then. You're going to have to skip it. I already told her and my father we would be there. My mother wants to talk to you about your clothes. It's about time, too."

Or, "Those pants, well"—a mean laugh—"they don't quite look right, do they? On someone who was built thinner than you, they might, but Cannonball, these aren't made for you."

And the worst, "Would it kill you to show a little enthusiasm in bed? What is wrong with you? I think it would be easier to have sex with an icicle."

And still I stayed. I tried to please him. That didn't work. I tried walking away. He came after me. I tried to fight back, but he squashed all my efforts. By the time I took off on our wedding day, I realized I hated him for making me hate myself.

"There is power in your breasts!" Lydia boomed. "Sit up straighter, Katie! Look for your power!"

I watched Katie struggle to sit up straight, her eyes at half-mast. Her face was more relaxed now than it had been, the wine having worked its wonders, her red hair only loosely held back by a rubber band, but even in the candlelight I could see her exhaustion, and I sensed her profound unhappiness, as if black charcoals had settled on her soul.

"I think my power was lost the first day I gave birth," she said with a groan. She picked up the mirror that Lydia handed to her and held it up to her large, tired-looking breasts. Her bra, I had noted, was tattered and frayed, a dull beige. Her bra and her sweatshirt were folded neatly behind her.

"I have nursed four children. One still reaches for me as soon as I walk in the door. Sometimes I think it's like having a pet leech. Oh, God. Did I just call my child a pet leech?" She groaned again, dropping the mirror.

"He's not a leech," she muttered, tears pooling in those dark eyes. "He's so adorable, I could cry. Yesterday he climbed on my lap and kissed me on the cheek and said, 'I love you better than the cat, Momma.' Better than the cat! And he loves that cat."

"You must regain yourself through your breasts, Katie!" Lydia admonished although I noticed that her voice was softer. "You have to make some choices."

"I've made a choice to sit in this house, on this floor, and drink a lot of vine. I mean wine. It's the perfect choice." Katie lay back down and giggled, balancing a mirror on her breast. "There are no children to take care of. I am doing no housework in my home right now, or anyone else's. I am not dealing with Mrs. Nunley, who told me today I wasn't a good grout cleaner."

"You're not a good grout cleaner!" Lara laughed, taking a break from her drunken mimicking. "Horrors. I am sure you will be going to hell for that! I will pray for you."

"That would be helpful, Lara," Katie said. "Pray also that I don't try to grout Mrs. Nunley's face."

"How many houses did you clean this week?" Aunt Lydia asked.

"Fifteen so far. Fifteen houses in Golden are bright and spanking-clean because of my vacuum cleaner and dust rag. See?" she declared, sitting up again and wobbling just a bit. "I have become what I wanted to become. A business owner! Whooo hooo! Katie's Cleaning."

But the whooo hooo came out weak, tired.

I knew something was up with Katie, and I knew the other women knew, too, by the way they looked at her, but no one said a thing.

"Mrs. Nunley said she is not going to recommend me to any of her friends unless I whiten the grout. 'Make it as white as my teeth' she told me. '*As white as my teeth.*' Then she pulled back her lips with those wrinkled hands of hers and showed me her teeth, sticking out her tongue so I could see right down her throat."

Katie started to laugh. I noticed the slight pitch of hysteria. "They weren't white! She had rows of those silver fillings, and her front teeth were yellow. And there she is, with a sick grin on her face, her fingers pulling her lips back to her ears and telling me to make her grout as white as her teeth. At least I have my won-der-ful husband to support me."

I did not miss the looks that Caroline, Lydia, and Lara exchanged.

"Oh, gag me," Lara said. "Just ggaaaagggg me."

Katie's laughter filled the room, but none of the other women seemed to think this was the slightest bit amusing.

The lights were still low, the candles burning, but the Breast Power Psychic Night group had broken up a bit. Lara had passed out on the couch after declaring that she could hear the state of New York calling her name through aliens. Lydia had pulled a sweater over her head and sat embroidering a pillow that read, "Sex is good for the skin. Men aren't."

Katie had wrapped an afghan around herself and was in a rocking chair by the window, staring straight out, not moving, not reading, just staring.

And Caroline and I were huddled on the floor, sitting across from each other. Caroline and I had both put our shirts and bras back on.

I had heard nothing from my boobs except that I was fat, with no job, almost no money, and had a Dread Disease and a sicko ex-fiancé I had had to escape from.

Caroline the Psychic didn't ask to see my hand to trace my lines. She didn't ask for my favorite number. There were no fancy-schmancy teacups or tarot cards, only a flickering candle between us and Lydia's quiet humming. I think it was a southern song, one the slaves would have sung in the fields. A song with an upbeat tune but words so tragic, so hopeless you wanted to cry.

Caroline stared at me. "Let me look at your knees."

"My knees?" She nodded. "Okeydokey. You're the psychic. If you can read knees, all the better." I pulled up my skirt. My knees were scarred in several places from childhood.

"What's this scar from?" Caroline asked, pointing to the smallest scar, shaped like a half moon.

"I was hit by a car."

"Hmmm," Caroline said, her shiny brown hair surrounding her head like a veil.

I thought I heard wisdom in her "Hmmm."

"And this one?"

"That one I got when I was a baby."

She arched an eyebrow at me. It looked like the wing of a blackbird.

"My mother said I was too fussy that day. She put me on the patio of our apartment when it was raining. I stood up in my high chair and fell over the top."

I didn't tell her the rest of it. Aunt Lydia had told me later what happened. She got the scoop from the neighbor next door, who heard my pathetic cries. The neighbor had rushed over and untangled me from the tray of my high chair.

There was a gash on my head where the tray of my high chair had hit me when it slipped off in the crash. My hands, elbows, and knees were also bleeding messes. The gashes required nineteen stitches. The new scrapes and bruises simply added to the old scrapes and bruises and two old breaks in my bones.

The neighbor had banged on the sliding glass door, but my mother didn't answer, being passed out in bed, upset and drunk because another boyfriend had walked out. So the neighbor had called the police, who called Children's Services and an ambulance. I went to the hospital and had eleven stitches put in my head and eight on my knees. I still have the scars.

Children's Services picked me up for the third time that year and deposited me in a foster home until Aunt Lydia found out about it and came and got me. She petitioned the court for custody, for the second time, but lost when my mother, Candy, who is very petite, except for her breasts, and can look like the most harmless, lovely woman anyone has ever seen, convinced the judge that she had mended the error of her ways, wasn't drinking anymore, and had found Christ. She was born again, praise the Lord. She was walking with Jesus and felt blessed to have this second chance at living a holy life.

The judge, a devout Christian, believed her, and back I went with my mother. Aunt Lydia was furious, she told me later, but my mother was careful from then on out. Not because she wanted me, but because she didn't want Lydia to have me. Then Lydia would have won. Candy couldn't have that. Ever. Even if her child's life was a miserable, terrifying mess. Lydia was quite a bit older than she was, they shared only a mother, and they had never, ever gotten along. "I don't get along well with sociopaths," Aunt Lydia had told me once.

I know Aunt Lydia lived with a massive amount of guilt for not rescuing me from my mother, but there was nothing she could do. She tried again and again, when she could find us, or when I could secretly send her a letter, to convince Candy to let me come and stay with her. But except for summertime, Candy always said no. And yet, I think my mother often hated me, especially when I became a teenager.

"Hmmmm . . ." Caroline said again. "It looks like a scar of inner pain. Of betrayal. The pain is still in you, isn't it?"

I nodded, but wasn't too impressed. It's not hard to discern from that story what really happened.

"That's one of the things you're running from, isn't it? Besides the fiancé?"

I swallowed hard.

"In fact, you have another scar here that was caused by your mother, wasn't it?"

I looked down at Caroline's little hand. She was tracing the largest scar on my knee and was studying it, as if looking through a microscope.

"Well, that one isn't exactly from my mother," I hemmed.

"Yes, it is," she insisted, rubbing it softly with her finger.

"Your mother caused this one. Again, it was neglect. Not the same sort of neglect, but neglect, right? Yes, I can see that I'm right. I'm very sorry."

I wanted to burst into tears. Sometimes a kind voice, a steady look, and a touch will make you cry, and this was it.

Yes, that was the worst scar, the tunnel to more scars, all of the same sort, all emblazoned on my heart as if I'd been branded by a cow poker.

"So." I tried to bluster my way out. "What kind of fortune do you see in my knees? What's my future?"

Caroline laughed. "Oh, I can't see a thing in your knees for the future. They were the door to the past, to your pain. I've already seen your future. I saw it when I walked in the door."

"You saw my future?" That was alarming.

"Yes," said Caroline. "And no. I saw a purplish haze around you and—"

"A purplish haze?"

"Yes. That stands for change, and for choice."

"What else?" I knew there was something else. She was pleating her fingers together and the eye-twitching was getting more intense.

It would be melodramatic to say that the candle between us flickered and went out, but it is the truth. That candle died. Just died, the wax swallowing up the wick, and though other candles burned in the room and Aunt Lydia had her embroidery light on, it was dark between me and Caroline.

"Julia, honey—" she began.

"Just tell me. It can't be worse than what I have now."

"I see blackness. A rim of black around the purple. All around you. It's a warning."

"A warning?" Fear danced its way from my toes to my neck, and I felt my heart start to palpitate again, my hands filling with blood that was filled with chunks of ice. My unknown disease, triggered by stress.

I couldn't breathe, couldn't get a breath.

"Someone hates you."

I nodded.

"Be careful."

I nodded again. "But what about the purple you're seeing?"

"It has something to do with chocolate," Caroline said seriously. "When the chocolate comes, your whole life will change. It's the impetus."

Suddenly my breathing stopped, then started again. Had she said "chocolate"? My heart stopped rushing, stopped racing, the ice melted in my veins, the curious blackness that often obscured the edges of my vision when this mystery disease attacked started to clear.

"You're on the road to chocolate," she told me, her mouth grim. "And there is no way to veer off course."

"Got it," I breathed, trying not to laugh. "Watch out for chocolate."

"That's right," Caroline said, holding my hands in hers, her eyes serious. "Watch out for chocolate."

≈ 4 ≈

If I could jump into the sunrise I'm sure all my problems would be solved.

I thought about this while I watched the sun peek above the row of blue mountains in the distance. The sun was the color of egg yolks, the pinks and oranges around it like cotton candy and squished oranges.

Part of me knows that I am losing my mind, but I am proud in a weird sort of way that I can lose it while still appreciating nature's beauty.

I pushed my hand over my hat, squishing it down on my curls. It was the crack of dawn, and I was feeding Aunt Lydia's chickens. I hadn't showered yet, and I was positive I stunk like chicken shit. I also had wet mud sliming down my legs and hay all over my plaid shirt, which hung almost to my knees, because I slipped when I was petting the piglets. They'd all gathered around at once, and I'd lost my balance.

Although I slept well the night of Breast Power Psychic Night, I did not sleep the next two nights for more than a few hours, and when I did, I dreamed of Robert chasing me with a pickax.

A pickax is an unusual object. It looks mean and nasty.

But there it was. I was not surprised in my dream to see Robert holding that pickax. Nor did it particularly frighten me. What frightened me was that Robert was smiling. A smile that was so gentle, so endearing, it made me feel sick with high-octane panic.

In my dream I started running. You know how in your dreams when you run, you just can't move, and the person who is chasing you catches up with lightning speed, and the reason you can't run is because your legs are all tangled up in your sheet, and you're sweating, a river of water gushing down your face?

It was not like that at all. In these pickax dreams, I ran. So fast, so hard, so long. I hid around buildings and waited. Robert would appear, pickax above his head, and grinning. I would turn at the last minute before my imminent death, run again, this time hiding behind a bridge, and there he would come again. Smiling. So gentle. So endearing. And he'd swing. He'd miss me by inches, and I would sprint at high speed to the country, and there, behind a tractor, he'd find me, and he'd still be smiling.

This went on until he finally got me. I saw my mother laughing in the distance, her dyed blond hair flying behind her. My father was on his motorcycle. He sped away.

I woke up cold—freezing, in fact—my whole body shaking so hard I grabbed the pink comforter on the bed and wrapped myself up like a caterpillar. A very scared caterpillar.

After ascertaining he was not near, that this was not another hiding place, I willed myself to breathe again, in and out. Then, when that didn't work, I gave up. I picked up a book on tending roses next to my bed and read. I read every single word. Forcing myself to concentrate. I learned about fertilizers, traditional versus organic, and all kinds of rose bugs, and different types of soil, and how to water your roses.

At some point I fell asleep, and in my next dream Robert was chasing me through a rose garden with that same pickax in his hand. In his other hand he carried a book on roses. I woke up with the rose book on my chest, the sunrise peeking through the wooden slats of my bedroom window.

Deciding I had had enough nightmares, I got up, dressed in a couple of old shirts Aunt Lydia kept in the white wicker furniture chests in the room, and headed out to the barns.

I knew Aunt Lydia was there already. She needed only a few hours of sleep a night, said sleeping was boring and she could get absolutely nothing done in bed. "After I'm dead I'll have plenty of time to sleep. Right now I'm alive, and I've got things to do."

Plus, 370 hungry chickens.

Aunt Lydia sold the eggs to the local store in town and to two stores in neighboring towns. People often called her "The Egg Lady." She loved it. Every day, for hours and hours, she would work with her chickens. Picking up their eggs, cleaning out the barns, making sure "the ladies" had time to run and play in special areas she had gated off for them.

She sent me to the smaller barn at first when she saw me. She simply pointed, and I knew where to go, and I trudged through to the barn after a short detour to the pigpen. Melissa Lynn snorted her way over and licked my hand. I bent down and put my hands around her neck. She nuzzled my face, snorting happily. The piglets snorted, too, and I laughed.

The laughter felt good, freeing, as if it had been held down by a lead lid and chains for years. I gave them all another hug, fell on my butt in the puddle, and the piglets snorted away, already busy with their day, things to do, troughs to eat out of, mud to roll in. The life of a pig is very busy, you know.

When I stood outside the barn—painted purple, of course, for good luck and good sex, Aunt Lydia had said—I could hear "the ladies" clucking, soft and comfortable, as if they were snoozing.

Then, as if they had a sixth sense and knew I was there and freedom and food were only seconds away, their clucking took a new turn, sounding shrill and strident, as if someone were dropping their bottoms into a pail full of ice and giving them a little shake.

I opened the barn door.

Shocked, I could only stare at what seemed like a million chickens flying out the door, their mellow clucking changing to high-pitched squawking. When one flew at my head, I ducked, stood again, then had to lean to my right to avoid another chicken, then to my left, then back down again.

Chicken after chicken flew out of that barn. I could almost hear their commentary: "Who the hell is that? She didn't open the door right! Where's Lydia? What is this barn coming to, when the servants quit?"

When the stampede was over, the ladies settled and pecked at the ground, I ventured into their domain. Lydia had told me the night before where many of the eggs would be. She had painted different bookshelves bright colors and lined them up against the walls or laid them flat against the wood chips and hay. She always put a golf ball on the shelves so the chickens would think they were looking at a real egg and, as she said, feel comfortable about dropping their insides.

The chickens loved it, laying eggs every day. When the chickens were too old and not laying anymore, Lydia gave them away to a group that would send fresh chicken breasts out to women's shelters and homeless places in the city. She hated sending chickens away and often kept them long after they were good for egg-laying.

On the day her friend Albert brought his truck around to transport the older chickens to the Chicken Slice and Dice business, as she called it, she would always help load the chickens, blowing them kisses, hugging them tightly, then go to bed for the rest of the day and cry and grieve as if she'd given away her best friends.

But the next day, it was business as usual. Did I mention that Aunt Lydia is a hard-core businesswoman?

So I went through the bookshelves and the nests, then looked for the "secret piles," as Lydia calls them—places where the chickens all like to lay their eggs. Every so often, she'll find a new "secret pile."

This, I think, is the ladies' way of keeping secrets. They all lay their eggs in some nook or cranny—between the bookshelves, behind them, anywhere—and finally Aunt Lydia will find the hoard. Usually there's about seventy eggs by that time, and even as she's pulling them out and putting them in her baskets, the ladies will wander over and lay more eggs.

So the secret gig is up, but the ladies know it's a good place to relieve themselves, so they carry on a bit more.

I heard Aunt Lydia come in the barn.

"Darlin', Julia," she yelled. "Saw the chickens flying at your face a bit ago. Too bad I didn't have my camera. Now wouldn't that be dandy? We could win a million dollars on one of those TV shows."

"The ladies were a little anxious to get out today."

"The ladies are always anxious to get out. They don't do much, but what they do they're used to doing. They like routines. Oh, now"—a chicken pecked at her hand when Lydia reached in to get the egg—"don't be hormonal, Tizzy."

Lydia names all the chickens as she goes. Who could remember all those names anyhow?

"There ya go, Jessalynn," she soothed as she took another egg from yet another late-morning riser, not so eager to get outside today. "This one is much kinder than the other, but I prefer Tizzy."

"You prefer Tizzy?" I saw a white egg sticking out of hay bunched together in a small cubbyhole created by a miniature bookshelf. I dug through the hay and found another "secret loot" area. I popped fifteen eggs into my basket.

"Yes, I do. Tizzy has spirit. She has a temper. She knows

what she wants and what she doesn't. When she doesn't like what's going on, she snaps. Yep. I like her."

We stared at the two ladies. Tizzy shook her head a bit, Jessalynn settled down in her nest. "Anyone who thinks chickens don't have personalities is wrong. We got the mean ones, the nice ones, and everyone in between in this barn. It's a microcosm of a woman's life, only the ladies shit out in the open and human women don't drop the eggs from their ovaries on the floor each morning."

I nodded. "We women generally like to keep our eggs close to home."

"Darn right we do."

We continued digging through the barn, silence settling on us, familiar and warm. I brushed hay and, undoubtedly, chicken shit out of my hair as I bent under a shelf to grab more eggs.

"I've had to get more roosters out here since you came last. But not *too* many. I learned my lesson years ago about roosters. Don't get enough chickens, and those roosters will run the ladies into the ground with all the matin' they do. They hop on the ladies' backs, hump around, and when they're through, they walk right over them. Almost every rooster will stomp on the lady's head on his way out and not think a thing of it."

"That's so like a man," I muttered.

"Damn straight it is. Some men will do the foreplay, but most of 'em don't really want to. They just want to be like roosters. Hump 'em, walk out the door."

"Personally, I don't want any more roosters in my life. I've been stepped on the head once too often."

"Yes, you have, but your head is done getting stomped on!" Aunt Lydia spread her arms out wide. "The world is sending you good karma, darlin', and a head stompin' is not in your future."

"Always nice to hear. Thank you, Aunt Lydia."

"Now, take a look at these eggs." Lydia pointed behind a

bookshelf painted blue at a hoard of eggs. About twenty of them.

"Chickens hide things. They like to keep secrets. Like these here eggs in their little secret hiding places. Chickens are like women in that respect. We all have secrets, some small ones that aren't really a big deal. Some we're ashamed about." She bent down and hugged a chicken to her like it was a baby. "Some we love having because we can visit them when we're having a rotten day and remember something we shouldn't have done but did anyhow. Those are the most interesting. We *know* we should feel guilty, so guilty that our insides should be burning up and smoke should be rightfully spewing from our ears, but at that moment in our lives, what we did was right. It was wrong, too, of course, deliciously wrong, or it wouldn't be a secret, but deep in the heart we don't regret it."

I didn't know exactly what she was referring to, but I knew about secrets. I wish I didn't. I've known all about the worst type of secrets since I was four. Secrets always hurt. When I was a child, anytime a man told me he wanted to share a secret with me I knew I was gonna get hurt. No other way out. The boyfriends who paid a lot of attention to me from the start were always the worst.

When I was older, I got smarter. When one of my mother's boyfriends said he wanted to share a secret with me, I'd leave. Anytime my mother took on a new boyfriend, I'd start looking around for places to sleep. I found out where the shelters were, looked for hiding places in parks under trees that I could safely sleep under, and figured out ways to stay in the town's library after hours, which was never too hard. I'd read books all night. I'd get to know the neighbors, too—feel out where I could go in case of emergency.

"Speaking of secrets, Julia, my dear . . ." Lydia turned toward me. She was wearing the same type of flannel shirt as me, her gray braids piled under her cap, the tilt of her head proud and strong, as always.

"Whenever you're ready to talk, I'm here."

I swallowed hard. Swallowed hard again. Looked down. I felt like a kid. Felt as I always had when I'd come to Lydia's farm for the summer, relieved beyond belief that I was with her, that I had escaped, if only for a while. I moved the egg basket from one hand to another as emotions roiled through me—fear, worry, pain, more fear.

"Jellybean Julia," Lydia said my nickname as soft as chicken feathers, and pulled me into her arms.

Jellybean Julia bent her head and cried.

He was huge.

Absolutely huge.

Not fat at all, but huge.

Tall, with shoulders as big as a car and a chest wider than a pillow.

And he smiled at me.

From the start I gave Dean Garrett a lot of credit. That huge man with his gold and white hair and his weathered, tanned skin, and his bright blue eyes that actually looked right at me instead of skittering away like most men who lose interest in me as soon as they're done marveling at my boobs.

He didn't laugh when he saw me in all my muddy glory, which was another point in his favor, but the sight of a man that big, that strong-looking, made my heart leap a bit with fear. I have never been comfortable with men, except for Stash, and after my experience with Robert and my mother's "friends," any man who looked like he could squish my face into gel made me particularly nervous.

This man not excluded.

"Dean Garrett!" Aunt Lydia boomed when she saw The

Huge Man leaning against her kitchen counter, drinking a cup of coffee with Stash. "I have not seen you in so long I was thinking about having a new concrete pig crafted and named after you!" She gave him a hug, and I watched as she seemed to disappear into his arms.

A smile stretched across his square-jawed face, his teeth white, little lines fanning from the corners of his eyes. He had that weathered, Marlboro-man look to him. I put him at around forty-two years old or so.

"It would be my honor to have a pig named after me, Lydia." He looked at me, then back down at Aunt Lydia. "In fact, I'll look forward to it. Put me next to Stash out there." He looked back at me.

Wonderful, I thought. *Splendid!* I must look even more mangled than I thought. Perhaps it was the mud adorning my outfit that caught his eye. Or the matted hair? Perhaps the stench of chicken poop? Perhaps I had a chicken atop my head that I hadn't noticed? The chicken was probably a great backdrop to the bruises that were still visible on my cheek and eye. I reached up and pulled at my hair, catching Stash looking at me with a smile. He winked.

"Ha!" Lydia pulled away. "Never! I have reserved that space only for Stash, who, I see, has come into my house again without an invitation. Never mind. You have brought one of my favorite people on the planet, so just this time"— she slammed her hand against Stash's behind—"I'll forgive you. You brought me my pie pan back, didn't you? *Finally.* Dean, this is my wonderful niece, Julia Bennett. She'll be here for a while. Hopefully forever."

Dean Garrett crossed the room in milliseconds, his long legs eating up that floor like a tractor. For a man who was huge, with shoulders the size of, yes, a piano, he moved well.

"Miss Bennett." He took my hand in his, and I watched it disappear. I now had no hand attached to my right arm. My heart pumped harder. Oh dear. Please don't let the Dread

Disease affect me now. Not while I'm covered in chicken poop, holding the hand of a man with blue eyes that were currently peering right into my soul and reading all my secrets.

"Mr . . . Mr . . ." I forgot his name.

"It's Dean Garrett. It's a pleasure to meet you." His voice was low and gravelly, like honey over crushed rock.

It would be a pleasure to meet you if I could breathe, I thought to myself. "Yes. Of course. I mean. Yes, I'm pleasured to meet you." I could feel the blush rising in my face. *I'm pleasured to meet you*? I sounded like I was having sex with his introduction. I tried again. "It's nice to meet you, too, Mr. Garrett."

I heard Stash cough to cover a chuckle in the background, but I couldn't see him. The only thing within eighty miles of my vision was this man. And the longer he stared at me, the longer his hand warmed mine like a hot-water bottle, the longer I was caught by those blue eyes that had X-ray vision into my soul, the more my heart pattered about like a loose pinball.

I saw one corner of his mouth tilt up in a smile. "Lydia must have had you up bright and early to help with the chickens."

He was still holding my hand.

"No. Yes. I helped with the chickens. Yes."

"Julia moved here from back East. Finally came to her senses," Aunt Lydia said. "She worked in an art gallery."

Dean nodded. "That's interesting. Who are your favorite artists?"

"My favorite artists?" I made the mistake of looking at his lips. The top one slim, the lower one full. Way full. Way kissable. Sheesh. "Uh. I. Well. I'm sorry. What was the question?"

He smiled. "Who are your favorite artists?"

Ah. Okay. I knew what an artist was. "Van Gogh. Vermeer. Faith Ringold."

He smiled at me again, then let go of my hand. The warmth was gone. I swallowed hard. If I'd had an Adam's apple it would undoubtedly be making a fool of me.

"And yours?"

"I'll take Picasso and the photographer Ansel Adams."

I nodded. Wise choices. I stared some more. The man reeked of testosterone. *Stop, Julia, please stop*, I pleaded with myself. *You've just run from one man—let's not start looking at another.*

I decided I had to go.

"If you all will excuse me . . . I have . . . well, I have to take a shower."

Now why did I say such a *naked* thing? I couldn't even look at Dean. "I've been with the chickens and . . ." Brilliant again. It almost sounded amorous. *I've been with the chickens*?

"Nice to have met you," I said, my voice quiet to my own ears. And, as if he were deaf, I said louder, "Good to meet you."

I should start digging a hole in the floor now so I could crawl into it.

"Oh, now, honey, don't you say good-bye yet," Stash said. "When you're through, you come right back on down here quick as a wink and have breakfast with us. I'm making your aunt and you and Dean my World Famous Stash's Omelets. They are the best Oregon has ever eaten, you know. If they had an omelets contest, I would win. Damn sure of it. So you get on in that shower and we'll see you in a jiffy."

I managed a nervous smile as the Dread Disease slammed into me suddenly. My heart rate sped up to 23,897 beats a minute, there was suddenly no air in the house, I was freezing cold, and I felt faint. All at the same time.

I turned, managed to bump into only one chair and the side of the doorway, then stumbled through the living room. Super. Now Dean would know I was a clutz, too. The stairs now looked mountainous, and I vaguely wondered if I would need crampons to help me climb them, as the air had been completely sucked out of my lungs with an invisible siphon.

I stumbled up the stairs, then collapsed on my bed, my hands over my head.

I could feel the Dread Disease get worse, second by second, until I thought I would never breathe again, my forehead breaking out in a sweat, that familiar tremble coursing its way through my weakened limbs.

What disease was it? Was it the first case of leprosy in hundreds of years? Would I suffer? Would I collapse dead away in the chicken coop, and all the chickens would cover my body with eggs and no one would find me?

I would be remembered as The Woman Buried By Eggs.

And Dean Garrett would probably read about me. How humiliating.

I tried to breathe, but it didn't work, and my head spun. Tried again. The air this time was gracious, and I felt my collapsed lungs inflate slightly.

Another breath came puffing on in, then another, and soon the sweet smell of jasmine potpourri wafted in, the curtain at the window fluttered, I heard one of Lydia's cats meowing, and the clucking of the chickens penetrated the thick fog of frightening yuck in my head.

Now, I realized I could go to a doctor about the Dread Disease, but I didn't want to hear that I had contracted a strange, deadly, breathing sickness from a tiny colony of ants that had somehow grown giant teeth and burrowed their way into my skin.

No, knowledge is not always good.

I heard Aunt Lydia, Stash, and Dean talking and laughing downstairs and knew I wouldn't be able to eat at all. Not in the presence of that he-man. Although I felt exhausted, and I knew the exhaustion would take hours to shed, I could think clearly enough to know that I was not going to sit next to a man who was as tall as a tree and had blue eyes that had stripped my insides bare.

But I would take it upon myself to shower. Dropping Aunt Lydia's clothes on the floor, I turned the water on, shampooed and rinsed my hair, then scrubbed any possible fleck of chicken poop off my body.

I toweled dry and put on my jeans and my one nice white blouse, although I certainly wasn't going down to breakfast. That would be too scary with Dean there.

I slipped on silver hoop earrings and my watch. And a little lipstick.

Although I certainly wasn't going down to breakfast. Way too scary.

Lydia came up, saw me sitting on the bed.

"I knew I would find you hiding up here."

"I'm not hiding."

"You are hiding. You must draw up your courage from the bowels of your uterus and come join us at breakfast."

"I'm not hiding," I said, trying to sound rational. "I am enjoying a nervous breakdown. I should be done in a couple of months. But until I'm done I'm not hanging out with any men, especially men related to Paul Bunyan. Does he have his blue ox outside?"

Aunt Lydia groaned. "Funny. Now that you mention it, he does. Although he calls it a truck. Don't be scared of him, Julia. He's a good man. A man who is not afraid of his testosterone. He rules his testosterone and does not let his testosterone rule him. His balls are made of steel, you can tell by the way he moves."

Steel balls?

"Moved here several years ago. He's a farmer and a rancher. Attorney, too, so he goes into the city for weeks at a time sometimes. Some big hotshot law firm. I don't know. Stash does."

Great. A rancher. Farmer. And an attorney. Oh, yes. I'm sure he would be excited to dine with someone like me. A nervous, paranoid, blushing, clutzy, bruised, muddy, plump, overly endowed ex-fiancée who left her wedding dress hanging from a tree and who sounds like she's been getting it on with chickens.

"All I know is that he is a damn good poker player. He beat Stash many times, and he's almost beat me. He'll play for quarters, not pennies, like all the other cowardly people in this town." Lydia snorted, then grabbed my arm. "I'm drying your hair."

"No, please, Aunt Lydia. Tell him I'm sick. Tell him I have leprosy. I'm certainly not going down to breakfast."

"You do look a little pale, Julia. Which is why you need to pump your womanhood full of eggs and cheese. They will restore the equilibrium in your inner core, which is what you need. And those jeans look good on you."

"I'm fat."

"You're not fat. You're curvy. Men like something to grip in bed, Julia. They like handfuls of warm woman. Mouthfuls, too, now that I think about it. But men are pricks!" she shouted, pointer fingers in the air again, as if she'd just remembered. "Sleeping with one of those skinny models would be like sleeping with a fence post with a head. You attracted to fence posts? Me neither. Now get in there so I can dry those curls of yours or I'm calling Stash in to do it."

"You wouldn't." But I already knew.

"I would. Sure as I would paint the north outbuilding orange, I would, which is what I'm going to do tomorrow. Now move."

I stood up, my knees still a bit weak from the attack of the Dread Disease.

"And, by the way, after breakfast, can you help me paint the back shed green?"

"Sure, Aunt Lydia." I'd work all day if I could. Nothing like work to take your mind off the fact that you're going to be hunted down by your ex-fiancé at the same time you're fighting off a Dread Disease and Paul Bunyan and his great big steel . . . thingies, who is down in the kitchen.

I shivered again. I wouldn't go there. Wouldn't think

about steel balls. If I did, I wouldn't be able to eat the sausages.

"So you don't like sausages?" Paul Bunyan asked me from across the table.

Stash had, indeed, prepared Oregon's best omelets. Avocado. Shrimp. Sour cream. Some type of sauce. Tomatoes. Spices. Delicious. Or at least it would have been had I been able to eat much.

Stash was on my left, Lydia on my right. Stash had also brought over blueberry muffins. "I cooked them for you, sweetie," he told me, giving me a hug before settling me at my seat. "You're my sweet blueberry girl. Always have been, always will be." Then he told Paul Bunyan about how I ate so many blueberries one night that they had to drive me to the hospital at two in the morning because my stomach hurt so bad that the doctors thought I needed an appendectomy.

I looked up into those blue eyes again. Cool. Smooth. Yet friendly.

I caught myself. *Breathe, Julia.*

"The sausages?" Dean asked again, smiling at me across the table.

I jumped. I had stared at him, not answering.

"No. Yes." I shook my head. I wondered if there was a Mrs. Paul Bunyan? Was she as big as him? "I do like big sausages."

Oh, deliver me, Lord. Had I said I like *big* sausages?

I heard Stash's fork drop to his plate with a clatter. There was a dead silence around the table. Then Lydia snorted.

I heard Stash trying to control his laughter. He sounded like a hyena who was being muffled with a pillow. I felt the blood rush to my face. Aunt Lydia had found a sudden interest in her napkin. It covered her whole face. Her shoulders shook. She made odd meowing sounds.

"Well, what I meant . . ." I protested. I looked into Paul Bunyan's eyes. They were laughing, but his mouth was very still. "I meant that I do like sausages, any sausage."

Aunt Lydia snorted.

"You know, there are different types of sausages. . . ." I sputtered, still trying to save myself. "Bavarian sausages, German sausages, French sausages, California sausages. I didn't really mean big . . . really didn't mean . . ."

Stash made a sound like a donkey braying. Lydia answered with her own high-pitched choking sound.

"But I don't like *spicy* sausages. . . ."

Please, I told my mouth, *oh please, stop*.

"Nothing spicy," Paul Bunyan said, those lips moving over his words like hot syrup.

"Right." We needed to get away from this conversation.

"So," Stash said, tears floating in his eyes. "That's a good thing for you to remember, my boy, Dean. She likes sausages of any kind."

Aunt Lydia didn't even try to pretend anymore, her laughter filling the room like sweet flowers on a cold winter day.

"But nothing spicy."

"Never," said Stash, laughter spilling from his mouth like caramel corn from a paper bag. "Women are picky about these things. Some women like one type of sausage, some another. Spicy sausages. Big ones, small ones, sausages from different countries. There's just no pleasin' these gals sometimes, Dean, no pleasin' them at all."

"Well, I like your sausage, Stash," Aunt Lydia said. "I like it right fine. Right fine."

I stared, astonished. Then I laughed. I couldn't help it. For all the time that Aunt Lydia was fighting with Stash, this was the first compliment I'd heard her give him in a long time. The tension rolled right out of my body with that laugh. I looked at Paul Bunyan, who did not seem the least bit embarrassed about my sausage comment. His eyes were still on me, but now they had a look in them, a considering look, a curious look.

"But you must remember!" Lydia boomed, holding her fork high in the air.

"I know, I know, darlin'," Stash said, still laughing. "Men are pricks!"

❦ 5 ❧

Caroline Harper's house was a study in surprise. Her home is actually a pole barn, painted brown on the outside. From the front, all you can see is a door and a tiny window. There's a red and white sign in that tiny window that says GUNS ARE LOADED. Outside another sign says NO TRESPASSING.

It looks like the kind of place where methamphetamine might be manufactured. At the very least, it looks to be a hideout for wicked criminals. I asked her about the signs later, when we were having tea over a lace-draped table, and she said they added humor to her life. The old man who lived here before her was slightly insane. He had twenty-two cats, was rumored to eat a full garlic clove a day, and made his own whiskey. He lived to be 104. Caroline knew him, liked him, and kept the signs in memory of him.

At first I was sure I had gotten the wrong directions from Lydia. Surely no one like Caroline Harper lived in such a depressing, dark, scary-looking place. And Aunt Lydia had said she lived in a dollhouse. This wasn't a dollhouse.

But Lydia had mentioned the signs, so I slammed the door of the truck closed and proceeded with caution.

And there's where the surprises started.

Caroline opened the door, a smile lighting her gentle features. She wore a red cotton dress that on anyone else probably would have looked frumpy, with its square neckline and flared skirt. I would have looked like a giant blood clot. But on Caroline, it looked stylish and hip and lovely. She had pulled her hair back into a ponytail, her cheekbones gracious curves. Her right eye winked at me, but slowly, gently. She hugged me as I walked in the door. And then I stopped.

As shocked as I had been at the outside of Caroline's house, the inside left me gaping. I remembered to shut my mouth after a long minute so I wouldn't look like an airstarved guppy.

"It's beautiful," I said, awed.

Though the outside of the house looked like a drug warren, the inside décor was English Country/dollhouse. The furniture was overstuffed and comfy and covered in flowered or striped fabric. It was old, and used, and plush and cheerful.

Tables held books and candles and lace doilies, and the room was filled with light from floor-to-ceiling windows and French doors everywhere. The walls were painted an eggshell blue, white, or pink.

It was one huge room, Caroline showed me, with two areas walled off, one for a bedroom and one for Caroline's "workroom." The door to the workroom was closed.

The kitchen was surprisingly modern, and she had painted all of the cabinets pink. It was clear she had been cutting bouquets, as flowers were scattered about the white counters. I looked out her back windows and saw an enormous garden.

I wanted to stay forever.

"Would you like to see the garden, too?" Caroline asked, her voice soft and cultured. I again felt like a water buffalo next to this petite woman, and I would have hated her if I could for being perfect, but I couldn't. She was kind, for sure, but more than that, I related to that twitching eye of hers. Twitch twitch. I was twitching on the inside, Caroline twitched on the outside.

"Come and see the flower garden first," she said, leading me to the most gynormous, lovely array of raised flower beds. "It doesn't look very good right now. Spring is much better."

I reassured her it was beautiful, as it truly was, and she gently pulled out a plant with long-stemmed flowers from one of the beds. "You like to garden, don't you?" she asked, and before I could answer, she piled yet another plant on, and another, rattling off directions on how to plant them, where to plant them.

Next we moved to the vegetable garden. This time she grabbed one of the crates she had stacked against a small shed. Within seconds I had enough vegetables to feed me and half of the third world. She insisted on helping me take my loot to the car. I wondered if the tires would pop.

"Now come in for some tea," she said, grabbing my hand. For an instant, right in the middle of the driveway of her drug house/English Country Manor, she stopped, closed her eyes, her hand tightening on mine.

"Caroline?" I asked. Her hand had gone cold.

Having a Dread Disease like I do is difficult. Not only do I have to deal with my own triggers that take away my breath, but if someone around me is upset, that can trigger an episode, also.

Her hand seemed to get colder by the second until I felt like I was holding ice. I could feel my own hand losing all warmth. Soon, I told myself, both of us would be freezing-cold. We would turn into ice women together. I wondered if she would think it odd if I asked if I could go to her bed and pull the comforter over my head and hide.

"It's nothing," she whispered. "Everything is fine. Every-thing will be . . . fine."

"But what is it? Please, Caroline. Aunt Lydia knows that

you can see the future. You're freaking me out," I said, hearing my own shaky voice.

She turned to me abruptly then, holding both my hands in hers, her green eyes luminous, close to mine, and yet real far away. She was clearly on another plane than me. I was not inclined to believe this stuff, but I didn't want to dismiss it, either.

"Your fiancé," she said, her face tight, her right eye twitching at a higher speed as soon as the words left her mouth.

Oh God. Not him. "Yes."

She stepped closer. She smelled like roses and tea and butter. Who knew why she smelled like butter? "I can feel him."

"Me too," I said. I wanted to jump into the house, grab a gun, and hole up, waiting for his imminent appearance.

"Julia, he's angry. I can feel it. He's hot. Very hot." Twitch. Twitch. Faster even.

I knew that Caroline knew I had an ex-fiancé. And she also knew that he had beat up my face, turning it lovely shades of purple and green. For her to say he was "hot" did not take much deduction on her part.

"He's burning. He's trying to find you. I see him."

Just thinking about Robert scared me. I could almost see my liver shriveling up in fear, my intestines frozen solid, the blueberry muffin I ate this morning hardening as the temperature dropped.

But, of course, I still wasn't convinced that Caroline was authentic. I mean, really, who can see the future? Everything she said could have been deduced by talking to Aunt Lydia for a few minutes.

"I see the dog, Julia."

The ice edged up my throat.

"He was small. White. I see pink, too." Caroline's voice was small, broken.

The ice leaped several inches, like a miniature glacier, choking me.

I knew a small white dog. He was mine up until three months ago. His name was Spot, though there was not a single spot on him. I had loved that dog, and he had loved me.

But one night I had voiced to Robert, again, my concern that his mother, well, detested me like vermin, although I left the word "vermin" out.

"She's so beneath you, Robert," I had overheard her say. "Beneath us as a family, beneath us as influential, powerful people in this country. And that figure of hers. For God's sakes, Robert dear, she looks like a hooker. I'm feeling disgraced already. Disgraced. *Disgraced.* Sleep with her if you must. I can see, from a very base and vulgar perspective, the rather animalistic attraction to someone who looks like that, someone who has come from such an *unusual* background. But must you *marry* her?"

"Robert," I had said. "I've tried to get your mother to like me—"

"You can't force my mother to like you, Boobs." Another favorite nickname he was so amused by. "It's you who needs to change. You. Not me. Not my mother. You." His hand tightened on my chin like a metal clamp as his cold eyes dropped to Spot, growling low in his throat. "And goddammit, Julia, quit clinging to that dog. I'm sick of it. Sick of him barking at me, sick of him biting me. Sick to shit of him." His other hand darted out and grabbed Spot's muzzle, holding the dog's mouth shut. "I am at my limit," he said, his mouth an inch from my ear, his voice soft. "Don't push me over the edge."

The next day Spot was gone. Two days after that my neighbor found him on her lawn. She brought him, shoulders heaving as she cried, wrapped in one of her own fuzzy baby blankets. His neck had been slashed. His license and collar were pink but you would have thought they were black. Black with blood. I cried for days. Still cry when I think about him. Shake, too.

When Robert came over that night, I told him through these wretched, heaving sobs about Spot. His fury mounted by the second, and he muscled me into my bedroom and informed me that Spot was "a pathetically annoying animal," and that I treated him like he was a child instead of a dog. "For God's sake, get over it, Watermelon Buns."

Not yet making the connection between Robert and my dead dog, I had said to him, "Robert, my dog was killed by some sicko and you want me to *get over it*? Just like that?"

His eyes got this weird, livid look, like fireworks were exploding in his brain, and he told me I was going to have to learn to get control of myself, that no one liked a baby, and he especially did not like to see fat girls cry because it made them look worse. "Fat girls shouldn't cry at all in front of other people, in point of fact. It's disgusting."

I thought of my poor, beloved dog in a little box, wrapped in that fuzzy blanket, buried in my tiny garden outside my apartment and felt sick. "Shut up, Robert! Just shut up! Shut up!"

In answer he spun me around, ripped down my pants, and shoved me against the back of an overstuffed chair. "Shut up yourself, bitch," he whispered as he bent me over the top. I fought for about thirty seconds, but he grabbed my hair, and exhaustion ran over me like a dump truck and I gave up. My nonresponsiveness seemed to turn him on even more, his pants and groans coming harsh and ragged.

When he was done, he steered me over to the bed, his breath hot and fast. I stumbled because my pants were around my ankles, and he swore and ended up carrying me, his arms around my waist. "Damn. You've put on even more weight, haven't you?" When I was lying flat, he straddled me, wrapped both hands around my boobs and glared into my eyes as he squeezed and fondled them.

"I'm glad that dog's dead, Julia," he said. "You paid more

attention to it than you did me. You're weird, you know that? You've got mental problems. Serious mental problems. You like an animal more than a real man. How do you expect me to stay attracted to a woman who's turned on by a dog?" He got off the bed, got undressed, then leaned over me, ripping the covers back down that I'd yanked up to my chin, then shoved his fingers up my vagina.

"You like it like this, don't you? It turns you on." He cupped my face with his palm, one finger gently stroking my face while the other hand hurt me. He did that often—one hand loving, one hand hurting. "Don't you ever let some dumb dog get between us again. Do you get that, cunt? Do you get that?" His voice was low and kind. And scary. So very scary.

"Every damn day I see that dog sitting on your lap. I'm glad it's just me and you now. Just me and you. Only me and you. And do not"—he shoved his hand up me harder and dropped three gentle kisses on my mouth at the same time— "do not even think about getting another dog."

And then I had this creepy, horrible feeling, and I had to ask the question, even though I knew Robert would filet me as he would a dead fish when he heard it. "Robert . . . Robert, you didn't kill Spot, did you?"

The look in his eyes skewered me to the bed. "Oh, Julia," he said, his voice a caress. "Oh, Julia." He smashed his mouth on mine so hard I could hardly breathe.

After a couple of minutes, when I began to really struggle, he lifted his head, and I could see that some of his anger had dissipated. "Why do you make me so angry? Why? You constantly provoke me. You know I love you. I can't live without you, Julia." He grabbed a fistful of my curls and kissed them, then kissed both breasts as I held my breath. One time he'd bitten down on me. "No, I can't live without you, and I won't. But this is your fault. You have to learn how to be a wife. A good wife. And you must learn to be more like my mother."

He lowered his head again, and this time he kissed me so sweetly, so soft, so gentle, it made me gasp with mind-numbing fear. Of course, he misinterpreted my gasps.

"I'll do you again, don't worry about it. You're always hot, always wanting it, aren't you? You have a need for constant sex. Who would guess that with someone like you?" He shook his head in wonderment as he ran his hands over my trembling-with-fright body. His cell phone rang then, and he answered it and walked out the front door, leaving me cold and half-naked on the bed.

When he left, I resumed my crying jag over Spot, which morphed into me not being able to breathe and my heart palpitating as if it were racing a hundred miles an hour, and I figured I was going to die.

I had found Spot three years ago, literally on the city street near to where I was living. He was sitting by a garbage can. Waiting, waiting, waiting, it seemed, for something to come his way. He was skinny and nervous and dirty, and I thought I was looking at myself in dog form, except for the skinny part. He must have looked at me and seen himself in human form because he came to me instantly. I showered him, fed him, doted on him, loved him.

That dog was happy when I woke up in the morning, happy when I came home, happy when I walked him. He was not happy alone and was often quivering with nerves when I came in from work, which endeared him to me all the more.

Growing up unloved and neglected is horrific. Not only because your parent doesn't love you, but because you know your parent doesn't want *your* love. You learn that your love is inferior. Unneeded. Worthless. You're inferior, you're un-needed, you're worthless.

But Spot needed my love. He needed me.

Robert had hated Spot on sight, as he hated all animals.

A voice in the back of my head told me that day that Robert had killed Spot. I knew the voice was right. As the days wore on after that incident, and the wedding loomed like a rusty pitchfork over my neck, I found breathing more and more difficult. I could almost see those points of that pitchfork imbedded in my neck, and I knew I had to escape it.

Caroline grabbed my hand, bringing me away from Spot and back to her. Her right eye was almost spasmodically twitching.

"I see clothes in a bag." Her voice was tight. "The bag is full. I see it being thrown. I see fire. It's hot. It smells. The clothes are burning. They're gone. I see red. He's furious."

Now I really was having trouble breathing. About two months ago, in a weird attempt to make him happy, and wanting to look better for him, I had gone shopping. I had bought two skirts that came above my knees, several lace camisoles, a bright red coat, black heels, and a halter top. The clothes were a huge departure from my usual jeans and a dull sweater and loafers.

When he came to the apartment and saw the bag full of clothes his face had turned almost purple with rage. He had turned the bag upside down, running his hands over each and every garment as if a woman were already inside them. "You're cheating on me, aren't you?"

After a long minute when I couldn't speak, from fear, he laughed mercilessly, as if that was a hilarious thought. When he released my hair from around his fist, I protested my innocence.

Robert had laughed again. "I know you're not cheating, Cannonball Butt. Who would cheat with you? You're lucky I'm with you, I'm the best you're ever going to get, the best you can ever expect." He held up the camisole and laughed again. "I hardly think you'll be able to get your stomach in that. Don't try to be something you're not. I don't need humor in bed."

And then suddenly I was furious, too. I was so sick of him criticizing my clothes, my hair, everything, and here I had gone out to fix the problem, and he was cruel again. "Well, if you don't want to see me in them, perhaps someone else will." I didn't know where the words came from, and, really, it was a preposterous thought.

Robert froze, his eyes darkening, and fear exploded in my stomach. He very quietly, very neatly folded each and every garment into the bag. Then he took the bag, shoved it into the fireplace and lit a match. I screamed at him to stop but he didn't, the fire smoldering against the material. I yanked at him and he backhanded me. Backhanded me again when I tried to pull some clothes out. He had to light a second match to burn them all.

When the fire was roaring, he picked up a nearby phone and smashed it into my face.

I lost consciousness. When I came to, Robert was bending over me, the fury gone, replaced by a concerned, loving, desperately sorry man holding an ice pack over my eye.

"You shouldn't have made me mad, Turtle. Shouldn't have threatened to cheat on me."

Shaking, I could barely keep from throwing up, my head throbbing. When I didn't say anything, he grabbed my upper arms. "I know you come from a white-trash family, and I'm trying to save you from them, can't you see? You don't know how to be a proper wife yet, but you will. I'm being patient. . . ." The lecture went on and on and on. He slept at my apartment that night and watched me carefully for days, taking time off work. When he did go back to work, he called every hour on the hour, then made sure that his horrible mother and her sisters monopolized every moment of my time with wedding plans.

His mother and her sisters didn't ask about the bruise, and I didn't discuss it. Those women were wrapped up tight in their secrets and were used to ignoring abuse.

Two nights before our wedding, he came by my apartment. He wasn't happy with the greeting I gave him, nor was he happy when I complained that his mother had taken over the wedding, so that fist came out once again.

He didn't call on our wedding day, left me alone, believing that I would never cut out on my wedding to a rich, eligible bachelor.

"I hear screaming, Julia," Caroline said, her voice low, sad. "It's you, isn't it?"

I nodded.

"He's coming, Julia, he's coming. Here. To Golden."

⚜ 6 ⚘

Aunt Lydia and I worked out a system over the next weeks. We'd wake up before dawn had even cracked, then head out to the chickens, pigs, horses, and sheep with Aunt Lydia's eight cats swirling around our legs. Cat 1, Cat 2, Cat 3, Cat 4, Cat 5, Cat 6, Cat 7, and Cat 8, were the most friendly cats I had ever known. They meowed at me all the time, and as soon as I sat down they would leap to my lap, snuggling in, even three at a time. They would meow again until I scratched their heads, and then they would fall asleep, purring contentedly.

I had never been much of a cat person, but I had made a radical 180-degree turn.

Of course, the chickens weren't real fond of the cats, clucking excitedly when they came near their hallowed houses, but the cats were scared of the chickens, scampering away in fright if a chicken came clucking. 'Fraidy cats, all of them.

Lydia and I went about collecting the eggs and caring for the animals. The morning was cool and crisp, although I knew it would become much warmer later on in the day. I loved mornings on the farm. The land was waking up. The sun was stretching. The trees waved their morning greetings at each other. Melissa Lynn and the piglets were softly shuffling about as if making too much noise would break the serenity of the moment.

It was so different from the cities I'd lived in. I breathed in deeply, the exhaustion that followed me around like a stalker still with me, but it wasn't as sharp, wasn't as invasive. Sleep had helped. Peace had helped. Mountain air had helped.

"Good to see you, young lady. How is your womanly health today?" Aunt Lydia would say when she wanted to discuss women's issues. This was my clue to the conversation topic of the day.

During the egg-collecting I would get information on all sorts of women's issues that Aunt Lydia had read about in *The New York Times,* the *Journal of the American Medical Association, Forbes, Science Digest*, and a whole array of obscure magazines. I would also get a lecture on the feminine healing powers of embroidery, cross-stitch, knitting, painting, and wreath-making.

She was most fond of quoting some hippie friends of hers who published a monthly newsletter listing sage advice on how to rid yourself of toenail fungus, how to reach your inner monster, cook for ghosts, and do cartwheels naked to improve acne.

Today's topic was fear.

"Fear will strangle the womanliness right out of you, Julia," she announced, petting a chicken on the head.

I had no argument for that. Fear had followed me for so long in my life. Being out in the country, among peace and gentleness, was making me well aware of how fear had guided almost every move in my life. And every mistake.

"Fear will turn your instincts to mush, making you doubt the wisdom that springs forth from your uterus. The uterus, your womb, knows the truth. The uterus tells the brain. But fear interrupts that transaction."

She looked under a battered pink dresser, found a batch of eggs. "Fear will smush your ability to choose your life's direction. Fear gets inside your brain like octopus tentacles and pokes into your brain cells."

I scooted my hand under a few ladies. No one pecked me today. I whispered, "Thank you, Hildy, Geranium, and Darth Vader." Aunt Lydia's funny way of naming chickens had grown on me.

"Fear will smother your creative energy, shaking your passions into nothing but warts."

I was not so lucky with the next three ladies. They pecked at me, then clucked, a secret sister language all their own. "I have never liked you, Queen Titty, Dog Face, and Sabrina," I said to them.

"Fear will prevent you from seeing the success that can be yours." Aunt Lydia shook her fists in the air. "It will blind you as good as someone with a fat ass sitting on your face will blind you."

Next she picked up a shovel. "Never, never let someone's fat ass sit on your face, my dear. Never."

I nodded at her. She was right, of course. I would not want someone's fat ass on my face.

When we were done, the eggs collected, the chickens happy, the cats petted, Melissa Lynn and her piglets cared for, she said, as she so often did, "Let's go and eat some pancakes, Julia. You look in need of some pancakes with lots of my maple syrup to get your secretions moving."

And then, as she often did, she pulled me closer to her as we walked out of the barn. But this time she said something different. "Sweetheart. There is one more way for you to conquer your fear."

I nodded, took a deep breath. Fear was killing me, day by day.

"You must attend target practice more often. Stash is coming over soon to help you. We both feel that you won't be able to hit this side of a cow's butt from ten feet away unless you spit more bullets out of the gun I gave you. So far you're a terrible shot. Don't look at me like that. You are a terrible shot. You must get for yourself the killer's instinct. My hormones are screaming that I'm failing you, my pelvic bones say that the child not of my womb but of my heart needs to protect herself better. Stash felt my pelvic bones the other day, and he feels the same."

I did not inquire into that particular statement on Stash and her pelvic bones.

Aunt Lydia kissed my cheek, then whispered, "Shoot to kill, Julia. Always, always, shoot to kill."

I nodded.

Shoot to kill.

Lydia had dubbed tonight Getting To Know Your Vagina Psychic Night. Caroline, Katie, and Lara were all coming over within minutes. Lydia had cooked dinner. We were having tacos.

"The taco shells are to symbolize the importance of filling your vagina with good health!" Lydia wielded two pans in the air as she said this, her gray hair pulled back into one long braid, stray curls softening her features. "We'll be filling our tacos with meat to symbolize our oneness with Mother Earth, and finely grated cheese to represent the milk our breasts hold to feed our babies, and avocados for healthy wombs, and fresh tomatoes because I like tomatoes, and hot sauce to kill vaginitis!"

I didn't know that hot sauce could kill vaginitis, but I was certainly game to try. My vagina had been feeling much better—cleaner, I would say—since being away from Robert the last weeks. It almost felt as if it belonged to me again, and wasn't just poised between my legs waiting for Robert's intrusion.

"We are also having strawberry daiquiris to release the fiery woman that lives in all of us, just waiting for a chance to escape and explore her sensuality!" She clanged the pans together three times, looking heavenward. "Daiquiris will let our femininity run wild as it should, the strawberries feeding our libidos and our lusts, since men so seldom do much for us with their teensies!"

I almost laughed, but I was eating some of the white chocolate I'd made earlier and didn't want to spit it out. Chocolate should never be wasted. It is a bite of heaven.

But, I thought, Stash obviously satisfies Aunt Lydia with his teensie.

Lydia and Stash spent quite a bit of time at her house, and often, when I came back from town or a walk, they would hurriedly rush from Lydia's room. Stash would wink at me, and Lydia would immediately start throwing orders his way. "You aren't to come over here again for three days, Stash! And get your tractor out of my driveway, and I need you to let me borrow your backhoe, and don't eat all the spice bread I made you in one day again."

"All right, my beam of light," he would drawl, kissing her on the cheek. "Not for three days, but I'll see you later tonight. Be by at seven. Henry and Casey don't like it when we're late for dinner."

Or he would tell her to be at his house by six for morning omelets, or he would hug her and tell her he would call tonight as he had to go to the city for a couple of days, and then he would lecture her about locking her doors, keeping her gun by her bed, thanking the Lord at that point that I had come to stay so he didn't have to worry about Lydia being alone. "Have you been target practicing, Lydia?" he asked on numerous occasions. "I don't like leaving you alone, but knowing you have the thirty-eight I gave you makes me feel a lot better. Remember, shoot to kill, not to maim."

She would interrupt him, even as she was slapping his butt with one hand. "I don't need you to tell me how to protect myself, old man. And I got better aim than you, and don't think I haven't thought about aiming a gun in the direction of your ass many a time!"

Stash would hug me before he left, his eyes full of warmth, and admonish me to keep an eye on Lydia while he was in the city. They would kiss again, with Lydia barely pausing to stop giving him orders. "Drive slow. Don't drive like the fires of hell are burning after your hide, Stash, you old man. I'll see you Wednesday night for dinner. Do not be late!" She grabbed his face with both hands, tilting his head down. "Not one minute late!"

Aunt Lydia would stand with her arms crossed tightly over her chest, and Stash would honk his horn periodically as he drove down the road. When she couldn't see him anymore, Lydia would semi-yell, "Stash! He will not leave me alone for a second. He is one ripe pain in the petoosy. Now, what needs to be done?"

And off we'd both charge. We'd fix a fence, clean out the Pigs Palace, as Lydia called Melinda's pigpen, paint a shed lime green, cook up four different meals to be distributed to four needy families in town, sew new curtains, or hang flowers to dry to make bouquets and other pretty house things. Aunt Lydia let her art projects be auctioned off for various fund-raisers in the county, so she always had plenty to do.

"When you're sad or depressed, you might as well get something done," Lydia always said. "Pretty soon, you're not sad or depressed, and darned if things aren't done."

We had spent about an hour in the kitchen getting the Cheers To Vaginas Tacos ready and making a fruit salad. She called it Fruit Salad For Fruitful Women. The green salad, with shredded cheese, dried berries, and nuts was called Greens For Clean Secretions Salad.

Like I said, it was Getting To Know Your Vagina Psychic Night.

So, as usual, the lights were turned down low, and pink candles dotted the room. The day was warm, so a couple of windows were open, cool breezes swirling through the house.

The dining room table was covered in a pink fabric. "Pink represents the inside of a healthy vagina," Aunt Lydia had told me. Over the table was a centerpiece in the shape of a wreath made with red apples, dried flowers, leaves, a little hay, and a pink ribbon. Lydia had whipped it up in about an hour, and it was stunning, made more stunning by the fact that it hung by cranberry-red ribbons from the ceiling, coming to a stop about five inches from the table.

"We're going to get half-naked and reawaken our vaginas," Aunt Lydia announced to the four of us, who were happily relaxed in the overstuffed furniture, drinking our daiquiris to release the fiery woman who lives in all of us and is just waiting for a chance to escape and explore her sensuality. Aunt Lydia had poured all the daiquiris into these tall, pink, curvy glasses.

"We're going to do what?" Katie asked, munching on another hors d'oeuvre of stuffed mushrooms wrapped in bacon. When everyone had arrived, Lydia had told us the stuffed mushroom was to represent our privacy, the bacon the outer shell of protection we all wear around our privates.

Lara sat next to me, again in a proper, red short-sleeved blouse, her blond hair piled in a bun on top of her head. She had dark circles under her eyes and a few flecks of purple paint on her face and hands. "Reawaken our vaginas? The way Jerry's after me, mine hardly has any time to sleep," she muttered, although not unhappily.

On the other couch, Caroline, whose eye seemed to be taking a break tonight, with no winking, laughed. She wore a jean skirt, a blue T-shirt, and white sandals. She had brought with her an enormous bouquet of flowers for each of us. Caroline was always, always giving.

I thought about all the times that I hadn't given, and should have. The neighbors who were kind to me, the old lady across the hall in my apartment building, the people I worked with, my two ex-friends that Robert had made me dump. All had reached out a hand. Some had tried to warn me about Robert. They all deserved a great big bouquet, but I had never given them one, being too wrapped up in my own problems to reach back.

I felt like crying, but I sucked it up. What a rotten person I am.

"I really don't think anyone wants to see me half-naked, Lydia," Katie said. "I don't even want to see my own butt." She wore an overly large red sweatshirt and baggy jeans. Her mermaid hair was swept back into a ponytail like a mermaid tail.

"Nonsense!" Lydia bellowed. "It's men who have made us embarrassed about ourselves. A woman's worth should not be judged by her bodily curves and valleys! That's what men have done to us!" She held up both fingers in the air, giving us the signal. "Remember!"

"Men are pricks!" Caroline, Lara, Katie, and I yelled back in unison. Soon we would probably have secret handshakes and rituals. Maybe we would sacrifice a man on a spit one night. I could think of one who would burn really well.

"A woman's form is merely what we've been given to get through this life," said Aunt Lydia.

"I think I know my vagina as well as I want to know it," Lara said. "It doesn't bother me, and I don't bother it. We exist separately except when I have to pee or have sex with Jerry."

"See! You just did it, Lara!" Lydia said, handing her another daiquiri. "You said that you exist separately from your vagina, except that's not true. Our vaginas hold our powers, our passions, our secret core. They are dear to us, and we must cherish them as we would our very best friend!"

"But I don't want to see my best friend's vagina," Katie said, flipping her red ponytail behind her back. "No offense to any of you, I'm sure you all have dandy vaginas, but I don't care to see them. Especially when I'm eating."

Caroline finally intervened. "Well, I think we can come to a compromise here, a give-and-take. Why don't we all sit down at the table and then take off our skirts and pants under the table and then we can be one with our vaginas during dinner, as Lydia suggested, but we don't have to actually see anyone else's vagina."

"Good idea," said Lara. "Let's eat. I'm starving. Naked or not, I gotta eat."

"Perfect! A perfect Vagina Plan, Caroline!" Lydia approved, clapping her hands together. "Now help me bring in the meal. We'll celebrate our vaginas without making everyone else celebrate them, too."

"Well, I'll strip down," said Katie. "But my personal vagina does not deserve any celebration. It has only gotten me into trouble. Vaginal irritation, yeast, bad sex, a baby, bad sex, good sex, more bad sex, another baby, yeast, bad sex, another baby, bad sex, still another baby. My vagina and I aren't speaking much, but I'll eat some of that chocolate cake you have in your kitchen that looks like this house and hope my passion and my vaginal strength come back."

"That is not my delectable creation, although I wish I could claim it," Aunt Lydia answered, turning toward the kitchen. We all followed her like she was the Piped Piper. "My brilliant niece Julia made that cake."

As they entered the kitchen, Lara and Caroline gasped, then their heads whipped over to me at the same time, like a line of Rockettes, before snapping back to my cake. For long, long seconds everyone at the Getting To Know Your Vagina Psychic Night meeting stood and stared in wonder at my chocolate cake. I had even recreated tiny chocolate toilets and the bridge on the lawn.

"It's like looking at art. Chocolate art," whispered Lara. "The pigs are incredible, Julia. They're even wearing their names."

"I'm telling you!" Aunt Lydia announced. "This chocolate cake is better than foreplay. My niece makes Better Than Foreplay Chocolate Cake, that she does."

"Oh, Good Lord," said Katie. "We're not supposed to eat that, are we?" And then she burst into tears.

Super. I had made Katie cry for the second time. I put my arm around her shoulders. A slice of chocolate cake would cheer her up. It had almost always worked for me.

I learned as a child that baking with chocolate can take your mind off life. It started when one of the young mothers in our neighborhood, Renee, gave me an old cookbook of hers with recipes for chocolate cakes, candy, muffins, etc. She taught me how to bake.

The walls of her kitchen were painted yellow. The cabinets were blue with handles in the shape of coffee mugs. Red tiles danced along the backsplash. She had a nice husband, three kids, two dogs, four cats, and a lizard that sat on the counter watching her all day. "I'm a hard-core Mommy, Julia. Hard-core. Want me to show you my new recipe book on making crepes?"

Using money from baby-sitting, I started buying my own ingredients to bake when my mother was gone for days or weeks at a time. When Renee got sick on her husband's birthday, I offered to bake the cake. I whipped up the eggs just so, melted the butter nice and slow, sifted the flour not once, but twice, mixed the dry ingredients with the wet ones a spoon at a time, then watched the cake as it rose in the pan in the oven.

I doubled the recipe for a thick, creamy chocolate icing, then decorated the cake with swoops and swirls—not so much it would look tacky, but enough to give it style.

Renee was so happy when I gave it to her, she blew her nose and cried. I had been sneaking out on Sunday mornings to go to church with her (her husband was a minister), and after that I started baking cookies, cupcakes, and muffins for their women's brunches, and I became close to the women there. They, in turn, reached back out to me with clothes and friendship and food.

And calls to Children's Services.

When my mother found out what was going on, we moved again. "They think they're better than you," she told me, shoving a trembling hand through her hair, one eye swollen shut from where one of her boyfriends had hit her. He had hit me, too, but had used his fist on my gut so my bruise didn't show. "You're their project, nothing more, nothing less. They think you're going to hell and they're gonna save you. How could they like you, anyhow? You're dirty all the time. You never smile. Your hair's a mess. . . ."

I hid my tears as we drove away from that neighborhood, but the minister's wife had given me something valuable to my heart and to my soul: a chocolate ticket to life.

Baking with chocolate calms my nerves. There is something about melted, warm, gooey chocolate, and the memories of Renee's red and blue and yellow kitchen with the ever-watching lizard that reaches deep inside of me. When I have felt despair crushing me into nothing, I have reached for chocolate with one hand, a recipe book with another.

Chocolate, you could say, has saved my life.

The Cheers To Vaginas Tacos, the Fruit Salad For Fruitful Women, the Greens For Clean Secretions Salad, and the hot sauce to cure vaginitis had all been eaten. The strawberry daiquiris had been drunk. I personally had three to make sure that the "woman in me" could escape and explore. We had filled our plates, slithered out of our pants and skirts under the table, and eaten, the candles flickering.

Within seconds we forgot we were half-naked and supposed to be celebrating our vaginas and chattered away. After an hour, I let my mind swerve to Paul Bunyan. I hadn't seen him for a week. I knew he had worked on Stash's farm the day I met him, and the next day Stash and his workers were on Paul Bunyan's ranch, and then Paul Bunyan apparently grabbed his great blue ox and went back to the city.

"Got a big trial that's going to start in a few weeks. He didn't tell me what it's about, but I read it in the papers. Man tried to have his wife killed. Hired a hit man. The hit man got to know the wife and liked her. Hit man told the wife what was going on. She called the cops." Stash shook his head. "The plot is too stupid and too overused to even use in a movie but there it is, in real life."

I was afraid to ask. But I did. "Whose side is Paul—I mean, whose side is Dean representing?"

Stash looked shocked. "Well, he's on the wife's side. Of course."

My body sagged with relief. Men who protected criminals were as creepy as the men they represented.

Those blue eyes of Paul's, and that smile, kept appearing before my eyes. Not that it meant anything, not anything at all. I am, after all, not into men anymore. The very thought of getting involved with any member of the male species made me feel ill.

Besides, Paul Bunyan was probably married or had been married eight different times. He wasn't the classically handsome sort. There was no way he would ever land in the pages of a magazine. But he was huge, his hair was good, he had those blue eyes and a nice, slow smile.

I told myself to rid Paul Bunyan from my mind. The man scared me. Those blue eyes that *really looked* at me scared me. That nice and friendly smile and that low, gravelly voice, and that laugh that made me want to laugh along with him scared me, too.

"You can stop kidding yourself anytime." The sharp tone shook me from my reverie, and my eyes flew to Lara, who sat across from me. Katie was at my left, Caroline across from her, and Aunt Lydia at the head of the table to my right.

"I'm not kidding myself, Lara!" Katie snapped, dropping more sour cream onto the meat in her taco. "I just know things will get better."

"When?"

"What?"

"When? When on earth do you really think that things will get better?" Lara took out the rubber band holding her hair back and shoved her hands through it. In the candlelight she looked pale, as if she hadn't slept in a week. "You've been saying that for three years, as long as I've known you. You smile when you say it, but you know the truth."

"Yes, I do know the truth! My husband is a good man, and he'll stop . . ." Katie's voice faded. "He'll stop drinking. Things have already gotten better—"

Lara rolled her eyes. "Katie, you told me earlier this week that J.D. had passed out on the couch after working his way through three bars. He just lost his ninth job. No one in town will hire him because of his drinking problem, and soon no one in Decateur or Rosemont will hire him, either!"

"So what the hell do you want me to do!" Katie turned red and tossed her napkin on the table. "You, of all people, should understand, Lara. I took wedding vows, I said all that stuff about forsaking all others, in sickness and in health, till death do us part, and I'm not going to just walk out because he's not perfect!"

"*Not perfect?*" There went another roll of the eyes. "Katie, he's not even got the 'p' in perfect going for him. You've been married how long?"

"Ten years?"

"Ten years? Four children in ten years and an alcoholic husband."

"He's not an alcoholic." Katie said, but her voice was as weak as a dying rabbit. "He drinks too much. There's a difference."

"I won't argue with you, not because I'm not right, but

because it's pointless. But the result is the same, isn't it? J.D. drinks. You work all day cleaning houses, often bringing Logan with you to work because you don't trust your husband to watch him. The man will be drunk, won't hear his cries, won't feed him—"

"Stop it, Lara." Katie covered her face with her hands.

"You work all day, pick up the other kids, take them to soccer and the community art classes, you volunteer at school, then you go home, try to get your husband off the couch, fix dinner, help the kids with their homework, clean your own house, pack lunches for the next day, and at eleven o'clock at night you start writing. Have I about got it?"

Katie didn't move.

"And this has been going on for your whole marriage. And he's a mean drunk, isn't he?" Lara asked, relentless.

I sat, frozen. Mean drunks were the worst. I would far rather have a friendly, horny drunk than a mean drunk for a husband. Mean drunks hit. I had seen that with precisely three of my mother's boyfriends/husbands.

Katie opened her mouth, then shut it. Opened it again. "I can handle this situation. I'm doing what's best for the kids."

"You're in denial, Katie."

"And you aren't, Miss Perfect Minister's Wife?"

"No." Lara took another big drink of her daiquiri. "I'm not perfect, and everyone here knows it. But I love you, Katie. You're one of the nicest people I've ever met. You're the best mother I know. Your kids are so good, so sweet, and it's because of you. Don't forget that people talk at church. Everyone loves you. Every time someone is sick or sad, they can count on cookies from you, help from you. And yet you never, ever help yourself."

"I *am* helping myself—dammit, I am! I am keeping my family together." Katie put her elbows on the table and bent her head for a moment, then looked Lara straight in the eyes, all vestiges of pretense gone. "I can't divorce him. If I did, he would turn on the charm for some other woman, get married, and then my kids would go and visit him, without me there to supervise. He can't take care of them. He yells at them, Lara. I would worry the entire time they were there. And what if his new wife didn't like the kids? What if she was mean to them? What if her kids didn't like my kids, and yet my kids are stuck there for the weekend with their father getting drunk and a mean stepmother?"

I didn't know what to say, but I knew enough about divorce to know that the father always got visitation unless he was an axe-wielding, drug-snorting, ex-convict son of a bitch. Katie was right about that.

"But what about you?" Caroline spoke up, her face pale, her cheekbones standing out in the light. "When are you going to choose you?"

"What do you mean, 'choose you'?"

"I mean, when are you going to see that you matter, that your happiness matters, that you don't deserve to be married to a drunk?"

"J.D. will get to a point where he'll stop drinking—"

"No, he won't," Aunt Lydia, Lara, and Caroline said together.

"Not unless he faces a crisis," Lara continued. "He has to hit the very bottom of the ladder, then fall off of it, then crack his head open, then wake up in his own vomit in a strange place with bars before he'll change, Katie. If then."

"When he's sober, he's nice to the children." Her voice faded. "Usually. Sometimes. Now and then."

"How often is he sober?" Caroline asked, but by the way she asked it, I knew she already knew. "He's an alcoholic."

"No, he's not. And if he is, alcoholism is a disease."

Aunt Lydia snorted. Lara blew air through her teeth and looked disgusted. Caroline's lips turned in on themselves.

"Bullshit," Lara said. "Letting alcoholics claim they have a disease lets them off the hook. It forces their families to feel sorry for them instead of kicking them out into the street. I've seen people with real diseases, and they did not find their disease, *they did not bring their disease on themselves*, by willfully drinking their way through thousands of bottles of liquor over a period of years. The only disease the alcoholics have is the disease of weakness and selfishness. And you're enabling him to stay just as he is, Katie."

Katie shook her head. "I can't support the kids on my own anyhow. He doesn't make much, but he brings in some—"

"But he drinks away all the money he brings in!" Lara snapped, clacking her fork on her plate. "You even have to pay a baby-sitter to watch the kids when you come here every week."

"She's a great baby-sitter," Katie intoned, as if that explained it all. "I don't have a choice. And anyhow, why are you so angry with me, Lara?"

"I'm angry because I'm so frustrated. Because you won't change this situation. You won't do anything about it."

"*Do anything about it*?" Katie looked like she was going to cry. "I *am* doing something about it."

"Is it working?" Lara was relentless.

A look of utter hopelessness settled on Katie's features. "I am not going to get a divorce. I'm not."

Her words fell into a silent void, I could almost see unspoken words floating over the table.

"Well," said Aunt Lydia, "I don't think you can claim to have a healthy vagina, then, can you?"

Silence again.

"You need a boyfriend, Katie," Aunt Lydia said, stabbing her knife in the air. "A little boy toy. A reprieve. A man who will understand the situation and give you some good lovin' till you're ready to dump that bastard husband of yours and move on with your life."

Katie looked up from the table. Her mouth twisted. Lara shook her head in a way that indicated she thought Katie was hopeless. Then she got up and hugged her tight and long. Caroline fiddled with her glass, then her hands stilled, her eyes widening as she stared at Katie. I gulped in air.

And then Katie laughed. Laughed right into Lara's shoulder. Laughed till she cried.

"I'm in heaven," Caroline sighed.

We women were all dressed again. Like the true girl-friends we are, we all insisted on cleaning up together. With five women, it took about five minutes. Now we were sprawled all over Lydia's comfy furniture like limp, engorged eels.

With tired vaginas. Vaginas blessed by hot sauce and cheese, but tired. It was late, after all, and outside the stars were twinkling, the moon full and peering into Aunt Lydia's darkened house.

After Lara's diatribe with Katie, Aunt Lydia insisted we change the conversation and discuss taking control of our vaginas, not letting the heat of passion with men get in the way of our strength as women, and not letting our vaginas lead us astray. Next Lydia encouraged all of us to pull away from the table, just a tad, and look at our vaginas.

It was hard to do. I am nowhere near as limber as Aunt Lydia, and my giant watermelons kept getting in the way. Finally, I pushed them out of the way with both hands and dared myself to catch a peek at my vagina.

Yuck. I am sorry. I do not know why men, and some women, would be remotely attracted to such a wrinkled, fleshy, sometimes foul-smelling organ. I do not.

I put my head up real quick. I noticed that Lara did, too. We both reached for our daiquiris in those long, curvy pink glasses.

"Visualize peace with your vagina," Aunt Lydia intoned. "Peace!"

I visualized my vagina and couldn't drink any more

daiquiri. Yuck again. Yuck that Robert had been there. Yuck that he'd squirted some of his stuff into me through that hole. Yuck that my vagina had never given me much pleasure, but had caused me a ton of pain.

Katie put her head up, too, then Caroline, then Aunt Lydia.

"Well, I looked at my vagina," Caroline said. "It looks the same as it's always looked. Would you pass the pitcher of daiquiris, Lydia?"

"You need a new awareness of your vagina, Car-o-line!" Aunt Lydia boomed.

"Let's take your vagina, Katie!"

"Oh dear God, let's not," said Katie.

"Dear God, thank you that Lydia didn't call my name," Lara muttered.

"You need to forgive your vagina, Katie! Forgive it! It got you into trouble before you realized what a lout J.D. is. A lot of trouble. You must forgive it. Here." She gave Katie a handful of strawberries. "Put these on your vagina, and tell your little flower that you forgive it, that the strawberries are there to offer it sweetness and comfort and peace."

"You have got to be kidding, Lydia," Katie said, pushing her red hair away from her face. "You want me to put these strawberries on my privates?"

"Yes! I do! None of us need to see, we don't *want* to see! It's between you and your little flower! You don't want your little flower to shrivel!"

"Well, I wouldn't mind shriveling a little bit," Katie said, pondering. "In fact, if I could shrivel off fifty pounds that would be pretty nifty—"

"You must concentrate, Katie." Aunt Lydia pleaded, spreading her arms wide. "Forgiveness is only an inch away! Put the strawberries on your little flower, and make this sound." Aunt Lydia made the sound of the ocean, the waves crashing back and forth.

"Why the sound of the ocean?" asked Katie. Her hands

disappeared under the table. I wanted to make very sure that those strawberries stayed on her plate and didn't go back in the communal bowl.

"Because the ocean's waves flow like forgiveness. *Feel* that forgiveness, Katie. *Be* that forgiveness. Allow that forgiveness to surge into your body, wave by wave. Now, Katie, strawberries down, your voice on! We must conquer our vaginas!"

Katie closed her eyes and did a very good impression of the waves breaking on the shore. Maybe in her past life she really had been a mermaid.

Next Aunt Lydia crooked a finger at Lara. "You need to allow your vagina to be all your vagina can be! She is trapped, lost, unable to escape. She feels such a responsibility toward the rest of the body, that she can't leave, even though inside she's angry and repressed. Here!" Aunt Lydia tossed a napkin to Lara, then shoved the salt shaker her way.

"Put this napkin under your rear and shake salt over your little flower."

"What?" Lara asked. "Salt my vagina?"

"You heard me! You are a damaged young woman who is still living under her father's fat ass. And don't deny it. You need to rid yourself of that man like I need to rid my shed of dry rot. Put the napkin under your rear so you don't get salt on my chair, and then shake salt over your little flower."

"Lydia," said Lara, taking another huge gulp of wine, "you have really lost it this time."

"Lost it? Lost it? *I haven't lost it.* You women all have issues, except maybe Caroline, and they stem from the bereftness, the desperation in the very core of your being, in your very essence, your very womanliness. You've let men make decisions in your lives for you, decisions you should have had the strength, the vagina strength, to fight back, to fight for yourself, to walk away. No!" She banged her fist on the table. "I'll correct myself! You should have had the strength to grab your vagina and *run* away!"

Lara sighed, grabbed the napkin, sat on it. We watched as she shook salt on herself.

"Can you tell me the significance of the salt, Lydia, before I turn myself into a hairy snowball?"

"Salt represents purity! Innocence! Strength! By sprinkling yourself with salt you are anointing your inner being, starting over, starting fresh!"

I tried not to laugh as Lara gave a few more shakes to the salt shaker, but the laughter bubbled in me until I thought it would burst out my ears.

"Now, Lara, make the sound of a rattler!" Lydia swung her fists through the air. "A giant rattler!"

"A rattler?" Lara asked, still shaking that salt shaker. "You mean a rattlesnake?"

"Yes, indeed I do!" Lydia said, her braids flying. "A rattler will swallow other animals whole. He's fierce and has a strong stomach. He's independent. He does what he wants. He shoots venom out of his mouth. That's what you need to be more like, Lara! A rattlesnake."

"Sounds good to me. I know there was that wily snake with Adam and Eve," Lara said, and then she made a rattling sound with her mouth. I was very impressed. She really sounded like a rattlesnake.

Katie made the sound of waves breaking, Lara made the sound of a rattlesnake. They weren't bad together.

"Caroline, you take these flowers, right here in this vase, and you twine the stems together, nice and easy. And when you have a long line of flowers, then you wrap them around your waist and let them droop toward your vagina."

"So I'm making a flower belt?" Caroline asked.

"No, not like a flower belt," Lydia said with a scowl. "A flower vibrator! You may have a healthy relationship with your vagina, Caroline, but you need some lust in your life, some hot and heavy and passionate lust, so you make yourself a flower vibrator! And when you're threading those stems together, you make a sound like this." Aunt Lydia made the sound of a bee.

"A bee? You want me to make the sound of a bee?"

"Yes, a busy, *busy* bumblebee!"

"So, this is a buzzing vibrator?" Caroline smiled. She was up for anything.

"It's a vibrator of passion. The bees buzzing represent your lust coming to life, your passion."

Soon the sound of the buzzing vibrator joined the rattlesnake and the crashing waves.

I laughed. I couldn't help it. Lydia's hard glare shut me up real quick, though.

"I am shocked at you!" Lydia intoned, no smile at all lighting her features. "Laughing at our healing! And you, with so much healing to do." Her face softened. "This is for you, Julia." She grabbed a salad plate and two forks. "Put the plate over your little flower."

"*What?*"

"Put this plate over your little flower. No, not like that, turn it the other way so it's upside down."

The laughter started bubbling in my throat again. Oh, well. I put the plate over my little flower.

"Take these." She handed me a fork and a knife. "Now drum the fork and the knife against the plate so your little flower can hear it."

"I'm sorry?"

"Pretend you're a drummer, Julia! The plate is your drum, the fork and knife your drumsticks. You need to drum the pain right out of your innards, pound the hurts from the soul of your womanhood, banish the tragedies from the memory of your vagina. You must start anew, but first you must get rid of the memories that have held your vagina captive, that have caught your vagina up in a vicious circle of fear. Take out the anguish and despair, and then give your vagina permission to have a new, safe, loving life, my dear Julia."

The whole idea was starting to sound good to me. At least

I was smart enough to recognize that I needed healing, and if silverware and a plate can help, I was game.

I closed my eyes and slowly drummed the fork on the plate, tuning out the buzzing, the ocean waves, and the rattler. It made a clinking sound. I desperately wanted to get rid of all the memories of my mother's boyfriends, wanted to get rid of the memories of all the times my own mother didn't protect me or, as Aunt Lydia would say, "my little flower." I felt a surge of fury rise in me, but stamped it down, as per usual. Long ago I came to the conclusion that fury with my mother and my childhood, and indulging the aching loneliness that seemed to follow me around like a dark phantom, never accomplished anything.

Knowing this, however, didn't prevent the dark phantom from wrapping himself around me and squeezing the loneliness and crushing pain right to the surface at various and unpredictable moments. It was at those moments that I often couldn't breathe and would have to put my head between my legs and wait for the tremors to stop shaking me like one might shake a bag of loose bones.

I hadn't spoken to my mother in years. The only reason I knew she'd run off to Minnesota with her latest boyfriend was because she'd sent me a postcard. "Moving to Minnesota with Blakely. Hope weight-loss program working for you."

Often during those years, I didn't even know where she was. I kept the same cell phone number in hopes that she would call someday, which is sick in itself, and that I still felt that way made me want to bang my head against a brick wall and cry. But, of course, she never called, and one day I took that cell phone, and piece by piece I dismembered it, then struck it with a hammer until it shattered.

I had said good-bye to my mother as I smashed that phone into nothingness.

And now I drummed on the plate with the knife, listening to a different type of clinking sounds. I thought of Robert. I thought of all the times he had made me feel fat and pathetic. He had even criticized the hair on my vagina. "You look like a monkey, Cannonball. Can't you get that bush waxed? God. A man could get lost in that—in a bad way."

I thought of all the times he'd hit me, or held me down, or accused me of cheating on him, or blamed others for all of his problems, which then became my problems.

And I had stayed with him. It didn't say anything good about me at all.

I speeded up my beat, drumming that plate now with both the fork and the knife. The ocean waves, the rattlesnake, and the humming bees were all keeping up with me.

I thought of romantic movies, and how the men in them were gentle and passionate and loving, and how they showed families laughing together on TV.

I drummed again.

Then I thought of Dean. Of those gentle eyes, those huge hands, those shoulders that went on forever. That smile.

My drumming stopped. For one glorious minute, I allowed myself to feel Dean in my head, allowed myself the time to see those blue eyes, the toughened skin, the rumbling laugh, the deep voice. I allowed myself to hope that men wouldn't always scare me to death. I didn't even know Dean, had only spent a day with him, but he represented to me what I hoped I would someday have if I hadn't made my vow to stay completely away from men: a kind and loving relationship.

The ocean waves stopped crashing in the middle of a crest. The rattlesnake became quiet, temporarily soothed. The humming vibrator stilled.

I saw Dean again, and he smiled at me, and in my mind I smiled back. I picked up the knife and fork and drummed to an entirely new beat, happy and hopeful.

And the waves, the snake, and the vibrator joined me again while Aunt Lydia got up and danced around the table, her gray braids flying everywhere, her little butt flapping about like a white mass of joyful butterflies.

When Katie had removed the strawberries from her little flower and Lara had stopped salting hers, and Caroline had picked up her flower vibrator and dropped it on the table and I had stopped pounding on my plate with a fork and knife, we settled in to eat my chocolate cake on Aunt Lydia's floor, our knees touching each others'.

I had worked on that cake for hours. It looked like a miniature version of Aunt Lydia's house, complete with a black front door made from licorice and a bridge made from striped, chewy candy and pigs I sculpted from chocolate chunks.

"This cake is better than sex," Lara murmured.

"My Julia makes the best chocolate on the planet," Aunt Lydia said, lighting a few more candles. "She has many talents, but this is the one that springs forth from the fountain of her womanliness. You can taste her sweet, loving soul in anything she makes with chocolate in it, yes, you can."

Tasting my soul sounded just a bit freaky, but I nodded. Aunt Lydia had such a way with words.

Katie didn't speak, just closed her eyes, leaned against the couch, and made a happy little moaning sound as she ate another bite.

Caroline was on her third piece. Skinny people can always eat like pigs. "Watch out for chocolate," she whispered to me, echoing the words she'd said before. "Chocolate will change your life. This is fabulous, by the way."

"Chocolate cakes like these could make you a million dollars, Julia," Lara said. "Or more. You gotta make more cakes like this and sell them."

I laughed.

Sell chocolate cake?

Ha.

❧ 7 ❧

We got our readings later, although I declined and Caroline didn't push. I'd had enough of her readings. It didn't freak me out that she was truly psychic, although I did see the mammoth personal problems this would create—like she would feel haunted by her future and everyone else's, and helpless, and torn on whether or not she should alter someone's future and all the consequences of that by telling them things—but I didn't want to hear more about me at the moment.

Caroline saw hay bales, a band, the color yellow, steak, and laughter in Aunt Lydia's future. Lydia thanked her, told her she could come again next week.

Caroline saw paint in Lara's future. Not unusual, since Lara likes to paint. But she specifically saw a painting. In the painting was a naked man wrapped around a sunflower. There was a little purple flower at the base of the sunflower. Even in the dark I could see Lara's face go pale.

When Caroline did Katie's reading she looked momentarily upset, then covered it up. Katie didn't catch it, too busy staring at their clasped hands. But by the end of Katie's reading, Caroline seemed more calm, then she smiled. Just a bit, but it was there, mixed in with a little bit of . . . well, was it relief? "I see a new house for you, Katie. I see paint cans. I see land behind the house. I see you working at a desk. You're at a computer. You're smiling."

Katie smiled. "I'll take it!" she told Caroline, as if she'd just bought a new car.

By the time I crawled into bed a few days later, my shoulders and arms were aching. Stash had met me when I got back from the library, two guns in his hands. He was cheerful and welcoming, but we got right down to business, walking to the far field of Aunt Lydia's property, where he stuck up a new target on bales of hay.

"I need to keep the family jewels for your Aunt Lydia, dear, so watch where you're pointing that thing," he said. Stash is a stickler for safety, so I had to reassure him I knew how to put the safety on and wouldn't accidentally shoot him.

We spent the next three hours practicing.

By the end of the night he gave me the ultimate compliment.

"You're not that bad."

And then, like Lydia, he said again, "Shoot to kill, Julia. Always, always, shoot to kill."

He threw a companionable arm around my shoulders, and I leaned against him, his words echoing in my brain.

It is difficult to drag oneself to a Bible meeting when you're not even sure God remembers who you are. Still, when Lara asked me and Katie several days ago to please come to a Bible meeting at her house because she was in major need of friendship and reinforcements, and when I looked into her exhausted blue eyes, all I could do was nod my head yes like one of those bobbing-head dolls.

But, as usual, the night before the Bible meeting, I didn't sleep much because ole Robert was chasing me, this time with a mixer, the silver blades whirling at my back, chocolate flicking off them at high speed. I hid behind a giant yellow pig, but he caught up to me, only now the silver blades were miniature pink knives, the same color as the tablecloth Aunt Lydia had used for vagina night.

I woke up from my dream drenched in sweat, my heart palpitating.

In the morning my face looked pale, although I was pleased to see the bruises were very pale now, like a bad makeup job. My hair, well, it was a mass of curls sticking out in 812 different directions. I fed the chickens, worked around the farm, then drove to get Katie, feeling like an exhausted blob of human existence.

Katie looked worse.

Logan, three years old, opened the door when I knocked. Like his five-year-old brother, Luke, and his two older sisters—Haley, age seven, and Hannah, age nine—he had the glorious red hair of his mother. All of the kids had dimples and chocolate brown eyes like their mother. They looked the same, but they all had their quirks. Logan wore his Spiderman outfit every day, and Luke insisted on dressing in layers: two T-shirts, a vest, and a sweatshirt. Sometimes more shirts. He often insisted on wearing three pairs of underwear, Katie told me.

Haley liked to wear toy antennas on her head with glittering purple eyeballs on the ends, and Hannah would only wear black.

"Hewwo, Miss Julia," Logan said opening the door to their home. Luke was right behind him. As expected, Logan was in his Spiderman outfit, and Luke, I could see, was wearing a couple of T-shirts, a vest, and a blue sweatshirt. It was about seventy degrees outside, and the sky was clear.

I gave them each a hug, then heard a sound that I can only

describe as the snort a wild boar must make while eating live prey.

I looked across the living room, spotlessly clean and tidy, and saw a lump of mankind that apparently was Katie's husband. He was in a robe, and the robe was open. I could almost see his goodies. He had stubble on his face, and a gigantic gut protruded from under a tight white T-shirt. If men got pregnant, they would look like this man.

He made the flesh-eating noise again when Katie entered the living room. Her kids grinned when they saw her.

Katie's eyes glanced at her husband, then at me. If I was tired from sleeplessness, Katie was one step away from toppling over. Her eyes were red, so I knew she'd been crying.

She'd told me that the only reason she was going to the prayer service today was to drum up more business for her housecleaning. "I'm a Christian, Julia, and I pray, but I don't think God's been hearing me much lately. I don't blame him. He's got the Middle East to worry about, the economy, abused children. Millions of people have problems worse than me, and I can handle mine. It would be nice, though, if he could bless me with a few more clients, so I'm coming with you to the prayer session."

Katie looked at The Boar grunting on the couch, then at me. "Come on in, Julia," she said, as if her husband had embarrassed her so many times she was past the point of humiliation and had given up. "I have to get the kids a snack to take with them, then we'll go."

So I smiled at the kids, trooped past The Boar with the serious gastrointestinal problem, and followed Katie into the kitchen. She closed the connecting door after me, and the kids entered. The kitchen was spotlessly clean. A germ would not dare to live in that environment. The cabinets were a pristine white, the counter battered and old, but Katie had colorful jars, a collection of tiny teapots, and a vase full of flowers on it, so it actually looked real nice.

I sat at the table, covered in a tablecloth with a cheerful floral pattern. On the counter was a cherry pie. Katie, dumping snacks into baggies, saw me looking at it. "I'm bringing it to the prayer session," she said, her lips twisting. If I didn't know better, I'd think she hated that pie. "I baked two yesterday, but J.D. took one of them."

"Oh." I didn't like the way she said that. J.D. took a pie? Where? Couldn't he just eat in the kitchen?

Katie grabbed a huge jar of pretzels, but the lid wouldn't come off. She said, "Darn it," then hit it three times against the counter, harder each time, her face growing flushed and frustrated. When she'd bent the lid back and it finally opened, she tried to put the pretzels in a Baggie but accidentally dropped the plastic pretzel jar, and pretzels went flying all over the floor. I got down on my hands and knees with Katie and the kids. She wiped her eyes.

"Mommy sad?" Logan asked.

"No, Mommy isn't sad," Katie said, so soothing. "Mommy's happy because I get to be with you two sweethearts today."

Logan hugged her leg and grinned, but he looked worried, his brow furrowed. If there were two little boys who were ever in love with their mother, it was Logan and Luke.

She wiped her eyes again.

"Don't cry, Mommy," Logan said, his voice scared and pleading.

"Mommy's sleepy. So sleepy."

"Were you up late writing your story last night?" Luke said.

"Yes." Katie wiped her nose. "Mommy was up late writing last night."

"Daddy's mean," Logan said, wrapping his little arms around Katie's neck.

"I hate Daddy," Luke told me in a conversational tone, as if he'd just said, "I don't like onions."

Katie sighed, ruffling Luke's hair. I knew that Katie's husband drank. I knew she wasn't happy. But I suspected something else. She had that look women get when they've absolutely had it. When they've given up on their husbands. When they're no longer in love with them, and, worse, they no longer love them even as a friend or father of their children. The look that said they're past being disgusted and disdainful, past anger, past hate, and into a zone where they're only trying to survive.

They're simply living day by day, their lives filled with work and kids and the impossibility of managing a husband who presents new problems every day.

"Go and get your backpacks, sweeties," Katie said, "and I'll pack your lunch."

The two scampered off, past the slobbering boar in the family room.

Katie tried three times to get the lid back on the peanut butter, but the tears prevented her from realizing that she was trying to put the jelly lid on it. I took the lid from her hand and put the peanut butter and jelly away.

She grabbed the bread, put it in the refrigerator. When she turned to wipe down the counter, I put the bread in the pantry.

When she put the lunch sacks in the microwave, I pulled them out and put them in the pantry.

It was not a good day for Katie.

"He found someone else."

"Who?" The Boar?

"J.D.," she whispered. "He's having an affair."

I felt my stomach drop. "An affair?" I knew I sounded like a parrot, but, really, who would have an affair with J.D.? A woman who liked sex with pregnant-looking boars who made guttural sounds?

But then I remembered what Aunt Lydia had said, that J.D. had that slick charm that stupid women buy into. That he was actually good-looking when dressed up, that he could make a tree talk to him. He was smooth. So smooth, she'd told me.

"Yes. I just don't know who with."

I nodded, feeling sick for her. But maybe now she'd leave. "I'm sorry, Katie."

"Me too." She wrapped her arms around herself, stared at the cherry pie. "I'm mad about that, too."

What could I say? Anything would sound inane. Condescending. "Perhaps you should consider removing his balls from his body when you get the chance."

"What?" She looked up, confused.

"You said you were mad at J.D. I suggested taking away his personal jewels."

She ran both hands through her hair, blinking hard. "I'm mad about the pies. I baked one to take to the prayer meeting today and one for the kids. They love my cherry pie. He took the pie. He actually took the pie that I baked to his girl-friend."

"What an asshole," I said. "Do you want to know who it is?" I just about swallowed my tongue when those words dropped out. How morbid. How inappropriate. Why did I ask that? Why am I an idiot?

"No." She was silent, a muscle jumping in her jaw.

"Katie!" A harsh voice, one thick with sleep and drink, one that I could only assume came from The Boar, grumbled through the kitchen. "Katie! Where the fuck are you?"

Katie rolled her eyes. "Just a minute."

She slid the connecting door open, then shut it behind her. I leaned my ear against the door so I could hear what was said, feeling sneaky as I did so.

I heard The Boar belch. Katie must have been standing right by him at the time. Then I heard him fart.

"I'm hungry."

There was silence. "I'm leaving to go to a prayer session, J.D. I left you a sandwich and soup. It's in the kitchen."

I could gag. The woman finds out that the meatloaf man she married is having an affair and she leaves him a sandwich and soup? Was it too much to hope for that she had added a pinch of rat poison?

But who was I to talk? I'd stayed with Robert even when he lurked outside the door of the gallery where I worked to make sure I was really there and thought that it was fun to sit on my back for long periods of time even when I complained that I couldn't breathe. I stayed with him even when he told me in this disgusted tone that my nipples were the size of dessert plates and said, "You eat too much dessert, Booby." I stayed with him when he bounced my face off the kitchen counter because the chicken I baked for dinner was burned. I hate when I'm a hypocrite.

"Bring it to me," he said, his voice slurred.

I heard the TV come on. The Boar farted again. I pictured black gas encasing that room.

"J.D., you can get your sandwich, I've got to get the kids ready."

"Dammit, bitch," he yelled. I heard something crash against the TV. "It isn't going to take you anytime to get your fat butt in the kitchen and get me some food."

"Logan, Luke," Katie called to her kids. "Get your shoes on. We're leaving. Grab a sweatshirt, too."

I heard the kids say, "Okay, Mommy," real quiet, then the sound of their little feet as they ran to their rooms.

"So you're leaving again, Katie?" The Boar said, his voice sounding like a meat grinder. "You got stuff to do, places to be? Can't spend even a second helping your husband? Shit. No wonder I don't want you in bed anymore—look at you. You're as fat as a cow."

Men are so unoriginal in their criticisms of the women in their lives sometimes. What came out of J.D.'s mouth had come out of Robert's, too.

I heard Katie coming toward the kitchen, so I scampered away from the door. Katie walked in, her expression calm and composed, as if she and her husband had just exchanged information on what kinds of vegetables they'd use for the garden that summer.

She smiled at me, her lips tight, her eyes watery, then wrapped foil around the pie. I heard The Boar's heavy footsteps coming toward the kitchen, and I braced myself, the old fear coursing through me even though J.D. wasn't Robert. Why were men such beasts?

"I ain't taking this shit, Katie," he roared, slamming open the kitchen door.

In spite of myself, I started to shake. The Boar wasn't tall, but he was thick and fat, with a slight beard and black hair. Even though he looked mean, I had to admit that his face was movie-star good-looking if you could get by the fat and the pissed-off look. A broad forehead, straight nose, sculpted lips, light blue eyes that looked straight at you.

Yep. I could see what Aunt Lydia meant when she said he could charm the skin off a snake.

When The Boar saw me, he froze, then shot a look in Katie's direction. "I can see we have a guest, Katie," he snapped. "It would be nice to know when someone is in my house."

I leaned against the wall for a little support. His fists looked to be about the same size as Robert's.

"I didn't want to wake you, J.D.," Katie said. "This is Julia Bennett. She's Lydia's niece."

He ran a hand through his thick black hair, his blue eyes raking me from head to foot, pausing on my breasts, my hips, my legs. "Well, now," he said softly. "Lydia's niece. It's a pleasure to meet you." He extended his hand. I paused, not wanting to touch him, but knew if I refused it would just make things worse for Katie. One time Robert had extended his hand to me after he'd told me I had embarrassed him at a party. I had argued with him. He became enraged, I tried to leave his apartment, and he freaked out, then offered me his hand in apology.

As soon as Robert had my hand in his, he yanked me to his chest, pulled my hair back with a rough hand and told me never, ever to walk out on him again or he would kill me. Did I hear that? he had yelled, right into my face. He would kill me.

Then he'd smashed his mouth on mine, and we had sex, right there, on his living room floor. Him on top, of course. It didn't seem to bother him at all that I kept saying no, that I kept pushing him away, that my head kept knocking against the wood floors, my whole body rocking back and forth as he forced himself into me, time and time again. He didn't even bother to kiss me, just glared into my eyes the whole time, until he finally came.

It was as if my fighting back made sex all the better for him. To top off that romantic moment he threatened to kill me again. The next day he told me he had been kidding. It wasn't long after that that I was throwing my wedding dress into a tree.

So when J.D. extended his hand, I took it, then tried to let go as soon as possible, but he gripped my fingers. I saw his eyes skate down my body again and felt as if a wet, slick snake had slithered over my naked skin.

"So. Aren't you a pretty thing! You got curves all over that body, don't you?" he asked me.

I felt like vomiting.

"So where ya from, Julia?" He still held on to my hand. I felt my hand grow sweaty.

"I'm from back east," I told him.

"Back east? Huh. How hoity-toity. What brings you out here, then?"

For a moment, my throat constricted. J.D.'s nearness, the harsh tone, and the overbearing personality overwhelmed me, but I was struck by the irony. I was becoming very close friends with a woman in the exact same situation I had just run from.

"I . . . I'm visiting my aunt." I stared at our hands. Katie obviously noted it, too, as she said, "You want to let go of her hand now, J.D.?"

He cast a seriously vile look his wife's way, but let go of my hand, then put both hands on his hips and glared at Katie. She stood her ground.

"You friends with my Katie here?" he bit out. "You friends with this woman who doesn't give a rat's ass about taking care of her husband?"

He was ugly. So, so venomously ugly.

"I'm good friends with your wife," I clarified. "Well, we should be off, Katie," I tried to sidestep around J.D., but he stepped to the left when I stepped to the right. When I stepped to the left, he stepped to his right.

My knees started getting that weak feeling.

"What's your hurry? I hardly know you. Did you bring your husband with you, Julia?" he asked, his rancid breath coating me. I took a step back. I could feel Katie behind me.

"No," I said, real soft.

"No?" He arched a black eyebrow at me. "No husband, or no, you didn't bring your husband with you?"

"I don't have a husband. I haven't yet seen that husbands can offer a woman anything of value." Where I found the courage to mouth off like that, I don't know. All I knew was that J.D. was one sick, mean son of a bitch.

I saw the storm clouds in his eyes. "So you're a smart-ass, huh? Just like my Katie. Woman like you looks like she would know what buttons to push with her man, like my Katie does."

"That's enough, J.D.," Katie said quietly, but firmly.

"That's enough, J.D.," he mocked. "I sure as hell don't ever get enough from you. But your friend here"—again the rake of his eyes—"she looks like she would know how to give a man enough, even though she's got the mouth of a shrew."

I took a quick step to the right, felt Katie's hand in my

back, and we pushed around The Boar, gathered up the children, who were cowering on the living room couch, and trooped out the door, The Boar's laughter following us out, sounding like the laugh of the devil high on speed.

"You forgot to give me my lunch, Katie-bitch!" he bellowed.

Katie, the kids, and I tumbled into the pickup truck. Neither I nor Katie talked much on the way. I shook, my hands laced tightly together. Tears slid down Katie's cheeks.

"I'm sorry," she whispered.

"Me too." I unlaced my hands, cold skeleton bones held together like tiny vises, and reached out to hold her hand. We drove that way to Lara's.

❧ 8 ❧

Lara's house was small but very neat and tidy. It's a ranch house with the same floor plan that millions and millions of people live in all over the country.

The walls were all painted a light beige, the carpet was beige, the furniture slipcovered in beige. A minister's budget does not allow for new furniture, so Lara had whipped out her sewing machine ("I practically learned to sew before I knew how to talk. Every good preacher's wife teaches her daughters to sew," she had told me, a tinge of bitterness in her words. "That way she can make all the kids' costumes for the Christmas Pageant each year.")

There was a small family room and nook area, a living room area in the front of the house, three bedrooms, and an attic space. Every room was sparsely furnished and perfectly dull. It had an old-fashioned, proper, stifling, creativity-sucking style to it, as if Lara had looked at a photograph of the perfect minister's wife's living room and copied it. I counted three Bibles and three crosses, two portraits of Jesus, and numerous books about faith.

I remembered how Lara looked with her hair down, how she acted while drunk, the things she'd said. The house did not fit her at all. It was like putting a peacock down in the midst of a desert. In fact, the house gave me the creeps. Everything had a place and everything was in its place. It was as if she was as much of a guest in it as I was.

"Did everyone do their Bible reading this week?" Linda Miller asked the nine of us sitting around Lara's kitchen table.

Linda had already told me she was a "devout believer . . . a very Devout Believer," as soon as I walked in the door. She wore a white sweater and a huge cross. The cross swung between her pendulous breasts. She had such huge boobs it was hard to look at her face. I swear the top half of her was almost all boob, and the rest of her was one gigantic no-nonsense bottom.

I almost felt flat-chested next to her. I could hardly restrain myself from sitting up straight and giving my shoulders a little wiggle.

She glanced over the tops of her wire-framed glasses at all of us. Her look alone made me feel guilty.

Lara had already briefed me on this particular Bible/ prayer group. Linda was about fifty and always took over the meeting, paying particular attention to praying for people in town that she knew were going to hell. She also prayed for people in church that had offended her with one thing or another. And she repeated town gossip about people and prayed for them, too.

"She uses God as a weapon," Lara had told me. "When she says she's praying for you it's because she thinks you've done something wrong—*you* are wrong—rather than she wants to share God's love or to show you she cares. It's her way of putting God on her side, not on yours. I'm sure she irritates the hell out of God." Lara had told us she was about ready to strangle the woman and our presence might prevent the aforementioned crime.

"Hmmm?" Linda asked again, picking up a small cross by her Bible and tapping it. "Who has done their Bible reading? A good Christian woman looks to the Bible for answers for her problems, for inspiration. Surely you're all good Christian women?"

I glanced around the table. Lara looked tense and exhausted and way too skinny, her cheeks hollow.

Two women, twins, about seventy years old, were on either side of Lara. They had been oddly delighted to see me when I walked in the door. It was as if I were a giant popsicle they would be able to lick and enjoy for days to come.

"A new face!" One of them shouted, peering into my eyes.

"A new face!" The other one echoed.

Then they laughed together. I didn't get the joke, but that was okay.

They had white hair, matching red-rimmed glasses, red dresses, and Lara told me they drove a red sports car. Fast. They were named Jacqueline and Rosita. "Mom was French, Dad was Hispanic. They each got a name," Lara said.

Three other women sat around the table. They had smiled when Katie and I walked in, seemed friendly. At least they did not say anything immediately rude to me like, "You look like the type of person who needs a lot of prayer," as Linda had.

Another woman looked as if she'd been struck by an invisible train when she saw Katie and I walk into the house. She was about our age, with short brown hair, a lot of makeup, and an annoying habit of whistling slightly through her teeth when she talked. I named her The Whistler. Not original, but there it is. I learned later that she had had a habit of picking, and marrying, the wrong kind of man, but seemed quite incapable of doing better. Her name was Deidre Marshall, and she actually dropped her punch when we walked in, the glass shattering, just like in the movies, right on the floor. There was a lot of hoopla at that point.

Katie went right over and helped her pick up the glass, laughing, saying she had done this herself so many times, and she was Katie, and this woman was? Katie reached out a hand to shake the woman's hand. The woman laughed nervously, then shook Katie's hand.

Katie even got the woman another drink and ended up sitting directly across from Deidre at the table. We all had a glass of punch. There were little breads cut neatly into thin strips on the table. I wondered if Lara had slipped a little something into the punch.

"Well, then, we'll find out who read the Lord's Word and who put other priorities above God in a few minutes, but first let's open with prayer," Linda said, folding her hands piously over her well-worn Bible and closing her eyes.

I glanced at Lara. Shouldn't Lara do the prayer as she was the one leading the group? Lara rolled her eyes and folded her hands.

"Dear Lord, my Father, my Savior," Linda began, "thank you for this opportunity today for us to pray together as women of faith. Please teach us to be more patient and kind and giving and to show Christ's love in our daily actions."

Well, the prayer didn't sound too bad yet. I bowed my head again.

"But, dear Lord, there are some people among us who need your grace more than others. You know who I'm talking about, Lord. So many sinners live in this town. So many people have not accepted you as their Savior, and they are going to go to hell. I've tried to help, Lord, I've stayed true to you, but the nonbelievers are difficult. So arrogant."

Lara made a sound in her throat.

"Please, Lord, let Sandra at Michael's Salon see the error in her ways. The way she cuts teenagers' hairdos is sinful, and the way she spoke to me when I told her I was praying for her very soul was sinful, so sinful, and please pray for Carl Seaton, who told me to get off his front porch. I had to tell him, Lord, that I had seen him at the tavern and the devil works through liquor. And, Lord, help the women of the sewing circle who don't seem to appreciate my help or want to hear my suggestions for how to improve their lives. And, also, forgive Daisy Canelly, who never goes to church and told me that she actually believes dinosaurs were here first and that anyone who didn't believe in science was hiding their heads in the sand. I know you will punish her, but please let her see the error of her ways, let her know that you created Adam and Eve, we did not spring from monkeys—"

"Thank`you, Linda," Lara cut in. "I'll finish the prayer. Thank you, Lord, for this time we have together, for this day we have. Thank you for the friendships we've made in this church and beyond its walls. Thank you for watching over us and teaching us how to walk with you, in your heavenly grace. In Jesus' name, Amen."

"Amen," the rest of us echoed, quite loudly.

"Mrs. Keene," Linda huffed, picking up her cross and jiggling it at Lara across the table. "I know you are young and have only been in this church for a few years and you have a lot to learn, but one godly thing to remember is not to interrupt another's prayer." Linda adjusted her glasses, sitting straight up.

"I appreciate that, Linda. Thank you," Lara said, her fingers tightly laced. "But we all must pray in the spirit of our Lord."

"Furthermore, young lady," Linda said, her face turning a lovely shade of poinsettia red, "You *must* include people from Golden in your prayers. Then the Lord will know that we're looking after others in our community and noticing the wrongs they've done and are praying for their souls."

I saw Lara swallow hard, her eyes flashing. "Praying for other people is what we all want to do. But we must pray for those people with love and forgiveness in our hearts, not with accusation and condemnation. Christ loves everyone. We need to attempt to live like Christ, and he did not call out other people's names for ridicule."

"No one, Mrs. Keene," Linda said, quivering again, "is ridiculing anyone. Especially not me. However, I will pray for you today, Mrs. Keene, so that the Lord reaches out and explains to you your purpose in life, as a servant to your husband and to Jesus Christ, our Lord."

"I understand my purpose in life, Linda, but this is my house, and as I speak with the love of Christ in my heart, I ask that you not use townspeople's names as you point out the wrongs you feel they've committed." Lara opened her Bible, her mouth tight.

Was this the type of person minister's wives had to deal with all the time? I wondered. Linda Miller was an overgrown hypocrite. No wonder Lara hated her life.

"Wrong Phrongs Thongs!" one of the twins yelled out, obviously hard of hearing. I think it was Jacqueline. "Let's get to the Bible readings."

"Bible readings!" The other twin announced, holding her Bible high in the air with both hands. "I'm so old I could die in a minute, and since I've had a lot of time to do a lot of sinning, let's get to the saving-my-ass part!"

"The saving-my-ass fart!" her sister echoed.

I sat up straight and glared at Linda as she opened that big mouth again. I looked at her gooey lips, smothered in bad lipstick.

"Mrs. Keene, we'll put our differences aside for the moment, I know your husband can enlighten you later in regards to prayer. I'll have Mr. Miller talk to him. As an elder in the church, I believe he'll understand this problem. We'll move on, and I will pray about this later. I don't think everyone has been introduced to your little friend yet, although I think we all know Katie Margold."

For a moment, I thought Lara was going to snap. Really snap. As in stand on the table and pour apple juice over Mrs. Linda Miller's overdone hair. But instead, she looked at her Bible, took a deep breath, then smiled at all of us. "Everyone, this is my friend, Katie Margold, who most of you know, and Julia Bennett. Julia is living with her Aunt Lydia outside of town. And this is Deidre, who just moved here, although she grew up in the area. Linda asked her to come today. They met at the hair salon yesterday."

All the women smiled at me and I smiled back. I tried to look friendly, like they did.

All except Deidre, who looked like she was about ready to faint, her mouth working spasmodically, and Linda, who looked absolutely askance. I paused for a moment, relaxing just a teeny tiny bit. The other women *looked* nice. Were they nice? Or would they all, as soon as I left, judge me as a regular heathen? I didn't know about these church women.

"Lydia Schmydia!" Rosita said, smiling, her brown eyes glowing. "I like that woman. She gave me a special cigarette one day when my hip was acting up and I felt wonderful afterwards. Ate six of her brownies that night. Remember that, Jacqueline?"

Jacqueline nodded. "Yes, I do!" she shouted. "I do! Best damn cigarette I ever smoked."

I stifled a laugh. The other women did, too.

Linda looked as if she might blow a gasket, which made it all the funnier. There was something very cool about watching Linda's lips tighten and almost disappear into the rolls of fat around her face.

I glanced at Katie. She had not smiled or laughed, but was staring across the table, not even listening. I followed her gaze. She was staring at Deidre while Deidre squirmed. What the heck was going on?

"Well, it's good you're here, young lady. Your Aunt Lydia . . . well!" Linda huffed. "She needs a dose of the Bible herself. She swears, she drinks, she plays poker. Going about with that man, Stash. Never going to church to praise our Lord. I'll pray for her. She needs it—I know it—God knows it."

I was speechless. Aunt Lydia was the kindest person I knew. Since I had arrived in Golden her home had been an open door to half the town. Everyone loved her, and for good reason.

"And you!" Linda pointed at me. "Have you been saved yet?"

Lara cut in, her voice sharp. "Mrs. Miller, that is entirely inappropriate. We are here to share in God's grace and love and to learn. We are not here to condemn, confuse, or condescend to guests."

"Guest schmest!" Rosita snapped, then looked at me. "Will Lydia be home after this Bible reading? I sure could use one of those special cigarettes!"

"Cigarettes migarettes!" Jacqueline cackled, tapping her hearing aid.

"Cigarettes migarettes!" Rosita echoed, holding her fingers around a pretend cigarette and smoking it. They both laughed, low and rumbly, then high-pitched as the laughter itself made them laugh more. They completely tuned out then and chatted about cigarettes migarettes between themselves.

"My Aunt Lydia," I began, my body shaking with anger, "is a wonderful person." I believed at that moment that I could remove the woman's head from her neck. "How dare you say anything about her?"

"I dare because it's true. I'm going to pray for you, too, young woman. I know a saved woman when I see one, and one who needs forgiveness and prayers. I'll ask God to make a special effort to enter your life."

One of the women next to me placed a friendly hand upon my arm, her nail polish a lovely pink. "I'm sorry," she said. "That's not how I feel, and I'm delighted you're here, and I've always liked your Aunt Lydia. My husband, Gavin, works for Stash as his accountant."

Another woman across the table said, "Linda, please do shut up—"

A third leaned toward me across the table, her brown braid falling over her shoulder. "You must ignore her. We all do. Your Aunt Lydia and I swap plants all the time."

"I think we'll find wisdom and patience in the Bible now," Lara intervened. "Everyone please open to Psalms, first chapter, first verse."

But I could not ignore Linda Miller, that sanctimonious cow.

"Mrs. Miller," I began, leaning across the table. "This is my first time here at Bible study. I came because my wonderful friend Lara asked me to come and for no other reason. You can attack me all you want. God knows I've committed my share of sins and have done so many stupid things in my life I could just cry thinking about it, but don't you dare, *ever* say a word against my Aunt Lydia. She is the finest, most honest, most caring woman I have ever met, and she leads a life far more reflective of Jesus Christ than anyone I've ever met."

"Really? What about the druuugsss." Linda Miller said the word "drugs" long and low, and I imagined steam shooting out of her nostrils.

"I think that God is far less worried about a tiny bit of pot than he is worried about people who speak in His name but don't act in His name. It is always easy to judge and condemn, so much easier than it is to live a true Christian life. None of us should be judging anybody else. Last time I looked, that's God's job. So, again, Mrs. Miller, do not ever, *ever* say anything rude or untrue about my aunt again."

The silence was deafening. The woman with the pink nails squeezed my arm. The one with the braid nodded, smiled. The woman across the table said, "Well said."

Deidre didn't move, seeming to be stuck like a statue under Katie's unwavering gaze.

The twins came back to the conversation. "I've never said anything rude about your aunt, dearie!" said Rosita. "Never. She brings me eggs all the time, and when I was sick last year she made me dinners. That woman made me laugh so hard one time I got rid of a wart. Do you remember that, Jacqueline?"

"Warts! Warts!" her twin answered, flicking her fingers about. "Wart begone! Wart was gone!"

"Wart was gone. Poof!" Jacqueline said, wiggling her fingers back at her sister.

"Well, I think we've got things settled," said Lara. "And now let's open our Bibles together. I will read Psalms."

Lara read. And read. And read. I knew she was trying to calm herself down, calm the situation down. When at last she put down the Bible, I was ready to clunk my head on the table and take a little nap.

"Now let's close with our own prayers. Miss Jacqueline and Miss Rosita, would one of you like to start?"

"I'll do it," Rosita announced. "I don't think that Jacqueline is fully awake yet from that long, very long, very very long Bible reading, Lara, dear, although you do have a wonderfully melodious voice." She cleared her throat with a little humming sound. "I'm going to ask you all to pray for my garden. Those darn worms are in there again and those pesky bugs, and if I don't get rid of those bugs, then I'm not going to be able to enter my squash in the county fair, and that would be a damn, damn shame."

"And I'd like you all to pray for my bowels," Jacqueline shouted. "I am having a terrible time with constipation."

"Oh, it is terrible. Horrible. Horrible, terrible, Lord," Rosita said with great reverence. "And the gas that I have experienced at home coming from my sister's anus! It's like she's got a dead animal inside her gut trying to pass."

"Thank you, Miss Rosita, Miss Jac—"

Jacqueline interrupted, her head bent over her folded hands. "Dear Lord, you know what it's like to be stopped up and gassy, and I'm afraid it's going to effect my bridge game tomorrow. Nobody is going to want to be my partner. Please also pray that Mr. Thompson will come over soon and he will have more luck with his bodily functions—you know what I mean, Lord. A woman has needs, but they can't be met with broken bodily functions."

I almost laughed. I coughed to cover my laugh. Lara did, too. The woman with the pink nails, the woman with the braid, and the woman who had told Linda to shut up all said quick, kind little prayers.

"Deidre?" Lara asked.

I stole a peek at Deidre. I noticed that her gray roots were showing just a bit.

"Dear God," she started, seeming very uncomfortable. "Thank you for today. Amen."

Then it was Katie's turn. "Dear God," I heard her say, her voice angry. "Please do not let my pies get into the wrong hands again."

I assumed she was talking about J.D.

"My pies are made with love and care." Katie's voice became more strident. "They are not made to be stolen, then given to someone who is deceitful and dishonest and unkind."

I looked up. Katie was still staring at Deidre. Deidre's head was bent. I glanced across the table at Lara. Lara looked alarmed, her gaze shooting from Katie to Deidre and back again.

"I don't care about the person who gave away the pie, but I also don't care to sit across from the recipient, so please keep her out of my view from now on. Thank you. Amen."

I never saw more than a blur of that Bible as it shot across the table from Katie's hand toward Deidre's face, but I heard Deidre's scream, I heard a bone crack, and I heard her plump body hit the floor.

Everyone crowded around Deidre, the blood spurting from her nose like a fountain as she wailed. I grabbed a pile of napkins, as did Lara, trying to stem the blood, while the woman with the braid and the woman with the pink nails darted to the kitchen for ice. Linda sat quivering.

I glanced back at Katie. She was calmly picking up the plates and cups from around the table and walking them into the kitchen. I heard her humming as she passed by me. Her face had lost some of that strained look I had seen earlier at her house.

The twins clambered out of their seats and stared down at Deidre, clearly stunned. They had not seen the Bible flying from Katie's hand as their eyes had been closed in prayer.

"God must be really, really upset with you," Rosita told a wailing Deidre. "You must have sinned something good, girl."

"Yeeeesss, something good," Jacqueline added, shaking her head, then clicking her tongue.

"Good schmood," they said together.

It didn't take long for Linda the Big-Boobed Bible Bitch to tell the entire town that Katie had lobbed a Bible at Deidre.

And it didn't take long for the town to figure out why sweet, lovely Katie the Housekeeper, with the charming children and the alcoholic mean-ass husband did it.

As Katie told me later, the longer she sat and stared at that cherry-pie stain on Deidre's blouse, the more furious she became. "She even had cherry skin in between her front teeth. My God, Julia, who eats cherry pie in the morning?"

The verdict on Katie: Innocent. Very innocent.

The verdict on Deidre: Slut.

Deidre left town the next week.

After she left, J.D. got drunk and disappeared for four days.

On the fourth day, the police called Katie at 2:00 in the morning to tell her they had found her husband trapped in a car in a ditch. He had apparently been there since the day he'd stormed out of the house calling Katie every name in the book, breaking all her housecleaning tools, and draining her cleaning supplies.

He was furious about his lover's nose being broken, but I suspect he was also furious that Katie (the money maker) had found out, that the townspeople looked at him as if he were vermin, and that Stash himself had calmly told J.D. he had never met another man who was less of a man than J.D. was.

"So he's not dead?" Katie asked the policeman, cuddling her younger daughter, Haley, who had crawled into bed with her hours ago.

"No ma'am," he said, his voice happy. He obviously did not know J.D. "He's not dead. He's hurt, but he's okay!"

Katie thanked the policeman and told him she would be at the hospital soon. Then, she told me later, she pulled the covers over her head and cried.

9

Being a newspaper deliverer at the age of thirty-four is not as humiliating as one would expect.

For humiliation, there usually must be a "who saw me?" effect. For example, "I am so humiliated because so-and-so saw what I was doing." Frankly, by the time I roll out of bed after my customary four hours of broken sleep to deliver newspapers, I am too exhausted to care what anyone thinks, even if they are up early enough to see me. Plus, I hardly know anyone here.

Two weeks after arriving in Golden, when my bruises were not quite so startling, I had started looking for a job. Jobs, I knew, were very scarce. Golden's lumber industry had crashed, and the main factory outside of town had closed. No new businesses had taken their place.

This, of course, made for a crummy job search.

I looked for a job in the local grocery store. No luck. I was told that an art history major is a "lovely major," by the assistant manager who sneered, her eyes narrowing as if I had personally offended her by even asking. "But no one who needs help finding Cheetos is going to care. Besides, you really aren't qualified to work the cash register. You have no experience at all."

Trying to get a job at the ice cream saloon didn't work, either. The owner had six daughters, he told me. They all worked there. But would I like to buy a sundae?

I also applied to be a receptionist at the dentist's and two of the doctor's offices in town. No luck. Same with the hardware store, the drugstore, a small clothing boutique, and the movie theater. The schools did not need any assistants for the next year.

Which brought me to the newspaper. I could write. Perhaps I could do obituaries or dog shows or town picnics?

Ha.

Did you know that even tiny newspapers only hire people with degrees in journalism or who already have existing journalistic experience? Sheesh.

Although they wouldn't hire me to write anything, their teenage newspaper delivery boy had just quit. Would I be interested in taking his place? I swallowed, said yes, and there I had it, my new career: newspaper deliverer.

Still, as I walked out of the newspaper office, my new paper route in hand, I was happy to have the job. I wanted to pay half of Lydia's bills.

Lydia argued, slamming pans together six times for effect, "You're family! Don't pay. You insult me. You hurt me. I am your aunt, and I will provide for you. . . . Here, have a brownie. Your complexion tells me that your womanhood is waning. Better yet, let's go target shooting together. We'll practice shooting to kill and bring Melissa Lynn with us. Melissa Lynn loves the sound of gunshots."

I didn't argue. I knew Melissa Lynn, and no one enjoyed the sound of a gun more than that pig. She made her pig noises whenever Lydia put a leash around her neck and took her to the firing range. Plus, I could see Henry, the beaver who lived on a little river that flowed through Stash's property, who came when Aunt Lydia called its name.

"I'm going to pay you, Aunt Lydia. Just think"—I laughed—"it'll be enough to buy yourself another pot plant."

She did not think my joke was funny and scowled at me as she dug her hands deep into the dough she was kneading. Stash needed more bread, and Lydia was a strong believer that milk and homemade bread made for a strong libido. "Young lady, I forbid you to pay me for anything."

I changed the subject, helped her knead, fixed a fence in the garden, trimmed some bushes, and then we both set about repainting the door black. There was no telling when a seedy man would drive up and try to con us into his evil ways, was there?

So I went to bed that night and got up way before the crack of dawn, collected the newspapers from the print shop, and was up and running my paper route, even though my body protested wildly at being up at this hour. The first time my paper route took me hours longer than it should have because I kept getting lost. The next day, I was better. By the end of the week—well, I had to pat myself on the back for being a good little paper deliverer.

And whose house was the last house on my route?

Yep. None other than Paul Bunyan's himself.

Dean Garrett's home is a sprawling, craftsman-style two-story home with floor-to-ceiling windows. Stash told me Dean owned a hundred acres and left a foreman in charge when he was at his Portland office working on different legal cases. The previous owner and Stash had had a falling-out because the other owner, Mr. Rekkum, didn't take care of his dogs the way Stash thought he should.

Those dogs were left outside regardless of whether it was hot enough to flip a pancake on the sidewalk or cold enough to freeze your nostril hairs. There was a very small, crude doghouse that could only hold two of the three dogs. They weren't always fed. They didn't always have water. Stash had talked to Mr. Rectumhead, as Stash called him behind his back, about treating the dogs better, but Mr. Rectumhead laughed, spitting tobacco juice very close to Stash's feet.

So one day Stash took the dogs. Mr. Rectumhead was pretty steamed and came charging over when he discovered that his dogs weren't chained up by their empty water dish anymore, but Stash and the men who worked his land and helped with The Biz were waiting, all in a line. Guns are the only things that Mr. Rectumhead really understands, so he backed off.

But when he sold the land, he did it on the sly, through a Portland Realtor, and Paul Bunyan bought the acres, not knowing anything of the feud between Stash and Mr. Rectumhead.

Paul Bunyan had the old house razed first thing, Stash told me, then started building his own home. Stash went over to visit him, and the two hit it off like they were long lost brothers. Paul Bunyan even liked the dogs. The dogs liked him, too, although they would never set foot on his property, the memory of Mr. Rectumhead being obviously too much for them. Even when Stash brought them over in one of his pickups the dogs whined and cried, refusing to get out of the truck. And when Stash drove off with them back to his own ranch, he told me, you could almost see those dogs grinning, their relief a living, breathing, doggie thing.

So as soon as I discovered I was to be Paul Bunyan's paper deliverer, I prayed that he wouldn't see me. His visit to Aunt Lydia's was still uppermost in my mind, and I couldn't quite get the look of his lips out of my brain, or of his hands, so strong and capable, and the thought of what it would be like to be kissed so thoroughly by Paul Bunyan you could barely stand, or of how heavy he would feel if he lay on top of me.

So I would drive past his home on the days when he was in town and had requested a paper, and I would shove the newspaper in that box real quick and speed off. On the fifth day of my route, I saw him in his house. Although it was the wee hours of the morning, he looked to be talking on the phone. I drove off even quicker then, missing a deer by about an inch.

But on the eighth day of my paper route, I darn near ran him over.

Since I was often chilled, which I attributed to the Dread Disease, I was wearing an old blue camping coat and a sweatshirt I had worn the day before to help with the chickens. (I had had to pluck chicken feathers off it before leaving.) I was also sporting a pair of baggy jeans and boots. Before leaving I had ripped my curls back into a ponytail and brushed my teeth to give my nose a break.

I couldn't have been more glamorous.

As usual, my heart started pumping as I neared Mr. Bunyan's house. I slowed, then stopped the car and got ready to shove the newspaper into the box and leave.

And that's when I saw the man, not three feet away, looming near the mailbox. My own scream almost scared the pee right out of me. It was piercing-loud and free-flowing, and it sliced through the cool silence of the country like a whip through ice cream.

I recognized Paul Bunyan, otherwise known as Dean Garrett, after I'd almost rammed him with the car.

I could hear his laughter low and sexy. "I'm sorry, Julia. God, I'm sorry. Are you all right? I didn't mean to scare you." His deep voice, rough around the edges, rumbled straight through my stomach. It was almost as if I were eating honey and pinecones.

"It's okay," I choked out, my heart racing at 1,845 beats a minute. "Really. I'm sorry I almost hit you."

He laughed, and when I could breathe like a normal human I dared a glance into his eyes.

"Good morning." Paul Bunyan leaned his arms against

the open window, which put him only inches away from me. He smelled like fir trees and a roaring fire and coffee and warmth.

I swallowed hard, then stared straight out the front window. No way was I going to risk my breath floating near that man. "Good morning. I, uh, I think I dropped your newspaper, I'm sorry."

"It's no problem."

I caught his smile out of the corner of my eye. He was so damn cute. The silence lingered, while I cast about for something non-inane to say. All I could get out was, "I, uh . . . well . . ." And then it hit me that Dean knew I had a paper route.

And it was about then that I felt humiliated.

"Can you come in for breakfast?"

I smothered a hysterical giggle. Breakfast? No. Absolutely no. He scared me to death.

"No, uh . . . well . . ." I gripped the steering wheel while my heart skipped 6,780 beats. "I can't. I have to . . . well, finish off the newspapers. I mean, I have to finish delivering the newspapers, and then I have to help with the chickens. Amelia and Miss Clarice and Queen Koo Koo will be waiting, and they get really uptight when they're not fed, and then Miss Clarice will peck at my hands . . ." *Please shut up.*

"Amelia and Miss Clarice and Queen Koo Koo have behavior problems, then?"

"I, uh . . . well, yes. They have behavior problems." If he stood there much longer I thought I would have a behavior problem. The fear had receded, and now that "woman in me" started to escape. Dean Garrett made my skin tingle and my nipples hard.

"They don't make chickens like they used to, do they?" he said. I saw his mouth slant upward in a semblance of a smile.

I shook my head.

"How many more houses do you have to go to?"

"Houses?" Why did his shoulders have to be so grippable?

"Yes. Houses. How many more houses do you have to deliver newspapers to?"

Why did he have such high, slanted cheekbones?

"I . . . well, I'm done with the houses. You're the last one."

Why did he have such long eyelashes?

"Oh," he said. "So you're done with your route? I thought you said you had to deliver the newspaper to more houses?"

Rats. Caught in a little lie. I hate lying. I rarely, rarely do it. I might not be the brightest light in the chandelier, I might get engaged to freaks, I might cut out on my wedding day, but I do not lie. Oh dear. Was not telling Robert I was going to make a run for it on our wedding day a lie by omission? I brought my attention back to Paul Bunyan.

"You're right. I'm done for the morning."

"Good. So come on in for breakfast."

"Oh no." *Oh, God, no!* "No!"

He looked taken aback by the vehemence of my answer.

"I didn't mean it like that. I just meant, that no way . . . I mean, *no*, I can't come in for breakfast."

"You can't," he drawled, and now I could see he was smiling. "Can't or won't?"

I won't because I can't stop looking at you and wondering how you would taste if I licked your lips, I thought. "I can't come in. I need to go, I really do."

He nodded. I thought his eyes looked disappointed, but I figured later I imagined that. Dean Garrett could probably get any woman on the planet to have breakfast with him. Naked. "I understand."

But he didn't understand. I understood that.

He smiled at me then, in the dark, his white teeth flashing.

"Maybe tomorrow?"

"No, I can't."

"The next day?"

"No, I can't."

He smiled. My skin tingled. In a good way. "Thank you anyhow."

He nodded, I rolled up the window of my car and drove off.

And that should have been that.

But it wasn't. Every day for two weeks Dean Garrett waited outside by the newspaper box for me. Every day we chatted, our chats getting longer and longer. Every day he asked me to come up for breakfast. Every day I refused, shaking in my shoes, not only because I was afraid of men, but because I was afraid of myself.

And then one day I said yes.

Well, I didn't really say yes. But my actions said yes. Dean gave me a bouquet of wild flowers, the flowers I had told him I liked better than any other flower. He also gave me this beautiful pink crocheted hat with matching mittens because I'd told him delivering papers was a chilly experience.

Then he got in the passenger seat of my car.

"Julia, tomorrow I'm leaving town for five weeks. I have to go back to Portland. You won't have to put up with being accosted at the mailbox for a little while, although I promise you I will return to my post the minute I get back. So, please. Do me the honor. Come to my house for breakfast. I'll cook. I'll clean. You relax."

I smiled, laughed, and then to my utter embarrassment, embarrassment that was so deep I wanted to nuke myself into a thousand bits, I put my head on the steering wheel and cried.

After a breakfast of omelets with shrimp and avocado, cranberry muffins, and bacon, we drank our second cups of coffee on a wood table in the nook of his kitchen. Outside

the sun had risen, golden and pure, surrounded by a purple and blue haze as soft as the wings of one of Aunt Lydia's birds.

"I can't believe you remembered that I only drink decaffeinated coffee. And that mochas are my favorite," I said. He smiled at me, and I felt that smile wriggle down my chest and into that private area that had felt so dead for so long. I tried to keep from swallowing my tongue. It was difficult.

"I remember everything you've told me."

Oh dear. That would not be good.

"I am hoping, however, Julia, that I will not always have to get up at the crack of dawn to see you."

I smiled back at him. I couldn't help it.

"I haven't minded, of course," he joked. "I always enjoyed our conversations."

I had, too. In that dark hour, after I'd passed him a newspaper, we had joked and talked about many, many things. I hadn't told him much about myself, but I had the impression he already knew quite a bit about my history.

"I have to tell you that I have not asked a woman out on a date in a very long time, but in the past, when I have, none of them have cried." He smiled at me, his eyes so gentle. "Why did you cry?"

What could I say?

I cried because I couldn't believe someone like Dean Garrett would want to have breakfast with me, much less meet me at the end of his driveway every morning for two weeks before the sun came up.

I cried because I could barely breathe sometimes and I was sick of it. You never know how wonderful air is until you can't have it.

I cried because I figured I had a Dread Disease and would probably be told soon that I had only six months to live.

I cried because I was scared of Robert. I cried because I hadn't had the guts to break my wedding off until the morning of it because I am really good at convincing myself a lousy, frightening situation is going to work out, and that quality scares me.

I cried because tears come easy when people are nice to you when your life is in ruins.

I could feel the tears welling again.

He held my hand across the table, his fingers intertwining with mine.

"Why, Julia? I promise I won't loom over the mailbox anymore if you tell me. No"—he stroked my hand with his fingers—"scratch that. I happened to enjoy my time at the mailbox. Please tell me why you're crying."

The tears fell then, without permission, right from my eyes.

What could I say? The truth? No way. Never. I looked at the hard planes of his face, the lines fanning from his eyes and the grooves around his mouth. I looked at his neck, his hair, those blue eyes.

"I cried because—" I stopped.

"What?"

"Well." I wiped my eyes with a napkin. "I—"

"Yes?"

I took a shaky breath, then looked at him. Right in the eye. "I was afraid you'd burn the bacon."

I felt his hand tighten on mine. Mine tightened on his.

And then he laughed.

I laughed, too, a sound that was foreign to my own ears, even as another rush of tears splattered our entwined hands.

❧ 10 ❧

"**H**ow are you, Katie?"
Katie stared straight ahead, her eyes on the winding road. Fir trees swayed above us, every now and then giving way to a sliver of river, the sun glittering off its surface, creating little diamonds on the water.

Aunt Lydia had offered to watch the kids while Katie and I went to get her husband, J.D., who was being released from the hospital today. She had not been to see him since she received the phone call two weeks ago that his car had been found in a ditch with his fat body still in it. He had been stuck, one leg jammed between the crushed door and the steering wheel.

By the way his car was positioned, the police didn't think he was driving back to Golden. Not surprising. Deidre had left for Portland, and J.D. had followed.

"I've had better moments," she said. Her skin was pale and drawn, and all that glorious hair looked limp. "I'm driving to pick up my alcoholic husband, who was leaving me for another woman. I don't even make sense to myself."

I nodded a little bit, patted her shoulder. This whole thing didn't make sense to me, either, but friends go along even when there's no sense involved.

The morning Deidre had told Lara that she was going to press criminal charges against Katie after the little Bible-throwing incident. Lara had taken a small moment to set Deidre straight, even as she'd held ice over the woman's nose. "Let me tell you how this will all go, then, Deidre." She moved the ice pack, not flinching when Deidre swore.

"You will file charges against Katie. Keep in mind that the chief of police is very close to both Lydia and Stash, and they, in turn, are close to Katie. If the chief does feel compelled to go forward with the charges, he will ask for a jury trial. That jury will find out that you've been having an affair with J.D. Margold, an unemployed, mean, abusive drunk who never works and everyone in town hates."

I saw Deidre's face flush.

"J.D.'s wife, Katie Margold, who owns a cleaning business and takes care of their four children and volunteers in the school and is a massive support to the wife of the town's minister, accidentally lost control of her Bible as she was praising God. That Bible hit you in the nose."

"She didn't *accidentally* lose control." Deidre's words were muffled.

Lara looked Deidre right in the eye. "I was there. She lost control. Katie was praying with great exuberance, and the Bible flew from her hands accidentally. Julia was there. I believe she thinks Katie accidentally lost control."

"I believe Katie lost control," I said. Lara lifted the ice pack. My. The bruising was going to be extensive on Deidre's face.

"Do you get what I'm saying here?" Lara asked.

Deidre's bloodied face got all twisted up in her fury. "I thought you were the wife of a minister!"

"I am the wife of a minister, and I'm going to pray for you, Deidre, pray that you understand that the jury will not sympathize with you at all." Lara let go of the ice pack and laced her fingers together in front of her stomach as if in prayer. "In fact, they will hate you. *Hate you*. And you can bet that Katie's court-appointed attorney will stack that jury with a bunch of middle-aged, heavy women who are single or divorced and struggling to make ends meet after their no-good husbands left them for the town slut. Katie will be found not guilty."

Deidre was ready to argue, I could tell, but she was not so stupid that she couldn't see the future. "Can I get you another ice pack before you leave?" Lara asked, sweetness running right out of her mouth.

Deidre nodded, took the ice pack, and left. Linda hopped along beside her. One of the twins yelled, "The devil's after your ass, Deidre! Watch out!"

"Watch out!" the other twin yelled.

"I think I *will* pray for her," Lara said. "I'll pray that J.D. goes to her, and she accepts him into her home." Katie was in the other room watching a soap opera, and the rest of us women filed in and listened to Lara's loving prayer about forgiveness and repentance.

And that was that. Deidre left town. No charges were filed, although the chief did jokingly mention to Katie that she should join a local softball team.

I was pulled back to the present by Katie's wistful voice. "It was so peaceful, Julia, not having him around." She snuffled. "It was just me and the kids. We got up. I got everybody out the door. I dropped the kids at the school and the baby-sitter's, cleaned houses, picked everyone up, came home. The house wasn't a mess with beer bottles everywhere, dirty plates and dishes everywhere. No one was drunk and mean and asking for dinner before I'd barely gotten in the door. No one yelled at the kids, or at me."

"Katie," I said. I'm sure Katie didn't realize it, but she'd slowed way down on that mountain road, and other cars were passing us, giving us 'the look.'

"At night, we had simple dinners. I didn't have to make sure there was a vegetable and a fruit and a main dish and dessert—J.D. always insisted on that. We had macaroni and cheese. Cheese sandwiches. Noodles and cheese. Everyone was happy. I cleaned up. We read stories, and off to bed everybody went.

She swallowed, her voice getting hard. "J.D. would sometimes whack them on the head when they missed their verses. I would grab the Bible from him, and then he'd turn on me—the drunker he was, the meaner. For some reason, he liked to hit me on the butt with the Bible."

We were now stopped at the side of the road, the mountains in the distance a bluish purple, a river bubbling by on the other side of the road. "He would get all dressed up for church on Sunday in a tie and jacket and insist the kids be dressed all nice. He'd eat the breakfast I made, read the paper, and go out to the car, honking the horn until I got the kids ready and out the door. 'You're not wearing that dress again, are you, Katie?' He hated the dress I wore to church but I was wearing the same dress because I couldn't afford another one. He drank all of our money. When I hid money, he would find it, as if he had another eyeball that hung around our house all day when he was out drinking and humping whatever female he could find."

She turned off the engine.

"Katie—"

"I don't think J.D. has said anything nice to me in five years. He doesn't even see me as a person, as a woman. He thinks we're married, and that's that. Ole Katie will be around forever. Who else would have her? I am there to serve him. Even if I were lying in the middle of the kitchen floor, exhausted, dying even, he would simply step over me to get a beer from the fridge, swearing at me for not getting him one."

"Katie—"

"He didn't really even hide the fact he was having an affair, Julia. Didn't care that he had lipstick on his cheek one night. Didn't care that I saw him talking to someone, laughing, on his cell phone. Didn't care that I was working all day and taking care of the kids and the house and was worn out."

She took a deep breath, wiped her tears off her cheeks. "I've been so much happier without him. I've lost seven pounds, did I tell you that?" She smiled at me, hope opening her eyes wide, her smile tremulous. "Seven pounds. I weighed seven pounds of apples the other day in the store and bagged them up, just to feel what it felt like. It's a lot of weight, Julia."

"It is. That's wonderful, it really is." I felt happy for her and morbidly, horribly sad. Why were we driving to go and bring that evil slug back with us? "Are you sure—"

"Yes. I'm sure. I can't do it. I can't do it."

I held my breath. "You can't do what?"

"I can't bring hate back into my life."

We were both silent for awhile. The trees on the mountains swayed. The river gurgled.

"Hate's a bad thing," I told her. I sound so immensely inane sometimes it drives me crazy.

"Yes. It is. I don't hate J.D. I'm past that," she said, her voice resigned. "But what I really hate is how he's made me hate myself, how he's made the kids hate him, how the kids know that an emotion as strong as hate exists."

I had heard those same words in my own head. Why do we let men make us hate ourselves? And why does it often take us so long to kick them out of our lives? Why do we cling? Why are we so scared to be on our own when hate is the only thing we have to come home to?

Why had I let Robert pound my face as often as he did? Life is better without a pounding.

"I hate what I've allowed him to do to me," Katie said. "I used to be happy. I used to have energy. I used to be fun. I used to laugh, Julia. I don't do that anymore. And I know why."

A huge logging truck barreled by us. Katie turned the engine of her old car back on, then looked both ways. No cars. We headed for home.

❧ 11 ❧

Every morning I run my paper route, then help Aunt Lydia with the farm. I must say I've become very attached to the chickens and even more attached to Melissa Lynn, the pig who follows me everywhere. If you could be best girlfriends with a pig, well, she would definitely qualify.

She's enormous, which is one thing I like about her. I feel darn slim standing next to that pig. The chickens aren't quite as enamored with her. I do feel there is evidence that they feel superior to Melissa Lynn, but Melissa Lynn doesn't give a rip about that stuff.

She operates on her own accord. When she wants to snort, she does so. When she wants to take a nap, she does so. When she wants to roll in dirt or poop, she does so, and if the chickens squawk angrily and run away from her, their little white bottoms up in the air, she couldn't care less.

Melissa Lynn is my kind of woman. I admire her greatly. Amazing what you can learn from pigs.

I don't even mind cleaning out her trough as she seems so appreciative of my efforts. She stands right near me, snorting her encouragement, and has taught her piglets to do the same. She is a mother who demands good manners from her offspring, and so many mothers don't these days.

Gathering the eggs can take a while. There are, after all, hundreds of chickens. Most of the chickens, as I've mentioned, are quite kind; others not so much. The other day, Aunt Lydia received by truck sixty new baby chicks. They are darling to watch and to hold. Their new homes are in the yellow shed. Plywood has been shaped into a number of different circles on the ground, and a circular light hangs straight over each one to keep them warm.

"I learned the hard way about chicks years and years ago," Aunt Lydia told me one day, wielding her pitchfork at a hay bale. "Ya can't put them into a rectangular holding pen or they'll climb all over each other for warmth and smush the little ones beneath them. Then all you get is flattened chicks. Plus the light has to be hanging just so, in the middle of a circular pen. If you put the light in a corner, you'll have the same problem. Smushed chickens."

She dug the pitchfork into the ground, then grabbed the gun that she had strapped around her waist for an earlier bout of target practice. She cocked it, aimed, shot, and a snake flipped into the air from about fifty feet away. "I hate when snakes get near my ladies," she said. "Anyhow, remember that chicks will pyramid, one right on top of another, Julia, so keep 'em in the right bins, and hang the light just so."

Still reeling from the unexpected gunshot and flipping snake, I assured her I would. Far be it for me to cause the death of a chick.

I went back to my egg collecting, admiring Aunt Lydia's target-shooting skills. I had not heard from Robert. However, I knew that my mother would shortly tire of her new boyfriend and move back to Boston. "My roots are in that town. Your great-great-great—some more greats—grandma was a maid who sailed over on the *Mayflower*. I'm practically damn royalty!" she'd declare, usually staggering about as she'd drunk enough liquor to drown her kidneys and liver.

Years ago I lived in hope that my mother would one day become sober enough, or have a lobotomy, or be attacked by killer bees and, lying flat on her deathbed, realize how hideous my childhood had been and would apologize for it.

It never happened. The last time she was in my life, she came to my apartment and demanded money. Her skin hung on her in drapes and droops, as if it no longer had the energy to stay close to her face. Her hair was blonder, almost white, like bleached straw.

She walked in without hugging me, without giving me a kiss, and I thought of all the other mothers and daughters I'd seen my whole life hugging and kissing each other. I cannot begin to tell you how much I longed for that. Such simple things: a hug and a kiss.

We chitchatted a bit about her current boyfriend, and she told me it looked like I still hadn't lost any weight, that no man would be attracted to a lump, that I should think about that real quick because I wasn't that young anymore.

I was on the verge of giving her money, my stomach cramping up as if she'd kickboxed me with those black knee-high boots she was wearing when I inhaled her familiar scent—vodka. Straight up.

The smell of vodka and bourbon and beer and cigarettes had swirled around my entire childhood, and it was the stench of that vodka that made me pause, that made me say what I did, misery wrapped around every one of my words like black glue. "Why didn't you let me live with Aunt Lydia, Mom? Why did you keep me?"

She had been staring at my massive collection of recipe books but spun around on her heel and said, with this ugly look on her droopy-skinned face, "I didn't give you to Lydia because I will never give your Aunt Lydia anything. Nothing. Even if it's a nothing that cost me a damn fortune to raise."

For some strange reason I became daring, for once, with my mother. Maybe it was because I hadn't seen her in so long. Maybe it was because I knew I wouldn't see her again for a long time. Maybe it was because I finally had the courage to ask the questions. "What do you mean, I cost you a fortune? I hardly ate, the church ladies gave me clothes—"

"Shut up, Julia. You have always been rude and ungrateful. Always. Even as a young child. Now, for once, I'm in need. Give me the money."

I whipped my purse behind my back, like a little kid would. "No."

"What the hell do you mean, no? You can pay me back for all those hellish years when I had to put up with you, the way you flounced around my boyfriends—"

The way I flounced around her boyfriends? Pain flashed through my body as if I'd been struck with a pickax in the heart.

"No, no, no!" My "no"s got louder and louder until I sounded like a shrieking hyena. "*No!*" I covered my ears with my hands like I used to do as a child. "I *never* came on to your gross boyfriends. Never. You allowed them, Mother, you *allowed* them to touch me. You knew what they did to me at night, but you didn't stop them!" I took my hands off my ears as one sad, hellacious image after another paraded through my head. "You didn't stop them!" I screamed.

"Give me a goddamn break. I had no idea, Julia. How could I know?" She crossed her arms across her chest, her black bra visible beneath the deep V of her black shirt.

"You *did*. You're lying. *Lying!*" My voice went up another notch, and I could feel hysteria speedily edging me toward a total breakdown. "And your lying makes it worse for me. My own mother won't even acknowledge that she let her boyfriends attack her daughter."

"No one attacked you," she snapped, then sighed, long and heavy. This conversation was so tiring for her. So dull. So nothing. "You flirted with them. You, with your young body and your huge boobs. They're men, Julia. What did you expect them to do?"

"Oh, God," I said, bending to hold my head in my hands as my head felt like it might very well implode. "I was a child, Mom. A *child*. And even now you won't admit what happened. You ruined my childhood. You turned it into a sick, twisted, scary nightmare. You, your viciousness, your abuse, your drinking, your men who were all over me—you ruined it. You ruined me. You ruined what I could have had with Aunt Lydia." I turned away from her and leaned against the wall before my knees gave out. "Get out. Get the fuck out."

Now that ticked her off. She dropped her hands to her sides and swayed a bit, the vodka affecting her balance. "Don't you ever use the word 'fuck' with me, you impossible—"

"Fuck," I said, tears making their way down my face like two little rivers. "*Fuck you*. Now get out."

Her hand struck from out of nowhere, my head thudding against the wall. When the white stars went away, I straightened, still fighting. "How could you do that to a child? How could you do that *to me*?"

"I didn't do anything to you." She put her face an inch from mine. "You did it to yourself."

"I did it to myself? I hit myself? I starved myself? Really, Mother?" The total breakdown loomed before my eyes.

"Yes. You got yourself into trouble. Always going to the neighbors for help, to your teachers for help, and then the stupid busybodies would call the police and Children's Services, and I would have to explain to them all what a liar you were."

"A liar? Me?" I choked past the lump of hurt in my throat.

"Yes, you." She pointed her finger at me.

"I didn't go to people for help. They came to me. They saw how thin I was as a child, saw the holes in my shoes, saw that my hair was a wreck and I was dirty—"

"How dare you judge me? I worked hard to support you—"

"Stop!" I yelled. "Oh God, stop. Stop! You never should have had me, never should have kept me. You had no right to keep me! None."

When she raised her hand toward me again, I raised mine and blocked the next slap. And the next. My purse dropped to the ground in back of me, coins scattering about.

When my mother realized I wasn't going to cower in a corner with my hands clamped over my head like usual she slammed out of my house—but not before she ripped a framed picture off my wall, a photo of an open box of chocolates, and shot it in my direction.

After she left I scrambled around and picked up every single coin, then lay on the floor until the crying stopped. When I could see through my tears, I went straight for a recipe book and made a chocolate mousse pie, my hands shaking as I crushed cookies for the pie shell, whipped the eggs, melted the chocolate.

When my mother landed back in Boston and got a new telephone number, Robert would call her. As I didn't know her boyfriend's last name or even exactly what town in Minnesota they were in, or if they were really even in Minnesota, I couldn't reach her first and ask her to keep quiet. She couldn't afford a cell phone, so that was another dead end.

But even if I told my mother not to tell Robert about Aunt Lydia, it wouldn't do any good. He'd pay my mother a visit, he'd smile and try to charm her, and of course, that wouldn't work. In terms of manipulation, my mother was a master. Even better than Robert.

But money would work wonders, and Robert tossed around money as if every dollar he spent guaranteed him another hard-on. My guess is that my mother would get about five thousand dollars from him. And then she'd tell him everything he needed to know, including the fact that he needed to look for giant pigs in front of Aunt Lydia's house.

And that would be all that Robert would need. He and my mother would exchange vile words, and off he'd go . . . his private jet waiting to fly him here to Oregon to terrorize me.

I felt my hands go cold and tingly, my body freezing as the Dread Disease took hold and a feeling of panic set in. I pictured my blood leaping through my veins as the air constricted in my lungs, the lack of oxygen making me dizzy. I dropped the basket of eggs I held and leaned against a hay bale. I was glad Aunt Lydia wasn't in the chicken house anymore.

Sweat laced my forehead, then dripped down the edge of my nose. My legs started to shake wildly, so I started shaking them myself, having found that that sometimes helps. I felt myself crest, the air now all gone, and I thought I was going to die. Again. I coughed, coughed again.

For what seemed like hours, I leaned against that hay bale, hoping to breathe, panicked that I wasn't.

I suddenly felt warm, hard arms surrounded my waist, and I screamed. One part of me was shocked that I could scream when I could barely breathe, the other was terrorized, believing that Robert had found me.

But it wasn't Robert's cold, hypercritical eyes I was staring into. It was Stash's warm, concerned ones. He wrapped his arms round my waist as he supported my now sagging body. I heard his gruff voice yelling at Aunt Lydia as he swung me up into his arms and carried me toward the house.

I was too exhausted to protest, too shaken by my Dread Disease to object when Stash carried me into the bedroom and onto my bed. Before I closed my eyes I noticed that Aunt Lydia's face was pale white. "Oh my God, what happened, Stash? What happened, baby?"

I assured her I was fine. I had simply gotten a little dizzy, hadn't been sleeping very well lately, was a tad bit stressed, forgot to have breakfast. Yes, of course, everything was okay. All was well. All was right.

But I knew things weren't right. Not right at all.

* * *

The paper route didn't pay much, so I talked my way into a job at a library two towns away, in Monroe, for four hours a day in the afternoon. I was going to run a Story Hour for small children, help shelve books, and help at the checkout counter. I was interviewed by five local members of the board who oversaw the library.

They asked me a lot of questions about whether or not I was good at working with difficult people, was I patient with children, was I good at working with difficult people, did I like to read stories to children, was I good at working with difficult people, and, by the way, was I good at working with difficult people?

I saw the writing on the wall regarding this particular job, but I was desperate, so I gave the right answers: Yes, I'm good at working with difficult people; yes, patient with children; yes, yes, I like reading stories to children; yes, and yes again. Working with difficult people? No problem.

I was hired.

On my first day of work at the Monroe City Library I was told by the assistant librarian, Roxy Bell, that the gal before me had quit because she hated the woman I would be working for. So had the woman before her, and the woman before her, and that particular woman apparently had three kids and no husband. "She told me she thought she was going to kill Ms. Cutter with the hatchet her ex-husband had left behind, and she couldn't see going to jail when her kids were so young," Roxy Bell told me, her white hair curling around the sweetest face I have ever seen. "I stay because when Ms. Cutter comes around, I just turn down my hearing aid and nod pleasantly at whatever she says to me, when she deigns to speak to me at all, which isn't often, and I watch her mouth open and shut and I keep nodding, and if she reports me to the board I don't care because my aunt and my sister's best friend are on the board, and I know I'll have a job here till the day I croak over the encyclopedias, but you need to watch out for her, dear, she's like a viper, and she doesn't like children, and she likes to keep it dark in here."

Roxy Bell obviously did not like periods in her sentences.

I looked around the Monroe City Library. It was a small building, in the center of the town, and had about as much warmth as a morgue. Rows of books ran the length of the library, with tables in between. Beige, dying curtains were down over all the closed windows, and the lights were dimmed. The walls were dingy white. Stuffy air filled the room like wet dust. The children's area was tiny. There were no beanbags or fun posters or paintings that might amuse children. It was simply a corner of the library—a dark corner, I might add.

Ms. Cutter and I did not get off to a good start my first day. "You're two minutes late," she said to me as I walked into the library.

Immediately, I felt like a little girl. A fat, clumsy, awkward, tardy little girl. Who was late. Two minutes so. I started babbling. "I'm very sorry, Ms. Cutter, I couldn't find a parking space, and I know you want us to park away from the library so the patrons can have those spaces, and I ended up parking at the far end of the road, then took a wrong turn walking here, and I'm very sorry . . ." Looked like I had lost my periods, too.

"Stop." Ms. Cutter stood to her full height of six foot one inches tall. Six foot three inches in her heels. She held up one hand about a foot from my face. She had short, butch hair, a long nose, and the coldest eyes I have ever seen.

"Please, Ms. Bennett, I have no time for excuses. I'm quite busy. Your job will be to shelve books, as we discussed. When we're busy, you can run the checkout counter with me. Make sure you are as quiet as possible. Your shoes look like they will be too noisy. Wear rubber soles. Do not wear clothes that make noise. No low-cut shirts or tight pants allowed. Do not let your boyfriends come and visit you here at the library. Leave your personal problems at home, I am not your mother or your counselor. Do not— Is something funny, Ms. Bennett?"

Oh yes. It was. When Ms. Cutter helpfully reminded me that she wasn't my mother I instantly pictured Ms. Cutter in one of my mother's more sleazy red outfits that shoved her boobs up nearly to her chin and exposed most of her thighs.

Now, that picture in my head was funny.

"No, there's nothing funny. Not funny at all."

"Good." She crossed her gangly arms and stared down her long beak at me. I was transported to childhood. "Get to work, then."

Ms. Cutter had told me in the interview that she did not believe that children should spend long amounts of time in a library, so she didn't think the space should be overly large. "Children are loud and messy in this town. Totally disrespectful."

Roxy Bell told me Ms. Cutter had initially run the Story Hour and scared away all of the children by reading the classics to them, which bored them silly.

There were not many children at Story Hour.

In fact, the first day I was there, there was only one child, a boy named Shawn Coleman. Shawn told me he was there because his sister was sick and he needed a book to read to her.

No, his mother wasn't home. She hadn't been home for a couple of days, he told me.

Unwashed blond hair stuck out around his pale face, his clothes too small on a frail frame. Bare toes peeped out of his shoes, and a battered backpack hung from his shoulders. A muttered "hello" is about all I got out of him. I smiled. He did not smile back. I held out my hand to take him to the children's area. He stuffed his hands in his pockets. I asked him if he liked books. "Carrie Lynn does," he said.

So I helped Shawn pick out a few books, then I offered to read to him. He hesitated at first because his sister was sick and he wanted to get back to her. "But she went to sleep right before I left, so we could read a few." He looked up at me, his eyes a murky green. "If you want to. If you don't have anything else to do."

I assured him I had nothing else to do. And, besides, this was Story Hour, wasn't it? So, Shawn and I read books. He was nine years old and could hardly read, so I read book after book to him. At the end I helped him to read a book. I chose a very easy one to help him gain some self-confidence, but he struggled through it. I was saddened by how poorly he read.

After exactly an hour had passed, Ms. Cutter returned, her back ramrod-straight. I wondered how it would feel to have a pole shoved up your rear all day long. "Story Time is now over, Shawn. Run along." Her glare was cold enough to freeze every hair in my nostrils, and Shawn's face got a pinched, worried look to it, just like the one he'd had when he walked in. "Go on home now, Shawn. Ms. Bennett is very busy. Julia, I'll expect those books to be properly shelved, and then you may start on the stack near my desk."

"I had a great time reading with you today, Shawn," I told him, handing him a stack of books after I'd helped him with his backpack. "Come back tomorrow. We'll read more books, practice your reading. Your teacher will be so happy with how much you've improved over the summer."

Ms. Cutter glared at me, clasping her hands in front of her. "Really, Julia. Let's not be false with our young people. Reading is a serious endeavor. Shawn, you must remember that a library is a serious place. Please show your respect by wearing clean clothes and brushing your hair before entering."

My mouth fell open.

Ms. Cutter took the books from Shawn. "You do not have a library card, Shawn, so you can't check out books. Your mother must sign for a card for you."

Shawn opened his mouth to say something, then closed it, looked at the floor.

"As your mother is never here, being so busy in *other places*, you must leave all the books here. Come along, now. Out you go."

Shocked into silence, I watched as Ms. Cutter led Shawn away, careful to keep her distance. She held out a hand, indicating that he was to precede her. Shawn shuffled out, his head still down.

I had to sit down in a chair for a moment. Had that really happened? Had she really been that bitchy? After a few moments, I stood and shelved the books Shawn and I had read, furious with Ms. Cutter for making Shawn feel so unwelcome, so unworthy.

Within minutes The Vulture was back, her long beak of a nose protruding from her face like a sausage. "Ms. Bennett." She had a sneer plastered over her face. She reminded me of the mother-in-law I almost had, her hands on her bony hips. "I know you're inexperienced and have a lot to learn, but, please, let's not cater to the riffraff of this town. We can't have this area turned into a little day care for the children of—how shall I say it?—the less desirable families."

I was stunned again. The town actually had someone like this in charge of the library? "I thought libraries were for everyone," I said. "Not just desirable families."

She huffed and puffed. "We have a certain atmosphere we're trying to promote here, one you're probably not familiar with. Our library is important to us out here in Monroe, very important, and people don't like to be distracted by problem children when they're here."

I glanced around the library. There were two people there. One looked to be about eighty. He was hunched over an encyclopedia. Roxy Bell had told me he came every day and read through the encyclopedias. He had read from A to Z. Twice. The other was a woman with graying hair. She had come in, chosen three books, and was now checking her books out.

"Shawn wasn't a problem child at all, Ms. Cutter. He was

very quiet, he listened to the stories well, and it *is* Story Hour."

"Stop!" Ms. Cutter held up her hand again in front of my face again. I stared at the backs of those wrinkled fingers. "You will not argue with me. I have been in charge of this library for twenty years. The board has given me their trust to do what's right, and this is what I believe is right. The discussion is closed. I will see you at the front desk immediately so you can begin shelving the books."

She turned on her heel and left. My heart ached for Shawn. I went to the front desk and, without looking at Ms. Cutter, shelved all the books. Roxy Bell and I chatted a little bit until The Vulture informed us that there was plenty of time we could talk when we weren't working on the taxpayer's dollar.

I arrived the next day, hoping that Shawn would come back, and he did.

Ms. Cutter's face turned a lovely shade of tomato red, but she said nothing when I greeted Shawn, a big smile on my face. He had brought his sister, Carrie Lynn. Carrie Lynn was very small, with hair the same color as Shawn's and badly matted. She had enormous blue eyes and hollows in her cheeks. She looked exhausted and scared and had this old look to her eyes that told me she'd seen way too much of life already. I saw her clinging to Shawn's hand with both of hers. Over her left arm was a dirty blanket.

"This is Carrie Lynn. She's six years old. She doesn't really like to talk," Shawn told me, shifting his backpack. "She's shy around people."

Carrie Lynn glanced at me, then down at the floor.

"But she's real good, Miss Bennett. She likes books, too. We have one at home about Cinderella, and she looks at it every day. Right, Carrie Lynn?"

Carrie Lynn nodded, then tried to duck behind her brother. I noticed that her clothes were as dirty as her brother's, her shoes also torn.

"I am so happy to meet you, Carrie Lynn," I said, getting down on my knees to be at eye level with her. I wanted to hug both kids. What kind of parents would let their children sink to this level? Well, actually, I knew.

Parents like my mother.

I remembered wearing shoes with holes. I remembered how the other kids had made fun of my dirty clothes. I remembered having hair that was so matted I couldn't brush it. I remembered having a dirty blanket just like Carrie Lynn's. And I remembered escaping to the library in town in every single place we lived. I spent hours in the library from the time I was about four years old when we lived a block from it.

The first day I walked in, the librarian asked me where my mother was. I told her I didn't know. She called the police, my mother showed up, told the librarian I could come to the library any damn time I wanted and if she called the police again she would be damn sorry. Then my mother whacked me across the face for causing trouble and yanked me out. I smelled alcohol on her breath.

The librarian always welcomed me after that. I have never forgotten Mrs. Zeebak's kindness, or the kindness of the librarians in my life that followed her.

"So you like books, Carrie Lynn?"

She nodded.

"What kind of books do you like?"

She glanced at her brother, tried to hide behind him again.

"She likes the book on Cinderella. She would probably also like books on animals."

"Animals?" I smiled at her. "Those are my favorite books! Of course, I'm a big fan of Cinderella, too. Shall we sit together and read both types? And what do you want to read today, Shawn?"

"Whatever Carrie Lynn wants to read is good with me because I had time to read with you yesterday."

My throat tightened. Shawn put an arm on Carrie Lynn's tiny, fragile shoulder.

So we read and read and read. A couple books on princesses and a couple on animals. Then I pulled out an easy-to-read book, and we worked on their reading skills. Carrie Lynn had fewer skills than Shawn, but they were pretty close.

When Hatchet Face arrived, pointing at her watch, her disdain oozing out of her skinny body, I was ready for her. I put the books away, took the children's hands, and kept up a steady stream of conversation as I walked them to the door. I told them to come back the next day.

Shawn said, "Thank you, Miss Bennett."

Carrie Lynn peeped up at me through a tangle of blond hair. I thought I might have seen a small smile.

Then they were gone, back to the apartment they said they lived in next to the library. Gone to parents, or a parent, who apparently didn't seem to care that a son's shoes had holes large enough for loneliness to seep in and a daughter who pulled her filthy blanket over her head to hide because she preferred to be invisible. Both children had the vacant, desperate, crushed looks of those who were never hugged and had truckloads of secrets to hide. How did I guess that? Because that was me. I was Carrie Lynn and Shawn.

I went home that day, helped around the farm, made tostados for Aunt Lydia and me, and then, because I was saddened by Shawn and Carrie Lynn, I made chocolate desserts for hours. Chocolate Amaretto Peaches, Pears in Chocolate Fudge Blankets, and Chocolate Red Currant Torte.

After about three hours of sleep, I went on my paper route, passed Dean Garrett's home, acknowledged I missed Paul Bunyan, helped out on Aunt Lydia's farm, then went early to the library.

At exactly 1:00, Shawn and Carrie Lynn showed up, Shawn with his backpack, Carrie Lynn with her dirty blanket, which she still sometimes pulled over her head. They showed up the next day after that and the next. Every day for an hour, despite The Vulture's withering looks, Shawn and Carrie Lynn and I would read together.

We read fairy tales, although Shawn pretended that he thought they were silly. We read books on earthquakes and hurricanes and sports figures. We read books on rocks and minerals, the weather, and life on an Oregon Trail wagon train. We read books about the stars and evolution and dragons and boys who got into trouble in school. We read everything.

And I had the kids read to me.

Within a couple of weeks Shawn had made enormous progress on his reading, and Carrie Lynn knew basic words. I could get her to read out of a book, but she still wouldn't speak to me.

One afternoon I asked Shawn what was inside the backpack he always carried. Inside was a beaten-up water bottle. An apple. A stained T-shirt, a sweatshirt for him, a sweater and skirt for Carrie Lynn. The clothes I had seen before. They were all dirty. Even the backpack smelled.

I remembered that smell, too well. It made me want to cry.

I knew from my own pathetic experience that the state would not take children away from their parents because they looked tired and dirty, but I didn't have to stand by and do nothing. So I started smuggling in food for them each day: apples from Aunt Lydia's trees, hard-boiled eggs with a little container of salt, two peanut butter and jelly sandwiches for each of them, two bottles of juice, and, their favorite, my chocolates. I always snuck a few to them while we read, and their sweet, tired, worried-looking faces lit up.

I got information on their lives in bits and pieces when I asked a few well-chosen questions. "You and Carrie Lynn look tired today, Shawn. Did you go to sleep late last night?"

He shrugged. "My mom's friends wouldn't go to sleep. They were up all night."

Or I would ask, "Shawn, what did you and Carrie Lynn do after Story Hour yesterday?"

"Not much. My mother was gone, so Carrie Lynn and I stayed at the apartment, and then when Bingham came over we went to the park and swang on the swings."

"What time did you go home?"

"I don't know. It was dark. No one else was in the park. Carrie Lynn got cold even with her blanket on her shoulders. Can we read about airplanes now?"

"Who's Bingham?"

"That's my mother's friend. Can we read about airplanes, please?" His eyes would sometimes get that worried·look, and Carrie Lynn would make these sad hiccupping sounds, so we would read.

But his mother's friend's name would change regularly, and he couldn't tell me much about the friends. "My mom says I'm not supposed to talk to her friends. She says they don't want to be bothered by a brat."

Shawn didn't say it with any resentment, nor did he seem to think that "brat" was a negative name. Just a fact.

On Mondays I noticed that Shawn and Carrie Lynn were especially hungry, so I started packing them bigger sacks of food for their backpack for the weekend. On Monday I also brought extra food. I bought them two new toothbrushes and a comb-and-brush set, and shampoo.

"It took me two hours to get the tangles out of Carrie Lynn's hair," Shawn told me the next day. "But look how good it looks now."

"Beautiful," I choked, thinking of Shawn brushing out Carrie Lynn's hair for two hours. "Beautiful."

๑ 12 ๑

"What happened to your arm, buddy?" I asked Shawn.

Carrie Lynn whimpered, held Shawn's hand with one hand and with the other pulled her blanket over her head. Shawn looked straight ahead. "Let's just read," he said, pulling away and sitting down on the floor. Purple and blue bruises lined his right arm. Carrie Lynn crawled over to sit in his lap, the blanket still on her head.

"Can I see your back?" I asked and then lifted his shirt before he could say no. I did the same with Carrie Lynn's shirt, then I quickly started reading a book, Shawn and Carrie Lynn cuddled up to me. I felt ill. Their backs were spotted with new bruises.

I called Children's Services after they left. They were very polite, said they would send someone out, noted that other people had also called about the children.

On the third day after that incident, the kids didn't show up for Story Hour, nor did they show on the fourth or fifth day.

On the sixth day, when I was thinking that maybe Children's Services had stepped up to the plate and done something, I looked out my window and saw Shawn and Carrie Lynn running for the library, Carrie Lynn's blanket swinging behind her.

I breathed a huge sigh of relief, greeting them at the door, ignoring the glower of Ms. Cutter.

I welcomed them back to Story Hour, even though I was surprised. I had assumed that they had been taken away from their mother. When I was sure that Ms. Cutter was back at work, I gave Shawn and Carrie Lynn the lunch I had brought them just in case they came.

They tore into the tuna sandwiches. They ate apples and bananas and yogurt and chips, and then they popped the chocolate truffles I'd made into their mouths. Carrie Lynn was positively scrawny. She sat as close to Shawn as she could without being right on his lap.

"My mom is real mad at you," he said, whispering, right in the middle of the story.

"Why?"

But, of course, I knew why.

"She said you called the police. The police came over to my house the other night and looked at me and at my bruises and they told her to shape up. She told them I got the bruises when I got in a fight with my cousins, but I ain't got no cousins, but she told me to say it anyhow."

"So did you say it?"

Shawn looked like he was about to cry. "I had to. Barber was there."

"Barber?"

"One of my mother's friends."

Carrie Lynn pulled her blanket over her head.

"Barber is really big, and he yells at us a lot, and he told me if I didn't say it that he would hurt my mother."

I kneaded the muscles in my neck. Shawn and Carrie Lynn were living my childhood all over again.

"I'm sorry, Shawn and Carrie Lynn." I hugged Carrie

Lynn to me. She still didn't talk much, but at least she let me hug her.

"Can we read about earthquakes again, Miss Bennett?" Shawn asked, wiping away tears with both hands.

I nodded yes and grabbed a couple of earthquake books, vowing to call Children's Services as soon as I left this dark tomb of a library with its shaded windows and bleak children's area.

I called, told them what Shawn told me. "We understand your concerns, Ms. Bennett, but these children are not at risk for bodily harm. Parents have a right to discipline their children."

"But their mother is disciplining her children with bruises."

"There weren't that many bruises, according to our social worker. We appreciate your call, but there's nothing we'll be doing in this case until a time should come where it appears the children are in danger."

"But what did your social worker tell you about their appearance? Their clothes? How dirty they are?"

"Ms. Bennett, we don't take children out of their parents' home when their clothes are dirty. Surely you know that? I have another call now—I know you understand." *Click.*

"Under the light of the moon is the best time to make chocolate," Aunt Lydia told me that night. It was about ten o'clock at night, and elbow to elbow we were whipping up a batch of Chocolate Cream Puffs for Rosita and Jacqueline, who had the flu. "I'm blowing snot out of my nose every hour by the gallon, and Jacqueline's got diarrhea, diarrhea, diarrhea," Rosita yelled at me over the phone when I called to check up on her. "We're sick as vomiting dogs."

We had earlier made Mocha Velvet Cream Pots for Marie, who was married to Dave, Stash's foreman and right hand man for "the Biz." Marie had lost her ninety-two-year-old mother the week before.

I wondered who else in town we could cook for. I was so upset about Shawn and Carrie Lynn I thought I might cook all night.

"When you're under the light of the moon, you should think. Think, think, think, Julia!" Aunt Lydia said, her braids, all seven of them, swinging around her shoulders as she heated the egg yolks and sugar. "Some people think moonlight is a splendiferous time to get romantic. They obviously have not fully evolved. When moonlight touches you, it's time for a woman to sit back and think, really think, about her life."

I looked right up into the face of the moon, bold and bright and sending out rays of light in four different directions like a cross.

I added cocoa and flour to melted butter. I didn't particularly feel like thinking about my life. Sometimes you just want to put all of your problems and worries and fears in a box and put that box deep inside yourself and shut the lid for a while, if only to get a little peace before the lid flies off and hits you in the face with another problem.

"See, love? Moonshine is lucky," Lydia said. "The moon is reflecting the sun. The sun is hidden. The moon isn't. It's just there. Right there. The light around it is asking you to put a light on your own life."

I knew what was coming. "So, Aunt Lydia, what is the moonlight telling you? What are you really, really thinking about?"

Aunt Lydia paused, then stopped and stared at me. "I'm really thinking about you."

I tried to laugh, but it came out like a tight wheeze instead. "I thought the moonlight was supposed to make women think about their own lives, not others'."

"You *are* my life, sugar." For once her voice was quiet. "I hope you can forgive me."

My hands stilled. "Forgive you?"

"Yes, forgive me."

"Aunt Lydia, what in the world do you need me to forgive you for?"

"For not kidnapping you." She flipped her braids over her shoulder, then melted more butter for the icing of the cream puffs.

I would have laughed, but she said it so seriously, I didn't.

"I should have come for you when you were a child."

"But you did." My voice sounded strangled. I didn't want to think about my childhood in Aunt Lydia's kitchen while we were making Chocolate Cream Puffs.

"I should have come and got you and kept you for good." She whacked her spoon on the edge of the pan four times. *Whack. Whack. Whack. Whack.*

"You tried that," I choked out. I was thirty-four years old. Surely I was over this?

"I know I did. Damn bitch!" Lydia yelled, "Damn bitch" into the sky, then swiped a hand over her face. Lydia had come and gotten me on four different occasions unannounced and brought me to the farm. Within days the police were there, taking me back to my mother, talking to Aunt Lydia about custody, kidnapping, etc. Even my cries and pleadings made no difference back then.

"I shoulda gone to Australia with you."

I stopped stirring the chocolate. Australia. Now that would have been nice. Kangaroos and the coral reef and clean beaches. And no boyfriends.

I pictured myself rescuing Shawn and Carrie Lynn and living in Melbourne with them. It might be my only recourse.

"At least she let me come and see you for the summer."

"Damn bitch!" Aunt Lydia boomed again. "Your mother moved you around so much, I couldn't always keep track of you. She knew I always wanted to know how you were, but it would be weeks or months before she'd call me."

My heart clenched. The times in my life when I didn't

have Aunt Lydia in it, when I wasn't getting calls from her, or gifts, or letters, had always been the worst.

It was during one of those times that Zeke, a boyfriend of my mother's would come after me every day once my mother left for work. She would kiss him passionately in front of me, smile, tell me to stay out of Zeke's way, and as soon as she left, Zeke would turn toward me.

It was innocent at first, and I was happy to have the attention. I thought he was kind. He brushed my hair one day, braided it the next, suggested we take a bath together, then he would massage my back later in the evening. One night his hands wandered everywhere. He told me he was massaging my whole body, that I was just to relax and enjoy it. I couldn't have been more than nine.

The massage on my back felt good; then he started playing with my breasts, which were growing even then. I felt sick. I tried to pull away, but he pushed me back down. The next day I told him I didn't want a massage. I landed face-down on the bed anyhow, one hand pinning me down as the other roamed all over my body and into places a man's hand should never be on a child.

I didn't know what to do. I couldn't tell my mother because I knew she would blame me. Plus, Zeke told me if I complained, he would hurt my mother.

There was no one else to tell. Two decades ago, practically no one talked about sexually abusing children. For many sane, normal people, it never occurred to them to do such a thing, so it never occurred to them it was happening to other people. If someone did find out about it, they often turned away, having no clue about what to do. Now it's different. Even in kindergarten, puppets are acting out "good touches" and "bad touches."

But there weren't any puppets around when Zeke's hands were violating my tiny body. His "lovin'" as he called it, took worse and worse turns. My little body ached all the time from then on out.

I could feel Aunt Lydia's eyes on me, one hand absent-mindedly heating the butter and chocolate mixture as one more horrible memory came back in fine detail.

It was raining. As Zeke's car was in front of our apartment when school let out, I didn't go home. I walked back to town and went to the library. When I was sure my mother was home, I went back. Zeke's car wasn't there, so I used my key and entered our shabby apartment. But Zeke was hiding behind my bed. When I dropped my backpack on my desk he sprang out and grabbed me. The buttons of my shirt popped off, my skirt flew up and then he tossed me on the bed. My mother walked in within two minutes.

I know that this was a good thing because she saved me from getting raped by Zeke. But it was a horrible thing, too.

My mother was absolutely, positively furious.

At me.

"You little bitch!" she screamed. I still remember that scream of pure rage as she ran into the room. Zeke scrambled off of me while she hauled me up and slapped me across the face. "Get your own boyfriend! Leave mine alone!"

Her ranting and ravings went on and on. I was a horrible daughter, a demented girl, a selfish bitch. Zeke sat back and smiled. When she turned on him, he told her that I had seduced him, that he'd had too much to drink that day, that he really wanted my mother and wouldn't she come back to the bedroom that second, please, so he could fuck her?

She slapped me across the face again, then slammed the door. I heard them in the next room and shoved a sock in my mouth so they wouldn't hear me screaming. I screamed all night.

My teacher asked me the next day if I was all right, and I wanted to tell her, but I couldn't. She was so pretty and so kind, and I thought she would think I was dirty.

A few days later Zeke tried to shove his way into my room. I could feel the screams welling up in me again, so I climbed out the window and jumped. Our apartment was three floors up. I hit a tree, then landed knee-first on the pavement, which was what gave me the gaping scar that Caroline saw. Still, it was better than landing on my head.

Several women saw it happen, and the police and an ambulance were called. I enjoyed my two-day stay in the hospital. The nurses comforted me when I screamed.

Zeke saw the police and fire engines, packed up his stuff, and left my mother immediately after that. We didn't see him again.

The Vermont State Police caught up with him when he went after the daughter of the assistant attorney general, whom he met in a video game arcade. Zeke was heading out of town on the freeway when the police boxed him in. Scrambling out of the car, he tried to run, but then he realized he was trapped and pulled a gun. The police pulled theirs, and that was the end of Zeke.

My mother and I watched the newscast together, and she cried, then glared at me. But she had a new boyfriend by then, Taryn. He didn't like children in a sexual sense at all, but he did like porn, and he often convinced my mother to bring her friend Marie Alice over for a threesome. I couldn't sleep when Marie Alice was over for all the noise those three made.

But at least I liked Taryn. He said good morning to me, he said good night, he bought us food, I saw him pay our bills on numerous occasions. He would often give me fifty dollars and now and then even stood up for me when my mother was screaming at me for one thing or another.

"Take it easy," he'd tell my mother, "Take it easy. She's just a kid." I'd go to my bedroom and shut the door, rocking myself on my bed. If I felt a scream coming on, I'd stuff a sock in my mouth.

But Taryn never touched me. Never looked at me in a weird, creepy way.

For Christmas he gave me a new bed set—a comforter made from a quilt, with two patching pillowcases, two new pillows, and a white dust ruffle. I loved it, truly loved it, the set being the only new item I'd had in a long time. But then Taryn left when my mother dumped him for Scotty, a giant of a man who looked like a humungous fart to me, and she took the whole bed set because it reminded her of Taryn.

She burned that bed set in the fire even as I screamed at her, even as I tried to pull it out. Scotty had to hold me back while I watched the quilt quiver and roll, the pillowcases shrinking and turning into black masses in the midst of the rollicking flames.

The first night without my bed set, my sheets and blankets looked even more ripped and worn than before. I put three layers of clothes on because it was freezing and my mother was out at some bar but had told me not to turn on the heat. I huddled under an old coat that one of my teachers had bought for me two years ago, and slept.

Scotty yelled often at me and my mother. That was when I took to leaving for school early. I had breakfast with a kind cook at school each day—Kathleen was her name. She always made sure I had enough food. Then I went to my teacher's class and helped out in the classroom. After school I made the rounds, asking if I could help this or that teacher, lapping up every single compliment and thank-you like a starving person does food. At about five-thirty, when the last teacher left, I'd go to the library and sit and read books. Teachers and reading books in libraries saved my life.

I would eat the dinner that Kathleen the cook packed me in a sack and then head home, hoping to avoid my mother, and succeeding about half the time. As soon as I approached whichever apartment we were living in, my stomach would start to ache, the pain depending on which man was living with us at the time.

I sighed. Aunt Lydia stopped what she was doing. So did I. We faced each other across the island in her kitchen, the moonlight streaming in. "I hope you can forgive me one day," she said.

"There's nothing to forgive, Aunt Lydia." And there wasn't. When I was sixteen I moved out of the rat-infested apartment I shared with my mother, and with the help of a counselor who had endured my kind of childhood, got myself declared an emancipated minor. I qualified for almost free housing, free breakfast and lunch at school, and food stamps. I was humiliated by the help but knew there was nothing else I could do. I went to school during the day, then waitressed forty hours a week.

I didn't have any friends. Not because people didn't try. The kids at my high school were nice to me in that they left me alone. But when you have been through what I went through, and you feel dirty from all the men who have grabbed at you and run their hands all over your body, and a mother who regularly ranted and raved in alcoholic stupors, and you're almost always hungry and worried, and your mind feels like it's snapping, well, that puts a damper, shall we say, on how well you're able to maintain friendships with people.

I was in the business of surviving. I bought used clothes. I cut coupons. I saved all the waitressing money I could because I was always petrified there would be an emergency and I would have no money for food. The fear of hunger stalked me, and I began to put on weight. Frankly, for a while I felt better. The weight meant I was eating. The eating meant there was food. Regular food.

But soon I was depressed by the weight gain, believing I was the size of a silo.

I channeled that frustration into school and received straight As. I literally worked until I fell asleep at night over my books during the first few months of my emancipation. Which left no time for thinking about anything else.

Why would I want to think too much, anyhow? I had a mother who had signed me away to the state. She had given me away. No tears, no apologies, nothing. I was a nothing.

And although I had to admit after living on my own for a

few months that being able to return to a safe home, a place where there would be no creepy men with sweaty hands and heavy bodies, no rampaging mother telling me how bad I was, no dirtiness and no chaos, was appealing, the fact that my mother didn't want me, and would go to such lengths to rid herself of me, was still a stupendous blow.

I could have gone to Aunt Lydia—in fact she pleaded with me to come to Oregon on a weekly basis, but I wanted to stay in the school I was in. I had been there for two years by then, and I liked the other kids and the teachers. I had the impression that as a group they had decided to look out for me. Furniture arrived for my apartment as soon as I moved in. Boxes of food. Clothing. A new backpack with tons of school supplies every fall. Christmas presents. They cared.

I graduated and received a full-ride scholarship to a prestigious college because I studied obsessively to keep my mother out of my head and nailed the SAT. "Have you got two brains in that head of yours?" my counselor had asked me, shaking her head over my score. "Maybe three? Anyone ever tell you that you're brilliant?"

I spent the summer with Aunt Lydia and tried to think and be and pretend I was a normal person like everyone else, then flew back to Boston with this admonition from her: A woman's estrogen is her strength. Capture that estrogen, embrace it, flow with it. Be your estrogen. You rule, Julia, girl, and I adore you.

At college I felt much like how an aardvark would feel among peacocks. I was fat, not stylish, not sired from a monied daddy with a salesman-like laugh, and I had never been on a yacht. Plus I still had all my secrets. The secrets kept me apart from the other girls—girls who partied really hard and slept around like you wouldn't believe, but you knew they would turn into proper society ladies the second they left campus.

"I'm going to have all the sex I can now," one gal told me,

"because when I'm married I'm going to have to stick with that one penis. Do you think I can do that, Julia? Stick with only one penis? For fifty years?"

I told her that was a difficult question to answer.

She nodded. "I think I might have to have a couple of penises on the side, Julia. They'll be my 'secret penises,' so to speak. For pleasure and fun and relief from the one-penis-per-married-girl rule."

Still, the girls were generally nice in an offhand way, even as they often studied me as one might a science experiment in which purple organisms are growing. And they loved my chocolate treats. They could not figure out why I took so many classes, and they thought that my waitressing was "quaint."

"It's spectacular that you're getting to know the lower classes, Jules," my roommate, Tabitha, said. "Spectacular. And it will look good on your résumé. Like you really can be counted on to know how to relate to poor people. You know—worked your way through school, that sort of thing. It's a smashingly good idea, although so dull, isn't it? Working, I mean."

I got fatter in college as I dealt with a lot of issues with my mother and my childhood and didn't date. In fact, men scared and often repulsed me. I went through a period of wondering if I was gay but figured I wasn't. I simply didn't want a man around me. Not that there were any men at my door anyhow.

After getting my art degree, I took a job at an art gallery with the help of one of my instructors and later had the grand privilege of meeting Robert.

I looked over at Aunt Lydia. She wiped both hands across her eyes, smearing chocolate right across her cheek. Aunt Lydia hardly ever cried. Of the two of us, I was definitely the Queen of Tears. For long moments, we both stood there. Sometimes things in life are so painful nobody can speak, so

I sang what I was thinking, low and husky. "I neeeedddd your love . . . I wannnntttt your looovvve," I sang and sang until Lydia laughed and then sang with me. We took a minute to dance around the kitchen, our hands waving in the air, and then we got back to work under the white light of the moon.

∽ 13 ∽

When I left the library the next day Shawn and Carrie Lynn's mother, Brandy, was waiting for me. She was about twenty-six years old, caked in makeup, and sporting stringy blond hair. She was appallingly thin, had several open sores on her face, and her hands shook. A maniacal smile was plastered on her face like one of those haunting clown dolls.

"Who you think you are?" she spat out, the smile still there. She scratched her back with both hands, up and down, up and down.

"Mrs. Coleman—"

"I ain't no Mrs. Coleman, bitch, and you quit calling the police on my family." She held Shawn firmly by the arm as Carrie Lynn cowered behind her brother, gripping his hand. Shawn's eyes were firmly on the ground. "You don't know shit about what's going on, so stay out of my business—you got that, girl?"

I looked at her. Didn't move, didn't nod. No, I didn't get that, 'girl.'

I wanted to say, "But do you 'get' your son's bruises? What about Carrie Lynn's? Do you get that she's scared to death of you? Do you get that they're starving? Do you 'get' that your children's clothes are dirty?"

But I didn't say anything like that. I knew that woman like the back of my hand. She was my mother, reincarnated with a drug problem.

"I'm sorry," I said, so contrite. "I think you have the wrong person about that police-calling business. I didn't call the police. I do Story Hour at the library with the children. That's it."

"You're telling me you didn't call the police?" Her eyes were narrow, like slits of hate.

"No, I didn't. Why would I call the police?" I opened up my eyes real wide and tried to look as innocent as possible.

"'Cause you're the only adult that spends time with them. Shawn and Carrie Lynn are always going to the stupid library with that old hag inside."

"Well, it wasn't me. What did you say your name was?" I extended my hand and shook hers. Her hands felt like ice, and I could feel the tremor. Sheesh. What was this woman on?

"I'm Brandy Wilshire. Me and the kids don't got the same last name. They're stuck with their retard fathers' names the sons of a bitchs' cows."

I wanted to slap her, to shake her, but instead I smiled. Above all, I wanted to help her children. "I'm glad you stopped by." I said it like I thought she was a concerned parent and it was so sweet of her to say hello to the local librarian. "I've been wanting to tell you what a smart boy and girl you have."

That stopped Brandy in her tracks. The smile even dropped. She looked better when she didn't smile. She had hardly any teeth on the top row. I couldn't see the bottom. "What?"

"Shawn and Carrie Lynn. They are so smart."

"Well that sure as hell ain't what Shawn's teachers have said. This kid is dumber than a board!"

"Oh no!" I wanted to tear her eyelashes out. What a bitch. But I smiled. "He's bright! So bright. He's learned to read! He can memorize anything. He never forgets what he learns. . . ." I went on and on, standing right there on the library steps. And then I launched into Carrie Lynn's intellect. Bright. Incredible reader. Advanced for her age. Wonderful listener.

"I gave Shawn a book one time, and he done never read it at all because he can't. He doesn't got much in the brain department, just like his daddy. Fact is, he reminds me of his daddy damn near every day. That man ripped me off, got me knocked up, then got himself jailed for murder and left me high and dry. No child support, no nothing. He's a piece of shit." She scratched at her neck, looked at her fingernails, scratched again.

I knew what to do. It was the same thing I did with my mother. And with Robert. That last thought gave me pause. I had spent so much time stroking Robert's ego, to get him to calm down, I was an expert.

I nodded gently.

"And Carrie Lynn's father ain't no better. He runned off, too, with another woman. I didn't much know him, but he knew I was knocked up again, and he didn't care about me or Carrie Lynn. And both my babies were screamers. All the time, they screamed."

I wasn't surprised. Babies tend to scream when they're not fed.

"Shawn and Carrie Lynn's brains must come from you," I soothed. "They are so sharp. Sharp as tacks. In fact, a little more time in the library would probably help out a lot. I know, being a good mother, that you probably want them at home with you, but I know you work and you're so busy—"

"You got that damn right. I am busy. And without school, they're always underfoot. I got things to do, I ain't no rich suburban bitch housewife who's got time to kill."

"Of course not. I'm sure you work very hard." Yes, having sex with one loser after another for drugs must be exhausting. I knew enough about drugs to know that they killed the soul of a person and replaced it with a version of the devil.

"Speaking of working hard, since the kids are reading so much now, I thought they would need a library card. Shawn, go on in and get two library card applications and bring them out here." Before Brandy could object, Shawn was off. Carrie Lynn stayed close by my side. Within seconds he was back.

"Just sign right here, Brandy, after you fill out your address, and I'll make sure that Shawn and Carrie Lynn get a library card. That way when you're working they'll have something to do and they won't get in your way."

At first I thought she was going to object, but then those mean little eyes got crafty and she nodded, signing her name and address. I took the cards from her.

I might have felt a little bit sorry for Brandy because of her drug habit if she wasn't such a miserable, pathetic, criminal loser of a mother.

"I'm here from one to five. They can come every day at one, and I'll send them home at five. They can help sort books. I can read with them. We're not busy."

I imagined Ms. Cutter's face if she could have heard me. She would look as if she'd sucked down an entire lemon in one fell swoop. Two members of an "undesirable family" in her library for hours! Shame!

"You want these two underfoot, fine by me, Trixie," said Brandy, her mouth twisting. She scratched at her face, then her arm, then checked her skin. I figured she was on meth. "But you tell whoever called the police that I got a gun and I ain't afraid to use it on anyone who gets in my business, you understand that?"

"I do understand that, ma'am," I said, all sweet again, at the same time praying that she would die soon. Like get hit by a Mack truck. "But I didn't call. We'll see you tomorrow at one, Shawn and Carrie Lynn," I told them, smiling. Shawn didn't look up, but I could tell he was smiling. Carrie Lynn caught my eye. A tiny little smile lurked at the corner of her lips.

Stash insisted on another target practice. I went to bed with the sounds of bullets whizzing through my dreams. For some reason, it helped me sleep. I woke up refreshed and calm.

And ready for Ms. Cutter.

Ms. Cutter did blow a gasket when Shawn and Carrie Lynn started coming in and staying from one till five. In fact, she blew a gasket right in front of them. I wanted to kick her. At that moment, I didn't know who was worse, Ms. Cutter or Shawn's mother.

The Vulture drew herself to her full height. "This is not a charity house, and we are not a home for wayward youth, either."

I turned and told Shawn and Carrie Lynn to wait in the children's section. It was a Monday, and Shawn looked pale and exhausted again, as did Carrie Lynn. Since they were both scared to death of Ms. Cutter, they ran off as quickly as they could. I knew Carrie Lynn would pull her blanket over her head as soon as she sat down.

I was furious. Couldn't Ms. Cutter see that they needed help?

"Shawn and Carrie Lynn are members of this town and have the right to use the library. They can help me shelve books."

"We are not a baby-sitting service, Ms. Bennett. I forbid this."

I stood there, thinking about her forbidding this. Thinking about forbidding children who were desperately in need of a respite from an abusive home from using the library.

Roxy Bell stood up behind her desk, then came to stand behind me.

"Ms. Cutter, you've managed to scare the children of this town away from the library, and their mothers—" I began.

Ms. Cutter looked as shocked as she would have if a naked man wearing an alligator mask had streaked through the books on tax law. "I have done nothing of the sort! I insist on quiet in my library, and young mothers today don't respect that."

"Young mothers today would probably like to attend Story Hour with their children. Other people would probably like to feel welcome in their own library. They would probably like to check out books," I said.

Ms. Cutter crossed her arms in front of her chest. "I've had enough. I am reporting you to the board. I'm sure they'll have a lot to say about your care of indigent children with a hooker for a mother."

I knew more about having a hooker for a mother than I wanted to know. And I had a pretty good idea of the life that mother was giving to Shawn and Carrie Lynn. And I also knew that all children should be welcome in the library.

I walked to Ms. Cutter's desk and opened up the bottom drawer with a key that was taped to the bottom of her pencil holder.

"Get out of my desk, this instant! You're fired, Ms. Bennett. Absolutely fired. Get out of here, and get out of my desk!"

I held up the bottle of vodka.

Ms. Cutter froze.

Roxy Bell's mouth fell open.

"I believe the board would like to know what you have in your desk, Olivia." I used her first name deliberately. "In fact, I'm sure it would amuse them greatly, as it would amuse the rest of the council. And the councilmen and councilwomen's spouses, and their friends, and in-laws. Even the in-laws' dogs might be interested. Can you imagine how people living here will laugh at this?"

The librarian's face went white, and I suddenly hated myself. I wanted to help Shawn and Carrie Lynn, but I didn't want to hurt or humiliate anyone. Even someone as bitterly mean as this woman.

"Surely," I said quietly, putting the vodka back in the drawer, locking the drawer, and retaping the key. "Surely we can find something around here for Shawn and Carrie Lynn to do?"

Olivia Cutter nodded her head, her shoulders slumped, her face now gray.

"I'm sure we can," she squeaked.

Roxy Bell clapped her hands and clicked her red pumps, her white curls bouncing around her head.

❧ 14 ❧

The tire blew out with a bang. I automatically covered my head with my arms, sure that Robert had found me and had shot a bullet through the tire and was reloading. The car plunged into a ditch, driver's side down. I heard myself scream, while at the same time I knew that on this particular country road no one would hear me. I dragged myself over to the passenger side, intending to escape, while I envisioned Robert running toward me, pickax or knives in hand, an implacable fury twisting his features into a gross mask of hate and revenge.

Already I felt my breath catch, knowing the Dread Disease was here again, but in a rare burst of courage I decided to fight through the disease, shoving the door open with my hands and feet and scrambling from the car.

It was still early in the morning, and I had another ten houses to deliver papers to, but I really didn't think about how inconvenienced those people would feel that morning without their papers. I didn't even look behind me as I tore up the bank and over the other side, running as fast as I could through a field. I remembered this field, knew that on the other side of it were woods that I could hide in, and a stream running through it that would eventually lead me back to town.

I heard my breath heaving in and out, sweat lacing my brow even though the morning was as cool as the inside of a refrigerator. I flew across that field into the woods, and when I could run no more, I looked behind me and saw . . . no one. I hid behind a rock, watching the darkness, trying to breathe, looking through the branches of every tree, all around, knowing that Robert could pop out from anywhere with his chosen instrument of torture.

I waited for what seemed like years, then peeled my body away from the rock I was clinging to for dear life and looked around. By this time the sun was starting to glint through the trees. The light took away some of my fear of sprinting through dark woods, and the thought of Robert sprinting after me was greater than my fear of any wild creature.

As soon as I thought it was clear and my breath was coming in a somewhat normal fashion, I ran through the woods, over a hill, and to the back side of town. I saw Donald, a friend of Stash's who looks like a giant, walking by the General Store. I darn near tackled the man I was so happy to see him and had him drive me back to Aunt Lydia's in his truck. He was almost stuttering in his efforts to calm me, to help me. Aunt Lydia called Stash, and he was there within seconds.

Stash told Aunt Lydia to get her guns out, and then he and Donald and Dave and Scrambler, one of Stash's favorite employees, went out to get my car and find Robert. He had five of his ranch hands surround Aunt Lydia's home while we were gone. Aunt Lydia pulled the blinds down in the whole house except where she poked a rifle out the crack of one window, her finger on the trigger.

Stash was gone for a long time, but when he came back, he was smiling, as were Dave and Scrambler. He hugged me when he told me about the flat tire that had sounded like gunfire. The rock was still in the tire. Dave clasped my shoulder. Scrambler said, "It's so unfortunate that this happened. Please, Julia, take it upon yourself to indulge in a nap and a small cocktail. You'll awaken feeling refreshed and rejuvenated."

Aunt Lydia sagged with relief onto the couch and didn't move for hours.

I went to bed. I was too exhausted to feel embarrassed.

It was only later that I realized that I had not been completely overcome by the Dread Disease. I had had trouble breathing from fear of Robert. It had been hard to catch my breath. But I had caught it, I had breathed. I had functioned.

I couldn't help it. As much as I had been scared right out of my pants that morning I was proud of myself.

I had won against the Dread Disease. Just once. But there it was.

You would never guess by looking at Carrie Lynn that she could draw outstanding dragons.

And suits of armor.

And castles.

And a princess that looked a great deal like . . . me.

But she could.

And I found that out when I was bending over a large piece of butcher paper making a sign advertising our new, daily, Children's Story Hour. I blew my curls out of my hair, my patience long gone with this little project.

For long minutes Shawn and Carrie Lynn watched as I attempted to draw a dragon with a crown on its head.

I had drawn the tail and body and head but could not get the face of that dragon. I erased the eyes for the third time, sighing in frustration. Stupid dragon. Stupid, stupid dragon. What did I care that he looked like an overgrown pig with snail eyes?

Carrie Lynn touched my arm, her little fingers warm. "Can I try?"

I gave her the pencil. What the heck. Anyone could probably draw a crowned dragon better than me. Carrie Lynn leaned over the paper and drew the dragon's eyes then proceeded to fix the body and the tail.

She handed me the pencil.

Stunned, I handed it back. "Why don't you finish up the poster?"

She needed no further prompting, taking the pencil from me and drawing a sprawling castle in the background across the whole page, complete with a turret and moat. Next to the dragon, she drew a smiling girl with curly hair wearing body armor, and holding a sword.

I looked close.

"It's you, Miss Bennett," she said.

"I'm not that pretty." The words slipped out. I wasn't asking for a compliment.

"Yes, you are," Shawn and Carrie Lynn said at the same time.

"It looks just like you," said Shawn.

Carrie Lynn put the pencil down, then picked up the crayons nearby and starting coloring. I watched as she blended the colors together, making the dragon and the girl come alive with color, even somehow managing to make the girl's body armor shine.

"Carrie's pretty good at drawing, isn't she, Miss Bennett?" Shawn asked, pride in his voice.

"No, Shawn," I said. Carrie dropped the crayons as if they'd burned her hands, her face flushing with color. Her eyes almost hit the floor as I hurried to tell her the truth. "Carrie Lynn is not *pretty good* at drawing. She's absolutely brilliant. Absolutely talented. Absolutely incredible. You're an artist, Carrie Lynn. An artist."

And at that, Carrie Lynn, tiny Carrie Lynn with her little hands and huge blue eyes that always looked on the verge of tears, wrapped her skinny arms around my plump waist and hugged me.

* * *

The front door of the library was on the main street of town, so I attached the poster to an easel and put it right out front at 2:00. Shawn and Carrie Lynn and I surreptitiously watched the townspeople looking at the poster while we ate our snack of White Chocolate Fudge Triangle Cookies and milk on the front steps. The Vulture had already had her lunch/vodka break.

Every time someone smiled when they saw the poster, I nudged Carrie Lynn. She looked so pleased—so small, so fragile, and so pleased! Her hair, which Shawn brushed every day now, shone in the summer light like gold.

I hadn't seen any more bruises, but I looked, and when I saw them again I would call Children's Services. Why does a child have to be half dead before the state will step in to help?

When our break was over, we put books back onto the shelves, and I read them both a story. By 3:00, the appointed time, we had two mothers and four children at Story Hour.

I chose my four favorite storybooks. After two books I taught the kids two songs about a naughty donkey and a princess who always got in trouble. I read another book, then put on a children's CD I had bought the day before, and we danced and I blew bubbles. To close Story Hour—we were ten minutes over time—I put the two puppets I had bought on my hands to say good-bye to the children.

The next day we had four mothers and their children. The day after that, nine mothers. By the end of the week eleven mothers and their children came to Story Hour. Each day I introduced Shawn and Carrie Lynn as my helpers. The mothers must have heard the town gossip and felt sorry for them, because they went out of their way to be kind.

And when they found out that Carrie Lynn was behind the wonderful poster, they were so complimentary that Carrie Lynn almost smiled. We decided that the children who came to Story Hour could put their names in a purple velvet hat I borrowed from Aunt Lydia. Whoever had his or her name drawn could keep the poster Carrie Lynn had drawn for that week. No one was allowed to win twice.

On Friday a four-year-old girl won the first poster. With braids flying, mouth open wide and screaming with excitement, she went up and hugged Carrie Lynn and Shawn, then grabbed the poster and ran out the door, her mother struggling to keep up with her.

Two of the other children cried.

I had Carrie Lynn and Shawn come early on Monday to make a new poster. Carrie Lynn drew a giant spotted dog surrounded by miniature kittens because we were going to read stories about dogs and cats. Up it went on the easel outside the library. By 3:00 the small Story Hour area was jammed.

Story Hour was a roaring success.

The only person who didn't like it was Ms. Cutter, but every time she said something sarcastic about "her" library turning into a children's zoo I would glance pointedly at her drawer.

At Golden's fiftieth annual town fair I decided I would sell chocolate truffles with a pink or white frosting bow on the top, and chocolates in the shapes of chickens, teddy bears, lizards, and cats. I had also decided that I would whip up Chocolate French Silk Pies, Chocolate Lemon Tartlets, Chocolate Mint Filled Cupcakes, and Chocolate Crackle Top Cookies. Might as well cater to every taste and see if I could make some money doing this.

"Those are some fancy-schmancy chocolate desserts you got there, Julia," Lydia said, dividing up all the eggs we had collected that morning into different egg cartons. The egg cartons all came printed with WILD EGGS FROM THE LADIES in red on the top, the name of her business. In each dozen-count carton she dropped nine white eggs, two brown, and one blue. "People love to see art in their egg cartons, and this is art!" Lydia declared. "Pure white, brown that looks like those mochas you like to drink, and blue as blue as those oceans in the advertisements for cruises. My eggs are art!"

She grabbed five eggs at a time in each hand and plopped them into the egg cartons. Already she had bound her elephant garlic together in white mesh bags and tied them with long purple ribbons and attached tiny tags with her company's name printed on them.

For someone who takes exactly eight minutes in the morning to shower, get dressed, and put her hair up in braids or a ponytail, and who thinks women who wear makeup and get dressed up are wasting their time on their looks instead of their "innards," as Lydia likes to call them, she was surprisingly picky about her "farm art," as she called it.

"Garlic is for lust," she told me. "For lusty lust. That's why I've called them Lusty Elephant Garlic. These will sell like you wouldn't believe, especially when I tell women their orgasms will be better."

A better orgasm.

Women could always use that type of thing.

"I'm off!" Lydia shoved several egg cartons in the refrigerator, tossed a bag of Lusty Elephant Garlic in a basket, and gave me a quick kiss. "I'm meeting Caroline today. She called last night, and I could tell she was seeing the future for many people and their tears and screams were upsetting her. I'm going to grab a joint and go. Are you sure you don't want to come, dearie?"

I shook my head. "I have to stay and prepare more Jumbo Chocolate Chip Cookies. Chocolate is an aphrodisiac, you know."

"Yes, it is!" Aunt Lydia agreed. "Chocolate is love and desire and passion all rolled up into delicious bites." She popped a chocolate cat into her mouth. "Delicious. I'm going to bring some to Caroline. You don't mind?"

I didn't mind. Aunt Lydia kissed me again and said good-bye to two birds who flew over her head. "Put the birds back in their cages after their morning flights, would you, love?" she called, and then she was off and I was back to my baking.

Aunt Lydia had taught me to cook and bake and can when I was a child, and ever since I was seventeen, making chocolates and chocolate desserts gave my mind a break from worrying about my problems and whacked-out emotional issues, the "life sucker" problems as Aunt Lydia called them. Chocolates were my escape.

But they offered no escape from thinking about Dean Garrett. In fact, I thought about Dean Garrett most of the time. I thought about that smile and the way he looked at me as if he thought I meant something, and the way he listened to me even when I sounded oh so inane. I let my mind wander just a tad to how warm his hands would feel sliding down my hips and how much my big boobs would fill out his hands and how he would be warm and snuggly in bed.

Now, I am not going to get involved with him, I told myself as I frosted a truffle. And I was sure he didn't want to get involved with me, especially not when he probably had another woman (or women) waiting for him in Portland, and my ass is rather wobbly and large, and my waist is none too thin, and my curls are always all over the place.

But I could fantasize a bit, because the Dread Disease would probably soon kill me, or Robert would, and I should enjoy my time on Earth as much as I could at this point. And, besides, Dean was supposed to be back tomorrow from a trial in Portland, which had gone two weeks longer than expected.

He had called every day. Sometimes two or three times.

He'd joked with me about my paper route, asked if I was having breakfast with anyone else. We'd talked about the farm, and an upcoming Psychic Night called Reinventing Your Pleasures and Passions—which he asked to attend, and I told him to forget it—and the chocolates I was making, and his legal cases, and life in Portland, where the traffic and the noise and the stress were getting to him. And we talked a lot about Carrie Lynn and Shawn and Story Hour and Stash and Lydia and the girls at Psychic Night.

Each time, though, there were silences between us. I could almost feel him smiling at his end. At my end I certainly was, and then I felt like a fool.

And I missed him.

Running a paper route is no fun if you don't have a Dean Garrett waiting for you at the end of it.

I frosted another truffle, this one made with white chocolate and a raspberry filling, and then dropped the frosting tube as the roar of Dean's truck coming down our country road filled my senses until I thought every nerve end would explode.

Dean was back.

He was one day early.

He was in our driveway.

I gripped the counter and watched through the window as he shut the door of his truck and walked toward the house, his stride long and sure. He climbed the steps to the door, and then there he was, standing on Aunt Lydia's porch, right outside the screen.

My breath caught in my throat when I saw him, but not in the way that makes me feel like my throat has closed up, shut down, and turned off, but in a heart-fluttering type of way.

He rang the doorbell. I swallowed hard. I remembered that my curls were piled up on top of my head, many of them falling out of the loose knot around my face. My blue sweatshirt and jeans were splattered with chocolate, and I wore zero makeup.

He rang the doorbell again.

Answer it, I told myself. *Please. Do. Answer it!*

I opened the screen. I knew I was smiling like a fiend. Dean had on jeans and boots and a blue shirt and a cowboy hat, and if any more raw masculinity poured out of that man I thought I'd probably land on my rear. Right splat in the middle of Aunt Lydia's entry, which was painted—appropriately, I thought—pink.

"Hello, Julia." And there was that voice. Honey over gravel. Yummy.

"Hi, Dean," I managed to squeak. Belatedly, I realized I probably smelled like a giant chocolate bar. I hoped he really liked chocolate.

He smiled at me.

I smiled back. *Breathe, Julia. Remember: air is your friend.*

"I missed you this morning."

Instantly, the thought of me curled up in his arms hit, and I blushed.

His smile got even broader, the lines near those bright blue eyes crinkling. "That didn't come out right."

I had another graphic thought, and my face decided it should blush even more.

He laughed, low and rumbly. That laugh went from my head to my heart and then to the nether regions where it lodged, hot and tingly.

He smiled at me.

I smiled back. I could almost breathe.

"What I meant is that I just got back from Portland."

"Oh."

Dean had a square jaw, a very square jaw. I wondered if it would taste a little bit like aftershave, a little bit like man, a little bit like fir trees and mountains, and a little bit like Dean.

"So I missed you on your paper route this morning."

"Ahh." And I liked his hips. He didn't have any fat on him, but neither was he thin. There was enough to grip. I didn't even feel fat standing there next to him.

"You do still have your paper route?"

He smiled at me.

I smiled back.

"Julia?" He laughed a little. I loved that laugh. I realized he'd just said something, and I thought quick.

"Yes! Yes, I do have a paper route!" I could die. Really die. "Are you looking for Lydia? Or Stash?"

I couldn't be presumptuous here. No need to make a fool of myself again.

"No. Neither."

I pushed my hair off my forehead, feeling brown chocolate streak across my skin.

"Would you like breakfast?"

"Breakfast?" His mouth tilted up on the left-hand side. Really, men who look this sexy should be illegal.

"Or lunch?"

"Actually, I haven't had breakfast yet. I left Portland early this morning. That'd be great."

I stepped back so he could enter the house.

He lifted a hand up to my face, his thumb rubbing across my cheek, then my lips. I felt so hot I would not have been surprised to see tiny flames erupt from my skin where he touched me.

Then he bent his head, and I didn't move, and his warm lips came down over mine, and I knew I was standing in heaven. He put one arm around my waist and brought me close to his body, every one of my curves sinking into his hardness, and he put his hand under my head and kissed me and kissed and kissed me.

When he was done and I was leaning heavily against him and smiling like a goon, he brushed a finger across my cheek and then licked the chocolate off his thumb.

"Delicious," he told me, smiling again. "Really delicious."

I have to say that I am proud of my pancakes. Years ago, one of my mother's boyfriends' father used to come over on

Saturday mornings and make pancakes. This boyfriend only lasted, I think, about a month, because my mother dumped him, but in those four weeks I learned how to make buttermilk pancakes from scratch.

As Aunt Lydia had pure maple syrup, and as I whipped up butter until it was so light and fluffy it could almost be used for angel's wings, Dean was delighted with the results.

I was delighted that he was delighted.

"Best breakfast I ever had."

Of course, the compliment made me choke up, so I got up to get us more coffee. I poured him some. I believe he had room in his cup for four drops, but it gave me a second to compose myself into some semblance of a normal woman.

"I'll bet you're glad the trial is over," I said. He had told me about it, and the trial had been in the newspaper, too. As the plaintiff's attorney, he had been quoted many times.

The paper had also discussed the "remarkable, decisive victory," noting that the jurors came back with a verdict in under an hour. His client won on all counts and was awarded an absolutely amazing amount of money.

"It went fine." He took another sip of coffee, looking at me over the rim of the cup, those eyes crinkling in the corners again.

"Congratulations."

"Thank you."

"It sounded very complicated."

"No, not really. Good versus evil, that type of thing."

"Are you tired?"

He fixed me with that blue gaze. "I was. I'm not today. How is all the chocolate-making going?"

"It's going well." I let him change the subject. "We'll see if anyone buys it at the fair."

"I'll buy some."

"Good."

"I'll buy all of it. Your chocolate is the best damn chocolate I've ever had. When I was in Portland, I went to three different chocolate shops to sample your competition, and yours was always, always better."

I almost chortled with glee. About the second week into our morning meetings by the mailbox, I had given him a bag of my chocolates. The look on his face when he tried one almost made my boobs dance with pleasure, and then picturing that he-man wandering through Portland sampling chocolates and thinking of me, well, that made me wiggle. "Maybe you're biased. I give it to you for free."

He thought a minute. "All right, I am biased about you. But I'm not biased about your chocolate."

I could hardly eat with him so close, but I managed to choke down a few bites as we chatted about everything fun and everything pleasant. He cleaned his plate.

"Stash told me about your ex-fiancé, Julia."

I dropped my fork, and it clattered onto my plate. A boulder the size of Colorado lodged in my throat. I reached for my coffee and knocked it over. Dean reached for it the same time as I did, and our fingers bumped together. He righted the cup, then took my hands in his.

"Julia."

I tried to pull my hands away, but he wouldn't let me. I couldn't look at him. I was humiliated. Lydia had told Stash, of course, and Stash had told Dean.

I felt a little angry, then smothered it. I could see how it had happened. Dean had probably asked about me, and Stash had told him what he knew because he cared.

"Julia." Dean's tone insisted that I look at him.

I raised my eyes to his, then wished I hadn't. Those sharp, honest blue eyes were why jurors believed him. They were also why witnesses probably withered under his gaze into squished prunes and spat out everything they were trying to hide.

"I wish he hadn't told you."

"I understand, but he did."

"What did he say?"

Dean looked down for the briefest of seconds, then squeezed my hands. At any other moment, I probably would have been melting into my chair, but my whole body was cold.

"He said that you left him." The left corner of his mouth curved upward. "That it was a rather abrupt departure."

I nodded, thinking of my wedding dress flapping on that tree, covered in dirt. I could still taste what that dirt tasted like.

"Yes. You could say it was rather abrupt."

"You're still scared of him, aren't you?"

So Stash had told him a little bit more. Was I scared of Robert? No. Not scared. I was petrified. And I was scared of Dean, too, for altogether different reasons.

Oh no. I could feel it coming. The Dread Disease was on its way. It must have been the mention of Robert's name. I took one last deep breath before I knew my air would be cut off. I felt my hands tremble under his, and I felt the pressure around my hands increase.

"Julia?"

I heard Dean's voice, low and concerned, but then it mixed with Robert's voice. I saw Dean's face, the blond and white hair, the square jaw, but then it morphed into Robert's face, twisted and ugly.

I remembered the time that Robert had held my hands together with one of his, then cracked me across the face with his other hand. He had put a foot under my ankles, and I fell hard onto the floor of my kitchen. I remembered seeing that the door of my refrigerator was slightly ajar. I remembered how I couldn't breathe under him. I remembered how I begged him to get up, but he wouldn't, and he pressed himself hard into me until black fog started to seep in around the corners of my vision.

"Julia?"

The air was now almost completely gone, my body freezing-cold. I clenched my jaw, one part of me scared to death of this mysterious Dread Disease, another part of me scared to death of what Dean would think, and still another feeling Robert's presence all around me and in between me and Dean.

I tried to look him straight in the eye while my body shook, my mouth going dry, the air so completely gone I could almost feel my brain cells shutting down and turning off.

"God, Julia, what is it?" Dean strode around the table and picked me up in his arms.

I made a gasping sound that was truly humiliating. My left breast was crushed against his chest, not unpleasantly, and I had one arm around his shoulder. Within a millisecond we were on Aunt Lydia's blue couch, with me on Dean's lap.

One large hand pulled my head down to his shoulder. I tried to breathe and couldn't, tried again through my nose. A shiver skittered right down my body, and I crossed my legs to control the other trembles and quakes that I knew would follow after a bout with the Dread Disease.

"Are you all right?" He said this with so much concern, I thought I'd bawl right there. Tears on his neck, mucus on his shirt. I bucked up. The latter was not attractive.

I breathed in again, as much to live as to inhale that man's scent. I rested for a second, then tried to pull myself off his lap.

"Stay a while," he drawled, settling me back in as my whole body shook.

The exhaustion that follows the trembling that follows the problem with breathing descended like a black blanket over my head, but this time the black blanket was comfy and warm and safe.

I snuggled in a bit, just for a moment, and felt Dean's arms pull tighter around me. Eventually I started breathing like a normal person. "What's wrong, Julia? God, honey, what is it?"

"Nothing's wrong," I said, automatically. A disastrous childhood does that. You get in the habit of telling people that "nothing's wrong" because no one wants to hear it anyhow. Except Aunt Lydia.

"Julia, if we have to sit here all day until you tell me why you're so cold, why your heart is racing and your body is limp, we will. I have all day."

All day? I sighed. Couldn't help snuggling up again just a tad. Now, that would be fun. I wondered if he'd play with my hair.

He laughed, feeling my body cozy into his.

But the laughter was short-lived. "It does have its appeal, Julia, but I'm not accepting that for an answer. You need to go to a doctor."

I shook my head. "How about if you and I play doctor?" The words slipped from my mouth the way melted chocolate slips from a spoon.

His forehead rested on mine. "I'll play doctor with you anytime but now."

I opened my eyes, and our gazes collided, and I noticed lighter blue specks in his eyes like dawn, and a blue-green like the sea. I noticed the height of his cheekbones, and the way his sun-bleached hair fell over his forehead. And I noticed his mouth inches from mine.

And I smiled.

And he smiled back, just a little. His mouth covered mine, and I closed my eyes as white-hot heat poured from his lips to mine and then landed in that toasty-warm spot between my legs. I wrapped an arm around his neck, my other hand on his massive shoulder.

Dean Garrett was not a follower, and he guided me through that kiss, and I followed along, enjoying every millisecond, his lips pressing against mine, each kiss more urgent than the next, his tongue doing a marvelous job of making me wonder what else that tongue could do on other parts of my body.

My breasts were pressed against his chest, and for once I didn't mind their size. Dean had a huge chest—he could handle those suckers. And then I just let my body melt, like the chocolate I had been making.

Until I heard Aunt Lydia's voice and Stash's laughter.

"Well, Stash, honey," Aunt Lydia drawled from the doorway. "I think we can surmise that Julia does indeed like Dean's sausage."

✿ 15 ✿

I was not having a good day at the library. Ms. Cutter was watching me like a three-eyed leech. Shawn and Carrie Lynn were tired and pale. Carrie Lynn kept putting her blanket over her head. I had seen new bruises on both children the day before. I called the police, and they referred the call to Children's Services. I was furious at the condition these children lived in and even more furious at Children's Services for doing nothing. The woman at CS sounded utterly annoyed with me.

"Ms. Bennett, I believe we have already told you that we do not remove children from their homes just because their mother is poor. We saw no sign of drug usage in the house."

I gasped. "Did you look at the mother? Didn't you see the sores on her body, how she scratches herself all the time, how skinny she is?"

"I don't think you understand what Children's Services does, Miss Bennett. We do not take children away from their mother because she has sores on her body and scratches. The children were clean and appeared well-fed." When I explained to the woman that the children looked well-fed because I brought them lunch and dinner and snacks every day and had also bought them brand-new clothes and shoes and brushes for their hair, she said, "Well that's all well and good, and we appreciate good citizens like you, but, really, we are busy. If you see a problem, you can call again, but until then this case is closed."

Click.

We had had several other Psychic Nights in the past few weeks. One had been called Organizing Your Orgasms, another had been called Dedicating Your Desires. Tonight's Psychic Night was titled Your Hormones And You: Taking Over, Taking Cover, Taking Charge.

I thought it sounded splendid.

"Hormones have ruled us forever!" Lydia scolded me as we worked that morning, the early morning sun cutting through the slats of the chicken house. I glanced at the chicken she held in her hands. She shook the poor bird in her exuberance, and I saw the chicken's eyes pop in fright. "Isn't that right, Hilga?" Aunt Lydia yelled at the chicken. She is usually so gentle with her ladies.

"Too much estrogen has robbed us of our inner souls. Hormones flow and fluctuate and dive and soar and make us go damn, damn crazy. I can hardly stand looking at Stash when I'm having a hormone rush. He walks in the door and I feel the need to throw my jam at his head."

I followed Aunt Lydia through the barn. She let the lady go, and we heard a very grateful-sounding *cluck cluck.* Hilga's chicken friends gathered around her and *cluck-clucked* sympathetically. "Lydia's off her hormonal rocker! Hormonal rocker! Hormonal rocker!" I could almost hear them say.

"Hormones take over our thoughts and actions. We must learn to control them!" Lydia jabbed a pitchfork into a bale of hay. I was surrounded by chickens, all clucking contentedly now that Aunt Lydia had released their comrade.

"Hormones are a nuisance," Aunt Lydia announced, picking up eggs from underneath squawking, resting, clucking chickens. "But with yoga, lots of walking, good sex, and a little pot, we can be in control. Of course, there's other ways to be in control of your hormones, but I'll save my womanly secrets for tonight!"

One chicken pecked at her hand. She grabbed that chicken's beak quick as a wink. "Now you listen here, Marie Jane, I'll have none of that pecking. I've talked to you about this before." She kissed that tiny beak, then moved on.

"Women need to vent their problems and trials and tribulations and hormone-fluctuation levels with other women. Men are hampered by the fact that they have thingies which make them naturally selfish and self-centered and boorish and unthoughtful," she declared, the chickens clucking at her raised voice. "Women, however, can do it all. Run companies, raise children, volunteer, tickle men's teensies at night. Our work is NEVER done!"

"So what time is Psychic Night?" I asked.

"Seven o'clock, over at Lara's."

"At Lara's?"

"Yes, at Lara's. I talked to her yesterday. She did not sound joyful. When I see her I will undoubtedly be able to ascertain where her hormone levels have taken her!" Aunt Lydia reached down and petted several of the ladies, calling them Honey Claws and Sweetie Beaks.

"Her husband is out of town at some minister's convention or something where they pray and pray and pray. I hope all that prayer does not take away from his testosterone-driven libido! Women need a man who can put out and up when their hormonal levels allow the passion lurking inside to run free."

I grabbed a few more eggs. A chicken pecked me. I thought about men who can put out and up. I thought about one in particular and wondered how far he could put it up, then grabbed a few more eggs as my face grew a tad hot. The memory of the kisses he had given me at the mailbox that day and his continual invitations for another breakfast made me hotter.

"Take these ladies, for example," Lydia said. "If I don't keep a few roosters around here, they get so uppity, so feisty. Every now and then they need to get laid."

I smothered a laugh, imagining the chickens at a bar, dressed to the teeth, but dressed sort of slutty, too, intent on having a one-night stand.

"Like other females, they need to get their orgasms out! If they don't, my ladies here start coming on to each other." Aunt Lydia shook her head. "Can't relate to that one myself. But if my ladies want a rooster around to satisfy their basic urges, good for them. They can have a rooster."

"You mean the chickens turn gay without a rooster?"

"Damn straight they do," Aunt Lydia said. "So I keep a few roosters around. The darn things cockadoodle doo all day, and I have come to believe it's their way of strutting their stuff, strutting their manhood. If they were smart enough to realize that my ladies only want them for sex I don't think they'd cockadoodle so loud."

I banged my head on the slanted roof, then looked behind a battered bookshelf. Sure enough, the ladies had hidden a hoard of eggs.

"Now, you, Julia. You need a rooster in your life. A man just for sex, nothing else. Men are good for sex and money, Julia." She looked under an old chair she had in the barn and grabbed four eggs. "But sometimes neither one is very good, so you have to take care of yourself. But if you can find a man who's good to you and wants to tra la la at night, super. But for heaven's sake, don't marry them! Men are best in small doses."

She must have seen my body language, which said, *Forgetaboutit. I don't need a man in my life, they scare me to death.*

"Now don't be like that, darlin'. They're not all insane

creeps. Most of them, but not all of them. Take Dean, for instance—"

"No, no, please," I said, flinching as a chicken pecked me on the hand. "Let's not take Dean at all." He was too tempting.

"All right!" Aunt Lydia said, her voice startling a few of the ladies. "We won't take him. But he would be a good candidate for a little sex now and then, and then you could send him on home. If you wanted to. He is one fine man, though, and big enough to warm a woman's bed for years. Otherwise, with the exception of Dean Garrett, look for a man in small doses."

"Right, Aunt Lydia. Got it. A small-dose man is what I need."

"That's exactly it! Have a lovely day, Agnes." Aunt Lydia let the chicken fly from her arms, both pointer fingers straight up in the air. "You need A Small-Dose Man."

I went back to work while Aunt Lydia burst into song about A Small-Dose Man, rhyming as many words as she could. It had a country feel to it, until she burst into an operatic soprano. The ladies fluttered around her. *Cluck. Cluck. Cluck.*

I might have kissed Dean a few times, but I was going to force myself to call it quits with him. I had to, I really did. And I would. As soon as I stopped having the time of my life.

I kept my head hidden by my hair, bending extra low to get the eggs from the ladies, who alternately clucked in a friendly way to me and pecked my hands.

Dean Garrett was impossible. Demanding but gentle, independent and strong, and very smart—smart enough not to be arrogant.

And we were going to make great . . . friends, I told myself. Great friends. As soon as he stopped kissing me every morning.

* * *

I went to work at the library, ran a splendiferous Story Hour, with kids roaring like lions and growling like bears, read an extra story to Carrie Lynn and Shawn, then packed their dinner in Shawn's backpack, as I did every night.

Shawn told me they always ate their dinner after their mother was gone for the night or "busy in her bedroom." If they'd been kicked out of the house, they ate their dinner on the merry-go-round in the park.

I had bought both of them a packet of new socks, and they seemed excited about those.

I then went straight to Lara's. I was early, but I had called her on my new cell phone, and she said it was perfectly all right if I came over. I knocked and heard her yell at me to come on in, so I did.

Again, I was struck by the sterility of Lara's home. Beige walls. Beige carpet. Blue accents, prim furniture. Heavy drapes. Freaky. I could hear her walking around upstairs, and I wandered into the kitchen to put the Double Chocolate Snowball I had made on the counter. I had been designated the dessert person ever since the gals had tasted my first chocolate dessert.

The kitchen was the same. Not a thing on the counter except my cake, a mixer, and a coffeepot. Spotless. Lifeless. The kitchen opened up to a family room with a tiny nook for eating. A plastic tablecloth with tiny red flowers covered the table. I went over to the curtains covering the backyard sliding glass door and opened them. Light streamed in like a tunnel.

It was about 6:00, but still bright and cheerful outside. For the life of me, I couldn't mesh the Lara I had met the first night at Aunt Lydia's with the woman who owned the house.

But I was about to see the other side.

"Hi Julia," she said, entering the kitchen. She was wearing beige slacks and a green crew-neck sweater. A thin gold chain with a tiny gold cross hung from around her neck. She smiled as she looked at the dessert. "Yummy. What did you make this time?"

I told her, and then we took off on the plane of polite chatter.

We discussed nothing of importance. It was the type of surface conversation that hundreds of millions of people engage in every day. Nothing deep. Nothing controversial. Nothing that reveals much of another person. And sometimes chatter like this can be comforting. Soothing. Sometimes you connect with another person.

But other times it's just a cover-up.

I let her indulge in the cover-up.

"So how's your work going at the library?"

"The library job is fine as long as I stay out of The Vulture's way." I thought about Shawn and Carrie Lynn's expressions when they saw their new socks. "Well, it's fine except for two kids who have a meth addict for a mother, no father, and aren't fed or bathed on a regular basis. Oh, and their mother, or someone in their home, beats on them, but Children's Services won't do anything about it."

"What?" Her voice rose three pitches.

I told her about the children, and then Lara stood in her kitchen and cried. She fingered the cross, and I wondered if she was going to rip this one right off her neck, too.

"Childhood sucks," Lara said. "Totally sucks." She leaned her forehead against the sliding glass window. Lara was young and beautiful, but sadness was definitely pulling on her face like a toilet plunger.

"Yes, childhood sucks," I agreed.

"There's nothing you can do as a child to fix your situation. You're stuck. It's all you know. Unless my father was at a prayer meeting, he would preach at my brothers and me for two hours every night, alternately screaming and making us cry when we couldn't memorize a Bible verse.

"I remember how the Rutulsky family infuriated him. They owned the best bakery in town, and they didn't go to church. 'Damned to hell!' he'd yell, 'The Rutulskys are damned to hell!' Then he would quote from the Bible for about an hour, ranting on and on while the three of us and my mother were forced to sit on the couch and listen to him. The Rutulskys actually came to our church once, and on the way out I remembered the kids looked positively horrified and the parents looked at me with pity."

"Pity?"

Lara kept staring. I noticed that she'd lost more weight. She was past scrawny now.

"Yes, pity. My father had given a sermon about disciplining your children, how to spare the rod was to spoil the child. He condemned others for not taking a firm hand to their children, talked about wives needing to be obedient to their husbands, how they must submit, obey, the man is the head of the house, that type of thing. Of course, he spoke on full throttle, screaming his lesson out to the congregation. 'Submit, women! Submit! Or you are sinning! God will punish you if you do not bend to your husband's will!'"

I nodded. I had watched my mother submit to men her whole life. Violent, mean, manipulative men. And I had watched how some men in her life seemed to submit to her. Sick. Her submission had had nothing to do with the Bible, I was sure of it.

"Those Rutulskys walked out of there pretty fast after the service, although Mrs. Rutulsky stopped to hug my mother. My mother got tears in her eyes, held Mrs. Rutulsky's hand for a moment. I heard Mrs. Rutulsky say to my mother, 'Our door is always open to you, Susanna.'"

Lara laughed, but it was that bitter laugh I was getting so used to with her. "At school the next day, Sharon, the Rutulskys' oldest, came up to me and told me that her family had prayed for me and my mother at dinner. I was so offended by that at first. Why did they need to pray for me? They were the ones my father said were going to hell. But I looked in Sharon's eyes, and it seemed like she was going to cry. So it made me feel like crying because I hated my life and my father and even my mother sometimes for not protecting us. Sharon invited me to spend the night, but, of course, I couldn't."

"Why not?" I didn't realize I was holding my hands together so tight until I noticed the fingernail indentations on my hands.

"Because the Rutulskys never came back to church, so my father considered them to be heathens. Absolute heathens. My mother said to him, 'William, I don't think they're heathens. Carolly brought me some flowers the other day and—'"

"My father held up his hand about six inches from my mother's face. 'Stop, woman. Stop now. I will not have you defending the Rutulskys in front of the children. Save your ridiculous comments for when we're alone so I can pray for your confused and unworthy and rebellious soul. You are so easily led astray, Susanna, and your compassion is misplaced, as usual.'"

Lara shook her head. "My mother shut right up, her head hanging about seven inches away from her plate."

"So, your father, a minister, someone who is supposed to love God and love Jesus and try to be kind to others, terrorized everyone who came into contact with him."

"Oh yes. Almost everyone was damned to hell. A couple of times, when someone stood up to him, questioned him, he would put his hands together as if in prayer." Lara showed how he did it. "And then he told the person that he would pray for them, that he would pray that God would show them the light, take away their ignorance, that they were unworthy to speak of His name until they repented. He used prayer as a weapon all the time. A way to make people feel bad about themselves."

"Yes, childhood does suck," I agreed. Lara had a raving lunatic for a father, and I had a raving bitch for a mother.

Perhaps we could introduce them to each other one day. Either Lara's father would become my mother's sex slave or they would kill each other.

"And, of course, gay people just sent him into a tailspin," Lara continued, her gaze still fixated out the window. She reminded me of someone looking out through the bars of a jail. "I had to stand outside shopping malls with him handing out anti-gay literature. So did my brothers. I read the pamphlets with my brothers at night. They presented as 'facts' that gay people had over a hundred partners each, that they were predators against children, had fetishes for animals, particularly sheep, and were otherwise perverted and gross. The literature also had detailed information about the fragility of rectal walls, the dangers of oral sex, and how gays were destroying America and had hidden agendas to take over the country and teach children how to be gay in the schools.

"A few times people would shake his hand, but almost everyone dropped the literature on the ground, in the trash, and kept going. Sometimes people swore at us, swore at my father, and he would simply stand there with his Bible and quote from it at the top of his voice. Half the time there was such a commotion that the store owners would beg us to leave. My brothers and I were always so relieved to see a store owner. We couldn't wait to get out of there. And all the way home in the car, my father would talk about how revolting gay sex was, and he would regale us with the physical details of gay sex, things no child should hear."

Lara turned to face me, her face flushed. "I cannot even begin to tell you how furious my father was when my brother called him from New York City and told him he was gay and had realized he was gay since he was fifteen. I thought my father was going to have a coronary right there in our little holy rectory."

"What happened?"

"He disowned my brother. Hasn't talked to him in ten

years. Isn't that Christ-like?" Lara made a choking sound in her throat. "My brother used to send cards and letters, but my father would send them all back. Now he just calls me and my other brother, who lives in Oregon. Jerry and I see Peter and his partner about twice a year. We go to museums, walk in the park, go out to eat, meet their friends. They're great people, certainly better people than my father."

I didn't know what to say. As someone who has also had a rotten childhood, I know that silence is sometimes the best comfort. No one can really say anything that will take the pain or inbred fear away.

"In fact, I miss Peter and Steve. Sometimes I feel like they're the only people I can talk to."

"What do they do in New York?" I asked.

Lara's face brightened. "They have this fabulous loft in Greenwich Village. Peter is a vice-president of a financial firm, and Steve is an artist and a teacher for the public school system, and they have all these liberal, wonderful friends who are always holding these great parties."

"They must know a lot of artists, then."

"Oh, yes, they do." As her face lit up, a new Lara emerged. "Yes, they're friends with artists of all types."

"You must have a lot in common with their artistic friends, then, Lara, since you've told me that you like to paint." I would later discover that saying Lara "liked to paint" was like saying Beethoven liked to fiddle with piano keys.

"Oh, yes, I like to paint." She looked at me, those huge blue eyes awash with tears so big a small squirrel could swim in them. "Hell, Julia, come on up. I've never let anyone see the attic except for Jerry, so don't laugh."

"I won't laugh." I couldn't imagine laughing. But, then, I couldn't imagine what was up there, either.

I trooped behind her up the stairs. We walked down the hallway, past two bedrooms. One was definitely an office for Lara's husband, and one was a sewing room. I peeked into their master bedroom. Again, it was perfect. And barren.

And bleak. I just could not imagine someone who looked and acted like Lara sleeping in that room. It was like dumping an orchid into a bagful of needles.

She took a key off the top of the door trim, inserted it into the lock, pushed the door open, and we climbed about ten steps into the attic. "Can't have any of the church ladies coming in here, I'll tell you that," she said, before a little hyena-like laugh erupted from her lips. Lara turned on the light, and I followed her in. Then stopped at the threshold.

I froze when I saw what was in that room. Stunned beyond stunned

In front of me was the most expansive, colorful artist's studio I could ever imagine. Every inch of it looked like Lara—the real Lara. "The previous owner had the room remodeled and the skylights put in," Lara said, looking relaxed for the first time. "He needed a third-floor office. Apparently he had a porn business. At least that's what two of the neighbors told me. He was a deacon in one of the local churches here, too."

On each of the four walls of the attic Lara had painted a mural. One was of the New York skyline, the way it would look if you were sitting on the top of one of the many tenement buildings. On all the other buildings, other people of all races and ages were out on the rooftops, too. Some were playing instruments, others were dancing, many were alone, staring at the sky.

In another mural, Lara had painted a group of people at a picnic together, only all of the people were famous historic and present-day figures: Abraham Lincoln, Rosa Parks, Tina Turner, Oprah Winfrey, Bono, Sandra Day O'Connor, Nelson Mandela, and Amelia Earhart.

On another wall, she had painted a huge quilt, and in every square of the quilt, she'd painted families from all over the world—Japanese, Chinese, African, and so on. Some were laughing, some crying, some looked tired, others happy.

On the fourth wall, she had painted a scene from an art

gallery. Every painting on every easel was different. And all the paintings had Lara's name in the corner.

The ceiling was painted a light blue with sunflowers. The sunflowers looked like van Gogh's sunflowers: distressed, unhappy, living, breathing things, caked with paint.

And scattered all about, against the walls, up on two different easels, were paintings that Lara had done herself. I walked around the easels, stunned at the paintings, then looked through the art stacked against the walls. I knew brilliant artwork when I saw it—had, in fact, been praised many times by my boss for noticing the quality of a new artist's work, or the lack of it.

One painting made me catch my breath. It was of a naked man, wrapped around a sunflower. The sunflower was taller than he was. It was exactly as Caroline had described it during one of the Psychic Nights. It had sounded ridiculous then, even though Caroline had said it with such seriousness.

The floor seemed to shake a little beneath my feet. Of course, maybe Caroline had heard Lara talk about her latest painting, but I had seen Lara's reaction to Caroline's statement: she had been shocked, but not surprised, and Lara had said she didn't let anyone up here, so I knew Caroline couldn't have already seen it.

I guess you get like that when you hang out long enough with a psychic. They shock you, but you're not surprised they know what they do.

While Lara had used only paints with some of the canvasses, like the one with the naked man and the sunflower, with others she had used bits of crumbled-up newspapers, buttons, confetti, twigs, a miniature bird's nest, crayons, pages from books, and dried flowers.

The effect was stunning.

I sucked in my breath. The woman was an *amazing* artist. I looked around the room. This was what Lara looked like to me, not the sterility of downstairs. Not the boring perfection.

This room was raw and emotional and throbbing with energy. It was alive, so very, *very* alive, as if a soul had been sprung loose from a cage and erupted with artistic enthusiasm.

"I don't even know what to say. . . ."

"Don't feel like you have to, Julia." Lara gathered up paints and brushes that had been left haphazardly around the room. I could tell by her tone that she had about as much confidence in her artwork as I did in ever permanently escaping Robert.

"It's incredible," I said. The words were so soft, I didn't think she would even hear me, but I was so awed, so dumbstruck, I could barely speak.

"Oh, please, Julia." She turned to face me, skepticism all over her classic features. "You don't need to humor me."

I stopped looking at the artwork, faced her square-on. "I'm not humoring you, Lara. People did that to me in the past, and I hated it. Hated the sanctimonious, patronizing looks on their faces while they lied to make me feel better about one thing or another. I told you your work is incredible because it is. I should know. I worked in art galleries for years."

"You really like them?" Her tone was so hopeful, so unsure. So like me. I felt myself connecting with Lara where before we hadn't.

"I'm positive. Your work should be in an art gallery, not hidden up here in your attic. You should share it with everyone, and you could sell it if you wanted."

She shook her head then, and I could see that latent anger and frustration rising in her features. She spread her skinny arms out, indicating her artwork. "How could I possibly do that?" she snapped. "Have you really looked at these? Some of the men and women are nude. Look at this one." She held up a painting with two women and a man. They were all lying down, the man between the women. One of the women was older, with gray hair and glasses. Alongside her were miniature smiling children, a house, and older couples that looked like parents and in-laws.

The other woman was young with flowing blond hair and huge boobs. Alongside her were a miniature cruise boat, jewelry, cash, and a fancy car. In between them was a man who was good-looking in a pretty, soulless, self-centered, annoying way. The two women glared at each other over him.

"How about my nude garden series?" she said, snatching up one painting, then another. In one painting, a nude woman, shown from the waist up, stood in her garden holding a birdhouse in front of her. She wore a straw hat and a smile. Birds swirled around her head.

In another a nude man tended his garden, surrounded by cornstalks. In the third painting, three middle-aged women sprawled on a quilt, roses in their hands and threaded through wreaths around their heads. They smiled at one another. "Can you imagine the outcry in this town if people saw this?"

Yes, I could. Small towns are not usually known for their liberal attitudes. But the paintings were so vibrant, so striking.

"My husband is a minister." She dropped the three women, then yanked up another of a couple naked and laughing and hugging on a bed of marigolds. "He's the head of a church. I teach Sunday school. I work half-time as the church secretary. I lead choir practice on Tuesday night. A very proper and boring choir practice, I'll have to say. Sometimes I feel like I'm going to go to sleep directing these people." Her shoulders slumped. "I can't possibly let anyone see these. And I'm not even thinking about what my father would do. God. He would probably set up camp here in the middle of my living room, not letting me or my husband out until we all died from starvation."

I dragged my eyes away from the art and thought about that. It actually didn't seem out of the realm of possibility. I envisioned myself rappelling down the fireplace to give her food.

"No. I absolutely cannot show these pictures to anyone." She flung a paintbrush across the wall. It clattered to the floor. Then she picked up another. And another. All of the paintbrushes went flying. I grabbed her as she reached for one of the water cans.

One dry paintbrush would not do much damage, but I couldn't let a bunch of dirty paint-water splat across one of these paintings. I had one arm around her waist, the other on her arm, as it was poised in the air, water splashing out of the can. She was so skinny, so very, very skinny, and pale and sad.

"I am losing it, Julia." She let the can drop, and all the water splashed on our legs.

I turned her around and hugged her, and she sobbed on my shoulder. I could feel her bones through her skin.

"I'm losing it, Julia. Every day I wake up and I grit my teeth and I wonder how I can get through the day. My schedule is insane. I am often meeting with people from seven in the morning until ten at night. They all need me, all expect me to be perfect, to have the answers, to fix their problems, to soothe their souls, to be prayerful. And I feel like such a hypocrite. I try to counsel people, try to guide them in their faith, but I'm not really sure I even believe in God anymore."

She pulled away, dragging both hands through her hair again and again.

"And if there is a God, he's either ineffectual or uncaring. Do you ever watch the news? There are millions of people who suffer every day, suffer horribly. How can I believe in a being like that? And all the time, I can hear my father's words echoing in one side of my head." She deepened her voice. 'Hell awaits you, Lara, as you waver daily in your faith! He knows your unbelieving heart, knows your many, many sins! You must repent and embrace the Lord before the devil takes over your soul.' And on the other side, I'm hearing the needs of everyone around me. All the time. God, I'm trying, but it's never enough. *I* am never enough"

I sank onto a nearby stool and pondered those words, *I am never enough.* It was exactly how I felt. Growing up with a mother who semi-hated me and a father who motorcycled off into the sunset, followed by a string of boyfriends and husbands who either ignored or criticized me, or followed me to bed whenever my mother wasn't home, had not done much for my self-esteem.

Robert had only reinforced my feelings of not being "enough," repeatedly telling me I was lucky he was interested in me, lucky he had even noticed me. "I'll train you, Turtle. Don't worry. We'll knock that white trash right out of you. You just have to listen to me and do what I say. Got it, Turtle? Got it? You're a nothing now, but as my wife you're gonna be a somebody."

I dragged my mind away from Robert. Thinking of Robert always brought on the Dread Disease symptoms. And thinking of how I had changed myself for him, had strived so hard to please him, how I had stayed even when he'd "accidentally" burned me with an iron on my butt made me feel ill. "Whoops," he'd said. "Sorry about that, Cannonball Butt. Didn't know you were that near, but don't worry, you've got plenty of butt to spare." He'd laughed when I'd cried. "Hell, don't be such a baby. I said I was sorry." I still had a slight scar on my butt.

Lara sank onto the floor, holding her head in her hands.

"Lara, do you love Jerry?" I asked.

She dissolved into another round of tears. "Yes. I love Jerry, but I don't think I love him enough to be a minister's wife the rest of my life. I can't live like this. But I love Jerry. I already said that, didn't I?"

"Yes, you did. What do you love about Jerry?" I moved and sat cross-legged on the floor in front of her.

"What do I love about him?" She looked shocked, as if I'd just asked her if she could take her intestines out so I could measure them. "I love everything about him. He's kind, he's funny, he's ambitious. Jerry knows what he wants to do, and he works until he has what he wants. In this case, he wants this church to grow so that everyone who wants to can know Christ. He tells me all the time that I am God's greatest gift to him, that he couldn't live without me, and he treats me that way."

"Have you ever told him how you feel?"

"Oh, God, no," she said. "God, no." She drove her hands through her hair again and again. With her hair pulled tight back from her face, she looked almost skeletal. "When we married, we had an agreement. He was going into the ministry, and I was going to help. I told him I was happy to do it, that I wanted a life in the ministry. Together, we were going to build this church. But I've come to hate my own life. I'm so tired, Julia. Tired and burned-out and utterly hopeless."

"But hasn't Jerry noticed that you're unhappy?" It had been patently obvious to me since the second I met her that Lara was miserable. Of course, she had broken the cross off her neck within hours of my meeting her, but still. Jerry was awake, wasn't he? He actually *looked* at his wife once in a while, didn't he?

"He asks me now and then what's wrong, but I tell him that there's nothing wrong, or that I'm a little tired, or that I'm worried about one person or another in the church, which I often am."

"When you tell Jerry that you're tired or worried, what does he do?"

She put a fist to her mouth to stifle another sob. "He makes me go to bed and read, or he gives me a backrub, or he goes and gets a movie, or he makes dinner."

Good God, I thought. One time I had told Robert I was tired, and he had whacked me on the butt really hard. "It's 'cause you're so fat, Possum. Get rid of that weight and you won't look so washed-out all the time."

"So does he suspect that you're not telling the truth?"

Another sob. "I think so," she said quietly. "I see him watching me really carefully. If he sees me doing house-work, he comes to help. He hugs me when we're going to sleep at night, and when I wake up he's still hugging me. He tells me to go upstairs and paint, and when he has to work, he brings his stuff up to the attic and works while I paint. He says he wants us to be together." She wrapped her arms around her waist and hunched over. "I spend so much time convincing myself that everything is going to be fine, that eventually this life will grow on me, that I'm doing what's *right*, that to do anything else would be selfish, that I have to go and have a drink or two until all my lies seem kind of fuzzy and it feels like I can manage my own hypocrisy."

Yes, I had seen that drink or two. Or five. "What does Jerry think of a drink or two?"

"He doesn't know. I get home so late after Psychic Nights, he's asleep. I go to sleep on the couch, then get up early and shower. I have a couple of drinks before he gets home or after he's gone to bed. It's no big deal. My drinking is no big deal."

But it was. I knew it. She knew it.

I didn't envy her her problem. Me, I would have cleaned streets with my tongue if I could come home every night to a man like Jerry, but Lara was different. Lara's passion was art. She could no more live without it than I could live with-out my heart.

We both heard the knocks on the front door. Lara wiped her eyes. I took a deep breath. I needed some chocolate.

"Please keep this between us."

"I will," I said, but then I grabbed her arm. "Have you ever had Psychic Night up here?"

Her eyes widened. "Oh no."

"You should."

"Oh no."

"Yes," I said. "Yes."

* * *

Lara was practically shaking in her shoes as we all trooped up the stairs to her attic after dinner. Aunt Lydia had made lasagna with garlic to kill off any excess hormones, Caroline had brought two delectable-looking salads, Katie had come a little later, after dropping the kids off at a sitter's. She brought cheese sticks as appetizers.

"I've never been to your attic before," Caroline said, her voice gentle and calm, her eye only twitching a bit tonight. "I'm looking forward to seeing your paintings."

"Me neither," said Katie. "I didn't even know you had an attic."

I looked closely at Katie. She didn't appear pale and exhausted tonight. In fact, she looked much better, her smile didn't have that tense, I-am-hanging-on-to-dear-life-with-my-fingernails look.

Lara looked rather ill, and I felt bad for convincing her we should have Psychic Night in her attic, but her art was incredible, and my gut told me that this was what she needed: outside approval of her art.

Lara pushed opened the door, then stepped inside. I followed her, keeping a close eye on Aunt Lydia's, Caroline's, and Katie's expressions.

I wasn't disappointed.

Their mouths dropped. Their eyes widened. They made I-can't-believe-this sounds in their throats. The bag that Caroline had brought upstairs for the psychic part of Your Hormones And You: Taking Over, Taking Cover, Taking Charge fell from her hands. No one noticed.

The silence was so loud, if a mouse had burped, we would have heard it.

"Oh my," Katie said, shaking her head as she walked with great caution to one of Lara's paintings, a portrait of a woman spread-eagled in the middle of a field, wearing only an apron, storm clouds churning above her. Tiny fabric squares had been glued to the canvas to form the apron.

"Good God!" Aunt Lydia declared, staring at a painting

with two women facing each other, their profiles identical except a snake wrapped around the neck of one, a flower chain around the other. Lara had used dried flowers for the chain and costume jewelry for the women's earrings.

"Incredible," Caroline whispered, as she stared at a painting of a woman holding a bird's nest. The woman's halter was made of newspaper clippings of horrible natural disasters that had occurred. Inside the twigs of the nest Lara had painted tiny ladybugs and worms and butterflies and birds.

Caroline toured the room, then flipped through stacked canvasses. When she got to the one of the naked man wrapped around a sunflower, she smiled, nodded.

Lara became noticeably less tense minute by minute as we exclaimed over her paintings and studied the murals with awe. An hour later I went and got the Double Chocolate Snowball, and we sat down to dessert, right in the middle of the attic.

"Damn, but you're good, Lara," Aunt Lydia said, shaking her head in wonderment. "Damn, but you're good."

Katie nodded. "Damn good."

Caroline smiled. Winked.

We poured ourselves more wine and offered a toast to Lara.

She cried.

The hormone discussion was put off for another night as we all discussed Lara's art. For the first time, Lara didn't drink too much, and her face lost that pinched, tight look. She even smiled, and it transformed her face.

To my surprise, Caroline seemed to have an endless stream of information and advice for Lara about selling her artwork. She even had a couple of names of people and galleries for Lara to call. Both places she mentioned were nationally prestigious. I thought this was a bit strange, since

Caroline had not mentioned being interested in art, but didn't think much of it in all the excitement.

Aunt Lydia said we should all pose nude for Lara. "It would be a testament to our Psychic Nights!"

Katie rolled her eyes.

I said, "Over my dead, fat corpse."

Caroline said she would pose nude as soon as Jupiter and Saturn changed places.

Katie kept shaking her head in disbelief. "I don't know anything about art, Lara, but yours is . . . yours is . . . well, it's as good as Julia's chocolate!"

We took another tour of Lara's attic, listened to her talk about the paintings, what they meant to her, what she had meant to convey.

I knew I was looking at brilliance.

When we all settled back down, Caroline did our readings. She saw paintbrushes, skyscrapers, taxis, blank canvases, and a river in Lara's future. She also saw her alone ice-skating. Then she saw her at a crowded party. People came and talked to her, then left. She was alone again.

"You'll work it out, Lara," Caroline assured her. "Listen to your heart."

Aunt Lydia had told me that once Caroline was done with her reading, she was done, and would not add further detail.

Caroline took Katie's hands in hers while they sat cross-legged together on the floor. Caroline closed her eyes, then gave a little jump, as if she had experienced a small jolt from the floor. She stared into Katie's eyes. "J.D. is coming back."

Katie groaned.

"I see you with Julia. And Stash. And Dave. Scrambler's there, too. You're leaving your home." Caroline closed her eyes. "You're happy, Katie. You're scared, but you're happy. I see the children on a porch. They're happy. Stay at the house with the porch."

She did Aunt Lydia's reading. "I'm seeing you at a long

table. I'm there. So is Stash. So is Julia and Dean. For some reason I'm seeing the faces of two children. I don't know who they are. They're not in the room with you, but they're there at the same time, too. You're angry, Aunt Lydia. Another woman is there. You hate her. I'm seeing the same kids' faces again. That's it."

Next it was my turn. Caroline and I sat down. We clasped hands. I looked into those huge green eyes of hers. The eyelid of one was twitching a little bit. By the end of our reading, it was twitching a lot.

But at the moment, she was smiling. "I'm seeing you in the kitchen. It's late at night. You're melting chocolate. I'm seeing you outside of an apartment building. You're staring up at an apartment. You're scared, you can't breathe. This is very interesting. I'm getting the impression of those two children again. The children aren't safe. Remember that, Julia. The children aren't safe."

I felt my blood run cold.

Caroline's smile was gone, her tiny hands went cold in mine, and she started to shake. "Your mail."

"What?"

"Your mail. From the post office. The mail that you receive is bad, Julia. And, again, I'm getting the same reading as last time. He's coming. *He is coming.*"

❦ 16 ❧

Story Hour was the talk of the town. More and more mothers and grandmothers and their children and grandchildren were coming. Ms. Cutter had been forced to acknowledge that we needed more space, so the children's area was expanded. Although Ms. Cutter was very upset to lose the tax-law section, none of the townspeople who had volunteered to help me move the books and shelves seemed the slightest bit concerned.

I also insisted on opening the drapes in the children's area, and I went to the board and received enthusiastic permission to decorate. I thanked them for the check. They thanked me for my outstanding work.

I must say I felt a little proud.

Lara came in and painted a giant jungle scene on one wall of the children's section. I next bought beanbags and a couple of huge rugs and blue tables and chairs in children's sizes. I hung mobiles of jungle animals and the planets. And I set up a reward system. Every time a child finished reading five books, he or she got to color a star and put it on the wall. Soon one wall was filled with stars.

Each evening, while helping Aunt Lydia with the chickens, the pigs, and all the other farmwork, I would make out a plan for the next day's Story Hour.

One time I read three stories on chickens and roosters. One nonfiction and two fiction books. Aunt Lydia came with me and brought in two chickens and a rooster. The chickens did their part to make Story Hour fun by clucking. Not to be outdone, the rooster cockadoodled. Not once, but eight different times. He was a huge hit. The kids loved it when the chickens pooped on the carpet. Story Hour lasted for almost two hours.

Another time I read a story about a giant chocolate cookie filled with candy that got so big the whole town had to come eat it. I did a cooking lesson, showing the children how to make Mint Chocolate Chunk Cookies. At the end, I passed out cookies I had already baked. Almost every mother there asked for the recipe. Some offered to pay me for a batch of them. I told them I would be selling my chocolate, including the cookies, at the fair.

For another Story Hour I had Stash come in, dressed in his farmer's overalls and plaid shirt. Stash read two books that featured farms. Then he told stories about animals on his farm: the cat who had to sleep with its paws straight up in the air, the cow who always licked his face when he saw Stash, and the cranky goose who came to his pond each year and chased him.

One day, after a rousing parade at Story Hour, Ms. Cutter marched into our little area, and I felt the children stiffen. I stiffened myself, bracing for a cool, cutting comment about how noisy Story Hour had become, how the crowds were wrecking the sanctity and peace of the library.

"Ms. Bennett," the librarian said, fiddling with the glasses that hung over her skinny bosom, the tie on her dress making her neck look more chickenish than ever. "I want to talk to you about the parade you led the children on today. There are adults in the library, and they did not appreciate all those children with those silly newspaper hats and instruments parading through the library."

I groaned. It wasn't true, of course. Ninety percent of the adults in the library at that time were parents or grandparents of the fifty children who had attended Story Hour. Most of them were also wearing "silly newspaper hats" and had paraded along with their children. The other adults in the library, many of them senior citizens, had stood up along the "parade route" and clapped their hands, cheering on the participants. It had been a beautiful moment.

"The library is a sacred place. A place for learning and knowledge and expanding one's mind. It is not for creating a ruckus."

"Ms. Cutter, I appreciate your concern," I said, holding my chin up. Not because I was particularly brave but because I knew that the vice-president of the library board, who was related to half of the rest of the board, had been bringing her grandchildren to Story Hour for weeks now and loved it. "However, Story Hour is one time a day, for an hour—"

"I beg your pardon!" Ms. Cutter's voice cut through my sentence like a hot knife slices through ice cream. "This Story Hour is getting absolutely out of control. It goes on for almost two full hours! Two hours of noise and cacophony with children everywhere!"

"But that's the nature of a children's Story Hour," I said quietly. "Children come to Story Hour to read, to learn, to play—"

"To play?" Her tone said that I was about one level up from a half-squished slug. "The library is no place to play!"

"The library is, however, a place to learn to love books. . . ."

"Your insolence knows no bounds, does it, Ms. Bennett? You're determined to ruin this library for everyone else—"

"I like your pin."

The small voice, coming from sweet, impossibly quiet Carrie Lynn, stopped both me and Ms. Cutter in our tracks.

"Wh-what?" Ms. Cutter leaned closer to Carrie Lynn. "What did you say, young lady?" She said "young lady" in that intimidating, I-wish-you-would-shut-up tone of voice that adults sometimes used with children.

Carrie Lynn suddenly looked panicked, her little fingers knotting together nervously. "I—" She swallowed hard, her eyes meeting Ms. Cutter's, then skittering away. She leaned into my side. "I . . . I like your pin."

The words came out in a whisper. A tiny, high-pitched, scared little whisper, and then the whole room went as quiet as the inside of a sunken ship. For once, Ms. Cutter was speechless, her mouth opening and shutting, then opening again, like a blowfish, as she stared at Carrie Lynn.

"My pin?"

Carrie Lynn flushed, her face turning red. She turned toward me and wrapped an arm around my waist, cowering behind me as if expecting a blow.

"What pin, Carrie Lynn?" I asked, putting an arm around her bony shoulders.

She pointed.

As if in slow motion, I followed the direction of her little finger to the flowered metal broach on the older woman's left shoulder. She wore it every day. Inside the middle of the broach were bright blue and purple stones.

Ms. Cutter's eyes seemed to grow to the size of oranges as she looked through the lens of her glasses.

Then she straightened up. Sniffed. Coughed. Sniffed again.

"I like the flower," Carrie Lynn whispered, her voice shaking.

I again felt a rush of impotent fury. Why did Ms. Cutter have to scare children? If she didn't say something nice to sweet, beaten-down Carrie Lynn pretty soon, I might just take it upon myself to knock shelves of books filled with the classics right to the floor.

"I like your pin, too, Ms. Cutter," Shawn said quietly, now

at my other side. "Carrie Lynn and I think it reminds us of this field we saw one time that had a bunch of flowers in it. We saw a rabbit in the field. It was real pretty."

"Well . . . I . . ." The librarian looked even more flustered than before. Again, we saw the blowfish: mouth open, mouth shut; mouth open, mouth shut.

"Well . . . well . . ." she fluttered again. "Thank you, Carrie Lynn. Thank you, Shawn." I saw her neck muscles moving spasmodically. "My mother gave me this broach thirty years ago. She died two weeks after that. It's my favorite pin, as it was her favorite pin."

We stood in an awkward circle then, me, Carrie Lynn, Shawn, and Ms. Cutter.

"Put the chairs away when you're done," Ms. Cutter ordered, then turned quickly away, her dress swishing behind her. I did not miss the fact that she wiped a tear from her cheek as she walked off, her back ramrod-straight, her low, sensible heels making hardly a tap-tap on the floor, the hairs ripped back in the bun she wore at the back of her head perfectly aligned, as usual.

Later I dropped the kids off at their apartment and waited until I saw them go in, feeling sick at the sight of the black hole they had to live in. I remembered Caroline's warning. But I had no idea what to do. I had called Children's Services. They had done nothing, refused to do anything. If I took the kids, the mother would call the police.

I had bought Shawn a sweatshirt and Carrie Lynn a sweater. Carrie Lynn actually dropped her blanket to finger the sweater. I made them wait to put them on until the next day as I didn't want Ms. Cutter to know I was giving the kids gifts. I had also packed them their dinner.

I worried about what their mother would say about the gifts, but my guess was that she wouldn't even notice.

The very thought of these children being in danger

brought on a minor attack of the Dread Disease. When it was over and I could breathe again, I drove home.

Caroline called the next day, and asked if I wanted to go with her to a neighboring town about an hour away. They had a Goodwill there, and Caroline wanted to shop.

As a child, I had loved Goodwill. I could walk up and down the aisles and think about what I would buy if I had money, how I would combine this or that skirt with this shirt and those heels and that purse. I could not remember getting any new clothing at all until I was in high school and could work and pay for them myself.

I happily agreed to go with Caroline. I had received another check from both the library and the paper route. I always wrote a check out to Aunt Lydia when I got paid. The first time, she refused to take any money, telling me that I had wounded her inner rose, the flower of protection. I left the money on the counter and told her I would tell Stash that in her dream last night she shouted his name.

"You are a pain in the butt, Julia," she told me, giving me a hug. I hugged her back, grateful that no matter how long I was away from her she always smelled the same. Like vanilla and lavender. "I don't need the money."

"And I don't need the guilt I would feel if you didn't take it, so take it, Aunt Lydia."

She hugged me tighter. "You inherited the honest gene from your Great-Great-Uncle Ace. Everyone in town knew that if they gave Ace a dollar, he'd give it back. Any time. Any day. Any year. He grew turnips, and all deals were made with a shake of the hand. Lived to be 106. Turnips are good for you, girl—now, don't you forget it. Your little flower will love you for it."

So I was actually feeling quite wealthy, comparatively, as Caroline and I sped along in her old car to Goodwill. It sputtered and clanked and rattled, but otherwise the ride was smooth. We inserted a CD and sang along with a female country singer about how girls can lie, too. They learned from the experts: men.

I loved that song. Caroline did, too, and we sang as loud as we could, the windows rolled all the way down to the summer sun as we ventured forth on our shopping trip. The next song was about redneck women keeping their Christmas lights on all year long who ain't no high-class broads. We loved that one, too.

As the Goodwill was about an hour away, we had plenty of time to sing.

When our throats were raw, we pulled over at a local store and bought some pop. "So what is it like to be able to see the future?" I asked, as the car sputtered back to life with a burp and something that sounded much like a fart.

Caroline didn't say anything for a long time. Then, "Horrifying."

Yep. That would be a good word for it. I couldn't imagine having a gift like that, although I don't really think "gift" is the word for it.

Her hands tightened on the steering wheel, and I was back to wishing we were singing about redneck women.

"I see the future often, but I can rarely place where it's happening. Sometimes I read about the things I've seen in the news, and I feel so ineffectual, so helpless. If I could only warn people, so many lives would be saved, but I can't."

"What do you see?"

Her lips tightened before she spoke. "Actually, Julia, I try not to see too much. One reason I do the readings for us each week at our dinners is because it seems when I look ahead on a regular basis, it sneaks up on me less. If I don't do someone's readings—like yours, Lydia's, Katie's, and Lara's—if I miss the evening, then I can expect that at least two to three times in the next week, I'll see something. I'll see the future."

"Is it always bad? The visions you see when you haven't been using your gifts enough?"

"No, it isn't. Sometimes I see good. I'll see a child being rescued from a river, the child is crying, but alive. Or I'll see a man emerging from an operation alive and his wife crying with relief, or I'll watch a person walking away from a hideous car accident. Those visions all engender huge emotions in people, which is what I think carries them to me. But I see much more negative. Probably because those emotions are so enormously strong, it's all the layers of civilization stripped away to reveal pain or loss or grief or hate or violence. I get sent those visions so much more."

"Do you know any of the people you see?"

She was quiet. "Yes. But very rarely. Often I can tell that what I'm seeing is happening in another country. I'll see Chinese people or Africans or a town that looks like it's in the South."

The wind whipped through my hair, and I pushed it back. "Why do you think you get these visions? Why you?"

"My mother can sometimes read minds. My grandmother and her mother could both see people's past lives. My grandmother told me that I've been a peasant, a servant in a castle, a warrior, a hooker, a factory worker, a wealthy socialite, a fortune-teller, a witch, and a nurse in past lives. One of my aunts can move certain things across the room, like lamps and silverware, just by thinking about it. Comes in handy when she's cooking. One time she lifted a table. She didn't like one of the women sitting at it, apparently."

"So it's genetic. Only it seems like you got the most difficult ability."

"In many ways, yes. I would far rather be able to move vases and vacuum cleaners or tell someone about the lives they used to lead than know when an earthquake is going to kill hundreds and be unable to stop it."

"When did the visions start?"

"I had them when I was a child, and I would tell my parents about them. They realized early on what gift I'd inherited. I'd tell them what I saw, and then they would read about it in the paper. Sometimes those things happened locally. Sometimes they happened in other states or countries.

"I didn't understand even who or what I was looking at when I was younger. I'd see women with black veils over their faces, screaming, and I'd hear gunshots. I'd see flooding and people running, their faces terrified. I'd see small children locked in dark rooms crying. I would see a war zone with men moaning in pain. All I knew, all my parents knew, was that it would make me shake and cry.

"Each summer, though, my mother and I would leave our home in Boston and go to the country to stay in our home out there, and the visions would decrease dramatically. Maybe it was because I wasn't in the midst of a city with the crowds of people and all their rampant emotions. Maybe it was because I was more relaxed in the country. I don't know."

"Which is why you moved to Golden."

"That's one of the reasons," she said quietly.

I did not pursue the other reasons. Somehow I didn't think she would appreciate it.

"But, with me, Caroline"—I sucked in my breath—"you saw Robert coming after me. Did you see him here, in Golden?"

Her face paled a bit. "Yes, I did. He's not here now, Julia. I hope I will know when he is, and I'll warn you. Then you can leave until he's gone."

I didn't say anything. I knew that she knew I was grateful.

The Goodwill turned out to be a gold mine for me. I bought several sweaters, two pairs of jeans, five shirts, and two pairs of slacks, one black and one beige. Someone must have died who was just my size, because none of the shoes looked like they had been worn. I bought fur-lined beige boots that I thought looked pretty darn stylish. I also bought a pair of black shoes for everyday, and a pair of bone-colored heels.

I had no idea where I would wear heels, but for three dollars, I wasn't going to ponder too long.

I also found a jean jacket and a long black coat, a black hat and black mittens and a bright red envelope-style purse that I thought was so cute.

Caroline found two skirts, three sweaters, a pair of purple jeans, and a pair of maroon jeans (skinny people can wear anything and still look cute), a stack of books to read, several baskets for organizing her closet, two baking pans that looked brand-new, and a set of blue ceramic dishes still in the box.

We were practically cackling with glee when we left. There is nothing like being poor and then suddenly feeling rich, like we did. We got back into Caroline's Blue Demon, as we had dubbed it on the way up, and headed for the grocery store for lunch.

"If you must eat out," Caroline told me, "a grocery store can often provide a cheap meal. Buy the special of the day, use in-store coupons for the rest, and you're set." To show me, she pulled out this huge folder full of coupons and ordered me to go through them before we arrived. "This grocery store takes everybody's coupons, so grab any that look good to you. I've got to do a little shopping before we get home."

So I grabbed a few coupons that looked good to me and handed the folder back. As soon as we entered the store, the Shopping Lesson began in earnest. Caroline's eyes didn't quite bug out of her head in her excitement to turn me into a bargain-shopping maven, but they came close.

"Look here, Julia," she would say, comparing the store brand and the manufacturer's brand, pointing out the price difference. She used an in-store coupon, other stores' coupons, and manufacturers' coupons to make her points as she gathered a few items together.

She regaled me with a ream of ideas for dinners I could make for practically nothing that sounded yummy. She told me eight different ways to use chicken and nine different ways to use ground beef as we lingered in the meat section.

She told me how to use chicken bones and asparagus ends, how important it was to grow herbs and vegetables, and how canning could save hundreds of dollars. She told me who in town would trade for services, which somehow dovetailed into a talk on how to make different kinds of household detergents for pennies.

In the produce department she told me the number-one, most important thing to do to save money: plant your own garden. "You'll save a fortune by growing your own food. Plus, you're creating an opportunity to both trade with your neighbors for other goods, and it's a way to give to others. There are many people in town—like Katie—who are struggling, and when you bring them something from your garden you can help them without hurting their pride."

We compared the store prices of fruits and vegetables to the cost of growing them in your backyard.

"That's why I have apple and pear trees, blueberry and raspberry bushes, and grow zucchini, squash, lettuce, arugula, carrots, tomatoes, spinach, corn, peas, pumpkins, cucumbers, radishes, and beans in my garden.

"You see, everyone thinks you need to have lots of money to live, but you don't really. It's all in appreciating the small things, the small gifts, and learning to live on less."

I nodded my head. A beautiful psychic who counts her pennies and bargain hunts. That was Caroline.

We were in that grocery store for almost two hours. By the time we were in line, my head was swimming, coupons and sale prices floating before my eyes, and I realized what a sick consumer I had been most of my life. Hundreds of dollars I had wasted shopping, I surmised. Hundreds. Maybe thousands.

Aunt Lydia had said that Caroline was frugal. She really, really didn't know the half of it.

We unloaded our purchases on the cashier's belt. I noticed Caroline staring at the family in front of us. She started whispering to me, but not in a quiet whisper. It was clear she wanted the family to hear her, her tone indignant.

"They shouldn't buy those expensive cereals. Oatmeal comes in huge bags . . . I can't believe they bought the manufacturer's spaghetti sauce. . . . This store's sauce is just as good, and they could have saved eighty-seven cents. Oh no. Look at those cookies. They certainly don't need that. Making cookies from scratch would save them at least three dollars. Why do parents let their children drink pop? It rots their teeth. Look at that. They bought the small packet of ground beef. A large packet is ninety-seven cents cheaper a pound. . . ."

Her gush of words suddenly stopped in midstream, and her face froze, her eyes riveted on one of the magazines on the stands near the cashier's. I followed her gaze and saw nothing out of order. Just the usual array of movie stars and entertainers and their continual parade of lovers and problems featured on slick magazine covers, a billionaire couple who had created their own massive computer business on the cover of a money magazine, and a sports hero on another.

"Are you all right, Caroline?" I touched her arm, but she didn't respond, instead taking a step forward and grabbing the money magazine.

She flipped through the pages to the cover story and read, completely forgetting that her precious coupons were moving down the conveyor belt.

I paid for our groceries. Caroline didn't even notice.

"Ma'am," said the checker, a bored teenager with purple stripes through her hair, chewing gum. "Are you gonna buy the magazine? Ma'am?"

Caroline didn't look up, so I touched her arm again. Her head popped up, and she looked at me, her gaze far, far away. "Do you want the magazine, Caroline?"

She looked completely confused, her eye winking and

winking. "Yes. I do." She pulled out her wallet. "How much do we owe?"

When I told her I had already paid, she paid for the magazine, and we walked out. She insisted on paying me back for the groceries.

"Don't worry about it, please, Caroline. You even drove us here. My treat."

But she would hear none of it. "Absolutely not. Take the money I owe you, Julia, or we're not leaving."

As I was expecting a call from Dean that night, that was not a pleasant thought, so I took the money. When we got to the car, we unloaded the groceries, holding on to the food we'd purchased for lunch.

She let herself in and started reading the magazine again. I had to knock on the window for her to unlock my side. She apologized profusely, then went back to her magazine.

We ate in silence. When she was done, she put the magazine with the computer couple on the seat between us, her eyes straight ahead. Neither eye winked.

"Caroline," I said. "What is it?"

She shook her head, her small hands fluttering on the steering wheel. "It's nothing, Julia. Nothing at all."

But it was something. That was obvious by the tightness of her pale face, the set of her lips.

I stared out the window.

So many of us have secrets.

As we drove back into Golden, I again saw the edges of rot around the town. Businesses that had gone out of business had not been replaced, and so many others were struggling. The economic bottom had fallen out of Golden. There were still some people making money, Stash, for instance, who had a growing organic food business, and Dean, apparently, who sold cattle. But Stash and Dean couldn't employ everyone.

Everything from the empty storefronts, to the unfixed potholes, to the bond that had failed last year to help prop up the schools, to the budget cuts that affected the tiny police and fire departments, to the fact that many people were out of work and either commuting to neighboring towns or had moved altogether, spoke of a struggling place.

On the one hand, Golden was an oasis for me. A place where, for once in my life, I could see myself belonging. On the other, it was a dying entity, a slowly drooping geranium that had bloomed to life and now needed to be dead-headed in order for the new flowers to bloom.

It saddened me greatly. Saddened me because of people like Aunt Lydia and Stash who had lived just outside the town for years. Saddened me for people like Katie, whose livelihood was based on her ability to attract clients who could afford to have their houses cleaned. Saddened me for Jerry, Lara's husband, who was trying to build a church but needed an influx of people to do it.

But what could I do?

For a moment, that thought startled me, and I had to sit and think about it. Me? Do something to help Golden? How in the world could I help? It seemed impossible.

I had always concentrated on surviving. Simply surviving, and not allowing myself to get pulled back down to my trashy apartment/trailer park childhood existence. Not allowing the memories of my mother's boyfriends or her complete lack of attention to swallow me whole. Managing Robert's manipulations had added a new depth to my fight for survival. Yep, fighting my way up and out of hell had taken all of my energies.

The thought of trying to save someone else, something else, had been beyond me. Selfish, but there it was.

I stared out the window. The scenery was beautiful. Rolling plains, mountains, farmland, space, the river. Perfect. But even a place that was perfect needed jobs.

I felt like eating my chocolate. In fact, I felt like eating a lot of chocolate.

What could I do for Golden? Me. A plump newspaper-delivery driver, Story Hour worker, chicken-egg collector, who knew her ex-fiancé would come charging after her momentarily and who was probably going to be dead sooner rather than later from the Dread Disease.

I needed my chocolate right away.

I don't know what triggered the Dread Disease that night. I had made all the birds go back in their cages after their evening flight and was sitting on Aunt Lydia's porch on one of six rockers she has out there. The night was cool, but not too cool, and I saw a car drive slowly in front of the house. For a moment, I froze, panicked, thinking that Robert was here already. But then I heard a whoop and a holler, and I could see a group of teenagers goofing around inside. I let out the breath I'd been holding.

Which made me start thinking about Robert. Which for some reason triggered the memory of what he had done months ago when I jokingly suggested that I was going to move to Tahiti and avoid all the wedding plans.

"Don't you ever joke about that, bitch," he whispered in my ear, grabbing my hair. "It's not goddamn funny."

His instant, uncontrolled rage sent me shrinking against the wall of my apartment. "I was kidding, Robert, just kidding."

I reached up and tried to loosen his hand from around my hair, but he simply caught my wrist and shoved it against the wall next to my head. His face was about an inch from mine. "Not funny, Lizard Head. Not funny."

He hadn't spoken to me for days after that. By day seven I'd turned into a pathetic mess begging him to talk to me, to work things out. He allowed me to make it up to him by having sex almost all night for three nights in a row. By the time he was done on Monday morning, my vagina was sore and raw. I had not had an orgasm, but, of course, he didn't know that or he didn't care. I am sure now, looking back, it was the latter.

Stress, I knew, could sometimes trigger the Dread Disease, and soon I could hardly breathe and felt dizzy as these memories came. The usual chill invaded my body, my hands turned to shaking ice cubes, and I wondered if I was losing my mind. I gasped and choked and coughed, and then things seemed to peak and I couldn't breathe at all.

I stood with what little strength I had and shook my legs as hard as I could, hoping to get the blood running through my body again. Blood is something you don't want to see, but you certainly do want to keep it flowing. Flowing blood, as long as it's in your body is a good thing. Very good.

Soon I could take a little breath, and another one, and a larger breath, and I stumbled back to the rocking chair and held my head in my still frozen hands, my body suffused with an exhaustion that was so complete, a few tears rolled out of my eyes.

I was sick of this. Sick of the fear. Sick of the symptoms of my Dread Disease. Sick of worrying about my imminent death.

I would have to go to the doctor soon. I didn't want a diagnosis. Didn't want to hear about the end of my life, didn't want to know about the treatments I was sure to have to undergo. Didn't want to deal with hospitals and doctors and needles.

But not knowing was getting to be worse than knowing and dealing with it. And maybe medication would help me to breathe again. Breathing, like flowing blood, is a good thing, too.

I leaned my head back on the rocking chair again.

I was running from two things: Robert and the Dread Disease. And running was getting so tiring.

*   *   *

Dean called me that night, as usual. The Dread Disease retreated a bit, and my heart warmed up past the temperature of a corpse.

I packed a lunch and dinner for Shawn and Carrie Lynn, added a box of my chocolates, and new sandals for each of them. I was past the point of worrying about whether or not their mother would notice and take offense. She obviously barely looked at their faces, much less their feet.

Today for Story Hour I read books on animals. All the kids made paper hats with dog, cat, rabbit, or bear ears. We had animal cookies for a snack, sang songs about frogs and a grumpy grizzly bear, then made the sound of our animal and hopped, jumped, or otherwise moved about the library.

I thanked everyone for coming, invited them back tomorrow.

The parents gave me a standing ovation.

I almost cried.

They liked me. A bunch of normal, happy, good, family people liked me.

Me.

Stash came over that afternoon and insisted on another round of target practice. Aunt Lydia came, too. I cannot believe how good those two are with their pistols. I think they could shoot the eye out of a spider hanging from a tree if they wanted to.

They were not real pleased with my performance, so we had to practice for a long, long time, and my arms ached.

"You must find the raging woman within you," Aunt Lydia admonished me. "And tell her to shoot to kill. You are not concentrating. The raging woman in you will help you to focus."

"Hold steady, aim, fire," added Stash, staring down at me

sternly. "When you are in danger, dear, don't hesitate to protect yourself. Shoot to kill."

Allrighty, I thought. *I'll try to shoot to kill. I really will try.*

Before I fainted on the front of Aunt Lydia's porch late the next afternoon, I could hear Stash and Aunt Lydia's voices encouraging me to shoot to kill.

In my hands lay a brown paper–wrapped package. It had been mailed from Boston.

I knew who had sent it.

I knew I shouldn't open it.

I vaguely remembered Caroline's warning.

But some sick, dependent part of me gently opened the package, as if the paper itself were priceless. My fingers shook, and I could hear death whispering in my ear. "I'm coming for you, Julia. Soon you'll be with me in a black, cold place."

I dropped the box with the dead chicken in it, the small knife sticking out of the center of its chest, the smell intense.

He knew. Robert had located my mother. He had located me. It would only be a matter of time.

❦ 17 ❧

"He got an attorney."

"What?" I stared at Katie across the red-and-white checkered tablecloth of the town's only café. Outside it was pouring. "Very strange," I was told by the residents. "It doesn't usually rain at this point in the summer."

Dave, Stash's foreman, told me that this signaled a cold winter.

Aunt Lydia told me it was a sign that all women should change, rise up against their oppressors, and be free of all testosterone. The young girl at the cash register told me with some bitterness that she figured her father had ordered up the rain so she wouldn't be able to go out with her boyfriend in a bikini anymore.

All of Katie's kids were in the Kid's Corner of the café playing with blocks and dolls and a castle. I bent to give each of them a hug and a kiss. They clung to me a little longer than normal and gave me wet kisses.

"Hi, Hulia," said Luke. "I'm wearing four shirts and three underwears today!" he said with triumph in his voice.

"Good for you!" I squeezed him tight.

"Joo Joo!" Logan chortled. His hands were sticky as he put

Cathy Lamb

them on my cheeks. He was wearing his Spiderman outfit as usual.

Haley gave me a kiss, too, her antennas with the glittering purple eyeballs whacking me in the face.

Hannah looked worried and pale. Dressed all in black, she gave me a quick hug and a steady look. I knew what that look said: "Help us, Julia. Please."

Katie smiled at the children, told them to go play, then lowered her voice. She was tearing a napkin to shreds. A pile of an already shredded napkin was next to her coffee cup. "He moved back in last night, too. Came by taxi. Just used his key and came back in."

"J.D. came back?" I confirmed, my stomach flipping.

She nodded, kept shredding, her eyes darting to the entrance as if she expected him to burst through the door of the café at any moment, which was a definite possibility. "You should have seen the kids' faces. Hannah burst into tears. Logan ran to his room. Luke hid behind the couch and shook. Haley started to hyperventilate. It was awful."

"Oh no! I thought he was gone for good." I noticed that her glorious hair was a mess. I'm not sure she'd even remembered to brush it. "I thought you told me that after he got kicked out of the hospital, he went to a motel, then an apartment."

"He ran out of money," Katie said. "He went right after me, leaning on his crutches. He could barely stand, Julia, but his face was beet-red. 'You listen up, Katie Bitch,' he was shouting, and swinging his crutch. Luke started screaming, 'Mommy, Mommy,' and Hannah stood right in front of me to protect me until I told her to go to her room. I was afraid he was going to hit her."

I closed my eyes for a second. J.D. was so like so many of my mother's boyfriends.

"He broke a lamp with his crutch, then my favorite bowl, and he tossed three plates against the wall and screamed,

'This is my house, and I'm living here. You can't kick me out. My attorney says I got as much right as your fat, sorry ass to live here.'

"He limped over to me, and I thought he was going to hit me, but I never let him get close enough. Hannah and Luke were screaming and begging him to stop, but he kept chasing me around the couch, yelling and screaming, saying that I was a bad, fat-ass wife who didn't even care enough to see her husband in the hospital and that he had told every nurse and doctor at the hospital what a lousy wife I was."

She paused for a moment, her hands clutched around her coffee cup for dear life.

"He finally tripped over one of the kid's toys. He picked it up—I think it was a train—and threw it right at Hannah's head. She ducked and didn't get hit, but you should have seen her face. She hates him, Julia, absolutely hates him."

"I would hate him, too," I said, but I knew she didn't hear me.

"He was swearing and screaming and telling all of us to help him. He told all the kids they were totally worthless and stupid, and he told Luke he was probably gay the way he protected his mother. As soon as he started in on the kids, I grabbed them and left. We stayed in a hotel last night on the highway."

She sighed, her eyes looking so tired, as if someone had taken them straight out of her head and left them out to dry and age. She had looked so much better lately, too, the spark back in her eye, a smile on her face. Katie Margold had even had a blush on her cheeks.

Now she looked bone-deep exhausted.

"Katie, we'll have lunch," I told her, taking a moment to hope that J.D. got hit by a steamroller. "Then we'll go and get your things and find someplace for you to live with the kids."

She nodded, her red ponytail slipping over her shoulder.

"The house is rented. I'll tell Bernie and Diane that I'm moving out and that J.D. is going to pay for it from now on. But where do I go?"

I thought for a minute, and then it hit me. Easy as pie. Chocolate pie, of course. Stash had a small cottage on his property with a nice front porch. It hadn't been lived in for years, and I was willing to bet he wouldn't mind if Katie moved in for a while, even for good.

I told Katie about the potential plan, and her eyes opened wide. "That'd be perfect. J.D. would be way too scared to go on Stash's property. Do you think he'll say yes?"

I grabbed my cell phone, called Stash.

"Julia, dear!" he said. "Wonderful to hear your voice! I just saw your Aunt Lydia!" I told Stash what Katie told me. "Of course! It's perfectly okay for Katie to come live here. I'd welcome having her little whippersnappers around!" Katie told me to tell Stash she would pay any rent he asked. I told Stash. He refused to let her pay. "That girl's been through enough. Tell her to come."

I put my hand over the phone and told her what Stash said. Katie's chin went up a couple of inches, she refused to live in Stash's cottage for free. She would pay what she had been paying before: $600 a month.

I told Stash. He was aghast. He told me to tell Katie that rent would be $100 a month, if she insisted.

I relayed this to Katie. She said forget it.

Stash refused to renegotiate. "I will not charge $600 in rent to a woman in distress with four young children. I will not." I told Katie. She lowered her amount. I told Stash. He refused but came up a tad.

Katie tightened her lips. "I don't take charity."

"I heard that," Stash bellowed. "Tell that stubborn girl it's not charity, and if she cleans my house now and then, we'll call it good."

Katie held her chin up. "Tell Stash I'll agree to the low

monthly rent but will clean his house on a weekly basis and provide two meals a week."

I told Stash.

"Done. Shake her hand, Julia girl, and do it on my behalf. I don't want her sneaking out of her deal. Lord knows I need some good dinners around here since your Aunt Lydia doesn't invite me over every night."

I reached out my hand, but Katie refused to shake it. "You tell Stash that he is to cash my check every month. I know him, and he'll just let my check sit there, but I'm paying for me and the kids."

On the other end of the phone I heard Stash sigh. "Why can't you women take a gentleman's gift? You're all so damn independent and feisty. Especially your Aunt Lydia. She is the worst. All right. Tell Katie I'll cash her checks."

Katie and I shook hands.

I told Stash, "She'll be there later today. We have to go and get her things before J.D. destroys more."

"Absolutely, positively not," Stash roared.

"I'm sorry?"

"Neither you nor Katie is to set foot in that house with J.D. in it. He's a drunk, mean son of a bitch, and I don't trust him. I'll come along with Dave and Scrambler and a couple of the other men with a trailer, and we'll load her stuff up. I repeat, Julia Bennett, you and Katie are not, *not*, to go there alone. We'll see you in two hours. I'll bring Oscar."

Oscar was Stash's favorite gun.

Dave, an African-American man who had been Stash's foreman forever, was six feet six inches tall and ran Stash's farm like it was his own. In return, Stash paid him enough that Dave and his wife had one of the nicest homes in town and a beach house.

Dave and Marie had been married for forty years. One son, Rupert, was a doctor in Portland at a teaching hospital, the other, Jordan, owned three car dealerships, and the third,

William, was a screenwriter. I had actually seen his name on several different movies I'd seen over the years. Rupert, Jordan, William and I used to run through Stash's cornfields and race tractors together during the summer. Rupert delivered me my first kiss. It wasn't bad, I'd told him. Not good, but not bad, either.

Rupert had not seemed disappointed by my pronouncement.

Every year Dave's chili won at the state fair. His wife's roses always won first place at the flower show.

I loved Dave, but if you want someone beside you who looks intimidating, he's your man.

Scrambler doesn't look like someone to mess around with, either. He's almost as big as Dave and has a murky past. "He's made mistakes," Stash had told me. "He had a lousy childhood and ended up robbing a couple of stores as a teenager. But he did his time in the pen, he's worked for me for eight years, and he's as loyal as they come. Teenagers do stupid things, he's paid for it, and he's changed. That's all anybody needs to know. Story over."

I personally had always liked Scrambler. He was a perfect gentleman. Very polite, very kind. And very, very loyal to Stash. But he was tough, too. Tell him not to smile, pull his cowboy hat down low, and even a strong man will shake in his boots when he sees him.

"Dave, me, Scrambler, and a couple of our other boys will be fine by ourselves. You tell Katie to meet us there so she can tell us what she wants to take, but she is not to get out of the car until she sees us. And make sure she's got a sitter for the kids. I don't want them anywhere near that house this afternoon."

I told Katie and then called Caroline, who offered to watch the kids for us while we retrieved Katie's and the kids' things.

We were set.

Katie pushed her red hair off her face, her brown eyes worried, but definitely relieved. "Stash is a saint."

I nodded. "You need to go to the bank before we leave. Close the checking accounts, the credit card accounts. You need to let them know that you're separating."

Katie nodded. "I'll go before we leave. Margo will take care of it for me. She's hated J.D. ever since he ran over her white picket fence, then blamed her for it. Plus, she's a single mom. She'll understand."

I nodded. Margo Fuller was a quiet firebrand who had been promoted to manager of the bank. Her husband had left her for another man. He had initially paid no child support for their four children, telling Margo that he was a new man, that country life bored him, that he had been suppressing his true self for years, and that he and his boyfriend, who had also been married, were forgetting about their pasts and going straight to their futures.

Margo's last words to him had been "Fuck you," and her attorney's last words had been to pay up or have his wages garnished. It wasn't long before that ex-husband, who had so wanted to go straight to his future, was losing half his paycheck.

Yep. Margo would take care of things.

Dave smiled at me when we drove up to Katie's small but impeccably cared for house. He was wearing jeans, a button-down sage green shirt, and loafers. At fifty-eight years old, he was fabulously good-looking in his own tough, take-no-shit way.

"How's Marie?" I asked him, as if we were at a tea party instead of standing outside a drunken lout's house, ready to go in to get an abused wife's belongings without anyone getting shot.

"Marie, my dear Marie, is as lovely as the day I met her,"

Dave said, that big smile shining. "But age has not diminished that temper. Just the other night she chewed me out for something. What was it? Oh yeah. Now I remember." Dave shook his big head.

"Does Marie ever let you be the boss?" I teased, already knowing the answer. Marie ran the ship, and her men loved her for it. She was the most loved and adored wife/mother I have ever known, and when she told her boys to do something, or when she told them to shape up, they did.

"Let me tell you something, Julia," he told me. "A long time ago I figured out that if I did what Marie told me to do, and if I taught the boys to obey their mother, we'd all be happier. So when Marie says jump, we jump. Except if it's on poker nights. But my Marie knows that those nights are sacred."

"A sacred time to lose money to Stash?" I laughed.

He spread his arms out like a giant eagle. "I beat him once, and I can beat the other men, so I don't walk home with nothing. One time, Julia, I came home with fourteen dollars in my pocket. Now, that was a good night. Of course, Marie took the money and gave it to the church on Sunday."

I laughed. Poor Dave.

Dave said hello to Katie as she reached us, and Katie gave him a hug. Stash and Scrambler were right behind her.

"Let me go in first," Stash said. Scrambler followed one foot behind Stash. Dave followed Scrambler. Next came three farmhands from Stash's business. They nodded a polite hello at both of us. I squeezed Katie's hand, and we walked up together. I felt the fear rise in my throat like bile. Abusive men can do that to me.

Stash used Katie's key to open the door.

"J.D., it's Stash." Stash didn't even wait, he just walked right into the house, his entourage following close behind him.

By the time Katie and I got to the door, we could see Stash bent over an inert lump on the couch. J.D. was snoring like a banshee, saliva dripping out of his mouth. Beer cans were scattered all over the coffee table. His left leg was in a soft cast, his crutches by the couch. I tried to summon up pity for a man who had spent four days trapped in his car, but I couldn't. J.D. was a Major Prick.

"Well," Dave drawled, "Looks like the man's deep into his sauce. We could wake him up or just move things out. What do you all think?"

"I think we move it all out. Let him wake up to nothing," I said. Katie nodded, as did Stash.

"What would you like us to grab first, ma'am?" Scrambler asked. "You just point, and we'll have your things out in a jiffy." I loved the way Scrambler talked, always so polite.

So we quietly started moving Katie's stuff out of the house. First went the dining room table, which had been Katie's grandmother's. Then went the oak kitchen table and five chairs which Katie's parents had given to her.

"I'll leave him one chair," Katie muttered. "The one he always sat his fat butt in." She turned the chair inward to face the corner. "Asshole."

Next we grabbed pots and pans and other kitchen items, including food. They jangled against each other, but J.D. kept snoring like a sledgehammer on speed.

The men grabbed the kids' two sets of bunk beds, dismantling them quietly. Katie grabbed some moving boxes she'd stored in the attic, and we went through the house, taking what she wanted to save, which wasn't much. We piled the kids' clothes, games, and stuffed animals into other bags.

This would have taken a normal person days to do, but Katie was the perfect housekeeper and believed in throwing all nonessentials out of the house immediately.

Katie showed us where her "office" was, where she was writing her book. An ancient computer slouched atop a rickety table in the same cramped, dark room where the washing machine and dryer sat. We grabbed the computer, her disks, her folders and writing books, and left the table

The men moved onto her bedroom.

"Don't bother," she told them quietly when they reached for her bed. "I don't want it. I don't want to ever see it again."

They nodded at her and moved out two antique pieces—a dresser and an armoire that had been willed to her by her Great-Aunt Zee Zee. Katie and I dumped her clothing into one big sack—she didn't have much, I noted—and I took it out to my car.

And still J.D. snored on.

We even moved the couch next to the one his enormous body was lying on like rotting meat, and he didn't stir. I couldn't help but hope he would quietly choke on his tongue or that his liver would be quickly pickled by alcohol.

It wasn't until Katie made the mistake of jarring his prized and most favorite possession, his stereo, that J.D. woke up like a cat that's had a mouse run over its back.

"What the fuck is going on?" he slurred, his eyes blood-shot, belly hanging over his pants. "What the fuck is going on, and what the fuck are you doing here, Dave? I ain't invited you into my home. And I don't want no criminals here, either, Scrambler, so get your ass out. This is my house, and I sure as hell don't need you two in it."

Dave and Scrambler spread their legs out and crossed their arms over their chests.

"Take it easy, J.D.," Stash said, his voice low and steady as he came into the family room. Stash had done two tours in Vietnam, fighting with a special unit that he never spoke about, and a drunk like J.D. didn't scare him at all.

"I ain't fuckin' takin' it easy, Stash. What the hell's going on? You took all my furniture! Dammit, Katie! What the fuck have you done now?"

Katie took a step forward, her chin high. "I'm taking my things, J.D. I told the landlord that you'll be renting this place from now on, not me."

"Me? Well, shit, bitch," he said, reaching for his crutches

and lurching to his feet. Dave and Scrambler took a step forward, standing between her and J.D. "You're leaving me when I've still got a cast on and I can't even work? What kind of lousy shit wife are you?"

"Don't talk to her like that, J.D." Stash said. "Do not cuss in front of a woman, especially not your wife."

"But this bitch—" The rest of whatever vile words were going to come out of J.D.'s mouth were stopped when Stash put his hand on the back of J.D.'s neck and squeezed. *The army will teach you wonderful things*, I thought to myself, trying not to smile as J.D.'s eyes bulged.

"I told you not to swear, J.D." Stash said, his tone calm, as if they were discussing a sunset. "I don't want to have to squeeze any harder. You don't want that none, either, do you?"

J.D. was turning a lovely shade of red, then purple. Finally he nodded, his eyes furious.

"I'm only taking my things, J.D.," Katie said. "The furniture my family gave me, the kids' things. I'm leaving the stereo that you bought. The bill for it is on the kitchen counter."

Stash released his neck, and J.D. gasped, bent over, then straightened as much as he could on his crutches. "How am I supposed to pay for it when I don't got a job? I can't work—look at my leg!" He looked around the room. "You've stolen everything from me!"

"No, I haven't. I've only taken what I walked into the marriage with and the kids."

"You're leaving me high and dry during the worst time of my life, Katie, you—" he stopped talking when Stash grabbed his neck again. "I'll get you for this," he wheezed after Stash let go.

Katie looked at him, strength in every line of her face. "You have left me high and dry our entire marriage, J.D. Plus, you were leaving me for Deidre when you got in your car accident, and you know it."

"I already told you I was going to the city for a break." He wobbled on his crutches. This was a man who was going to have to fend for himself. I almost giggled. "I had to get away from your constant nagging."

"For a break?" Katie snorted. "You took all the money out of our checking account that we had, J.D. and you knew I had rent due in three days. You packed all your clothes. You took photographs of your mother. You didn't even bother to say good-bye to the kids, I might add. You were leaving me. Worse, you were leaving the kids."

"That is not true, Katie." J.D.'s face paled.

"I went to the bank today and closed our account and told Margo I was separating from you. I have my own account now."

"You have your own account?" He looked stricken. "You took my money?"

"No, I took my money. The money I've been earning. There wasn't much in there. You do know that rent is due again soon? I told the landlord that I am moving out today."

"Katie," J.D. said, flustered, confused.

"Well, you probably didn't know that, because I always paid it, but I'm letting you know now."

"You take the money, you take the furniture, you take the kids." He blinked, as if he'd just thought of something. "I gotta right to the kids, too."

"You have a right to the kids?" Katie laughed, so bitterly, I cringed. "Tell me, J.D. What's tomorrow?"

He looked totally confused, and at the same time crafty and sneaky. "What's tomorrow?"

"You don't know what tomorrow is?"

"What is this, a quiz?"

"Yes, it's a quiz. Why is tomorrow special?"

"I don't have time for this, Katie," he muttered, but he looked like a rat caught in a trap.

"Tomorrow is Haley's birthday, but you didn't remember, did you? You never have. And you don't need to anymore.

The children hate you, J.D., as I do. You want this house, that's fine. It's yours for as long as you can pay the rent. Now, if you'll excuse us, we're leaving."

"You can't leave, Katie!" J.D. yelled, pointing a crutch at her and swinging it back and forth. "You can't leave!"

"I am leaving, J.D. Call Deidre. I'm sure she would be happy to come and take care of you."

J.D. flushed.

"In fact, I'm sure she'll find you more and more attractive each day. Especially if she has to work full-time so that you can sit and listen to your stereo. And I'm sure she'll love cooking for you, and cleaning, and doing your laundry, and if you criticize everything she does and tell her she's a tramp and useless and you can't ever figure out why you got together with her, well, I'm sure that Deidre will stick around for more of the same."

J.D. finally realized when Katie picked up a stack of books to take with her that she was serious.

"Katie, now look here, honey . . ."

"It's too late for that," she snapped at him. "Way too late. You haven't called me 'honey' in almost ten years."

He hung his head, and I could almost hear that tiny pea-brain of his whirring away. His remorse was so fake I wanted to laugh. "I've made mistakes, Katie. Big ones. I'm a sinner. As God as my witness, I admit that I've sinned. Sinned badly against you, and I'm praying about it, I really am, and I know you can't forgive me right now, but I'll work every day to make it up to you."

Katie froze. "What will you do to make it up to me?"

J.D.'s eyes blinked furiously. "I'll do anything," he finally announced.

"Well, really, specifically, J.D. what are you going to do to make it up to me?"

J.D. bit his lip. He thought. I could see him thinking real hard. "I'll get a job."

Katie laughed.

"Of course you will. And soon I'll see pigs jumping over the stars. Good-bye, J.D. Good luck."

"Katie!" he yelled, shock turning to hate on his face. "Katie! You call yourself a Christian, but you're no Christian. A Christian wouldn't walk out on her injured husband leaving him with no money!"

"You're wrong, J.D. God helps those who help themselves. I am helping myself to a peaceful life, a life without abuse, which is what God intended me to have. My only problem is that I've been so busy taking care of the kids and you and cleaning houses and running my home that I couldn't hear God's voice telling me to get the hell away from you."

"You bitch," J.D. whispered. "You total bitch."

J.D. screamed in pain when Stash grabbed his neck again. Then he slumped to the couch.

Katie grabbed a set of coasters off a coffee table.

"You can't take those!" J.D. squeaked at her. "You can't take nothing! This is my stuff, too. I'll make you pay for this, Katie. You're gonna pay. You can't just walk out when I can't pay the rent!"

She headed for the door. "J.D., I have supported you for years. You have drunk through every penny you ever made, and much of the money that I made. You have been a lousy father to the children. I mistakenly believed the children needed a father, and forevermore I will regret my own stupidity, my own fear of being alone. You left me and the kids to fend for ourselves years ago. And, yes, I can walk out on you. Watch me. I'm doing it right now."

She held her head up high and walked out.

"Do you have a moment, Mr. Margold?" Scrambler asked, his voice so even, so well-modulated that if I couldn't understand English, I'd have thought he was offering some soothing advice on how to grow orchids. "You're a right fine major loser, and if you come on Stash's property even by only one foot I will be compelled to break your neck with one hand. I learned how to do this when I was asked to take a brief sojourn at the state pen for an extended period a few years ago. A criminal, as you called me earlier, has special talents in that area. Have we got that clear, Mr. Margold? We do? Wonderful. You have a pleasant day."

J.D's mouth fell open, and he sagged further into the couch.

Scrambler turned to follow Katie out, a box on his muscled shoulder, but he stopped, took a few paces back toward J.D.

I saw J.D. swallow hard.

"Oh, one more thing, if I may, Mr. Margold? If you come near Katie, ever, I will feel compelled to snap your spine. We're clear on that, too? Again, splendid."

J.D. made a choking sound.

Scrambler turned toward the door, then held up one finger, his voice as smooth as hot buttered rum. "Oh dear, Mr. Margold. I forgot the most important rule of all. If you harm any one of your children, *ever*, or try to take them away from Katie, I will personally remove all of your limbs and put you in a little lake I know intimately up in the mountains. We're still clear? Fabulous, Mr. Margold, fabulous. Again, you have a pleasant day."

"I could call the police on you, Scrambler, and tell them what you said to me," J.D. whispered. "I could tell."

"I didn't hear Scrambler say anything, not anything at all," Stash said, eyes open and innocent. "Did you, Dave?"

"Nope. I didn't hear a thing. Not one thing except that J.D. seems to think it's okay to leave his wife and kids for another woman and clear out the checking account before he leaves, and then he uses foul language in the presence of women. Funny thing is, I know Carl Sandstrom and Doug Meachan down at the police station, ya know those two men, J.D.? Carl's been married to Julie for forty years and has four boys, as you know."

J.D. seemed to be getting smaller before my eyes.

Dave slapped his forehead. "Of course you know that! I

remember when you tried to pick on Carl, Jr., and got the tar beat out of you. Anyhow, Carl and Julie's anniversary is the same as me and my wife's, and we celebrate together each year. I bring my chili, Carl bakes the bread and whips up a salad. The wives get the dessert together. It's a real special night for all of us. And you know Doug Meachan, too, his assistant? Doug's been married for twenty-five years and is the part-time youth pastor at church."

I watched J.D. shrivel right into that couch.

"Anyhow, those two men don't take too well to men who walk out on their families, but you should feel free to go to them with your complaints. Fact is, when I see Carl and Doug at church on Sunday, I'll tell them how you feel your wife has done you a wrong by leaving you after years of abuse and neglect and your chronic drinking. Those men will be particularly sympathetic when they hear you cleaned out the checking account before abandoning your children to go after your rather slutty-looking girlfriend, I'm sure."

Now J.D. looked like a shriveled man who was about to vomit.

"That's a fine idea, Dave," Stash said. "A fine idea. You always do reach out to help people in your own godly way."

"Yes, you do, Dave," said Scrambler. "God's word has certainly reached your heart. You even put out your hand to the worst sinners among us."

"I do my best," Dave drawled. "I do my best. Be sure to tell Carl and Doug your problems, J.D. Right after church would be the perfect time. I'm sure they'll have great sympathy for a drunk, abusive adulterer."

We filed out. I met Katie on the porch. She had been listening in, and her eyes sparkled like, well, like sparklers on the Fourth of July. Later she told me that she felt lighter than she had felt since the day she met J.D.

"I felt positively skinny," she told me. "Sticklike, even."

* * *

That night I made chocolates in the shape of tiny bunnies with pink frosted ears and a fluffy looking tail made from icing. Then I made chocolates in the shape of miniature whales with pink tongues and little blue icing eyes. Next I made chocolates in the shape of little brown cats with licorice bows around their necks and green frosting eyes.

I must have been in an animal mood.

At 2:00 in the morning I stepped back and studied my handiwork. I must say I was pleased with myself. So I ate a bunny and a whale and a cat. Scrumptious. My chocolate is rich and dense and yet tastes so light and creamy it makes your mouth want to orgasm.

The fair was in three days. I had made enough chocolate to feed an army. I knew there was no way I could sell all my chocolates, and I was already thinking of places I could give them to. I would find out if there were any women's shelters anywhere within a hundred-mile radius and drive there with the extras.

I had spent a small fortune for all the ingredients, but making masses of chocolate animals, chocolate brownies with chips, fudge with a hint of mint, chocolate cookies with creamy chocolate insides and an array of other chocolate desserts had given me a break from my mind's devouring fears of imminent death.

And that in itself had made the whole endeavor worthwhile.

I cleaned up the kitchen until it damn near sparkled like one of those detergent commercials. Some women can't stand cleaning, but I often find the rote motions soothing. I can let my mind wander.

And of course it wandered, for the hundredth time that day, to Dean Garrett.

First I let my mind think of how utterly gorgeous he was. Then I told myself to think of the man, not the package.

I knew that Dean Garrett was an honest man. Plus, he was interesting, and surprisingly easy to talk to once I got past being scared. He's strong and smart and laid-back and yet intense, too.

But I didn't really *know* him. He hid much of himself, letting me see only what he wanted me to see. As a major secret-keeper myself, I could recognize the same traits in someone else.

I knew there was more to him than he was sharing, and I think he knew it. There was more to me than I was sharing, and I knew he knew it.

I almost smiled. We were quite a pair.

But the time hadn't come to spill our guts, and maybe it never would. It seems to be that way sometimes. Somehow, some way, it's okay to take a person where they are at that moment. Everyone has baggage. Is it really necessary to unwrap and dissect all of the baggage in detail?

With Dean Garrett, I was comfortable with what I knew. And I felt comfortable with whatever baggage would arrive.

Although my mind was willing to do all this introspection, my body was now throbbing at the very thought of a Naked Dean. And though whenever he was around I had to think about things like Albert-Einstein hair and the taste of chalk and dogs who slobber and complex mathematical equations so I wouldn't have a tiny orgasm right there and then, I decided, on an intellectual level, that I could not have sex with the man.

I had jumped into one man's bed, refused to see what a psychopath he was, and now was being hunted down like prey by said psychopath. I was not in any emotional shape to handle another man, no matter how kind and smart and upright he appeared to be.

I sat down when the kitchen was clean and stared at the chocolates on the counters. The rest were piled up in boxes in Lydia's spare bedroom. Each would be sold with a white doily. On every single doily, JULIA'S CHOCOLATES was printed in gold.

My body wanted to make love to Dean, to have and to hold him. My mind said forget it. For now.

I sighed heavily, then suddenly, maybe because of the late hour, or my lustful thoughts about Dean, or my fear of Robert, or the fact that I'd had little sleep the night before, my heart raced and my breath caught in my throat. The Dread Disease had arrived again, but this time, I stood up and grabbed the counter with my hands and shook my legs back and forth as fast as I could. I had learned that walking or running in place—just moving—could sometimes make the attack lessen.

So I shook my legs, and I started counting chocolate animals, and I thought about all the chickens and Aunt Lydia and Stash and the Psychic Night Girlfriends group and Shawn and Carrie Lynn, and before I knew it I was breathing normally again, with only a fine line of sweat beading my brow.

Maybe I was truly going to learn how to control the Dread Disease. Now, wouldn't that be something?

I sank back down into my seat and stared out at the black night, proud of myself for a millisecond until I remembered Robert could be out there now, looking in, waiting and watching, wanting to put his hands around my neck and squeeze.

I turned my back to the window, thought about target practice and how good I was getting.

I checked the locks again, turned off the lights, and crawled into bed.

Sleep came quick and deep.

❦ 18 ❧

As always, it was dark when I woke up a few days later. Dark when I ran my paper route, dark when I kissed Dean outside his house, his arms pulling me close until I was happily breathless. Dark when he leaned in my car and kissed me again and again. Dark when he told me he would see me later that day. Dark when I drove off, my lips tingling, my body on fire.

But the darkness had a pink and orange glow to it by the time I returned to the house. Aunt Lydia and I waved at Scrambler and Dave as they passed by our house en route to the chickens and pigs in the back. They would care for the animals this morning.

Aunt Lydia and I had better things to do.

Without saying much at all, which is unusual for us, we packed up every single piece of chocolate I had made over the last weeks and packed all the chocolate desserts into boxes so they wouldn't squish each other. I grabbed another stack of doilies, and another stack of gold stickers that said JULIA'S CHOCOLATES. Back again we went to the house, back again to the truck, our arms full of chocolates. Then we started on the egg cartons, dozens and dozens of them, filled with white, light brown, light blue, and light green eggs. We piled them into a pickup we had borrowed from Stash.

When dawn was stretching lazily overhead, we drove to the center of town. Unlike other days, the center of town was a hive of activity. Friends and neighbors waved as we parked our trucks. We set up our tables, then used drills to set up the fabricated storefronts that Stash had hammered together with plywood and Lara had painted.

In my humble opinion, Stash and Lara had outdone themselves. My storefront was cut like a chocolate truffle. Lara had painted it, of course, a rich chocolate color, complete with JULIA'S CHOCOLATES painted in gold at the top. Stash had made Lydia's storefront look like a giant egg, and Lara had painted hers a light blue with little chickens and roosters and chicks around the edges. On the top it read WILD EGGS FROM THE LADIES.

Golden's fiftieth annual town fair actually attracted towns-people from fifty miles away and from the city. The farmers sold fruits and vegetables, apple cider, potatoes, tomatoes, lettuce, corn, and other veggies. The craftspeople and artists sold their wares. Stash told me that Minnie Bachman sold her nasal-cleaning horseradish and told everyone who bought from her that she had learned how to make authentic horse-radish from her German grandmother.

The high school band played in the afternoon and early evening. Three churches sent their choirs over. Old men played the harmonica. Young men and women sang their rap songs. Bernie, the town's dentist, showed off his juggling skills to the children. Elizabeth, his wife, painted kids' faces. Henry, their son, made animal hats out of balloons.

And every single townsperson showed up and stayed all day, according to Aunt Lydia. Fireworks were the last hur-rah.

I grabbed several boxes from the truck and put them be-hind my display. I hoped someone would buy my chocolates, I really did.

* * *

The fireworks shot through the night sky.

Aunt Lydia and I, from our booths, could hear the crowd oohing and ahhing. Literally. Someone had started yelling, "OOOHHH AHHHHH," and everyone had joined in unison. *They're a bunch of hams in Golden*, I thought, and then I laughed, pure and sweet.

A bunch of hams who had loved my chocolate.

I had completely, utterly sold out. Every single piece of chocolate, every single dessert. Sold.

"I don't believe it," I said to Aunt Lydia, pushing my curls off my forehead.

"I do." She hugged me, then swatted my rear. "I do."

In the sixteen hours I had spent at the fair today, neighbors, friends, the mayor, the fire chief, the fire chief's wife, their children, teachers in town, the school principal—almost everyone I had met in Golden—bought my chocolates. Most had come back more than once.

Caroline came by, but she looked upset, distracted, her right eye winking spasmodically. "I'm getting . . . something's wrong," she said shakily. "I can't place it. I don't know who. Or where. But something is very wrong. . . . I'm seeing children. They're hurt, but I can't place them. Their faces are in shadows." She waved her hand, tried to smile, looked ill. I hugged her, then she left. I momentarily felt sick and worried, but then a crowd came up and I turned back to selling my chocolates.

I had not taken a break except to pee.

Miracles, I thought, *do happen*. Even to stressed out, plump, scared newspaper-delivery/Story Hour leading/ex-fiancées on the run.

Yes, indeedy, they do.

On Sunday morning I ran my paper route. Dean met me at his newspaper box. I got out of the car and, with a flourish, handed him the newspaper. He took the newspaper, dropped it on the ground, and gave me a kiss. "Congratulations, honey," he said. He looked so happy for me all I could do was blush at him. "I told you that you make the best chocolate on the planet. But I guess it took hundreds of people to reassure you of that fact," he said, kissing me again, his smile easy and suggestive and tasty, so tasty.

He had been at the fair, but I hadn't seen him much. One time he came by with Stash and Dave. They all bought chocolate. The next time he'd come around, I'd sold out of his favorites. He bought my last box of fudge. He had helped me load my boxes into the pickup that night, making me kiss him every time we passed each other.

I must say, it was the most erotic box-loading experience I'd ever had.

"Thank you." I almost wiggled with delight. "I'll make you more black-bottom pie."

"You do that." He kissed me again, and I hate to sound like a wimpy woman in a romance novel, but my knees actually did feel weak. "Why don't you serve it to me for dessert after dinner, and then after dessert we could have a sleepover?"

A sleepover? I smiled. Oh yeah. I'd like to do that, but since the very thought struck fear deep into my heart, I couldn't. Make love to Dean Garrett? To that he-man? Me? Cannonball Butt? Possum? Cold-as-an-icicle-in-bed? I had too many sex fears to make love to Dean.

"Even the very thought of making love scares you, doesn't it?" Dean asked.

I actually heard myself gasp in his arms. I put my forehead against his shoulder and closed my eyes. Oh, that man knew me too well.

"You're not ready yet, are you, Julia." He said it as a statement, not a question, and I knew exactly what he was talking about.

My body was ready. My mind was not. My heart was not.

My emotional health was certainly not. I shook my head. "I'm sorry."

He kissed my hand, then clasped it between both of his. "There's nothing to be sorry about, sweetheart."

The endearment made my breath catch in a good way, and I looked him straight in those blue, blue eyes. His lashes were black and thick. This was a man who would still be gorgeous at ninety years of age.

"When you're ready, you're ready, Julia."

I nodded. The problem with getting older is that you realize that unbridled lust can get you into serious, serious trouble. You get pregnant with the wrong guy, and your child has a lousy father for the rest of his/her life. You marry a jerk and get stuck. You waste your life trying to turn what should have been just a one-night stand into a relationship that really was never meant to be.

Lust is a great feeling. It sharpens everything in life. Rainbows are brighter. Snowflakes more intricate. Ice cream creamier. The little annoying things in life are even covered in this lust, and they simply cease to bother you any more. All you can think about is sex, and when you see that person you feel those smoldering sex embers in your body flare into a burning inferno.

And then, well, it's over.

And you get to deal with the aftermath.

But this time, this once, I, Julia Bennett, was going to be smart. I wanted Dean Garrett more than I had wanted any man in my life ever. But I wasn't going to jump, wasn't going to mess myself up further.

"I don't feel strong enough to handle you," I said, then nearly choked. That hadn't come out the way I'd planned.

"What? I think you can handle me just fine." He laughed and hugged me closer, tipping my head up with his palm.

I avoided looking at his eyes, though. The image of me "handling" him was too much. I tried again.

"What I meant, Dean, is that I don't feel . . ."

"You don't feel what?" His tone sharpened, and I instantly knew he thought I was breaking things off with him, that he thought I was telling him I didn't feel that he was right, that we were right.

His arms dropped, and I suddenly felt cold and alone.

"I'm not saying this right at all, Dean. I . . . I . . ." *Please, words*, I begged, *come out of my mouth the right way*. "I don't feel that I have a lot to offer you right now."

He shook his head. "You have everything to offer me."

"No, I don't. I have a paper route, for heaven's sake, and you're an attorney. . . ."

"Julia, that stuff doesn't matter to me at all, not at all."

"But it matters to me. You're so . . . so strong all the time. And you're smart, and you're obviously an incredibly successful attorney, and I'm, Dean, I'm a wreck, I really am." I couldn't even tell him how much of a wreck I was. How could I? How could I explain to him that I had a Dread Disease and would probably be a corpse in only a matter of months?

"I'm not sophisticated like you, I don't live in a world like yours. I don't have a background like yours, and I don't feel like I'm all together, if that makes any sense. I'm a mess, my life is a mess. I can't meet you on even ground right now. I have to get myself in order before I get involved with anyone else. Am I making even the slightest bit of sense?"

Dean Garrett looked at me long and hard. "I think you're saying that you recently broke things off with a violent fiancé, and you're still reeling from that experience and need time to recover. In addition, you want to get yourself to a place where you're secure and steady before you get involved with me or anyone else."

I marveled. I did not know that men like Dean existed on this planet. "Yes, that's about it. I need to be independent, I need to find myself, find out what I want to do, get a real job. . . . I'm sorry, Dean. I want you so bad I feel like I'm going to explode, but it's just not the right time for me. I would wreck it. I would wreck us. And I can't handle any more trauma right now."

He nodded. "I understand. I do, Julia." He kissed me on the forehead, then cupped my face and kissed me on the cheeks and landed a sweet, warm one on my mouth that went on and on and on until I felt all my good intentions slipping away. . . .

"Julia," he tipped my face up to his and waited until I opened my eyes. "I'm not going to push you into anything. But I'm not waiting forever, either."

I nodded.

"It's not my intent to be alone the rest of my life," he said, his voice low and quiet. "I know you're scared, but I give you my word that I will never, ever hurt you."

I nodded, wondering if I'd made a huge, enormous, gigantic, terrible mistake in not going into Dean's house right then and there and insisting we spend the next three days in bed getting to know each other.

But I knew I was right. I was too screwed up to be involved with anyone. That's, again, the problem with getting older: you don't throw caution to the wind, because you know that wind can come back and hit you in the face so hard you land on your butt and can't get up for years.

I put my hands on his chest and took a deep breath. I would sound stupid, but as this is not abnormal for me, what the heck. "I don't understand . . ."

"You don't understand what?"

How in the world did I say this without sounding pathetic and needy and like I was digging for compliments? "I don't understand why someone like you would be interested in me in the first place."

There. I said it. The silence was deafening.

And then he cupped my face with both of his hands. "Look at me, Julia."

I looked.

"You are the first person I've really been able to talk to

my entire life. I relate to you more than you know. You're a strong person, Julia, and you're not giving yourself enough credit for that strength. Yes, you have a paper route, but I see that as a strength. You wanted to make money, you couldn't find a decent job here, so you took what you could get and didn't complain. And you found yourself another job, too, which as I hear it, is a huge success. Your Story Hours are mobbed. Kids love you. Their parents love you.

"You help your Aunt Lydia for hours every day, and a bunch of women in town already love you and call you their friend. You joined your Aunt Lydia in her one-woman crusade to help people in town who are struggling by bringing them meals and food. You make me think. You make me laugh. You bring a calm and peace to my life that I've not had." He kissed me, sweet and gentle. "Plus, I love your chocolates. You're an incredible woman, Julia, and I hope one day you realize it."

Okay, I asked myself, *now why in hell aren't you in bed with this guy right this minute? Please explain it to me again, you fool.*

"And when you do realize it, I hope that you'll come looking for me."

Sometimes life just takes the words right out of your mouth and all you can do is nod, and that's what I did.

And then I turned to Dean Garrett, put both arms around his neck and kissed him.

When the kiss was over he put his forehead against mine and held me close. I kissed him on the cheek, got into my ratty car, and drove off.

I tried real hard not to cry.

When I got home, I helped Aunt Lydia in the yard, then she and I sat down to a celebratory meal of omelets with Katie, who had brought the kids with her, and a cinnamon coffee cake, and with Caroline, who had brought a spice loaf and banana bread. Katie hugged me, Caroline kissed my cheek, and the kids danced around me calling me The Chocolate Lady and Aunt Lydia, The Egg Lady.

Aunt Lydia had sold all her eggs, too. The city folk had been out in force, and they had loved the different eggshell colors. "Doesn't take much to turn them on, does it?" Lydia said.

Luke showed me that he was wearing four T-shirts, then pulled two pairs of pants down to show me he was also wearing three pairs of Superhero boxer underwear. Logan circled me in his Spiderman outfit, arms out at his side. Haley jumped up and down, and the purple glittering eyeballs on her antennas be-bopped about on her head, and Hannah, dressed in black as usual, looked happier than I'd seen her in a long time.

Lara darted in to our Egg and Chocolate Celebration after parking her car behind the barn, telling us she had told Jerry she was sick and couldn't go to church today. "I have to be home before the last sermon ends," she said. She gave me a huge hug and a bouquet of flowers from her garden. She gave Aunt Lydia a bouquet, too. Then she brought out two bottles of champagne.

My Psychic Night friends and Katie's kids toasted me, and we laughed our way through breakfast. Lara had a few too many, but Katie was going to drive her home. We did not know how she would explain the smell of champagne on her breath to her husband, but we didn't much worry—we were having too much fun.

The laughter stopped only when we got the phone call from the state police.

Hospitals have always made me feel ill. Doctors have always made me nervous. It does not take a psychotherapist to figure out why I avoid hospitals as if they're covered in germs from the Black Plague.

I ended up in hospitals several times as a child. Once after one of my mother's boyfriends knocked me across the room and I hit my face straight on and blacked out. A neighbor, high as a kite on pot, but a kindly soul nonetheless, was there when it happened. Over my mother's objections, the drugged-out neighbor called the ambulance.

I stayed in the hospital for five days. The boyfriend fled the state, and my mother admonished me for making him mad when she finally visited me on the third day.

"You always, always piss him off, Julia. Surely you can learn to keep your mouth shut around men when they're already in a bad mood? You didn't need to butt your big nose into our business."

"But, Momma, he was hitting you!" I whispered through swollen lips the size of bananas.

"Haven't you learned nothin' yet? They all got tempers, and you can't make a fuss every time you get a little knocked around." She drew out a cigarette, but a nurse, who was making sounds in her throat during the whole visit as if she was disgusted with my mother, told her to put it out. Now.

"I can take care of myself, Julia, you just make things worse for me. Look what you done now. Trayce's gone to who knows where because of you. If you looked at yourself more often in the mirror I would think you would be focusing on yourself instead of me. You don't get rid of your holier than thou attitude and do something with all that hair, there ain't gonna be any man who will come near you."

"Good," I muttered. Very good.

"What did you say?" My mother snapped. "Are you giving me some of your lip?"

"No, Momma," I said quickly, my head starting to ache again, as if a thousand needles were being pounded into it. "No Momma, no lip."

"The police came lookin' for him 'cause of you, Julia, and now I ain't got my man. What do you have to say for yourself?"

I just looked at my mother, sitting across the room from me in a tight pink dress, her white-blond hair piled on top of her head, her makeup thick. She was working as a dancer at that point, which was where she had met this latest creep.

"Well, what do you have to say for yourself, girl? I get ya a roof over your head, your clothes, your food. . . ." she went on and on about what she provided, and my neck was aching and my head was pounding as if needles were being poked into it with a sledgehammer, and I didn't want to argue with her.

But if I had had the energy to argue, I would have pointed out that the women at the local church had been bringing me their children's clothing, including a brand-new coat they'd all pitched in to buy, and the school gave me a free breakfast and lunch every day. I often got dinner at one of two neighbors who felt sorry for me: a gay man who was trying to become a ballerina and who had lots of nice artsy-type friends who were always kind to me, and a transsexual who worked as a mechanic by day and wandered around town like a woman by night. The transsexual made great meatloaf, spaghetti and meatballs, and cous cous.

"Well? I'm talkin' to you, Julia. Your smart mouth lost me another man, so what do you say to your momma?"

"I think I'll say that it's time for you to go, Miss Nudley," one of the nurses said, having caught the tail-end of my mother's diatribe. The nurse stood straight and tall by my bedside. She had gray hair and a young, flushed face. I could see she hated my mother.

"You can't tell me what to do," my mother protested, her eyes wandering down the woman from head to foot. It was her "you sure are ugly and worthless" look that she had down to a science. But it didn't faze the nurse.

"You may not be aware of it, Ms. Nudley, but your daughter suffered severe injuries when your boyfriend threw her across the room. She has a concussion, bruising—"

"Oh, please!" My mother cut in. "The doctor already told

me about her injuries. She'll be fine. And I'll leave when I damn well want."

The room was starting to swirl around for me now, as my mother's hatred seemed to seep into me like the stuff in the IV that was plugged into my arm.

"No, ma'am," the nurse said. "You. Will. Go. Now."

At that, I opened my eyes.

"You fat bitch," my mother said. "This is *my* daughter, and you can't order me around. Get out of this hospital room. Get. Out. Now." My mother mimicked the nurse's voice, her little eyes narrowed.

The nurse reached down and pressed a button near my bed, not taking her eyes off my mother. Within a millisecond I heard feet rushing down the corridor, then three men entered the room.

One of them, young and handsome, looked to the nurse. "What is it, Nora?" he asked, his voice kind, his eyes kinder.

"Ms. Nudley is overstaying her welcome, I believe," the nurse said, her tone calm, but I could hear that hard steel in her voice. "She is angry with her daughter because the police are after her boyfriend, Trayce"—she said the name *Trayce* as if he were vermin—"because he threw our patient, Julia here, across the room, severely injuring her face and chest. Ms. Nudley is upset because now she has lost 'her man.'"

My mother's face became beet-red with fury. I wanted to cry. If Momma was pissed off she would take it out on me. Here, at home, wherever, somehow it would be my fault.

My mother took a deep breath, stood up, straightened her dress, and stuck her ample bosoms out. She took several steps toward the young doctor and the two other men with him, who I assumed were also doctors.

She smiled, a smile I'm sure she thought was sexy. "Doctor." She looked at his name tag. "May I call you David?"

"You can call me Dr. Horner," the young man replied.

My mother blinked, surprised. This was not the response

she usually got from all the men she had met before in any number of bars.

She tried that smile again. "We have a misunderstanding here. This nurse"—she shot a venomous look at Nora—"is overstepping her boundaries. I am here to visit my daughter. This nurse is telling me to leave. Surely you can inform the nurse that it is not her job to decide who comes and goes here at this hospital?"

My mother's voice was smooth as honey. Even her speech was different. But she could do that. She would sound one way in front of me and her boyfriends, the speech of her rough childhood, but she also knew how to sound formal and polite, slightly southern, which I assumed she got from her grandmother, who spent a lot of time raising my mother when her mother ran off with various abusive men for months at a time.

My mother blinked her eyes, holding her hands behind her back so the doctor could get a better look at those huge boobs.

The doctor smiled at my mother, and I figured she had won over another man. And just when my mother smiled back and swayed left and right a bit, kind of like a little girl might do, his smile dropped.

"Miss? Mrs.?"

"Oh, honey," my mother said. "You can call me Candy."

He paused, as if he didn't like that name. "Candy it is, then. Your daughter has been here for three days. I know we talked on the phone the first day she was here, but I don't believe you've been to see her until now, is that correct?"

My mother swallowed, her swaying stopped for a millisecond, then she started up again. Smile in place. "I've been very busy, Doctor."

He nodded. "Yes, I'm sure."

"Single working mothers don't get very many breaks, as you know."

"Yes, I do realize that, Candy. But as I understand it,

Trayce has been living with you, is that correct? Did you know that on your daughter's body we found many signs of past injuries? Can you tell us where those injuries came from?"

The smile faltered a bit. "Julia has always been a clumsy child, falling down all the time—"

"Ah, well, then," said the doctor. "That would explain why she broke three ribs some time ago. When children fall down they often break their ribs." Even I caught the sarcasm.

My mother flushed slightly. "I didn't say nothin' about her breaking ribs when she fell. I didn't know she'd done broke her ribs!"

"You didn't know?" He raised an eyebrow at her. "Did she ever complain about her side hurting her?"

The flush became darker. I was so exhausted now, my head aching so bad, one of my eyes drooped shut.

"That child is always bitchin' about everything, all the time. Something's always wrong."

"Your daughter may well have been complaining about her stomach hurting, because there's bruising there, too, not to mention the bruises up and down her arms, a few scars from recent burns, two of which look like cigarette burns, and several scars that appear to be from a whip or a belt. Which one was it?"

It had been a belt, I wanted to answer, but my mouth didn't seem to want to work. I knew my mother knew that it was a belt, too, because her eyes lit up a bit with her answer, but then she snapped those red lips of hers tight shut.

"There wasn't no belt, no whip, Doctor."

"Can you explain the injuries?"

"No, I can't, and I don't have to. The kids at school probably hit her. She annoys me—she probably annoys the hell out of them, too."

I wanted to raise my hand and argue that point, but that head of mine felt like it was going to explode. I noticed Nora coming over to my side. She put her hand on my forehead, looked at the IV, added something to it. I really liked Nora.

"Candy, how long has Trayce been living in your home?" The doctor said it like Trayce was a little black leech that had attached himself to our walls with his gooey, sticky body.

"For about a year, off and on."

"Off and on?"

"Yes, Trayce comes and goes as he pleases, but now it looks like he's gone for good since the police is after him." She shot me a look. Yes, Momma was very pissed off, no doubt about it.

"I am making a note of your daughter's injuries and the fact that Trayce gave them to her. I hope the police catch up with him, because although you don't seem to agree, any man who does this to a child deserves to be in jail."

"*In jail?*" My mother sounded shocked. "For God's sake! Trayce just lost his cool with a kid who's got a smart-ass mouth and a bad attitude. He didn't do nothin' wrong."

Now the doctor and Nora, the nurse, looked like they were going to lose it. So did the other two men standing by the doctor.

"People lose their cool all the time," Dr. Horner said, "but that doesn't give them the right to pick a child up and fling her face-first against the wall, giving her a concussion. Your boyfriend could have killed your daughter. You don't seem to understand that."

The doctor was staring at my mother as if he couldn't understand her, talking to her as if she were an idiot. She had had me when she was seventeen, and I had always thought she was so pretty. I still thought she was pretty. I thought all men thought she was pretty. It was clear as day that no one in this room thought my mother was pretty.

"I understand it plenty damn fine!" my mother shouted, crossing her arms. "Why don't you mind your own business? Trayce is outta my house—that's all you need to know."

"No, that's not true. What I need to know is that you're not going to let this happen to your daughter again. You're her mother. It is your job to protect your child, and you failed miserably. Many women tolerate getting beaten up from time to time from the men in their lives, but most draw the line when their men send their children flying across the room like paper dolls."

Sensing probably that there was zero chance she was going to get a date with the doctor, Candy let her fuse burn out. "Oh, shut the fuck up, you know-it-all shit. What the hell do you know? You're blaming me for my daughter's injuries, and it ain't my fault at all."

"It's not? You are living with a man who has abused your daughter, it looks to me, on several, if not many, occasions."

"Look, you hyper-educated busybody, I'm Julia's mother, and I take good care of her, and I don't have to listen to any of this shit anymore."

She pushed through the doctors without saying good-bye to me. I felt a tear slip out of the closed eye, then another tear slip out of the other eye.

"We've reported you to Children's Services," the doctor called after her.

Before she left, my mother turned around to laugh and say, "What the hell do I care? What are they going to do? Trayce is gone—there ain't no threat there anymore. I never hit her."

That wasn't exactly true, I thought. I did get hit upon occasion. And beaten. And slapped. It was her words, however, that always lacerated my heart to pieces.

After my mother left, Nora and the doctors and the other nurses comforted me, brought me ice cream. Nora held me as I cried, then slept. When I woke up, another nurse, named Marci, was there to take care of me, and to hold me while I cried again. On the next shift I met Gabrielle, who did the same. Then I was back to Nora.

My mother came to get me a few days later, and I cried when I left the hospital.

The next year I was back in the hospital again, but we

were in a new state by then, and the doctors and nurses were different. I went in once when I hurt my leg. I had been running from home, away from Trayce, who had found his way back to our home. I ran right into the street and was hit by a car. I got bashed up some, but the only lasting scar was from a gash on my thigh.

The other driver was appalled and sorry and cried all over me. My mother, however, thought it would be wonderful if she took that man's insurance company for everything she could, so she got herself a lawyer, and she sued. I still went down the street to another church for my clothes and my coat, and I still had free lunch and breakfast at school.

Another time I was in the hospital when I was critically sick with pneumonia. My mother ignored how sick I was, ignored the school's calls, ignored the pleas of the women at church who begged her to take me to the doctor. Finally, two of the women from church came by our gross apartment when I didn't arrive at church on Sunday morning, picked me up, and drove me to the hospital.

I was there for seven days. My mother came to pick me up.

So now, every time I went into a hospital I felt ill because of my memories. Not of the doctors and nurses, who had almost always been kind. Not of the treatments, the tests, and the needles. Not even of the pain of injury. No, I had learned to hate hospitals because of the memories that made me face up to the fact that my mother really didn't give a damn about me.

But when I got the call from the state police, I flew to the hospital, located in Monroe, the same town where I worked at the library.

And that's when I learned a hell of a lot about methamphetamine.

Methamphetamine use takes a hold of a person and shakes the goodness and generosity and sanity right out of them, and turns them into a dangerous, pathetic, moral-less, desperate, criminal, altering their brains so there is little chance of going back to the cool person they used to be.

It was a meth addict, a friend of their mothers', who put both Shawn and Carrie Lynn in the hospital the night before.

As Aunt Lydia, Stash, Caroline, Lara, and I stared down at the sleeping children, sobs shaking our bodies as we looked at their bruised faces, IVs, and tubes going in and out of their bodies, I blamed myself.

I should have taken Shawn and Carrie Lynn away from their mother, away from her boyfriends. I should have insisted the police come, again to their apartment. I should have insisted that Children's Services come again, and when they didn't, I should have written letters to everyone from the governor on down. I should have forced their mother, by blackmail if need be, to let the children come and live with me.

I felt totally, completely responsible. I had failed them. Failed them utterly and completely. I had allowed this to happen. But I knew one thing for sure as I cried my eyes out over those two kids: come hell or high water or a move to Australia, I would not allow Shawn and Carrie Lynn to live a life like mine for one more minute.

Aunt Lydia and Stash and Caroline and Lara must have been thinking the same thing. "We're taking them home with us," Aunt Lydia said, her voice cracking like dead twigs. "We're taking them home."

Shawn and Carrie Lynn were in the hospital for a week. I took off the week from the library. I was joined at the kids' bedside by Aunt Lydia, Stash, Dave, Scrambler, Caroline, Katie, Lara, and Lara's husband, Jerry. Dean came, too. I held him as we both cried.

The local and state newspaper carried the story, and the kids were inundated with presents. Every time I think of it, I cry. Goodness in the face of horrible evil, that type of thing.

New clothes came for the children. New books. New toys. New games. New coats. The response from the parents at the library was overwhelming. New sheets and comforters with matching lights and teddy bears from the mothers at the library who had taken up a collection.

"So the kids can have something new, something to start over with," one of the mother's said, her eyes swollen from a thousand tears. The newspaper had reported that the children had lain in their own blood, in their own beds over the weekend, their mother never noticing how hurt they were, as she was strung up on meth.

A fund for their college educations was set up. I expected to see a total of $2,000 in the accounts. These were not good financial times for people, after all, and the kids really didn't know that many people. But by the end of the second week, $121,000 had come in for Shawn and Carrie Lynn, to be kept in trust for their college education. There was a rumor of two anonymous enormous donations, but there were also hundreds of smaller donations from the townspeople.

I could not have kept Ms. Cutter away from that hospital with an army. She was there every single day, twice a day. She brought books, all nonfiction or classics, of course, which she read aloud to the children. One time they were both sleeping when I walked in on her reading Shakespeare. "Children can learn while they sleep, I'm sure of it," she said, her voice pinched and pain-filled.

When the children got a little better, she taught them how to crochet. She brought little painting projects. She brought crafts.

And every time she left, Olivia Cutter would press their little hands together in hers. She tried to hide the tears in her eyes the first day that Shawn and Carrie Lynn were in the hospital, but that only lasted until she left their room, and then she collapsed in a heap on the hallway floor, her body shaking with sobs. She had to be medicated at the hospital and held overnight, because her heart was beating so fast they thought she was zooming her way into a heart attack. She took the rest of the week off from the library due to her health problems, but she still visited the kids every day, twice a day.

By the sixth day she was able to get halfway down the hall without sobbing and gasping for breath. Me, Stash, Dave, Aunt Lydia, Roxy Bell from the library, or one of the doctors or nurses always made it a point to catch her before she sagged to the floor, and when she was stable again, she and I would go to the chapel and pray together, kneeling before a statue of Mary, crying our eyes out.

Dean Garrett came from Portland and read to the kids, bringing little puzzles and games with him. He would read to Shawn, and I would read to Carrie Lynn; then we would switch places. The children always fell asleep in our arms.

By the end of the week, almost stumbling from exhaustion, I decided to go home and sleep, knowing how well the nurses cared for them during the night. I had met all of the nursing staff, and knew I was looking at Nora and Marci and Gabrielle, the nurses who had treated me as a child, reincarnated.

"I'll take you to dinner," Dean said.

"I think I'm too tired to eat."

"You're eating, honey," he insisted, wrapping an arm around me as we walked into the cool night from the hospital. "You're going to make yourself sick if you don't eat. You're not taking care of yourself. You're losing weight, Julia."

I laughed. "Well, that's a good thing." The watermelons on my chest still looked huge, I knew, but my pants were actually a little looser. *Hip hip hooray*, I thought dully. That's what staring at two innocent children who have been beaten to within an inch of their lives will do to you.

"No," Dean said quietly. "It's not a good thing. I like you the way you are." He stared down at me in the parking lot, the stars bright and shiny above us.

"You like me fat?" I was tired, tired all the way into my

bones and ligaments, but I still managed to smile. I couldn't help it. Anytime I was with Dean Garrett I felt like smiling. And if I wasn't smiling on the outside because he still made me nervous, so very nervous, inside my heart was always smiling, I could feel it.

"I like you the way you are, Julia Bennett, just the way you are."

"And how's that?"

"Beautiful."

I laughed. "You're good for a woman, Dean Garrett. I have barely slept in a week. I have no makeup on, so I look a little like death. I hardly had time to brush my hair, and I just noticed I'm wearing the same shirt I've worn for three days. My teeth feel like moss is growing on them, and I'm sure if I lifted my arms, the odor could knock a small bull to his butt."

Dean Garrett stared down at me, the corners of his mouth lifting up. "I happen to like bulls, Julia, and moss. So don't worry. To me, brushed hair or not, wearing the same shirt every day for a month, I don't care. You are the most beautiful woman I have ever met in my life."

"I don't feel beautiful." I leaned against his truck and crossed my arms over my chest. He placed both of his arms on either side of me.

"Why? Why do you not feel beautiful, Julia?"

I gritted my teeth, the guilty hysteria bubbling in me. "I failed them." The words came out in a gasp. "I failed Shawn and Carrie Lynn."

"Oh, honey." Dean sighed and pulled me close.

"I should have done more. . . ." The sobs shook my body, again and again, and Dean just held me in that dark parking lot, rubbing my back, hugging me close.

"You didn't fail anyone."

"I did. I failed Shawn and Carrie Lynn. I called Children's Services, and I called the police, but they wouldn't do anything." I cried into his shoulder again. "I knew what their lives were like at home, I know that sense of fear and loss and loneliness, because I lived through it myself as a child." I choked. I wondered how I would ever live with myself again.

He cupped my face in his hands. "We have something in common, Julia. My childhood was like yours."

"It was?" I pulled away. *It was*?

"My childhood was lousy, Julia, and I left home at fifteen. Suffice it to say that my mother died when I was two, and my father spent the next thirteen years making sure I was miserable. He had a belt that whipped across my back more times than I can tell you, and I have the scars to prove it. You would know if you had ever tried to take my shirt off."

I bit my lower lip, and he kissed me.

"He would often put me in a closet when I was a kid, Julia, for hours, sometimes overnight. I am the most claustrophobic person you have ever met because of it."

The thought of a young, motherless Dean in a dark closet by himself made tears come into my eyes.

"We lived in Idaho, and I worked every single hour from the time I got home from school until about eleven at night on our farm. In the summers, I worked sixteen-hour days. Nothing I did was good enough. He threw a bottle at my head once, which is how I got the scar on my forehead. My earliest memory is how he kicked my cat across the room. The cat pulled itself into a ball and died right in my arms. He did the same thing with a puppy I received from a neighbor."

Dean shut his mouth with a snap. I began to cry again, held him tight. I ached for him. Ached for me. Ached for Shawn and Carrie Lynn. Why are so many people so brutal to children, I wondered. Why? I felt an instant, intense connection with Dean, that sad understanding that comes through shared terror and misery.

"I know your ex-fiancé beat up on you," he said gruffly. "I know that you survived both your childhood and him, that you didn't let anyone crush you.

"And you still care, really care about people. I see it in your eyes when you talk about Katie or Lara or Shawn and Carrie Lynn. Lydia and Stash adore you. Katie told me you're her very best friend. Lara told me she never had confidence in her art until she showed it to you. Shawn and Carrie Lynn love you. The chocolate you have given to townspeople who are sick and older is the stuff of legends."

He smiled at me, kissed me on the lips until the passion was welling so hot and heavy in me I thought it might just bowl me right over. It was a passion for Dean, mixed in with a crush of overwhelming and conflicting emotions.

"I love you, Julia. I know it's more than you want to hear right now, more than you're ready to handle, but I still wanted to tell you where I stand."

I nodded at him. I liked knowing where he stood.

❦ 19 ❧

It is amazing what an intimidating lawyer who knows everyone can do for you.

Dean Garrett was both intimidating and knew everyone. I hadn't known this fact until we started fighting for custody for Shawn and Carrie Lynn.

Though several nurses and two doctors had known Aunt Lydia for decades (because of a garden club they all belonged to), and though Stash was close friends with two of the doctors (because they had been on hunting and fishing trips together), the hospital couldn't simply let us walk off with Shawn and Carrie Lynn.

I had thought we could—since Shawn's biological father was a guest in a Texas State Penitentiary for killing a police officer who had had the nerve to raid his crack cooking company, and Carrie Lynn's father had "disappeared," according to police reports. Their mother was now also in jail, along with the psycho-violent boyfriend, and there was no other family we knew of. It should have been a slam dunk. I figured we should have been able to walk out of the hospital with the kids, and that would be that. But the state has to have its piece of the action. A child welfare representative came and informed us that the children would be going to a foster home when they were released.

When Aunt Lydia heard that, she made a comment about how Shawn and Carrie Lynn were going to a foster home over her dead, rotting, maggot-infested body and then launched into a recitation of her gun collection and her talents as a mother. The welfare worker got a little pissy and walked out.

The pissy woman came back the next day with a couple of other welfare workers, and we all met in the hospital conference room: Aunt Lydia, Stash, Caroline, Lara and her husband, the nurses and doctors that knew Aunt Lydia and Stash, Dean Garrett in all his intimidating, cool glory, and I.

Although I felt sick at the very thought of losing Shawn and Carrie Lynn to a foster home while I fought for the right to be their legal parent, I took a second to look around. Stash was actually wearing a suit and looked like the affluent, gentleman-farmer he truly is. Aunt Lydia wore a bright purple dress and red heels, her gray hair pulled back into a loose bun. She looked lovely—furious and irritated, but lovely.

Lara and her husband looked proper and caring—the perfect minister and his holy wife.

And Caroline? She looked like a tiny fashion model. My mouth actually dropped open when I saw her in a silky beige suit and fine gold jewelry. Her heels looked like they probably cost her a fortune. If I didn't know better, I would have thought she was a high-fashion, rich socialite.

I was wearing a burgundy-colored blouse and a black skirt and black heels, the only nice outfit I had brought with me to Oregon. I had taken care with my curls, and they tumbled to my shoulders. When Dean saw me he did a double-take, then kept staring at me.

But I couldn't stop staring at Dean, either. We were quite the staring pair. I had seen Dean only in jeans and cotton shirts, jean coat, and cowboy boots. Casual. Sexy. Wonderful. But in a dark suit, crisp white shirt, and dark tie, he was devastating. Intimidating, but devastating.

We sat together at the table in the conference room, his foot in front of me at the table, so I had to put both my legs around his. If I hadn't been panicked and worried sick about losing Shawn and Carrie Lynn to a foster home, I would have enjoyed all that sensual stuff.

He leaned in close as everyone got settled. "You look beautiful, Julia," he said quietly, his blue eyes crashing like a heat wave into mine.

I bent my head, tried not to blush. We were here for serious business. I wanted Shawn and Carrie Lynn to come home with us so desperately, so completely, I was ready to dance naked on the table and do a backhand spring to the floor if that's what it would take, but I couldn't resist smiling at him.

And Dean Garrett smiled back, slow and easy. My thighs were hot, and my vagina felt like it was leaking. I wanted that man so bad it was all I could do not to jump him right there on the table.

He grabbed my hand for just a second, and I felt all hot again. *I am such a mess*, I thought. Hot flashes, followed by cold freezes, heart palpitations, a frequent feeling that there was no air in this galaxy anymore, and trembling of all sorts. And Dean still seemed to like me.

The meeting started when the three people from the state walked in. Introductions began, and I couldn't remember their names. I could only peg them as Miss Tight Ass, because she looked like she thought a lot of herself and was as skinny as a stick, Mr. I Have A Small Penis, so dubbed because he looked like he hated women and the world in general, and then Ms. Cuddly, because she was tiny, like a doll.

By the end of the meeting, I knew I had named them all wrong.

Dean introduced himself as my and Aunt Lydia's lawyer.

The three from the state cringed a little as he shook their hands, towering over each of them.

"Mr. Garrett," said Ms. Cuddly, smiling, her shock over at seeing Dean Garrett here. "I've followed many of your cases through the news. Your most recent victory was stunning, absolutely stunning! Congratulations on your victory."

"Thank you," Dean said, his hands clasped together on the top of the table, his expression serious.

"I am such an admirer of your work! I am so very impressed!"

The woman spoke in exclamation points, and it was beginning to annoy me. Plus, she was cute. Sparkling, cheerful, blond-haired, and cute. I started to dislike her.

"Thank you," Dean said again, then tried to divert her from the subject of himself. "In regards to the matter of custody of Shawn—"

"In the case before this last one," Ms. Cuddly gushed again, "with the sewage companies dumping wastes into the river, I read your closing argument, and it was truly inspiring, a wonderful testament to the freedoms we Americans take for granted!"

My dislike grew.

"I appreciate that. Now, if we can discuss Shawn and Carrie Lynn . . ."

"I believe I heard that your wife is an attorney, too?" Ms. Cuddly asked.

The silence in the room almost blew my ears out. His wife? Dean had a wife? My stomach pitched down to my feet, and I felt ill.

A wife.

A roll of depression, of despair, so thick, rolled over me, I closed my eyes. I could almost feel the blood leaving my head and pouring south to my toes. When I opened them, I saw Dean.

"No," he said, looking straight at me. "I don't have a wife."

The air left my body in a whoosh, and I sagged against

the chair. No wife. Dean had no wife. As quick as the despair had caught me up in its thick claws, it was gone again, Ms. Cuddly chattering about still another case.

"I think we need to get to the business at hand," Dean said in a clipped voice.

"About time," Stash agreed, folding his arms over his chest and looking somewhat intimidating himself. "We can pass out membership cards for The Dean Garrett Admiration Society another day, ma'am. Now, look here, Julia Bennett has known and been a friend to both Shawn and Carrie Lynn for months now. She's the librarian in town and brings them lunches, dinners, gifts. They know her, they trust her, they love her."

Ms. Cuddly had, at first, blushed after Stash's rebuke, and now, I could tell, she had it in for Stash for his sarcasm.

She didn't look so cute anymore when she spoke again, the condescension dripping from each word. "Mr. Hookland, is it? It is? Let's see, you're a farmer, aren't you?" She said it as if she thought being a farmer were one step up from being on welfare. The smile came back but disappeared instantly. "Our job as child welfare workers is to protect children. Just because someone wants to raise someone else's child doesn't mean we automatically hand over custody." She laughed, as if Stash were an immature, stupid child.

"Ms. Hawthorne," Dean cut in, his voice harsh and low. "As you know, the state always looks to place children with family and friends during times like these."

"Yes, I do know that, Dean," Ms. Cuddly's smile was back and she leaned forward, resting her boobs on the table. *Oh, please*, I thought. *Please*. "But none of the people here are family, and as I understand it from the mother, none of you are friends, either. In fact, the children's mother has told us that she does not want any of you to have custody of the children."

There was a collective gasp in the room, then Stash swore, stood up, and started pacing the room. Miss Tight Ass looked up, interested, but not afraid, her eyes moving from one person to the other in the room. Mr. I Have A Small Penis looked slightly alarmed.

Caroline's mouth fell open, her huge eyes shocked. Aunt Lydia slapped both hands on the table. "This is bullshit! A drug-addicted mother who used her children as punching bags, then lets them lay in their own blood for two days while she gets high and turns her tricks with her boyfriend, who also gets his swings in at the children, gets to say where her children are placed?"

I was too shocked to say anything. But this is what I thought: *That bitch. That heinous, selfish, horrible complete bitch. I hope she rots bone by bone in hell. That bitch!*

"So, it's your intent to follow the mother's wishes, is that correct?"

"Yes, Dean, it is," Ms. Cuddly said, her voice like honey. "I take the law very seriously, as I know you do, too. The mother has not been convicted yet—"

"Have you read the police reports?"

"Well, yes, Dean, I have, but the mother of Shawn and Carrie Lynn has expressly asked, in no uncertain terms, Dean, that this family not raise the children while she is in jail." Ms. Cuddly smiled again, cocked head to look at Dean, as if she was beckoning him. Her attraction to him was so blatant, so cloying.

I hated her.

"More bullshit," Aunt Lydia said, shaking her head.

I saw the muscles in Dean's cheek clench. Ms. Cuddly rattled on about the mother's rights, that the mother was sorry, that drugs were to blame, etc. etc.

Stash paced more, Caroline kept making protesting sounds, and Aunt Lydia said again and again, "Bullshit, bullshit, bullshit."

"I'm sorry," Ms. Cuddly said to Aunt Lydia, her voice high and patronizing. "I've forgotten your name already, but please do refrain from using such vulgar language in our presence. We know what we're doing. And we know the law. I assure you that the welfare of children is our topmost concern. We know what's best in these cases. We've had years, absolutely years of experience. . . ."

"And your experience has taught you nothing but bullshit," Aunt Lydia told her.

"I will have to ask you to leave if you use that abusive language again," Ms. Cuddly said. She lowered her eyelids and looked at Aunt Lydia as if she were one fine, interesting bug.

Stash leaned across the table, both hands curled into fists as he addressed Ms. Cuddly, his gaze never wavering. "Do not speak to Lydia Thornburgh in that manner again. Do you understand me? Do not ever, ever speak like that to her."

"This meeting will end, here and now, if you people are unable to control yourselves—"

Dean held up his hand, and everyone stopped talking as if a lightning bolt had crashed through the room. "If I may?" He arched an eyebrow at Ms. Cuddly.

Pulling several sheets of paper from a folder, he read aloud the children's history. The past abuse reports, not only in the state of Oregon, but reports he had also managed to get hold of from California, where the children had previously lived.

"Despite the abuse, the children were not taken from their home," he said, then waited for Ms. Cuddly to nod her agreement.

"No, the children were not taken." Ms. Cuddly smiled. "Because we felt—"

Dean held up his hand again. "Let me finish, if you wouldn't mind?"

He then, in almost a monotone, detailed the concerns that had been expressed to the state by the children's current school and three of their teachers. "Despite these concerns, and the physical injuries the school and teachers noted, the children were not removed from the home." He arched his eyebrow at Ms. Cuddly again.

"That's correct, but again—"

"If you'll let me finish," he said again.

He detailed the information I had shared with him about the multitude of phone calls I had made to report the bruising and injuries on the children, and the poor state of their health. "This time a caseworker went to see the children, but, again, the children were not removed from their home, is that correct?"

Ms. Cuddly rolled her eyes.

"Excuse me," Dean said. "The children were not removed from their home, is that correct?"

Ms. Cuddly said, "That is correct, but—"

Dean held up a hand. "Is it also correct that no one checked to make sure that the mother's current boyfriend wasn't a pedophile or a violent criminal?"

"That's not really something we do. . . ."

"He was both—you do understand that, don't you?" Dean then listed the injuries that both children had suffered over the last two years in this state, using hospital records and anecdotal evidence from the people who had been in the children's lives. Then he discussed how over a three-day meth binge the children had been beaten and starved and refused critical medical treatment by their mother and her boyfriend.

He noted that it was a neighbor who had called the police when he heard Shawn screaming, allegedly at the boyfriend, "Get off of her, get off of Carrie Lynn!"

Dean quoted the doctors and nurses who had treated Shawn and Carrie Lynn, both their physical injuries and their very frail emotional health. Even Ms. Cuddly was sinking in her seat by the time Dean was done. Mr. I Have a Small Penis held his face in his hands, and Miss Tight Ass just cried. I handed her some Kleenex. When she blew her nose it sounded like a foghorn.

"So, in conclusion, I would have to say that the state has not, as you have declared today, handled this case with any amount of competence. Your years of experience should have told you that the children were in grave danger. As I read the law, it clearly states that in the condition that Shawn and Carrie Lynn were living in, they should have been removed from their home for their own protection."

"We cannot predict the future, Mr. Garrett," Ms. Cuddly said, her face flushed.

"No one asked you to. The children's past clearly foretold a tragedy in their future. At this time I would like to request that you allow Julia Bennett and her aunt, Lydia Thornburgh, to care for the children until we can get adoption papers processed. A home visit can be arranged and the paperwork completed and forwarded to the state immediately."

"That sounds like a good idea to me," Miss Tight Ass said, blowing her nose again. This time it sounded like it came from a very *large* foghorn.

"Perfect," said Mr. I Have A Small Penis. "Absolutely perfect. I'm sure we can work something out here."

"No." This came from Ms. Cuddly.

We all sucked in our breaths. Aunt Lydia mentioned something about cursing the woman. Stash grumbled.

"I'm sorry?" Dean arched that eyebrow at her again, then carefully folded his hands together.

"I said no. We cannot allow Miss Bennett and Ms. Thornburgh to take the children with them to their home. This is a long process. We must run criminal checks, background checks—"

"Good," Dean said. "You mean, like the criminal and background checks you ran on the mother's boyfriend, who proceeded to nearly kill both Shawn and Carrie Lynn?"

Ms. Cuddly flinched. "I will not allow you to make a mockery of this state, Mr. Garrett, or the laws that govern them. Truthfully, I am not convinced that Miss Bennett or Mrs. Thornburgh are what the children need in their lives."

"You don't think my aunt and I are what the children need in their lives?" I was so furious I thought my head would blow. "I love those children. I have been with them five days a week, four hours a day for months, I—"

"You are even meaner than you look," Aunt Lydia said, "Your womanhood is a shriveled and lifeless thing. . . ."

"Just a minute!" Dean's voice cracked through the room. He picked up his cell phone, hit one number on speed-dial. "Hi, Charisse. It's Dean. . . . It has been a while." He smiled at the phone. "Don't be mad. . . . I know. . . . I promise I'll think about coming to your next party. . . . Yes, I said I would promise to think about it. You know I don't like parties. I was out on the ranch. . . . How's your mother doing? Good, that's great to hear. . . . Can I talk to that useless husband of yours? You, too. . . . Hi, Marc. . . . Good to hear from you, too. Say, I have a problem. . . . Yeah, you do owe me a favor, big guy, so here it is. . . ."

Now, I could not figure out why in the world Dean was making a call on his cell phone in the midst of this conversation, especially when he could tell I was an inch from throwing myself at Ms. Cuddly and permanently removing that smirk from her face by way of tearing off her lips, but there it was.

But then the unusual name, "Charisse," came to mind, and the only Charisse I knew of was the governor's wife. And his name was Marcus. And then everything fell into place as Dean succinctly explained the problem, including who the children were, the crime, and who was sitting at the table with us from Children's Services.

"Thanks, buddy. Yeah, I already promised Charisse that I'll think about your party. . . . We'll hit the slopes then. . . . you'll just have to force the legislature to take a break. Tell them you need to go and be a ski bum. That'll sit well with the voters. I'll call you back."

Dean hung up. Laced his fingers together.

"Was that . . . ?" Ms. Cuddly looked like she'd swallowed a canary, I thought with great glee. "Was that the governor?"

"Yes, ma'am." Dean answered. "It'll be a few minutes. So, how 'bout those University of Oregon Ducks?"

Stash leaned back in his chair, understanding real quick what had happened. "Well, I'm real proud of them. The quarterback isn't half bad this year. What do you think?" he asked I Have A Small Penis.

I Have A Small Penis, still looking flushed and upset at the children's abuse report, nodded at Stash. I got the impression that he did not like Ms. Cuddly, for he launched into a full discussion about the Ducks' offense.

"Excuse me," Ms. Cuddly cut in. "Can I ask why on earth we're talking about football, Mr. Garrett?" Her cheeks were flushed, red as cherries.

"We're waiting for a call," Dean said, smooth as molasses.

Ms. Cuddly flushed more. Now she really did look like a cherry. "From who?"

"From Teresa Gonzales, who is the head of Children's Services for this state."

Within three minutes, Ms. Cuddly was glancing down at her waistline, where she had hung her phone on her belt. She checked the number, grabbed the phone, and pushed a button. "Hello, Teresa," she said, her voice sounding sick and wobbly. "Yes. Yes I am. No, I did not recommend that they could take the children. . . . Well, because of the mother's wishes. . . . Yes, the mother is in jail. . . . assault . . . meth user. . . . Uh . . . uh . . . her record is a bit extensive . . . well, quite extensive. . . . Yes . . . yes . . . I'll do that."

She hung up. Coughed. "It appears there's been a change of plans," she began.

When Shawn and Carrie Lynn were released from the

hospital, Aunt Lydia, Stash, and I brought them straight home.

The chickens proved to be great therapy for Shawn and Carrie Lynn. So were Melissa Lynn and her little piglets, who took an instant liking to the children. Carrie Lynn got a real kick out of the fact that she and Melissa Lynn shared a name.

And the birds that were let loose in the house in the morning and evening for their daily hour flight also brought smiles to their faces.

But it was the year-old golden retriever that Dean gave the children that brought the most smiles. Shawn and Carrie Lynn played with that dog for hours, walking it around the farm and even inside the house on a leash. He let them put flowers in his collar, a white bonnet on his head, and pink socks on his feet. Alphy was a very naughty dog, chewing on everything in sight and barking at the birds that flew through the rooms and Aunt Lydia's favorite green vase, but he licked those kids on a constant basis and couldn't stand to be without them.

Alphy slept with Carrie Lynn in her bed, and more than once I found both children crying into his neck. Sometimes I joined them, rocking both kids and the dog in my lap, and other times I just let the kids cry, that big golden dog licking their tears away as fast as they came down their faces.

Day by day Shawn and Carrie Lynn got better, although I knew from my own experience that they would never be completely healed. The cast on Shawn's arm was removed, as was the cast on Carrie Lynn's leg. Their stitches were pulled out. The bruises disappeared. The haunted, hunted look in their eyes faded a bit. They spent their time helping Aunt Lydia on the farm, gardening with Caroline, playing with Katie's kids, and making chocolate with me.

If they had any question about how Ms. Cutter felt about

them, it had been settled at the hospital and at her three-times-a-week visits to our home. At first she sat stiffly on a chair by their beds reading the nonfiction books and classics she brought with her. But the kids couldn't see the pictures very well, so when Carrie Lynn held the sheet of her bed up with one hand, an invitation to the gray-haired librarian to snuggle on in, Olivia Cutter didn't hesitate.

From then on, if the kids were in bed or on the couch, she sat right next to them. They continued their crocheting, too, and both kids made a scarf. Shawn made one for Stash, and Carrie Lynn wrapped hers up real pretty and gave it to Ms. Cutter.

Which, of course, made the woman cry all over the place. She wore that scarf every day from then on in.

I blamed myself for not protecting the children, the guilt almost overwhelming. I should have taken those kids and moved to some tiny island in the Pacific. My recriminations went on endlessly, often into the wee hours of the morning. Sometimes I even cried into Alphy's neck.

He was one great dog.

"It has to be tonight," Caroline said, her voice strident over the phone. "Tonight. I had a vision, Julia. But I don't know who it is."

"Who what is?" I gripped the phone, Caroline's hysteria strangling me like talons in my throat. "I don't understand. Slow down, Caroline. You're talking too fast."

"I had a vision. Yesterday. In my garden. Of a woman. She was naked. I couldn't tell who it was, but she had cancer. I could see a black spot. A tiny, tiny black spot. Oh, God. It's someone I care about, because I saw myself crying. Call the Psychic Night group, Julia, please."

I assured her I would, then dropped the phone and ran out to the chicken coop to Aunt Lydia. She listened gravely, her face tight, fingers clenched around a shovel.

"Go, Julia. Call Caroline and Lara. Now."

❧ 20 ❧

Katie, Caroline, Aunt Lydia, Lara, and I sat around three burning candles on the floor of Aunt Lydia's darkened family room with our shirts off.

None of us was the slightest bit embarrassed. Some might have feared that Caroline had gone right off the deep end and into a deranged pit, but we knew her, which is why we were all scared shitless—too scared to be embarrassed.

The Dread Disease started creeping up on me again. I assumed that the cancer Caroline sensed was mine, which would explain my months and months of breathing problems, my heart issues. I could feel my throat start to close, and my hands were freezing-cold and trembling. I told my body to calm down, to pound out the disease, to take control, but my body did not respond. Neither did my brain, which seemed to be knocking around in my skull with fright. I knew something bad was coming. We all did.

Caroline closed her eyes, her right one blinking at frantic speed even while shut.

I shook, my huge boobs quaking, and I noticed that Lara shook, too. I noted the dark circles under her eyes, her pale, strained-looking face. Her hands fluttered in her lap. I knew that this meeting was not the only thing stressing Lara to a breaking point. It did not take a psychic to determine that Lara was ready to implode. Steadily over the last few weeks, she had seemed to become more nervous, more uptight.

Plus, every time I saw her, she was fidgeting. Fidget, fidget, fidget.

Katie looked better than I'd ever seen her, although she was scared to death like the rest of us. She had lost weight, and the strain was gone from her features. It was as if J.D. had drained the life out of her, and without him life was oozing back into her soul.

I asked her how the book-writing was going.

"Better. Much better. It's so much easier to write when tears aren't spilling onto the keyboard." She spread her arms out. "My main character doesn't seem to have an underlying hatred of men anymore. In fact, she's turning into a down-right funny gal who doesn't take an ounce of baloney from anyone."

I hoped with all my heart that the cancer did not belong to Katie. With four children and an alcoholic, phlegm-infested, fart-filled, rutting pig for an ex-husband, who would automatically get custody . . . I shuddered.

Caroline held her arms out, both of them palms up, her eyes tightly closed. She pointed them toward Katie, then moved to me, then Lara, then Aunt Lydia. When they were pointed at Aunt Lydia, they shook. With her eyes still closed, Caroline told us to quietly change places, so we did. Again, when her hands were pointed toward Aunt Lydia, they shook. Then they pointed at me, Katie, Lara.

It seemed so new-wave, so abundantly weird to be sitting half naked in front of a woman with her arms stretched straight out, but I could feel the authenticity of the moment, the cold tragedy about to hit us all in the face.

Caroline took a deep breath, eyes closed. "One more time. Switch places." We did so, my heart pounding with fear. Same result. Her hands shook when they were pointed toward

Aunt Lydia. They were still when pointing toward me, Lara, and Katie.

She pointed her hands at Aunt Lydia again.

They shook.

Caroline opened her eyes.

"I'm sorry, Lydia," Caroline said, her voice breaking. "I'm very, very sorry."

Radiation treatments began immediately after the mammogram results were in. Aunt Lydia had never had a mammogram. Stash accompanied her to her mammogram appointment, literally dragging her, he told me later. When Aunt Lydia saw the mammogram machine, she threw her hands up in the air, then placed her palms over her breasts protectively.

"I refuse to have my breasts smashed like pancakes!"

The doctor assured her it wouldn't hurt.

"How would you like your jingle bells smashed in a machine while someone took photos?" she asked him, leaning close.

The doctor was apparently very experienced and used to working with all kinds of people. "Mrs. Thornburgh, the mammogram is not going to hurt—"

"Can you guarantee me that machine will actually let me take my breasts with me when we're done?"

He could guarantee that.

"What if the machine catches on fire?"

He could also guarantee her the machine would not catch on fire.

The day that followed the Mammogram Torture Machine, as Aunt Lydia dubbed it, passed by so very, very slowly.

And then the call came.

The doctors had found a tumor in her right breast. She would need radiation, surgery, chemotherapy.

Stash and I sat in shock in Aunt Lydia's living room. Caroline did not look shocked. Pained, anguished, worried—

but not shocked. Her eye betrayed her fear, winking on hyper-overdrive.

Aunt Lydia was the only one who didn't seem bothered at all.

"It's just a little cancer," she told all of us that night at her kitchen table as she worked on her needlepoint. She had created a beautiful scene of her home, complete with the rainbow bridge and two of her giant concrete pigs. In the center she had stitched the words, "A Black Front Door Will Ward Off Seedy Men."

"Hell, I've fought off worse than cancer before. Everything is going to be fine. Damn fine. You'll see."

We all nodded. The word "cancer" must be one of the scariest, most devastating words on the planet. I already hated that word with a passion.

"Woman, I know it's going to be fine," Stash suddenly declared, hitting both hands against his knees. "We don't got nothing to worry about at all. We're getting you the best care we can get in this damn country and you're going to be goddamn fine."

He was pissed off, I could tell, but I have learned that when men feel powerless, they get pissed off. That's why it's hard to tell a man a problem. They want to fix it all up, nice and tidy, and move along to your next problem. There. All done. Can I have a beer now?

But looking at Stash's face, and the stark fear he couldn't hide, I knew that a beer was not going to cut it.

"It's a small spot. One spot," he said, more to himself than to any of us. "We're strong, Lydia, and this is gonna be gone before you know it."

"Damn straight," Aunt Lydia said, not looking up from her needlepoint.

"Yep," Stash added, sitting up straight in his chair next to Aunt Lydia's and rubbing her leg. "Doctors can make miracles happen. Not, of course, that we need a miracle here, because the cancer is so small."

"Very small," Aunt Lydia said. "Tiny. Probably hasn't spread a whit."

Caroline's eye kept winking.

"You're gonna have that surgery on that tiny tumor, and I'm gonna move in here and take care of you, and, no, don't you even start arguin' with me. This is the way it's gonna be."

"You can't tell me what to do, Stash," Aunt Lydia said, but there was no force behind her words. She brought the needlepoint canvas up closer to her eyes so she could see better.

"I can, and I am, Lydia. I'm taking charge of things between us from now on. You've been running the show for too many years, and now you're done."

"Stash, I've been running the show because I know best how to run it!" Aunt Lydia dropped her needlepoint on her lap, but she still had that needle in her hand and she pointed it at Stash for emphasis. "You're not taking over my life."

"Yessiree, I am. From this moment on. I will take you to your appointments, and you will rest when I tell you to rest, and you will eat healthy foods with a lot of corn and peaches and zucchini when I tell you to eat them, because that's what's good for you."

"All you need is a club and a dead animal over your arm and you'd fit right in with the cavemen," Aunt Lydia muttered.

Stash leaned toward her, patting her knee. "I like cavemen, always have, and I admire the way they took control of their caves and all the people in them. I also wouldn't mind a club." He kissed her on the cheek. "Please, Lydia."

Aunt Lydia smiled then, tucked the needle into her canvas, and put her arms around Stash's broad shoulders. "I love you, old man. You're a pain in the butt, and I love you."

I bowed my head, not wanting to intrude on their moment, even as I felt my heart cracking.

I heard Aunt Lydia laugh, then she pulled away from Stash, looked deep into his eyes, and once again, for the thousandth time since I moved here, I saw that bond the two of them have, that steady, hard-core love that never dies.

Then Aunt Lydia flung her braid over her shoulder and looked at me, Caroline, and Stash each in turn as she said, "I think we need to visit the basement, don't you all?"

We followed her down the steps to the basement.

A little pot now and then sure can take the edge off life's stresses.

I didn't bother telling Aunt Lydia or Stash or Dean that lately my cell phone would ring, the Caller ID would record an anonymous number, and when I picked up, all I heard was silence. A living, breathing . . . silence. I didn't tell them when I found an envelope to me in Robert's handwriting in the mailbox with no return address.

I was unprepared for the terror that one white, blank sheet of paper inside the envelope brought to me.

The next envelope contained the same. One blank sheet of paper.

And the next.

And the next.

Every day an envelope awaited me. Inside the envelope was a white, blank sheet of paper.

I knew what Robert was trying to say. He knew where I was.

He had found me and would be coming soon.

The Dread Disease took over, and I was soon squatting on the ground by the mailbox, rocking back and forth, the letter clenched in my hand as the air whooshed out of me.

When it was over, I went back to the house. I worked at the library that afternoon, confirmed with Ms. Cutter that, yes, she was still invited to dinner the next week and, yes, I did think that Aunt Lydia would like a new, flowering begonia plant for her front porch. We made pizza that night for dinner and I got ready for work at the library.

I acted as if nothing had happened.

No sense worrying anyone. Aunt Lydia and Stash had enough to worry about, and there was no sense telling Dean, who was currently in the city working on another high-profile case. I didn't want him to become involved in this messy, humiliating, dark part of my life.

So I kept on keeping on. What can you do?

When Katie left J.D., it was as if she had also left a giant, black, abusive umbrella that had hung over her head every day since she'd met the creep.

Katie could now be Katie, and that was no more evident than in the house on Stash's property she was renting. Stash had given her the okay to paint away, so paint she had. The kitchen and family room were painted a lemon yellow, the loft upstairs a sage green. The girls' room was pink, the boys' blue. She painted her bedroom, the smallest of the three, a pure white. "For freedom," she'd told me. She had even stenciled a leaf design around the kitchen and family room.

People in town had cheered J.D.'s departure from Katie's life, and furniture seemed to appear out of nowhere. The pharmacist whose house Katie cleaned suddenly decided that she didn't want her family-room furniture anymore, so she gave Katie a dark blue couch, a red loveseat, and a red and white flowered overstuffed chair.

The dentist, whose house she cleaned, decided that she didn't want her old bedroom set because her fiancé's was much better, so Katie got a new bed, dresser, and two nightstands. She was thrilled even though the bed took up almost the entire room. "I sleep in the Land of Luxury," she said as we tried out the bed with the lace canopy.

A carpenter in town gave her his twin boys' bunk beds as they were both off to college, so Katie got rid of the oldest bunk bed, which wobbled, and used the new one.

Another cleaning client, ninety-seven-year-old Edith

Williams, even gave her an antique buffett and matching hutch for her nook. "They'll be shipping me off to a nursing home soon," she cracked, "so ya might as well take the good stuff now, Katie."

But what had really changed was how Katie kept house.

"When I was living with J.D., the one thing I had control over, the only thing, really, was how clean that house was, so I cleaned. And cleaned. And cleaned," Katie had told me once. "When J.D. came home drunk, I'd clean for hours. When he yelled at me, I cleaned. When he criticized the kids, I could have cleaned my own house for days if I hadn't had others' houses to clean. He was like a giant carpet stain that I had to keep sanitizing, but the sanitizing stuff was old and useless, and the stain kept spreading."

I looked around Katie's home as she grabbed a pot of coffee from the kitchen and poured both of us another cup. Sunlight tunneled into her cozy nook. I could hear Shawn and Carrie Lynn and her four children playing outside. Before there was not a speck of dust or mess in her home. Everything had a place, and everything was in its place. It was almost too clean. Now, it was clean, but only fairly tidy.

She settled down next to me. I knew she had something to say, so I waited.

"I sent an editor the first three chapters of my book."

I set my mug down. It thudded on the table. I waited.

"She likes it. She wants to see the whole thing."

Fabulous, I thought. "Fabulous!" I grabbed her hands across the table. "Absolutely splendiferous! Is the book done?"

Katie laughed, her red hair piled on top of her head in a loose twist. "No, not at all. I've only got the first three chapters written. I assumed that it would be rejected."

"But why would you assume that? Editors have asked you before for your books."

"And then they rejected the book." Katie wrapped both hands around her mug, looked out the window. She should have been happy, but she seemed sort of defeated to me. "I

don't know, Julia. This book is entirely different than the other
ones. All I've written before has been historical romance.
This is a romance, but it's modern-day, and there's a mystery
to it, too, and it all takes place within a week. . . . Anyhow,
part of me wants to write it, and part of me wants to call it a
day. I don't know . . ." Her voice faded.

"You're afraid of getting rejected again?"

She bit her lip, thinking. "I'm not afraid of getting rejected again. My books have been rejected many times, and
I've become rather used to it. I'm just not sure I want to waste
any more of my life with this. I want to build my cleaning
business. I want to spend more time with the kids. I want to
save for a house and plant a garden and see you and Caroline
and Lara. I want to help Lydia."

"But then you'll never know, Katie. You'll always wonder
if this book could have been it, if it would be the one that
sold." I was appalled. Quit? Now? When some editor in New
York had asked to see the book? "Please, Katie, don't quit."

"I've been thinking a lot about quitting. I am not a quitter.
But sometimes I think in life when you continue to fail, you
have to take a realistic look at what's happening. I'm taking
that realistic look, and I don't think I'm going to succeed
with my writing. And it's okay. I would far rather get to be
ninety years old and look back and say, "I tried my damnedest"
to succeed, rather than get to be ninety and think, "I wonder
what would have happened if only I had done something different.""

I nodded, but I really thought she was insane. I would let
her know that in a moment. She had even told me the plot of
her book, and I loved it. I could barely wait to hear how it
ended.

"And I've loved writing the books while I was doing it,"
Katie said. "It allowed me to escape from my life, from J.D.,
from my own exhaustion. I could escape four hundred years
into the past. I swear my writing kept me sane even though

J.D. criticized everything he could get his hands on that I wrote. It was my hobby."

I leaned forward in my chair, my hands clasped in front of me. Katie looked back, her eyes calm, which bothered me. Sometimes people told you they were going to quit something, but they didn't really mean it. They just needed encouragement, needed to vent. But Katie's eyes were peaceful. She was okay with this decision.

"Katie," I said, before launching into a motivational lecture, learned from my own despair, that left her speechless and sputtering. I finished with, "Don't be such an idiot."

The next day she told me she'd stayed up till three in the morning working on that book.

A few days later, after Stash, Aunt Lydia, Caroline, Lara, Scrambler, and Dave took the children to their first day of school, I got a call from a man named James who operated a candy store in Portland. He would like to place an order for my chocolate, he told me, his voice high and excited. He was particularly interested in the chocolates shaped like cats and dogs because a doggie day care was right across the street from his own business.

I could barely speak.

"Ma'am?" his gentle voice prodded me back to reality.

"Yes? Yes!" I said, a bit too loudly. "Of course. I would be happy to send you some chocolates. How many?"

He named a number that again made me speechless.

"Ma'am?" That gentle voice was back, prodding again.

"Yes? Yes! Of course. I'll have them to you as soon as possible."

He asked what I charged, and I pulled a number out of that great blue sky and gulped.

James did not hesitate. "Wonderful! Your chocolates are scrumptious, simply scrumptious, a slice of heaven! Dean

Garrett so kindly gave me a bag not long ago at all. How long have you been in business?"

"Uh, well, uh . . . not very long at all."

"Good, lucky me, then! The stars are shining brightly in my direction! I owe Dean a favor. Seems like I owe him a lot of favors," he mused, then snapped back to business. "So, I will look forward to receiving your order."

I made the appropriate answers, thanked him while trying not to sound too overly joyous and sickeningly grateful, and said good-bye.

I grabbed the keys to Aunt Lydia's truck and headed out the door for Dean's ranch. On the porch I turned around.

When would I ever, *ever* remember to brush my hair before leaving the house?

"Dean Garrett, I want a word with you," I said, loud enough so that he could hear me, as could the four ranchhands who were standing around.

He looked at me and smiled, slow and easy, and I saw his eyes run from the top of all my blond curls, then down my light blue, blouse and jeans to my black boots.

That man could turn my body to mush in no time, and because I was turning to mush, I smiled back. What else can a gal do? Mush and smiling go together.

Dean nodded to the men he was talking to and sauntered over.

I smiled and tried real hard not to let those blue eyes devour me, and I tried not to think of what those shoulders would feel like when I gripped them or what that body would feel like on top of me or how those hips would move or how those thighs would be so strong and hard and what those lips could do to my body.

Yes, I tried real hard to stay mad at him for interfering with my life, and even when he looped an arm around my waist and pulled me into that beautiful house of his I tried to look stern and pouty, but it really hardly worked at all because I had a hard time holding his gaze for very long because I thought he would see I Want You So Bad I'm Melting in my eyes.

And when he pulled me to his length and stuck one of those sexy thighs between mine and kissed me on the mouth with such passion and warmth and possession, well, it is hard to stay mad when your breasts are throbbing and you want to strip off your clothes in record time.

But I took a deep breath and pushed away.

"I just got an order . . ." I breathed heavily as Dean tried to pull me closer again. "From James at Cool Chocolates in Portland. . . ."

"Hmmmm," Dean said, kissing my neck. I arched my neck a bit, telling myself I would let my body indulge for a few minutes.

"And he told me that he and you went way back, and you had brought him a bag of my chocolates . . . ohhh." I moaned a tad, but that was because he was kissing my collarbone, and one of his hands had dropped to my hip, pressing me firmly against his very aroused self. I could not help one more little moan from escaping.

"And I wanted you to know, Dean Garrett . . ." Oh, the man knew how to make love to a woman, I thought, slowly, my mind becoming fuzzy and warm. ". . . that I think it's wonderful that you've helped me, but I don't want you to feel obligated . . ." I groaned.

His hands were now caressing me from shoulder to hip, his lips kissing me senseless. Yes, I had lost all brain cells to Dean Garrett. I could barely think.

"I don't need help from a man. . . . I am doing fine on my own. . . ."

He kissed my lips again, my hands pressed flat on his massive chest. I could hear his heart tripping away, fast but hard, and it gave me a little thrill, even though, of course, I was going to get down to business here, in just a second. . . .

I allowed myself one more kiss, then pulled away, my breasts screaming their frustration. "Dean . . ." I wanted to tell him that I was independent, that I didn't want to be indebted to him in any way, but I couldn't get the words out. "Dean . . ."

But soon I couldn't even remember what I had wanted to talk to him about. I simply wrapped my arms around his neck and kissed him back, and before I knew it we were in his bedroom and all my clothes were lying on the floor and I forgot to be embarrassed about my body.

I just acted on instinct, and as soon as I could I had that man's shirt and his pants off and I kissed his mouth and worked my way lower until he couldn't stand it anymore and pulled me back up and kissed me again, his hands on my breasts, my nipples, my hips, and for once I didn't regret the size of my breasts as they filled Dean's hands and then spilled over.

"You're perfect, Julia," he said, his blue eyes staring into mine as he pulled me close to him like I weighed less than a box of chocolates. "God, you're so perfect, so beautiful." And he kissed me hard, and my body thumped with desire, my breasts arched against his chest, my insides so wet I was sure it would get all over Dean's manly bedspread, but I was past the point of thought as I enjoyed that big, delicious body.

And then I hesitated, ever so slightly, my lips freezing where they were.

I could hear Robert's voice as clear as day. I was too fat. I was cold in bed. He would rather jack off on a fish than inside my body. I was clumsy, didn't know how to make love any better than I knew how to be a ballerina. I didn't know how to turn a man on. I, Julia, was lucky to have him because other men would not put up with a woman who felt like a middle-aged lizard in their arms.

I tried to banish that voice, and I kissed Dean again, then stopped and felt ice creep from my heart to my head to my toes, Robert's scary, threatening, critical voice following that ice.

And I stopped kissing him again.

Dean sensed it and raised his head and studied my face. He closed his eyes, and I saw a pulse leap in his temple, and then he rolled away and I was left with nothing but the cool air covering my body.

He rolled to his side of the bed, groaned loudly, and flung an arm over his eyes. His breath was coming as fast and furious as mine.

My body started to shake, and I yanked the covers up over my huge watermelons, my humiliation totally complete, my self-esteem in threads. After about two minutes of deafening silence, I flung a leg over the side of the bed, intending to make an immediate escape and never look at the man again.

At the very thought of not seeing Dean, my heart squeezed, tight and painful. Whoever said you couldn't really die of a broken heart was terribly, horribly wrong. I could see exactly how it happened.

The tears started to rise, and I knew this cry was going to be a doozy.

As I tried to get up, Dean's hand caught my wrist in a viselike grip.

"Where are you going, Julia?"

I didn't face him, couldn't face him. I thought of what he was seeing from his prone position on the bed. He would see my back, half my butt, my huge breasts. Not a pretty sight.

"Let go of me, Dean," I said.

"Julia, we're going to talk about this." I could feel the bed shift as he sat up. He tightened his grip. Lord, the man was so strong.

"Please, Dean, just let go." I could hear the exhaustion in my voice, the defeat, and I vowed to buck up. No one liked people who wallowed in self-pity.

"No."

"What?" I said, still not turning around. He could see my crack. Just the upper half. I looked at the floor. If I wished hard enough, would it open so I could fall into it and bury my shame in the center of the earth?

"I said, no, I'm not going to let go of you."

Dean's voice was gruff, broken.

I turned around. He had tears in his eyes. Strong, sometimes intimidating, smart, sophisticated Dean Garrett had tears in his eyes.

He used my stunned amazement against me, pulling me toward him, cuddling me against his side, my head on his shoulder.

"Julia, sweetheart," he said. "I want to make love to you so bad I hurt. But more than that, much more, I don't want you to send another wedding dress sailing into a tree."

Shocked into speechlessness, I could barely grunt out an answer. I wanted to make love to Dean Garrett more than I wanted air. But that was about all I wanted. No, that was about all I could handle. Scratch that. I wanted more. No I didn't.

Sheesh.

I sounded blisteringly confused even to myself. I wanted Dean. So much. But I couldn't handle being in a relationship with him. Couldn't handle the intimacy.

"I'll wait, Julia. But, just know"—he kissed my lips again, my cheek, my eyes—"know that every day I miss what we could have together if you'd trust me."

"I'm trying, Dean, I really am."

He smiled, sweet and gentle. "Try harder, love. Please, for us, try harder."

❦ 21 ❧

Aunt Lydia and I both heard the car before we saw it. It grumbled and roared, alternately sounding like a wheezing possum and a mini-jet. Caroline's car took the curve into Aunt Lydia's a little too fast, almost hitting a concrete pig and a flowering toilet.

We both went to greet her. Aunt Lydia had another radiation appointment the next day, so, in true Lydia fashion, we had been working our butts off. "No sense dwelling on a problem you damn well can't fix on your own," she told me. In the last few days, after our usual chores, we'd painted all the chickens' "houses" red to remind the ladies to be daring with their lives, and we had painted the doors yellow, to remind the ladies to always look on the bright side of life.

We had also finished sewing three little quilts Lydia was donating to the hospital for sick babies. All the quilts had baby chicks on them.

"I plan on being out here each and every day, Julia, so don't think I'm going to slow down a damn bit just because of this silly Roaring Radiation," she told me that morning. She had named the radiation Roaring Radiation so she could fight it like a "real woman."

And although she had professed to hate hospitals and doctors, she had fallen in love with her doctor on sight. It was a good thing he was thirty years younger, or she might well have dropped poor Stash. She called Doctor Ray, "Ray of Sunshine" even to his face.

Young, cute, a little shy, and the son of a minister, I had seen him brighten up every time he looked at Aunt Lydia. Even on the first day when she told him in her booming voice that she didn't trust any man who wore a white coat, and she thought doctors were overeducated quacks, they got on well. He proved to be the only one who could convince her to start the radiation and follow the recommended schedule rather than have one dose of radiation, wait a couple of years, then do another, as she suggested.

Aunt Lydia and I had just painted Melissa Lynn's fence a lime green so that Melissa Lynn would know that it's best to look for the green in one's own yard rather than to long for the green in a neighbor's yard, when Caroline came careening around that corner.

She did not ever drive fast, preferring to take life slowly, so this was unusual. When she screeched to a halt, she flew out of her car and ran straight toward us, wearing a purple flowered skirt, white tank top, blue jean shirt, a long red scarf, and white tennis shoes.

Skinny people can get away with any kind of outfit at all and everyone thinks they're stylish, of course. If I wore what she was wearing I'd look like a grape with a ghost wrapped around my boobs.

In her hands, she held a plate full of what looked like sliced bread. There was no foil on the top or any kind of wrapper.

"Good morning, Caroline!" Lydia yelled, although she was only a few feet from her. "Because of my radiation, Ray of Sunshine tells me that my cancer is now being eaten alive! That is a reason to celebrate! My body is a cancer-killing machine. Now, don't tell me you made me my favorite bread."

"No," Caroline said. She ran a hand through her hair, breathing hard. She must have forgotten that she had pulled her hair into a bun because her fingers got caught in the ball of the bun for a second. "No. This is just bread-bread. Only bread."

She took a deep breath. "Hello, Julia." Her eye was twitching pretty fast, and she pulled at the hem of her shirt with the hand that had been freed from her hair.

"Well," Aunt Lydia said, a little confused. "Would you like to come in and eat it? We could all sit down for a cup of coffee—"

"No, no," Caroline said, and then stood there. Staring at both of us. The tip of her tongue wet her lips, and she took another deep breath.

What in the world is she so nervous about? I thought. If she didn't stop breathing so hard, I was afraid she might, by suggestion, give me an attack of the Dread Disease.

"No coffee. Um." She looked at me, those murky green eyes huge, begging.

"Can we help you then with something, Caroline?" I asked.

"Well. I don't need any help. . . . No, *I* don't."

I could feel Lydia freeze beside me.

"But you're a little upset today," Aunt Lydia said.

"Oh, just a tad. People have problems sometimes. We all do. Our friends, Lydia, sometimes have problems."

"Yes, they do. Problems abound for us women, and we must strike back at them with our full arsenal and not wallow in self-pity!" Aunt Lydia stomped her foot.

"But, of course, well, you know I have always had that one concern about that one particular person that I talked about with you that one particular time," Caroline rattled on, the hand holding what I knew now was regular sliced bread shaking a bit.

"Yes, I do know," said Aunt Lydia, her face grave.

"And you know, I try not to interfere with other people's lives unless it's life or death but . . ."

"I see," said Aunt Lydia.

"Well, I don't see," I protested. "What's going on?"

They both looked at me. Caroline nodded. So did Aunt Lydia.

"It's best if she goes with something, don't you think?" Caroline asked Aunt Lydia. "Then no one thinks that, well, that I'm spying on them, prying into their lives. It would be just a little visit."

"With plain sliced bread?" Aunt Lydia shook her head. "You're losing it, Caroline. Stay right here. I'll get some of my jam."

"No!" Caroline's cry made both of us jump. "There is no time to get any jam." She shoved the plate of regular white sandwich bread at me.

"Julia, take that bread on over to Lara's house," Aunt Lydia said. "Now! Quick! It will give you an excuse to be there. Tell her you wanted to bring her some bread."

"But this is sandwich bread. . . ."

Aunt Lydia and Caroline looked like they were going to explode.

"It doesn't matter, Julia! Breathe in, and capture your woman's strength and grace as you will need both for this situation. Go, go, go."

Caroline handed me the bread, then grabbed my elbow and started leading me to Aunt Lydia's truck. She did not stop when two of the bread slices fell to the ground.

"I must have missed something," I said to Caroline and Aunt Lydia, even as I was being hauled away. "I couldn't quite understand your English!"

"Go see Lara," Caroline said, her voice high-pitched and tight. "Go to Lara's house."

I looked into Caroline's eyes. My stomach clenched.

"Go, Julia. Now."

I went.

* * *

Lara was in that sad place all of us get to in our lives when we're sobbing and hiccuping and gasping all at the same time. Her eyes were swollen like two miniature grapefruits, her cheeks red.

"You're leaving for New York? Today?" I asked. I deposited the plate of sandwich bread on the counter. Lara had stared at it for a moment, perplexed, then apparently decided not to deal with it. She hiccuped and walked to her bedroom.

The bedroom was as neat and tidy as the rest of the house. Blue flowered bedspread. Two crosses. Another portrait of Jesus. Old brown dresser and desk. Tired-looking blue flowered curtains that matched the bedspread. No dust anywhere. It was so devoid of Lara's personality, I felt like I was in a hotel, and a not so nice one at that. She opened another suitcase, tossed in socks, underwear. She pulled out a red negligee.

Now, the red negligee was more like the Lara I knew—fun and daring and lively.

Then she took that fun, daring negligee, wadded it into a ball, and cried her eyes out. I rushed over, put my arms around her.

"Lara, tell me, please—"

"I can't live like this." She brought the red negligee up to her face. "I'm trapped. Every day I feel like I'm acting the part of someone I'm not. Do you know what my schedule was like yesterday?" she demanded. She stood up, paced the room, hitting the wadded red negligee with one hand.

"At seven o'clock I led a prayer group for working women at the church. At eight-thirty I brought out the tables and made lemonade for the women's ministry group. At nine I led a Bible study for another group of women which lasted until eleven. While the ladies ate lunch, I went to the church office and did paperwork, ran to the bank to deposit money, came back and did three counseling sessions, one right after another with parishioners. One couple is on the verge of divorce because the woman is gay and has a girlfriend in the city. Her husband thought she was going to a twice-a-month Christian Women's Workshop.

"Another woman was in because she just can't seem to stop herself from stealing licorice from the local pharmacy." Lara tossed the red negligee into the trash can, then yanked a dresser drawer open and pulled out two other negligees. I saw lace and satin go flying right over my head to the trash can.

"And another woman was in because she doesn't think she believes in God. She's been going to church her whole life, she told me, and believes in God because that's what her parents believed, it's what her husband believes, but she says that in her mind there is either no God, or God is someone who is powerless, or God is someone who doesn't care about the suffering that goes on all the time. She says she has little faith in a God that doesn't step in and help those who are in huge need, and she's beginning to think that people believe in God because they need a crutch."

"She came to you, a minister's wife, and told you that?" I was aghast. This did not seem like the type of thing to admit to a minister's wife.

"She did. And you know what, Julia? All I could do was cry. I related to what she was saying too much. I couldn't even counsel her. To tell her to open her Bible to find her answers sounded pathetic. She ended up comforting me."

She grabbed a couple of sweaters, one beige and one gray, from her closet, dropped them into the suitcase, then said, "I hate these ugly things," and tossed them back into the closet. She did this with five other sweaters, four pairs of slacks, and two pairs of shoes.

"I don't even know if I believe in God, Julia," she whispered, finally collapsing beside me on the bed. "Look at Lydia and what's happening to her. Why her? She has helped more people in this town than I can count. Do you know how many people she gives free eggs and garlic to? How many times she has given me bouquets of her cut flowers to give to people in town who are having troubles? She doesn't deserve it. And she's not the only one. Look at the whole world. It's falling apart. Look what happened to Shawn and Carrie Lynn. Why didn't God intervene there? Of all things, why doesn't God at least protect the children?"

Lara sobbed again, hiccupped, then slid to the floor, her arms wrapped around her legs as she rocked. I slid down next to her.

I couldn't think of anything to say that would help her. It would sound trite and sanctimonious, and she sure wasn't in a place where she wanted to listen.

"All I do all day, seven days a week, except for Psychic Nights, is talk to people about God, about trying to pattern their lives after Jesus, about living a life of servitude for God. I pray all the time, with others, with my husband, and yet I don't even feel God in my own heart anymore. There was a time when I did, but not now. Not for so long. Is there a God, or did people invent God because we want to believe in heaven, want to believe that someone can make things right? Do we simply, desperately, stupidly want to believe that some other being is in control because if we don't, we won't be able to stand living on this planet any longer?"

I put my arm around her as her voice crescendoed again. "I can't stand this any longer. I can't stand the hypocrisy, the constant work. I can't stand not being me."

"You're not just going on a trip, are you, Lara?" Why did I ask such a dumb question? I already knew the answer.

"No. I'm not going on a trip." She got to her feet, took a coat and two pairs of jeans out of the closet, put them in the suitcase, and snapped it shut. "I'm leaving."

She pointed to a pair of boots next to the bed, and I handed them to her. She wiggled her feet into them.

"You're leaving? Does Jerry know?"

She cried then, made great, gasping, choking sounds, then shook her head.

"No? Aren't you going to tell him?"

"I can't stand it," she choked out, barely able to talk. "I can't stand the thought of what his face will look like. I don't want to hurt him."

"I've always thought you loved Jerry." Heck, if I had met Jerry before her, I would've loved him and if he wanted me teaching Bible lessons all day long while doing cartwheels and tossing around crosses, I would. The man was good-looking and smart and kind and funny. The whole town loved him.

"I do, I do love him, but look at me, Julia, I'm a nervous wreck. I can't live like this any longer. I work all the time, I handle people's problems, teach Sunday school, run Bible studies, organize the teenagers' activities, and I'm the choir director. I can't do it anymore."

She stared at the lingerie in the trash can as if she couldn't quite remember how it had gotten there.

Oh God, please don't pack that, I thought. *Who would you wear it for?* For a moment I wondered if there was someone else Lara was running off to, but dismissed the idea. Lara was not the type to cheat on her husband.

Then again, Lara was not the type to leave her husband, either.

"The worst of it, after Jerry, is that I feel awful, just sick about leaving Lydia! I can't believe what a horrible person I am!" She sat down on the bed, burying her head in her hands. "I'll send her cards and gifts and, oh, *stuff*!"

"Lara, you need a break, that's all. Time off. You're completely burned out. I read once that ministers have the highest burnout rate of anyone because they're always taking care of other people. Maybe you and Jerry should get away." I sounded so inane, so shallow that I wanted to kick my own shins.

"No, no." She curled up in the fetal position on the bed. "That isn't going to do it. He wants to be a minister. I don't. There's nothing else to work out. Weeks ago, Julia, I was in church in a women's Bible study class and I thought that I didn't want to live anymore."

Oh God. Please, no.

"And I wouldn't hurt myself," she gasped between more broken sobs. "But I don't want to live—does that make sense? I told God that if anybody else had to die, it would be okay with me if it was me, because I am so tired and so depressed, and I am so tired of being tired and depressed. I am so tired of living like this."

"I'm sorry, Lara, I am so sorry."

"I'm sorry, too." Hiccup, hiccup. "A few days ago I was talking to my brother in New York, and I told him how I felt, and he told me to come and stay with him and his partner, so I am. They had another roommate, but he moved out, so I'll have my own room, and he says mine even has a window for light for my painting. Can you help me with something?" she squeaked.

The abrupt change in conversation startled me. I wanted to say no, I will not help you to leave that dear husband of yours, who probably got great joy knowing Lara had peed and her bladder was more comfortable, and yet Lara had always seemed unhappy to me, and she looked like she was one step away from completely snapping.

"Yes, I will, of course."

"Give this to Jerry." She handed me a letter.

"Oh, no, please, Lara." Not that one. I didn't want to see that poor man's face, either.

"Julia, give him the letter," she pleaded. "Tell him I love him, tell him what I told you. . . ."

"Oh, Lara, please talk to him. This isn't fair to him."

"No, it's not fair." She took a deep breath, ran her hands through her hair, grabbed the suitcase and her purse, and headed for the stairs. "It's not fair at all, but this is the way it is. I love you, Julia." She stopped in the entry, where I had followed her, and gave me a hug.

I locked and closed the door to her sterile house as I watched her drive away. Her car kind of hiccupped, blew a little smoke out of its tail, and was gone.

I looked at the letter in my hand.

God help me, I thought.

When Jerry saw my face at the church, he immediately excused himself from the group of people he was talking to, crossed the small atrium, and led me to his office. We sat down across from each other at a table. I grabbed his hand and held it. His face paled. I saw a pulse leaping in his temple, his jaw tight.

"I'm sorry," I said. I blinked rapidly. I was so sick of crying.

He nodded. I saw that hard jaw of his quiver.

I didn't want to, but I pulled my hand away and handed him the letter.

He didn't open it for a while, simply flipped the pink letter forward and back, from one hand to another.

"Is she coming back?"

I swallowed hard and told the truth. "I don't know."

He nodded.

He bowed his head, not in prayer, but in defeat. I got up and patted his shoulder as I left.

Men don't like women to see them cry.

After I told Lydia and Stash what happened, Stash, not a churchgoer, took it upon himself to call Jerry that night, whom he had always liked, even though "the man won't play poker. He's got a great poker face, too."

Jerry arrived at the house almost immediately, and he, Aunt Lydia, Stash, and I gathered around the table for eight-layer lasagna (to conquer the layered complications in our lives), green salad with a few raspberries (raspberries caused miracles, Aunt Lydia believed), and bratwurst (I don't know why we had bratwurst, too. I don't question Aunt Lydia).

Aunt Lydia had lit eight candles representing hope and love, she told me. "Hope and love are the great saviors. They save the soul from shriveling up and dying like a dried prune, and Jerry needs to feel this hope and love. Damn Lara," she muttered. "Now, don't take that wrong, I don't blame her, but I love that boy, even though he's so insanely religious."

Aunt Lydia offered Jerry apple pie, but he wouldn't eat it.

Stash offered him a little Scotch, but he wouldn't drink it.

The kids colored him pictures. He hugged them, then looked like he was going to cry as he watched them march off to bed.

Aunt Lydia then offered him a little pot.

He smiled at that, refused politely, thanked her for offering.

"I knew she was unhappy and stressed. I knew she was tired," he said, rubbing his shaking hands over his face. For a calm man of steel, as Jerry was, this trembling was truly heartbreaking to see. "I tried to get her to cut back on some of the things she was doing at church, but she wouldn't do it. She'd smile at me and laugh, give me a hug, tell me everything was fine." He stood up and paced the room. "I knew everything wasn't fine, but she wouldn't talk to me about any of it. I always encouraged her to paint, to show people her work, but she refused."

"She thought her artwork would embarrass you, embarrass the church."

Jerry shook his head. "Nothing Lara could ever do would embarrass me. Nothing. Not even this. I just want her back. I don't care how long I have to wait. I don't care what she does in New York. I want her back. I'm leaving in the morning."

No one spoke around the table for several minutes.

"Don't go after her, Jerry," Aunt Lydia said, drinking her mint tea, which she had told me was good for the ovaries. I don't know how she knew that. "Give Lara time. She needs to become her own person. She needs to paint. She needs to be an artist. When she's ready—"

"*If* she's ready," Jerry interrupted, his voice bitter, defeated.

"That's right, if she's ready, she'll come back to you." Aunt Lydia patted his hand. "I know she loves you, son, she really does. She talks about you all the time."

"But she didn't love me enough to stay."

"No, that's not quite it. Lara doesn't love *herself* enough to stay. She has to find Lara. She has to find out what she likes, what she doesn't like, what she believes in and what she doesn't. She has to take time to be the artist she has longed to be."

I stared at Aunt Lydia. A speech like that—without talk about a woman's secretions and libido and hormones—was so unlike her that it made it all the more heartfelt.

Even Jerry sensed it, and he started to cry then, burying his face in his hands. Aunt Lydia held on to him on the right, I got the left. Stash awkwardly patted his back, kept telling him that a little Scotch would help, maybe a lot of Scotch? In fact, was Jerry wanting to get drunk, by any chance?

By the end, we were all crying. For Lara. For Jerry. For Aunt Lydia, who was going in for radiation tomorrow. For the chemo that would follow. For Stash's worry about Lydia. And me, I cried because I had gotten five blank letters from Robert today, which scared me to death.

We all certainly had a lot to cry about, and hot tears feel good sometimes.

As long as you know that after a good, hot cry, you've got to buck up and tackle life once again.

❧ 22 ❧

The great thing about a small town is that people will, truly, look after each other if someone needs help. They notice if an elderly neighbor hasn't been outside. They notice if someone breaks an arm or a leg. They notice if someone is suffering from a broken heart. And they help out, even if they don't like the person.

But gossip flies. Hard and fast. And mean. Within hours everyone knew that Lara Keene had left Jerry, the minister. A neighbor had seen her walking out with a suitcase. Jerry had cancelled all of his appointments for that day and the next. His secretary's sister's best friend, who happened to be at church for some meeting or other, reported that he looked upset.

And the rumor mill started to grind.

The gossip about Lara was relentless. Some said she had a lover. Some said she was gay. Some said they had always known that she had a wild, uncontrollable side.

Some questioned whether or not she was a "real" Christian and said she would now be damned to hell if she didn't repent. Of course, that one set me off no end, and when I heard two women talking about her in the grocery store I felt like pelting grapefruits at their faces. Instead, I smiled and asked them what made them think that Lara wasn't a real Christian?

The two women looked shocked. One was in her mid-forties and had that hard-core mommy look to her. Very short brownish, gray hair, about fifty extra pounds, a light blue blouse and stretchy black pants. The other looked about the same, only she had a giant cross around her neck, a sour expression on her face.

Perhaps they thought Lara wasn't a "real Christian" because of all the time she spent teaching Sunday school class? I asked. Perhaps it was all the Bible studies she ran? Perhaps it was all the time she spent with several elderly parishioners? Perhaps it was the way she made home-cooked meals for people when they were ill? Perhaps it was the way she had recently planned the fall chorus presentation?

True Christians walk the walk, they don't just talk the talk, I told the women and could they please tell me who they had recently helped in this community? Whose lives they had made better? No? They couldn't think of a single good deed they had done for anyone? Since they were such good Christians it was really a shame that they weren't more involved with helping the needy or desperate, as we are here to serve the Lord. I smiled sweetly. By the time I was done I could tell that the women wanted to disappear into the tomatoes.

"And please don't tell anyone else you think Lara is going to hell. I know you think you have the lock on heaven, but it's Jesus who decides all that, not two housewives clutching coupons in the grocery store, making judgments against the minister's wife."

I knew those two would never acknowledge my presence again, but I was okay with that. Mean people suck, as the bumper sticker says.

I missed Lara. Aunt Lydia missed her, but Lara was true

to her word. Every week something arrived for Aunt Lydia. A card, a little present, paintings and sketches that she had made. A bouquet arrived when Aunt Lydia got home from her operation.

For Shawn and Carrie Lynn, Lara sent new outfits and art supplies.

Over the next weeks, we received e-mails from her, although she was not in contact with Jerry, which broke his heart again. She had settled in with her brother and his partner. New York was wild. And exciting. And dirty. And dangerous. But she was painting, and her brother's partner knew someone who knew someone, and that someone was coming to see her work.

We wrote back cheery letters, wishing her well, keeping her up to date on Aunt Lydia's progress and the farm, and Shawn and Carrie Lynn, who were finally smiling.

Jerry called or came over now and then, bringing presents for Aunt Lydia. The operation had worn her out more than we had expected it to. He tried to keep a strong facade, but he often broke down and cried.

Shawn and Carrie Lynn did not ask for their mother very often, but when they did ask about her, we told them the truth—well, the truth that a child is old enough to handle.

We told them gently, oh so gently, that, no, they would not be living with their mother anymore. We knew this for a fact because their mother, and her boyfriend, were both going to jail, not only for the assault against the children, in which they had both taken part, in a methamphetamine-fueled rage, but because they had decided that weekend to also rob a liquor store at gunpoint. The store owner had been shot, though not killed, as had his assistant.

That had about wrapped things up for their mother.

Shawn and Carrie Lynn looked sad and lost for a moment, and I sympathized. Even though my mother had been abusive and neglectful, there is something so innate in all of us that wants to be loved and protected by our mothers.

"What about . . . what about . . . ?" Shawn asked, his voice quavering a bit

We knew who he was talking about.

"Your mother's boyfriend is going to jail for a long, long time," Aunt Lydia said. "You will both be old before he gets out. And by then I'll have taught both of you how to shoot a rifle!"

Both children nodded, not speaking.

"Do you have any other questions?" I asked, hugging them close.

Neither one moved for a second, then they shook their heads. Carrie Lynn took a second to pull her blanket over her head, but in a few minutes she took it off again, leaning against Aunt Lydia.

We decided to go out to the garden to pick a few of the last tomatoes, the fall weather getting chillier and chillier.

Later that evening, Aunt Lydia and I found the kids huddled in Carrie Lynn's bed, all their new stuffed animals around them, Carrie Lynn's thumb in her mouth, her eyes staring straight ahead. Shawn had his arm around her and was rocking back and forth. Alphy licked Shawn's face, then Carrie Lynn's, then back again, his whine worried and high-pitched.

I snuggled into bed with the kids and could feel both their little bodies trembling. Stash found us there when he walked in from working all day on his ranch and immediately ordered pizzas. We invited Katie and her kids over for a Bed and Pajamas and Pizza Night. Scrambler came, too.

After pizza, I brought in my chocolate and watched the love that was surrounding those kids slowly beat back the terror.

* * *

The cancer had been shriveled down. Dr. Ray of Sunshine deemed the radiation a great success.

Then we were on to the chemotherapy treatments.

As everyone knows, the intent of chemotherapy is to kill the cancer. The problem is that it kills the good stuff, too. One day in the future I think the chemotherapy treatments we have will be considered barbaric and inhumane, but it's all we've got now, all Aunt Lydia had, and so, under the comforting eye of Dr. Ray of Sunshine, Aunt Lydia agreed to undergo chemotherapy. She named it Crappy Chemo.

"I'm going to beat cancer, Julia, and I'm not going to let Crappy Chemo get me down. You watch me. You just watch."

And so I did.

On the third day after chemotherapy started, Aunt Lydia couldn't get out of bed. She was too sick, too tired. "Crappy Chemo has made me tired," she told me weakly, before I got some juice down her, "but I'm fighting mad now, fighting mad. When I'm up to it, I will whip Crappy Chemo's butt. It will regret the day it trapped me in my bed, sucking my energy from my bones—oh, how it will regret it!"

Then she fell back asleep.

There was no reason for her to get up anyhow. We were bombarded with offers of help from the townspeople. So many people brought us meals, Stash had to buy a new refrigerator for Aunt Lydia's garage to store them all. The chickens were fed, the house was cleaned, and her car was washed and taken for a lube job in town by one of her ex–poker buddies. Another ex–poker buddy mended her fences. Someone else gave the toilets in the yard a good scrubbing and filled them up with chrysanthemums.

On the fourth day, when Aunt Lydia was able to walk, she saw seven people in her yard and garden weeding, raking fall leaves, and trimming. She walked out on to the porch and yelled, "You all make the woman in me want to cry!"

Then she sat down and did just that. When she was done everyone came in for hot chocolate and cookies—cookies, of course, that someone had brought by the night before.

Lydia said that Crappy Chemo hated laughter, so she insisted we laugh our way through the afternoon, and that's what we did. The high-grade Scotch that Stash brought in also helped.

When she wasn't feeling sick, Aunt Lydia was up and out the door. She didn't bother with a hat or wig except on our cooler fall days. "Wigs itch and make me look like I'm wearing a dead gray and white cat on my head, and hats are too hot. I'm bald because I'm fighting cancer and Crappy Chemo, and I'm damn proud of it. No need to hide."

In December, on a snowy night when Aunt Lydia went to bed early, Dave and Marie, in whispered voices, reminded me, Stash, Scrambler, Katie, Caroline, and Jerry, who often escaped to our house, that Aunt Lydia's birthday was coming up. I had thought we would have a small celebration.

Stash had forgotten all about it, as he was too whacked-out about Lydia having cancer in the first place to plan anything other than to get up in the morning, make sure all day long that Lydia had everything she needed, then to stumble into bed at night, ready to go again if Aunt Lydia needed anything in the wee hours of the morning.

Dave thought we should have a big surprise party, and the more we all talked about it, the better it sounded. Aunt Lydia loved parties.

"We'll have it in the barn," Stash said, his voice low and raspy. "Hell, that's the only way we can handle all those people."

"I will be pleased to handle the music," Scrambler said, his voice as well-modulated as usual.

We all stared at him.

"You're going to handle the music? You mean, you got CDs and stuff that we can play?" Stash said.

"Something like that," Scrambler answered, leaning back

in his chair. "I will have an appropriate selection of music available for Lydia to enjoy. I will begin the preparations now." And, like the man of few words that he was, he smiled at all of us, took time to nod and wink at Katie, and shut the door quietly behind him.

"Well! Okay!" Stash said looking around at everyone and scratching his beard. He looked so tired. Tired but excited. "Scrambler is doing the music. So, for the food, I'll get steaks for everyone."

I decided, with the number of people coming, that it should be potluck. Everyone would be asked to bring their favorite side dish. I'd make enough chocolate cake for everyone. I made a note to talk to Sylvia at the bakery and ask if I could borrow her kitchen for a while in exchange for some of my chocolates.

Katie would do the decorations. We were going to have an old-fashioned barn dance, complete with hay bales, a stage that Stash's farmhands would build for the occasion, and long tables full of food.

"I'll do the party favors," Caroline said.

I turned to look at her. We were expecting probably five hundred people. "Party favors? That would be really expensive, Caroline." I thought of her clutching her coupons.

"Don't worry. I'll take care of it." She nodded her head, her right eye not blinking much at all, her face at peace. "I'd love to do it."

I opened my mouth, shut it again. Frugal Caroline, who had made her living from doing psychic readings and selling breads and vegetables and fruits at the farmer's market, was going to do party favors?

So it was.

We were set.

Dean was in Portland working, but when I got home, I took a deep breath and called his office in the city. We had not had more passionate interludes when he came to Golden on the weekends. In fact, he hadn't even tried to kiss me much, and I certainly couldn't blame him. Being the pathetic emotional wreck I am, it would only be a matter of time before he gave up. The giant manila envelope I received in the mail today filled with about a hundred blank sheets of white paper had only tipped me farther into the pathetic emotional wreck zone.

Still, this once, I would try to be courageous. I would try not to let the fear that I could feel creeping from my toes up my legs prevent me from doing something I wanted to do.

"Dean Garrett's office," the perky voice at the other end said.

"Could I speak with Dean Garrett, please?"

"He's in a meeting. Can I have him call you back?" Still perky. I pictured someone young and beautiful and sleek and sophisticated. I felt sick. What in the world was I doing calling someone like Dean Garrett? I was insane. I thought about hanging up.

"I'm sorry. Ma'am? Are you still there?"

"Yes . . . uh . . . could you tell him that Julia Bennett called?"

There was silence on the other end of the line.

"Julia Bennett?"

"Yes, my number is—"

"One moment, please, Ms. Bennett," Perky interrupted. "He's available."

And in exactly one moment Dean picked up the phone.

"Julia," he said, his voice entering through my ear, then my brain, until it lodged, I'm sure, somewhere in my vagina. Oh, the man was so, so hot.

"Dean," I squeaked. "How are you?"

"I'm better now." He chuckled. "It's good to hear your voice. You've never called me before."

"Yes . . . I mean, no, I haven't."

"Is something wrong? Is that why you're calling? How's Lydia?" I heard the instant concern in his voice.

"Oh, she's doing well. Tires more easily, but she's fine.

She told Mrs. Taylor at the bank yesterday that she had always thought the woman was too much of a priss and needed to liven up a bit before she died. Then she dragged her out to Mike's Saloon, and they both got sloshed. Mrs. Taylor had a great time. She even tried the karaoke machine and sang a love song while Aunt Lydia danced. Apparently Mrs. Taylor got a standing ovation from the other people in the bar."

"They didn't drive, did they?"

"Oh no. Mike took Aunt Lydia's keys from her. She didn't notice. Then he called Stash. Stash came with Dave and Scrambler and Katie, and pretty soon they were all trying out the karaoke machine. And then other people in town heard what was happening, and pretty soon Mike's is hopping and it's only about four o'clock in the afternoon. Mike invited them to come back the next day, too."

I could hear Dean laughing in the background. "That certainly sounds like a better day than what I'm having here."

"What's going on there?"

He paused, then told me. He was involved in a trial, the defense attorney was a dick, the media had got wind of it and wouldn't stop calling him, he couldn't wait to see the defendant in jail. . . .

"So, sweet Julia, I know you've called for a reason and not just to chat, although I will say right now you are always welcome to call me anytime you want. In fact, if you want to call me again soon and breathe over the phone, I would appreciate that, too, as then I would know you think of me, if only a little, when I'm not in Golden."

"No, I . . . well, I will. . . . What I mean is that I'm not going to call you to breathe over the phone, but maybe we can chat tomorrow . . . well, not tomorrow." *Oh, I am an idiot. Please stop blabbering*, I told myself. I felt sick, scared to death, my throat tightening as if a metal vise were squishing it. I told him about Aunt Lydia's surprise birthday party. "And, well, we don't have to . . . I mean, I don't want you to feel like you have to say yes . . . and you probably would rather bring someone else . . . but, well, I was wondering . . . if you wanted to . . ." I was dying.

"Oh, just say it, Julia." I could almost see him smiling.

I took this huge, mongo-sized breath. "Dean . . ." another breath before my lungs completely collapsed in fear. "Dean, would you go with me to Lydia's birthday party?"

I heard nothing but silence.

"Dean? Are you still there?"

He sighed. "I'm savoring the moment, darling, just savoring the moment."

"What?"

"I'm imprinting this moment in my head forever."

"This moment?"

"Yes. This moment. I want to remember every little detail about it. Where I'm sitting, what I'm doing, what you said, how you said it."

"Why do you have to remember this?" I took a trembling breath. Simply thinking about Dean Garrett made me quiver.

"Well, I want to get it exactly right."

I sighed, then laughed. Felt myself blush. Why the torture?

"Are you going to say yes or no? Surely you have better things to do than this? You know, people to sue, papers to file, depositions to run, other attorneys to yell at . . ."

"When our grandchildren ask, I want to tell them exactly what happened when their grandma asked me out. Down to the littlest, sweetest detail."

Our grandchildren. That would imply children first. Children with Dean Garrett. Now, life wouldn't get sweeter than that.

But I couldn't imagine that could ever happen. I'd have to get rid of the Dread Disease. I'd have to learn how to breathe like a normal person. I'd have to make sure my ex-fiancé didn't fling *me* into a tree like a dead white wedding dress and leave me to die.

"They'll love the story," Dean continued. "I know it."

I would love the story. "But what about the party?"

"What about it?"

I took a deep breath, the smile I could never control around Dean finally reaching my lips. "You want me to ask you again, don't you?"

"Yes, as a matter of fact, I do."

I took another deep breath, but this time I laughed. "Dean Garrett, do you want to go with me to Lydia's birthday party? Please?"

"Yes. I do."

"Good," I said, very little breath in my body left, but I was so happy I was tingling. "Very good. Thank you."

"You're welcome. And, Julia? I do, also."

"You do?" The man confused me often. In fact, I could often barely think around him.

"Yes. I do." He paused. "I'm practicing ahead of time."

My ex-white wedding dress fluttered into my mind like a ghost, but I banished it quickly. If I ever did get married again—*if*—I would wear red. Bright, happy, freeing, bold red.

It was almost impossible to think that so many people could keep Aunt Lydia's surprise birthday party a surprise. But miracles do happen, and the town of Golden experienced one that week. Aunt Lydia was clueless about the surprise party.

Everyone else was in a tizzy, especially about what to give Lydia for a present. Although Stash, Dave, Marie, Scrambler, Katie, Caroline, and I had made it a point to call everyone and invite them, and ask them to bring a side dish to share, we had specified that people were not to bring gifts.

No one listened to that part.

When Stash and Dave went to the liquor store to talk to Pat Haines about the beer for the party, they could barely leave. Pat is tall and thin and wears glasses without any rims.

He runs a book club here in Golden. The women love him because he acts just like one of them. Although he sells beer and hard liquor, he's a major wine connoisseur, and he had decided a special bottle of wine for Lydia would make the perfect gift.

"I've got a Riesling in the back, at least ten years old, and I'll be bringing that to Lydia as my gift." Pat then put a hand over his heart, Dave told me later, and said, "No, I've changed my mind. Not that one." His face scrunched in concentration, his glasses lifting a bit off his nose. "I have a pinot noir that's twelve years old. That one would be much better—the grapes were perfect that year. No! I've changed my mind. Not that one." His face scrunched up again. "I will give her the Riesling from 1972. A splendid wine, the very best. No! That one won't do, it simply won't do." Face scrunched again, he put a hand to the bridge of his nose. "It will be the chardonnay. . . . No! I have a better one than that, how could I forget?" He moaned.

Stash told me he and Dave left Pat in an absolute tizzy, anguishing over which wine would be absolutely the best for the best damn poker player in the West.

When I went to town the next day, I was accosted.

"Do you think she would like my jams?" asked Becky Pines, a tall, thin woman with three degrees from a top notch university who had decided she preferred farm life to corporate life. "You do? Then what kind? I have strawberry and blueberry and raspberry. Does she have a preference? Two cases of each, then? Three?"

I told her it wasn't necessary to bring a gift.

"Of *course* it's necessary!" Becky looked at me as if I'd told her I would be needing her left arm for about three years. "That woman is one of my best friends. So, back to my jams. I thought I'd put them all in a basket with a giant ribbon. Or do you think a silver bucket would be better? More in keeping with the farm theme of the party?"

I told her I liked the bucket idea to make things easy.

"I need a word, lickety split with you, Julia!" Geoff Miles interrupted. Becky walked off muttering to herself. Geoff was an expert wood carver. He could make absolutely anything. He could also sing, often bursting into song in the middle of the town's square. He had a deep baritone, had even spent time on the stage in his younger years, so he always drew a crowd. "I need to talk to you about Lydia's gift. I was thinking that I would make her a new bench for her porch in the shape of a giant pink pig? What do you think?"

I thought it was a fabulous idea, I told him, but he didn't need to bring a gift. . . .

"Oh, that's ridiculous. I would never come to a birthday party for Lydia without a gift. I love her. So, now, all is wonderful! You like the idea of a giant pink pig bench? I thought I'd paint an apron over the pink pig, just like the one that she wears, you know the red one with the chickens on it? At night her and Stash can sit out there and look at the stars and argue in peace. . . . Now, my girlfriend, Sarah—you do know Sarah?"

I nodded. Sarah was tall and willowy, an ex-stockbroker who had had a nervous breakdown and was now a happy seamstress. She made beautiful pillows and tablecloths and curtains and sold them in the pharmacy.

"Well! Sarah's making a blanket that will match the bench. Stash and Lydia can put the blanket over their legs when they're sitting out on the porch. What do you think of that?" He clapped his hands, smiled gleefully.

I thought that was wonderful, so I hugged him, gave him a kiss for Sarah.

Corinne Mathers caught up to me in the aisle of the pharmacy. I was holding a tube of vaginal irritation cream in my hand. "Julia, dear, tell me. I'm going to embroider a pillow for Aunt Lydia and I don't know what she would like better. I could embroider a rooster, chickens, a barn. Or all three. I could even take a snapshot of her home and embroider that, I am just a wreck. I can't decide!"

Corinne had seven daughters. Her husband, Gavin, had been the financial officer of a local factory and lost his job when it closed. He was now doing whatever odd jobs he could find. I knew that Stash had had him look at his own books at the farm. Gavin worked hard, he was honest, he was kind. He was simply a victim of the economy.

But back to the seven daughters. I could not imagine how Corinne would have time to embroider a pillow. "Corinne, people really aren't supposed to bring gifts—"

"Nonsense. Everyone is bringing a gift. But what do you think of my pillow idea?"

I smiled at her, I couldn't help it. She was so sweet and so eager. "Whatever you do will be lovely, but I don't want you to have to work all night. Embroidering a pillow takes so much time. . . ."

"Nonsense again! My girls are sewing the pillow as we speak. I'll make the design, and then we're embroidering in shifts. A wonderful project!"

"Well . . ." I said and thought for a few seconds. "Maybe the house design?"

"Perfect! We're on it right now, Julia. And, dear, this type"—she reached behind my head and chose a different vaginal irritation medicine—"this type works much better. Trust me and my daughters. We know our vagina medicine. See you Friday!"

Friday arrived with the people of Golden almost dancing with excitement, and Aunt Lydia in happy ignorance.

On that same Friday a dead cat also arrived at our home in a box for me, and I promptly ran to the bathroom, threw up, then endured another episode of the Dread Disease. When I was lying flat on the floor, my freezing-cold face pressed to the cold tile and could actually move again, I did so, crawling out to the front room, where I had dropped the box, grateful that Shawn and Carrie Lynn were in school.

I put the lid on the box, but it tumbled from my hands twice more as I cried for the poor cat. With eyes so blurry with tears I could barely see, I took the box to the very edge of Lydia's property, along with a shovel, and buried it.

The cat's neck had been slit with a wire.

Inside the box was another white envelope, but this time inside there was a note.

It said, "Missing you."

I had run my paper route, then hurried back to the barns, where I met Stash. He had insisted that Aunt Lydia stay in bed for the morning to celebrate her birthday, and then he would be taking her out on a "hot date" in a neighboring town. I had taken the day off from the library and was glad of it. Ms. Cutter was closing early so she could come to the party, too. She had, of course, bought Aunt Lydia a whole new stack of classics—along with a bookbag with her name sewn on it.

Stash would bring Aunt Lydia to the barn later that evening with the excuse that he had a present there for her.

"She'll probably think I've bought her a tractor," he muttered, shaking his head, as he and I moved through the barns, the morning sun shining through the cracks. The ladies clucked at us as we took their eggs.

"I hope not," I said. "Johnny Cain is already bringing her one of his, complete with a giant red ribbon wrapped around the whole thing. He says she needs it for her back field."

Stash shook his head. "I take care of her back field. You know what I got that woman for her birthday?"

I shook my head.

"This." He placed the basket of eggs he held on the ground, then reached into the upper pocket of his overalls. I caught my breath.

The diamond on that ring was huge.

After a quick shower, I told Aunt Lydia I was going to see Dean, who was arriving this evening to be my date for the party. It was the first lie I had ever told to Aunt Lydia, but I couldn't think of any other excuse that she wouldn't see through. She would think that the reason I looked uncomfortable was because she believed, and rightly so, that Dean had taken control of my feminine hormones and estrogen-plagued brain cells.

She smiled at me from her bed and nodded with approval, her bald head gleaming in the light. "Good for you, girl!" she said, nice and loud. She was having a good day, her old energy back. "Dean Garrett is a real man. He's like your chocolate fudge batter. Delicious to feel, nice and silky and warm. Delicious to taste. And when you leave it alone, it hardens up perfectly. Plus, it's got a good shelf life."

I nodded. Yes, Dean was a bit like my chocolate fudge.

"I've told you before that he has tapped your inner womanly power source. But you have something that you must banish from your life! Banish it!" I had made Shawn and Carrie Lynn buttermilk pancakes before school, and Aunt Lydia was eating a stack of them now. She brought her fork and knife up to punch the air with conviction.

"What? What is it that I have to banish?"

"Fear! You have fear. You're scared of Dean Garrett, scared of yourself, scared of your past and your future. Fear runs rampant, like raging she-dogs, through your body."

I thought about that. But not for long. Those raging she-dogs were yapping and barking at me in alarm that I had to finish icing a bunch of cakes down at Sophie's Bakery, and, raging dogs or not, I was going to get it done. "You're right, Aunt Lydia. I do have fear running like raging she-dogs through me."

She dropped her fork and knife, hugged me close. She smelled like buttermilk and vanilla and coffee and a bit of pot. I hugged her back. "And I don't blame you one bit, Julia. Your childhood consisted of one nightmare after another." She kissed me on the cheek, then spoke, for the first time, at less than full volume. "Dean Garrett is a good man,

Julia. I've known him for years, I've watched him, I've listened to him. He loves you. He can't take his eyes off you when you're in the same room with him. He won't ever hurt you."

I nodded, my throat closing up as emotions threatened to turn me into a ball of tears.

God, how I love my Aunt Lydia.

"And he looks like he's got big *cojones*," she whispered. "That'll be fun in bed."

I had a zillion errands to run for the party, and I didn't have time to cry. So I wiped my eyes on the way out the door and told myself to buck up.

"Do I look like a cowgirl?" Carrie Lynn tipped her little face up to mine. With a red cowboy hat, a plaid shirt, jeans, and cowboy boots, all bought for her by Ms. Cutter for the party, I had to admit she was a dead ringer for a cowgirl. Ms. Cutter had embroidered on the brown vest, "Smart Cowgirls Read Books."

"You sure do, honey," I told her, setting her up on one of the bales of hay that had been placed strategically around the barn for the party. "So does your brother." I picked Shawn up and set him right next to Carrie Lynn, then snapped a photo. They both smiled without being asked.

At first, they had been stiff and uncomfortable when Stash or Aunt Lydia or I took their photo. No one ever had in the past. But they had gotten used to it.

They had not gotten "used to" their past. They still had nightmares, and it often took all of us—Stash, Lydia, and me—to calm them down. They refused to sleep in separate rooms, so they were in two twin beds in one room. Carrie Lynn still reached to hold Shawn's hand all the time and was prone to pulling her blanket over her head. They both started at loud noises and seemed to shrink when large men were in the room.

Although their physical injuries were gone, both often seemed nervous, wary, scared. When they went to their bedrooms, we would give them a few minutes, then go in and comfort them as they were inevitably under their covers, arms wrapped around their little bodies, and crying.

They still had scars on their backs from being whipped with a belt by their mother's boyfriend, but the doctors said they would fade. Lydia used a combination of herbs and honey, massaging it into their skin every night. On the nights that she couldn't do it because of how the chemo had made her feel, I did it.

But they had learned to trust Stash and Aunt Lydia, Katie, Caroline, Dave and his wife, Marie, and Scrambler. Scrambler was as kind to them as he was to Katie's kids. He always got out his guitar and sang to the kids when he saw them, making up silly songs. His singing voice was incredible, and the kids loved him.

I snapped another photo. They were so darn cute.

I took a deep breath as I looked around Stash's barn later that afternoon.

We were ready for a great big hoedown.

Stash's farmhands had set up tables and chairs. Katie had spread yellow tablecloths on the rented tables. The centerpieces were pumpkins, gourds, Chinese lanterns, wheat, and fall leaves. She had made scarecrows and propped them up in the hay. Giant pumpkins were mounted around the wooden stage that Stash's workmen had constructed. Orange and yellow streamers drooped through the rafters. A hundred strings of white tiny lights wrapped around posts and beams. A poster Shawn and Carrie Lynn and Katie's kids had painted hung from the center of the barn: HAPPY BIRTHDAY, LYDIA!

I had only two problems. One was that Scrambler had said he would handle the music, but I had seen not hide nor hair of him. The second was that I had not talked to or seen Caroline for three days.

Katie read my mind. "Where the heck is Caroline?"

I shook my head. And then we heard it. The wheezing and coughing and burping of Caroline's car.

We rushed out to meet her. Behind her she was pulling a small trailer.

"Whew! I'm here in the nick of time," she said, her face bright and cheery. She wore a red dress, cowboy boots, and a cowboy hat. "Come back and see what I got for party favors."

I looked at Katie, and she looked at me. Katie had on one of Scrambler's cowboy hats, jeans that showed off her new-found figure, and a plaid shirt. I was dressed about the same, only I had let just one more button go on my shirt. After all, I did have a date tonight.

Katie leaned in to whisper, "I hope she didn't spend her life savings on this, Julia. I am so worried about this. Caroline does not have money to throw around at all. Not one cent!"

And, if Caroline had had any money to throw around, she surely couldn't have any now. Piles and piles of yellow T-shirts were inside the trunk. Imprinted on the front was "Happy Birthday Lydia!"

Caroline swung around to the trailer, her skirt swishing behind her. "Now come look and see what else I got." She swung open the doors. Out poured hundreds of cowboy hats, all yellow. Imprinted around the edge, "Best Damn Poker Player West of the Mississippi."

"What do you all think?" Caroline asked.

Katie couldn't speak.

I couldn't, either.

But we could laugh, so we did. We laughed when we watched Caroline pull on a T-shirt and hat, we laughed when we pulled on our own, we laughed when we got Shawn and

Carrie Lynn and Katie's kids in their shirts and hats, and we laughed when Dave and Marie and a bunch of ranch hands put theirs on, too.

"This is going to be one shit-kicking good party," Dave said, smiling. "One shit-kicking good party."

Dean showed up later looking so good and tasty in jeans and boots and a denim coat I thought I would soon dissolve into liquid heat. He pulled me behind the barn, then picked a few pieces of hay out of my hair, smiling that yummy smile at me as if I were the only person who currently existed in the galaxy. He hugged me close, kissed my cheek. "Hi, honey."

Honey. You had to love that word.

"Thanks for coming."

"Thanks for inviting me." He kissed me on the lips, warm and gentle, then with more passion. He sighed heavily, lifted his lips from mine. "I've missed you."

I had missed him like I would miss my liver or my kidneys or my heart or my guts, but that didn't sound too romantic, so I settled on, "I missed you, too."

"I'm getting tired of living in Portland."

I was not expecting that, so I just told the truth. "I'm tired of you living in Portland, too."

He nodded, his blue eyes sparkling. "We'll have to fix that soon."

So what's a girl to say? "The air here is better."

He laughed.

"Would you like a shirt and hat?" I held up the shirt and hat I'd grabbed when I saw him. My words came out shaky and nervous, but I was too happy to see him to feel like a gooey fool.

"Yes, sweetheart, I would," he drawled, looking right down at me with those blue eyes of his, so intense, so all-seeing. "Why don't you help me get this shirt on?"

I smiled and tried to leave, because the very thought of

Dean Garrett half naked was—oh—too much yum all at once, but he yanked me into his chest, and I couldn't help myself. I let him mold every curve of my body to him and I kissed that man like I have never kissed another man in my whole life. And when he pulled off his shirt so he could put on Aunt Lydia's yellow Happy Birthday T-shirt and hugged me to him again, I felt like I'd found home against that truly splendid and muscled and hairy chest.

Yes, a great big, warm, secure home.

Right there, right in Dean Garrett's arms.

It is difficult to hide five hundred people in a barn. Even more difficult to get them to be quiet when they're all ready to party and wearing new bright yellow T-shirts and hats, but we did it.

We heard Stash's truck, and I shushed everybody, and everybody shushed everybody else, and, finally, when those car doors slammed, everyone was quiet and we could hear Stash and Lydia come into the darkened barn.

The last thing I heard was Aunt Lydia saying, "Oh, you old Stash. Whatever are we doing out here? Did you buy me a tractor?"

And then someone plugged in those sparkling white lights, and someone else hit the drums, and hundreds of people leaped up and yelled, "Surprise!"

It was priceless.

Aunt Lydia's mouth dropped practically to her shoes. She stood there, staring at all of us in our bright yellow Happy Birthday shirts and yellow cowboy hats, proclaiming her the boss of all things poker.

"Well, I'll be damned," she said, tears flooding her eyes. "I'll be double damned."

And damned or not, we all sang, "Happy Birthday" to her, not once, not twice, but three times for good luck, as she had sung to me every summer when I came out to see her.

She threw her fists up in the air, shaking them in victory when we finished, and cried some more. And then, like a giant yellow blob, hundreds of people rushed to wish Aunt Lydia a happy, happy, *happy* birthday.

"Where is Scrambler?" Katie asked, a worried look in her eyes, as she scanned the barn, filled with people already having a shit-kicking good time. "This is not like him, not at all. When he says he's coming over, he comes. He's the most reliable person I've ever met."

I was getting nervous, too. Not because I was worried about the music. We had CDs, great country music, already blaring through the barn, but Katie was right. When Scrambler said something was going to get done, it got done.

But then again, timing is everything, and Scrambler knew that, too.

In a large barn, filled with hundreds of people it would be almost impossible to get their attention, but one by one they froze as those barn doors slammed open not two seconds later.

No one recognized Scrambler at first. He had a cowboy hat pulled down low over his head and dark glasses for effect. Behind him were eight people. Five of them later made up the band; three were backup singers.

Now, we all knew Scrambler had secrets. And one of those secrets happened to be that he had grown up with a best friend in Idaho named Bryce Williams, although Scrambler knew him as Duncan Davis. Anyhow, Bryce liked to sing, and pretty soon Bryce had a recording contract and a few hit songs, and now he sang them like there was no tomorrow right there in that barn for Aunt Lydia, and we danced the night away.

Old Agnes pulled her sister Thelba's wheelchair out to the middle of the dance floor and danced around it while Thelba danced with her arms. Dave danced with Marie. The kids danced with each other. Katie stole a couple of dances with Scrambler when he himself wasn't singing along with Bryce. I danced with Dean, his blue eyes rarely straying from mine. Men did the hoedown together, women swung each other around. People danced in groups and pairs and alone. And everyone danced with Aunt Lydia. In fact, she led the bunny hop, her special pink cowboy hat bouncing right around that barn.

And at 10:00, when Stash stood on the stage, we had all determined, like Dave had said, it was the best shit-kicking party any of us had ever been to.

Stash took Lydia's hands in his own. He towered over her, his shoulders huge, his back ram-rod straight, and his face more serious than I had ever seen it.

"Lydia Jean Thornburgh, I have loved you since the moment I met you twenty years ago. And even though you are stubborn and have never thought it right to keep even a single opinion to yourself, you are the most beautiful woman I have ever met. And tonight you are more beautiful than you have ever been."

"Oh, Stash, you old fool," Lydia croaked, whacking him on the arm, then readjusting her hat.

"I am an old fool, Lydia, and I love you. We've walked through life together for twenty years, and they have been, by far, the happiest twenty years I have ever had. I cannot imagine life without you because it wouldn't be worth nothing. I have asked you to marry me once a year since we met, and you have always turned me down because you are so damn feisty and independent. But I want to ask you one more time. Here. In front of all of our friends and your niece, Julia."

So I'm crying, and all the women around me are crying, and even a few men look choked up, like Dave, and like Caleb Dirks, who spent thirty years in the army and looks like a grizzly bear, and Michael Sparks and Stewart Adams, who are marines just back from Iraq.

Stash, still holding Aunt Lydia's hands, got down on one

knee in front of her. "Lydia Jean Thornburgh, would you please, please, you stubborn woman, please marry me for once and for all, forever?"

And Lydia stood there, shaking her head, laughing and crying at the same time. "Well, a man who wants to marry a gal with no hair and a face like a skeleton must be one great man, indeed. So, yes, Stash, after twenty years, I will. I will marry you."

And the cheer that went up from that crowd was so loud the kids put their hands over their ears, but we kept on cheering. Stash got out the ring box, and he put that ring with the gigantic diamond on Aunt Lydia's finger, and she cried some more, and Stash cried, and the marines cried, and then he hugged her and twirled her around, and we danced the rest of the night away.

Sometimes, for a moment, life is truly beautiful.

❦ 23 ❧

The kids had long been asleep on hay bales when Stash, Aunt Lydia, Dean, and I finally left. Stash and Dean carried the kids to the cars and drove them back to Aunt Lydia's.

There was one more gift left to unwrap. It had been delivered that day, and I had hid it in my back closet.

We settled the kids into bed, and I poured a little wine for all of us, then brought the large, flat present from Lara out and put it on the wicker coffee table in front of Lydia and Stash. I must say that she looked rather regal with that bald head. When she was done with chemo I was going to suggest she keep her head shaved.

"The diamond on this ring is too damn big, Stash," Lydia said. She gave him a kiss. "Too damn big. I can barely lift my hand. How am I going to drive the tractor and shovel Melissa Lynn's shit?"

"You're not going to shovel shit or drive a tractor until I say you can, Lydia, so just hold your horses on that part. You're also going to bed in five minutes, so unwrap that present from Lara damn quick. You can unwrap the other hundreds of presents another day."

For once, Aunt Lydia didn't yell at Stash to quit telling her what to do. She clapped her hands together with great glee. "It's from Lara, my sweet Lara, the woman who is in search of her soul." She ripped that paper right off, and then her hands stilled.

Stash leaned forward, as did Dean and I.

Lara had used every ounce of talent she had to paint a picture of Stash and Aunt Lydia sitting together on the porch outside Lydia's front door. Stash's arm was around Lydia, their faces smiling and relaxed and happy.

It was stunning. An exact likeness, the painting radiating the love, the memories, and the history that the two of them had together.

"Happy Birthday to the most courageous woman I have ever met," Lara had written, right on the painting. "I love you. Lara."

"It's perfect," Aunt Lydia said with great reverence. "She has captured my womanhood and your manly manner, Stash. The testosterone and the estrogen, the essence of the woman and the soul of the man."

"Yes," said Stash, patting her hand, his voice gruff. He took a swipe at his eyes. "She has done all that."

Aunt Lydia cocked her head to look at the painting. She looked frail next to Stash. She had lost weight and lost her hair, and her body was fighting like hell to save itself, but I knew who was the stronger of them.

"Lara has captured one more thing, Stash," she said, a smile lighting her face and transforming it into lines of gentleness, a look that my Aunt Lydia rarely wore.

"What's that?"

"The love we have. She captured the love."

The blank letters kept coming. I took it upon myself to practice shooting my gun once a day. At least.

* * *

I knew there was nothing he could do, but I went anyhow.

I had always found Golden's police chief, Carl Sandstrom, to be somewhat intimidating. People in town joked that if you jaywalked and he caught you, you could expect a ticket.

No one got off with Sandstrom. Not the fire chief's son who drove drunk. Not Allison Baker, who worked at the supermarket and who slugged her husband on a regular basis. When Sandstrom found out, he locked her up. "She's gotta be locked up," he told Lydia later, who then told me. "We gotta lock that woman up until her husband comes to his senses and leaves her. No one deserves to be pummeled, especially not little Clark Baker. Man wouldn't hurt a spider."

It was even reputed that he wrote his wife a ticket for staying too long in a city parking space one time, but no one seemed to know if that was true or not.

Yes, the law was the law with Chief Sandstrom, and everyone had to follow it. Everyone.

At Aunt Lydia's party, though, I saw a less intimidating man. All four of his children still lived in Golden. As the economy worsened and one after another of his boys lost their jobs, the rest of the family rallied around them. All four boys were now commuting long distances to work so the family core wouldn't break up. There were fourteen grandchildren.

Watching that big man dance with his wife, Julie, and their children and grandchildren had been heartwarming for me; I thought that any man who loved his wife and granddaughters that much might be sympathetic to an increasingly paranoid and very panicked woman like me.

So I called to make an appointment. Margaret Zimball, the longtime secretary, put me on hold—I assumed to look at the chief's calendar.

"Come on in now, sugar," she told me. "He'd be happy to see you."

So I came on in, and there I sat in front of Chief Sandstrom, who had spent twenty years in the navy and had had a short career as an amateur boxer. He was perfectly groomed, his black and white hair brushed right down, his uniform flawlessly ironed.

And I told him.

I told him about running out on my wedding day. I expected to see judgment in his eyes, but he just nodded. I told him why I'd run, that I'd been hit one too many times. "Wise idea," he said, his voice like a bass drum. "Late, but still wise for you to take action. No innocent being deserves to be pummeled unless they're a boxer."

I told him about the blank letters, the dead cat, the dead chicken. The letter that said "Missing you." I told him that I knew Robert was on his way.

And I told him that I didn't think he could do a thing to stop Robert.

"Young lady, if there is even the smallest thing I can do for you, you are to consider it done. I don't take to wife beaters, or husband beaters. Now, I don't suppose you have a photograph of him."

I did not, but I referred him to the Web site of the family business.

"Is that him?" the chief asked when he had pulled it up.

I didn't want to look, but I did, and instantly felt vomit rising in my throat. I sank into a chair, nodding.

"He's one pretty-looking boy, isn't he?" The chief eyed me. "You just relax now. Margaret, would you bring our friend Julia some coffee and a doughnut?"

Margaret came in with the coffee and doughnut, giving me a little hug.

"Have you told Dean about this?"

I shook my head.

"Why not?"

I felt my face heat up but decided on the truth. "I'm embarrassed. I don't want to involve him."

He nodded. "You need to tell him."

"I can't."

"Here's why you should, Julia. Dean Garrett is a big-time attorney in Portland. He'll know what legal steps you can take. I'm going to handle the criminal end of this, which means I'm going to call his hometown police station, I'm going to get someone to talk to him at his office or at home, and I'm going to report back to you. But Dean can write some nasty legal letters, too, that hopefully will get this creep off your back."

No, no legal letters of any kind from anyone would get Robert off my back, but it was a nice thought. "I would tell Dean but . . ."

"But what?" The chief prodded. Margaret patted my shoulder.

"I'm so embarrassed." How to say it? I didn't want to put Dean in the position of rescuing me. I didn't want to have to be the type of woman who needed rescuing. Our relationship was too new. I didn't want to involve him in my messy, messy past. It was too much to ask of anyone, anyhow. Robert's family was rich and powerful.

"Tell Dean. I'll call back east and get things moving on this end. This is a crime. It's a crime of harassment and intimidation, and it's a crime against the cat that was killed, and if there's one thing I've learned in this business it's that hurting animals enrages the public like nothing else. Robert's family is not going to like the publicity that this generates."

I thanked him, held out my hand. He gave me a hug. Margaret gave me a hug.

"I'm sending Doug over to your house today. You give him the letters, show him where you buried the cat. We'll need all that when we go after this guy's ass."

It was only later that Chief Sandstrom told me that as soon as I left he immediately got on the phone to talk to an acquaintance of his in Boston. His acquaintance found that Robert, unbeknownst to me, had been kicked out of no fewer than three elite prep schools, had spent some time as a teen in juvenile hall, and had been headed for jail on assault charges against two women when both of them mysteriously moved out of state and refused to talk to investigators.

"The women were beat to shit," his police buddy said. "Both landed in the hospital for a week. Broken ribs, broken bones in the face, internal bleeding. That they didn't die was a miracle. One managed to pull out her cell phone and call nine-one-one after he dumped her under a bridge. The other was found by a bum."

"A bum?" the chief asked.

"Yep, a bum. Stanfield dumped her body in a trash heap—probably thought she was dead—and a bum looking for food found her. He was hysterical, apparently it triggered something from his experience in 'Nam, but he still managed to get the police and ambulance there."

"And then that was that?"

"Apparently. That family has money and power. Has almost single-handedly put every Republican candidate in office in their area. Without their backing and support, the candidates didn't have a chance. So Stanfield got off. Twice. Money exchanged hands, the girls were paid off, dirty chapter closed."

"That isn't how it works out here."

"Maybe. Maybe not. Bottom line, that guy's on the loose, and if you've got a woman out there he's gunnin' for, you better get some protection. This guy's a true psychopath."

After a follow-up call, Chief Sandstrom's anxiety rose another ten notches. The chief's acquaintance had begun his preliminary investigation and found that Robert Stanfield III had taken an abrupt vacation from work ten days ago. No one had seen or heard from him since.

Chief Sandstrom later told me his whole body went cold and clammy when he heard this news. He made more calls.

*   *   *

"She isn't planning on coming back, is she?" Jerry Keene, Lara's husband asked, his face bleak. The lights in Aunt Lydia's dining room were dimmed, a few candles in the center of the table offering a soft, flickering glow that revealed the hard, harsh angles of Jerry's face. He had lost weight in the weeks since Lara had left, and a hopeless look had set up camp in his eyes.

Stash, Aunt Lydia, and I had all read the article in the magazine that Jerry brought us. A week had passed since the barn party, and when Jerry dropped by and saw the painting Lara had given Stash and Aunt Lydia, he had had to look away, his jaw tight.

A two-page spread in some art/literary magazine in New York City had a feature article on Lara. Her paintings were showcased, there was a biography, in which it was mentioned she was married to a minister and was the daughter of a minister, and then the writer of the article had darn near swooned in admiration—which, of course, he should. I had seen the talent oozing out of Lara's work myself.

Brilliant. The most up-and-coming, artist in New York City. Burst on the scene . . . paintings all sold out before opening night. . . .

I recognized the paintings as ones from the attic.

Jerry explained, "After she left, a shipping company contacted me and came and got all the paintings. They even wrapped them all up. They were very nice. They had no idea they were ripping my insides out." He brushed a hand through his hair. "I take that back. I think when I leaned against the wall and cried, they might have had a clue. One of them offered me a cigarette. I actually smoked it." He sighed.

I covered Jerry's hand with my own. I had heard that he was working all the time. Even the parishioners in his church were becoming alarmed. He looked ill, positively ill.

Shave all that brown curly hair off his head and you'd think he was going through chemo along with Lydia.

Aunt Lydia was wearing a pink cotton scarf over her head that Old Agnes and her sister Thelba had knitted for her, but only because, she told me, it was "so cold it could freeze a pig's tail right off his pig butt."

I glanced down at Lara's photo in the magazine. Her blond hair flowed over one of her shoulders like liquid gold. She wore a black shiny tank top, a pink crocheted poncho, black leather pants, and knee-high black boots. She looked like Lara, and yet she didn't. She wasn't smiling and didn't look particularly happy, which would, of course, make her even more appealing to New Yorkers. They like angst and despair and misery to drive their artists. Lara looked sexy, but not warm.

I must say I was darn proud of Lara. She had broken out of the tight, jail-like, constrictive cell she had been brought up in, then she had left a situation that she could no longer bear. I must say I related to the woman.

And yet, Jerry was a hell of a catch. Even Lara had told me that he was always kind and loving and thoughtful. She had told me he was great in bed, and her only complaint was that he wanted sex all the time. "He'll do anything to get it, too," she said once, laughing. "He makes dinner with three courses, gives me a massage beforehand, brings me coffee and omelets stuffed with every sautéed vegetable under the sun. . . . Oh, yes, the man really knows how to get laid."

I couldn't imagine a woman ever letting someone like Jerry go. Watching him sink day by day further into a black pit of depression made me feel like I was getting hit with a sledgehammer in the head every day.

"Her father keeps calling me. Lara won't return his calls. He just rants and raves. He swears it's her brother's gay influence that has done this to Lara. He thinks her brother has seduced her into 'his lifestyle.' " Jerry shook his head in disbelief. "Her mother calls me and cries."

I thought of the horrible things Lara had said about her father, how he had raised her with the Bible in one hand and a belt in the other, how her mother had stood by and let that domineering man control her daughter as if she were a cow and he the rancher. The mother's cowardice was revolting.

"Two weeks ago he called me and screamed that Lara would go straight to hell unless I exercised my husbandly rights and dragged her back here to the church. 'She needs to submit to you, her husband, submit, submit,' he kept yelling. Then he started quoting the Bible and saying that Lara had always been rebellious despite the hours he had made her pray for forgiveness on her knees as a child. The way he has always treated Lara made me sick, and I couldn't take it anymore."

"So what did you do, son?" Stash asked, pushing a straight shot of Scotch Jerry's way. Jerry nodded politely, but I knew he wouldn't drink it.

"I told him to shut the fuck up."

Shocked silence greeted his announcement.

Jerry laughed, but it was a bitter, dry laugh, like lemon mixed with dead leaves "That man is a tyrant, her mother a weak, sniffling ghost of a woman, and I swear, *I swear*, I will not let those two near Lara again if she ever comes back. I moved her away from her father's constant criticisms and her mother's subservient attitude because I didn't want those two screwed-up, hypocritical people to be able to hurt Lara anymore."

I didn't know what to say. Jerry had tried to protect Lara from her parents. I wonder if Lara even knew.

"I don't know how Lara even turned out how she did. Kind and caring and loving and smart and open-minded. Not judgmental and sanctimonious like both her parents. Her father has probably turned more people off of Christianity than on with his constant ravings about hell and sin and wrath. He is the epitome of what we don't need in back of a pulpit."

"Son, you didn't say that to him, did you?"

"Yes, I damn well did, Stash. He needed to hear it. He needed to know that he cannot think of his daughter as his own personal emotional slave, that his parenting was both abusive and controlling, which is why neither his sons nor his daughter wants anything to do with him. He needed to know that God does not want us to try to bring people to His Son through fear and manipulation and anger. He needs to preach of a kind and loving God, a God full of forgiveness. He needs to help people to live more Christ-like lives, with generosity and love, not talk about how we're all headed to hell unless our thoughts align exactly with his."

"What did the man say after that?"

"Nothing. He couldn't think of anything to say by the time I was done. No one has ever spoken to him like that, I'm sure, and I haven't before out of respect for his position as Lara's father, but I couldn't hold back any longer. The man is a hate-filled, obsessed, sick shit-head."

"So then you hung up?" Aunt Lydia asked.

"I hung up after I told him that I also felt that cutting off his son for being gay was sinful, that the hatred and disgust with which he had treated his son was exactly the opposite of how Christ would have treated him. That his son could no more help being gay than I could help loving his daughter. That his son was one of the kindest people I had ever known." Jerry got up and paced in front of the table, his face flushed. "Did you know that Lara's brother and his partner have a massive toy drive every year for one of the children's hospitals in New York? Anyhow, I told him that his son was living a far more Christ-like life than he was, and he could shove his self-righteous anger right up his butt because I didn't ever want to hear from him again."

"And then?" Stash asked.

"I hung up."

There was silence for several seconds. Then Lydia nodded, raised both hands, and started clapping. I joined her. So did Stash.

"You've commandeered your role as a true man, Jerry," said Stash. "You've taken hold of your rights as a husband and told that shit-head to take a hike. Well done, young man, well done."

Jerry shook his head. "I should have done it sooner, should have taken action sooner, and I blame myself for the pain that man has caused Lara. I blame myself for not protecting my wife. I blame myself for not taking action when I could tell Lara wasn't happy. She refused to tell me why, but I should have figured it out. I was too busy to *really* look at my wife. I was too afraid of what I would see."

He stopped and stared at the painting of Stash and Aunt Lydia.

"I blame myself for not letting Lara be Lara."

There was a deep silence at the table when Jerry stopped talking and sank back into his chair. "So what do I do now?"

Stash leaned toward him. "Son, go to her. Go to Lara in New York City. Tell her you love her. Tell her what you've told us. And be prepared to change your life if you have to in order to be with her."

"Stash, she won't even take my calls." Jerry's voice sounded like it was coming from an aching, despairing heart. "I've left messages with her brother and his partner, left messages on her cell phone, and nothing happens. The only time she has ever called back is when I've left messages telling her I'm coming to New York. Then she calls back right away telling me I am not welcome in New York, that she needs time away from me. I've begged, I've pleaded, I've told her I'll leave the ministry, that we'll move and change our lives together, that she can be an artist and I'll get a different sort of job, but nothing works. One time I talked to Steve, her brother's partner, and he started crying because he was so upset about how upset *I* was. Two grown men crying on the phone together who have never even met."

Aunt Lydia, Stash, and I all looked at each other. We were all hoping someone would have an answer here, but no luck.

Jerry leaned back in his chair. "I'm praying about this," he said, so quiet. "I'm praying that I don't go straight out of my mind."

✆ 24 ✇

I was almost ready to give up my oh so glamorous paper route. James, who owned Cool Chocolates in the Pearl District of Northwest Portland could not keep my chocolates in stock, they sold out so quickly, and neither could another store, in the Hawthorne area of Southeast Portland.

The thought of not having to get up at 4:00 in the morning for deliveries was quite tempting, although it would eliminate my morning chats with Dean when he was here for the weekend or on vacations.

But then I thought of that steady money. It wasn't much, but it was a little bit, and I decided not to quit. Chocolate-selling or not, I had been poor, been desperate too many times in my life, and I hated it. I heard once that poverty, or the fear of poverty, never truly leaves a person once it lodges like black sludge in your body, and I believe it.

But the money coming in from my small chocolate business was truly exciting.

"I had a lady in here yesterday who had a vivid and rather ugly fit because this was the third time she'd come by and we'd sold out again of Julia's Chocolates," Penny Grayton said, the owner of the candy shop in the Hawthorne area.

"She took off this huge red hat with feathers on it, then pointed the longest finger I've ever seen in my life right at my head, and told me that she would sue me if I did not get your chocolates in. I am not kidding, Julia. *She threatened to sue me.* I told a few regulars we were getting a shipment of your chocolates in last week, and they were waiting outside the shop when I came to work. Please, Julia, I need more."

"Allrighty, more are coming. Any in particular that you want?" I had expanded my menu to include chocolate tulip-shaped cups with little square chocolates wrapped in gold piled up inside, chocolate champagne glasses, chocolate boxes with pink and yellow wrapped truffles inside and chocolate vases that held candy flowers.

"The penis and boobs chocolates are particularly popular."

I laughed. I had made a mold in the shape of a penis and in the shape of breasts and had shipped a bunch of them off to Penny as a joke. She had thought I was serious and put the phallic symbols and the chocolate boobs in the display case. They sold in the first hour to a woman who couldn't stop laughing as she made her purchases.

Penny told me the woman brought them to a party with her girlfriends that night, and the next morning four of her girlfriends came in to ask for the "penis and boobs chocolates." "It's the only setting where people can come in and say 'penis and boobs' and not get embarrassed. Get started melting that chocolate, Julia."

So I melted. Chunks and chunks of chocolates.

And it was never enough.

Awakening The Baldness In You Psychic Night ended with Caroline curled up in a ball on Aunt Lydia's floor, white as a sheet, pleading for me to leave town, Aunt Lydia trooping down to her basement for a little pot, her bald head gleaming in the light, Katie declaring she was going to make herself gay, and me leaning over a toilet after a massive attack of the Dread Disease.

Even Alphy seemed upset. He didn't even bark at the birds when they flew around the room.

Since "baldness" was the underlying theme of the evening, in honor of Aunt Lydia, she insisted that everyone bring food that was bald.

This threw me, Katie, and Caroline for a loop for a bit but not for long. Being the dessert woman, I made flat, chocolate, round cookies, then created icing faces on them with different colors to represent each of the women. Aunt Lydia's cookies had green eyes, black scarves around their necks to fight off germs, and yellow T-shirts from the barn party. Caroline's cookies had huge green eyes, pink lips, dangling hoop earrings, and a lacy-looking collar. Katie's cookies had a pencil behind one ear to represent the writing she was doing on her romance novel, brown eyes, and a huge smile. I also attached four little iced chocolate cookies to the big ones to represent Katie's kids.

I stared at the cookie I had made of myself. It looked scared.

I shrugged, told myself I was getting used to living with fear. After watching Katie's brave move away from her husband, Lara's escape from a life that suffocated her, and Aunt Lydia's brave fight against cancer, my fears of Robert, the Dread Disease, and my entire future didn't seem too significant.

But Caroline did get me going that night. She arrived looking pale and wan with a black medical patch over her right eye, the eye that always twitched. Caroline was naturally beautiful, and so unaware of it, it sometimes struck me as odd, but it made her more endearing to me, also.

I got a bad feeling in my gut the second I saw her. Perhaps it was the scared-shitless look she sent my way.

"What happened to your eye, Caroline? You look like a pirate dressed in drag," Aunt Lydia said.

We had turned down the lights, as usual, so we could get to know the soul of the woman lurking inside of us, and candles were burning all over the place. Aunt Lydia had kicked Stash out, back to his house for the evening, along with Shawn and Carrie Lynn, who were always delighted to go and visit Stash and Scrambler and Katie's kids.

"I'm having a little problem with my eyes," Caroline said, her gaze shooting to me once again.

That pretty much did it for me. I felt all the air in my lungs flush out like a hose.

"My girl, what's wrong with you?" Aunt Lydia asked, taking the round pan from Caroline and lifting the foil. "Very clever, Caroline! This pizza does look bald! Only cheese, but it smells heavenly. Is there garlic in here, too? A bald pizza—this will be a happy experience for our uteruses, as our uteruses are bald in spirit, also, as no one is with child here." Aunt Lydia sensed the silence then, her head shooting back up. "So what is it, Caroline? Something is amiss. Are you hearing people screaming again? Are you feeling their fear?"

Aunt Lydia wrapped an arm around Caroline, kissed her cheek. "What is it, dear? You must share your problems with women whose inner essences are the same as yours."

Caroline looked right at me, and her body shuddered.

"Oh God!" Aunt Lydia cried, following her gaze, her expression filling with horror. "Oh God, no."

When Katie arrived seconds later, we all went to the living room and sat down on the pillows, Caroline across from me, Aunt Lydia to my left, Katie to my right.

Caroline held my hands in her shaking ones, her one eye huge in her face, and twitching like the light from a lighthouse. It was her right eye that always twitched, but that was covered by the black patch. That her left eye was now twitching too sent a special sliver of terror racing through my steadily weakening body. Not only had all the air left my lungs, my heartbeat was in a dead sprint, my hands were freezing, and my mind was shot. *I am such a wimp, such a wimp, such a wimp,* I thought. *Such a very, very scared wimp.*

Caroline's lips tightened. "Write his name down."

"*What?*"

Katie made a whimpering sound, then found a pen and pad of paper for me. I noticed vaguely that she had lost more weight. You sure couldn't say that Katie Margold was fat anymore. But then the Dread Disease grabbed me again, and I concentrated on writing.

It's funny, but when I was in love with Robert, I used to practice writing his name. Then my name with Robert's last name attached, Julia Stanfield. All the time. It was a hobby. After he hit me or had verbally destroyed my self-esteem— which he did as easily as one might smash a rotten tomato against the side of a barn—it would take me a few days to start writing my new name again, but I always did. The magnetic pull of the escape that Robert offered me from my life was that strong.

But tonight, under the warm glow of candles, I could barely write that name. I wrote a capital "R."

Caroline's tiny, soft moan hit me in the heart like a bullet.

"Are you all right, Caroline?" Aunt Lydia asked. "Maybe you should lay down? You want some vodka?"

Katie hugged me. "Oh! Oh!" she kept saying, "Oh! Oh!"

I wrote the "o." Caroline made a groaning sound.

I wrote the "b." Caroline buried her head in her hands.

I felt like running. Like hiding in Aunt Lydia's basement and smoking pot till I couldn't see anymore.

Aunt Lydia's hands clenched and unclenched, then she leaned over and hugged me. "That's good enough. That's good enough. We know you have to leave."

But, call me sick and a sucker for punishment. I wrote the "e."

Caroline started to sway. I thought about stopping for her but knew she wouldn't want me to.

I wrote the "r," then the "t."

Caroline fell forward, wrapping her arms around her knees, moaning softly.

"Oh! Oh!" Katie cried and tried to pull Caroline into her lap. "Oh! Oh!"

"Julia," Caroline whispered, "You have to leave."

I nodded.

"I can't tell you when he'll be here, but it will be soon. The color around you isn't even purple anymore, it's black. All black. Black, and it's swirling, and it's dangerous. God, it is so dangerous, Julia. I'm seeing a dark building. Your back is turned. I see chickens. You're alone."

I felt like the star in some cheap horror flick. Caroline's hands shook again, Aunt Lydia got up and checked for the fortieth time that her shotguns were in the right places, and Katie burst into tears. How strange could this whole thing get? A psychic with a twitching eye, a bald woman chasing down her guns, and a mermaid-type mother crying.

"I can't leave—"

"Julia, you are leaving," Aunt Lydia declared, wrapping her arms around me. "Stash will let you use one of his trucks, and you can take my thirty-eight and my rifle. Just drive, sweetheart, anywhere. Go to a big city and get lost, and we'll call you when Caroline thinks the threat is gone."

"Oh, Julia," Katie whimpered. "This is awful. You have to go. God, I am going to turn myself gay."

This distracted all of us for a moment. From horror to homosexuality. And I thought I had seen Katie and Scrambler gazing at each other with lust and affection. "You're going to turn yourself gay? Why would you do that? Don't you like the feel of a penis anymore?" Aunt Lydia asked.

Katie shifted, her tears still falling. "I might still like the feel of a penis, but I haven't felt a good penis in years, and men can be so damn scary, so damn hurtful. It's like they exist to make women miserable! Julia can't even get rid of sicko Robert when she comes all the way across the country. Julia, run, *just run*."

Aunt Lydia got up again and handed me a gun. "Remember what I told you, Julia. Shoot to kill. *Shoot to kill*."

Caroline pulled her knees up to her chest, swayed, and then lay down on the floor with Katie clucking over her, stroking her hair.

I would have helped Caroline, too, but by that time my air was completely gone and my vision was blackening on the outsides. I knew I was in faint-mode, but I fought to stay away from that particular abyss.

I vaguely saw Aunt Lydia go downstairs to the basement. When she came back up, she handed me a joint, then slipped one between Caroline's lips and told her to inhale.

We both took long drags.

"I was serious about the part about turning myself gay," Katie said, eating the last of her children in the cookie I had made her.

Caroline, pale and wan, sat in one of the chairs at the table in Aunt Lydia's kitchen. Her left eye was still winking. I didn't even want to think of what her right one was doing, hiding behind the patch.

Aunt Lydia had eaten her bald cookie and was now twining together dried flowers into a wreath for each one of us. "These wreaths will shield us all from dangerous testosterones floating through the air," she declared, dropping three types of ribbon onto the heap of dried flowers. "We will reawaken the fierceness, the strength that lives in our estrogen, and we will conquer the males in our lives." Her hands shook as she worked, but she never stopped.

She made my wreath first, filled with dried lavender and white roses and all three colors of ribbon. When she was done I knew the wreath would cover my entire head.

Caroline took a small puff of the joint we were passing around.

"I don't think I'll ever conquer a male in my life," Katie said. "And I don't think I want to. That's why I think it would be better if I turned gay."

I swallowed hard. It was about the five hundredth time I'd swallowed hard. It was as if Caroline's raw terror had lodged in my throat. I tried to speak. Tried again. "But do you like breasts?" I asked.

I did not particularly like breasts. My whole life men had stared at my breasts with wonder as one might stare at the Grand Canyon. The attention from those men had made me feel cheap and ill and threatened.

Except for Dean. I had to give the man credit. I knew he had seen the size of my knockers, but he didn't make me feel like one giant breast waiting to be fondled and sucked and bitten.

No, Dean had actually seen my mind. Seen me. Heard my thoughts. Heard my fears, my hopes, my endless chatter about my chocolate and my small chocolate business. And he still liked me.

But I had no desire to see other women's breasts or to touch them. I had enough breast in my own life.

"Do I like breasts?" Katie pondered this, then took another puff of the joint. "I'll take a puff for Lara. I feel neutral about breasts, but I have no desire to touch them."

"That would be a problem if you were gay, then," said Aunt Lydia. "Gay women like boobs. If you don't want to touch a boob, I would suggest that you stick with penises." She wrapped another yard of ribbon around my dried wreath.

"I like a good penis," Katie said, contemplating the smoke from the joint with a little too much interest. "But I don't like the man attached to the penis before and after sex. I don't like the beast he becomes. Really, the best type of man would be one with a great penis, enough money so you didn't have to work seventy hours a week, and one who didn't hit and didn't speak, but always smiled and helped around the house."

"You want a man who doesn't speak?" I asked.

"Right. No talking. Ever." She inhaled again. "Unless it's to say hot and romantic things in bed."

"But then you would never be able to hear the words 'I love you,'" Caroline said, taking the joint from Katie. Her hands still trembled. She looked at me with accusation. I knew Caroline had wanted me to leave that instant, but I couldn't. Wouldn't.

Katie looked disgusted. "So what? The words 'I love you' are just that—words. It's so easy to say 'I love you.' It takes less than a second. We say 'I love you' to our pets, to our friends, to the people we work with sometimes. They're words. The way a man acts, sure as day, tells you if he really loves you or not. Is he kind? Is he great to the kids? Does he notice when you're tired and try to do something about that? Does he do something for you even if it inconveniences him? Does he see you as a woman, or as the cleaning lady and baby machine? Does he realize that you have feelings? Most men don't want to rise to the occasion and believe that the women in their lives have any emotional needs. They certainly don't want to address them. That's why I thought I should become gay."

We all nodded. What could we say? I personally had a fiery attraction to Dean Garrett that darn well threatened to eat me alive. My vagina almost always felt on fire—as long as I wasn't dealing with the terror of Robert. But men could be major assholes. Horrible assholes.

Caroline gave me the joint. I almost cried when I looked at her. She looked so fragile. I thought about love. I loved Caroline and Katie and Lara, even though I'd known them for less than a year. They were the best, really the *only* friends I had ever had. But I didn't want to kiss them.

"Julia," Caroline said, rocking herself back and forth, her arms locked around her waist. "If Robert isn't here in

Golden, he'll be here very soon. Very soon. Maybe tomorrow. I feel his hatred, I smell his obsession, I can taste the revenge he wants. He's lost it, completely lost it. His rage is uncontrolled. You are in danger."

I nodded. After Caroline had curled into a ball, and after I had smoked a little pot, I had had to crawl to the toilet and lean my head over it as everything I had eaten that day—and for, seemingly, six years before that—came up. A toilet can feel so cool and soothing, but I generally prefer not to curl around it, although I have experienced that particular position several times before in my life, twice after Robert insisted that I drink more alcohol than I'd wanted to drink.

It was freaky and scary that he'd made me do that, but what was freakier and scarier was that I'd done it.

"I'm not leaving." The words left my mouth before I knew they were even there.

Aunt Lydia's fingers froze over the dried flowers. "Yes, you are, young lady," she snapped. She never snapped.

Katie said, "Oh! Oh! You have to go!"

Caroline's fingers loosened around the joint, and it dropped to the floor. I picked it up, but no one noticed.

"Didn't you hear what I said?" Caroline said. Wink, wink, wink. "He's coming here. He wants to kill you."

Aunt Lydia nodded. "This wreath was meant to protect you as you leave Golden, my dear. *As you leave*. It's to protect you until we see you again, after we've gotten rid of Robert."

"I'm not leaving." I put the joint in the ashtray. I felt ill. What did I mean, *I'm not leaving?* I wanted to scream. I wanted to jump into a pickup and drive at a hundred miles an hour to nowhere, anywhere. I wanted to grab Shawn and Carrie Lynn and hide in a cave. "I'm not leaving."

"You are leaving, young lady," Aunt Lydia said. "Or I will curse you."

I stared at Aunt Lydia. I am not superstitious, but I am not stupid. I did not want to be cursed. She wouldn't really do that, would she?

"You have to leave, Julia," Katie said, tears falling. "I'll watch Shawn and Carrie Lynn for you."

Caroline winked at me again and again and again. "He is coming for you. He is violent and furious. You are in grave danger." Wink, wink. Wink!

I shook my head. As much as I wanted to join an expedition to Antarctica, I couldn't leave. I couldn't leave Aunt Lydia when she was battling cancer. I couldn't leave Shawn and Carrie Lynn, nor would I be able to take them with me. They were not even legally mine yet. And I could not, would not, leave the life I had finally built here.

I liked living in Golden, a place where people knew my name. Some even seemed to like me. I loved living with Aunt Lydia and Stash. I loved this house and the chickens and the pigs. I loved my friends. I loved Dean Garrett. Yes, I loved Dean Garrett. So very, very much.

I loved working at the library, loved Story Hour. I loved how the kids and their parents were always so happy to see me. I loved making and selling chocolate. I even liked my paper route.

I loved that I had a life filled with caring people. I would not abandon them. I would not abandon this life.

I got a little teary then. "I love you all. I know you care. I know you're worried. But I'm not running away from Robert again. No. I. Am. Not. Leaving."

Aunt Lydia protested, but I saw the respect in her eyes, the pride.

Caroline looked like she was about ready to faint again. She dipped a napkin into her water glass and laid it across her forehead.

Katie cried. "Come and live with me, then, on Stash's ranch. Dave and Scrambler will protect you."

"No, thank you, Katie." I reached for her hand. "I'm staying here. Right here."

Aunt Lydia wound the flowers through the wreath, her fingers flying. "Damn well better get this wreath done for you, then. I'm going to imbed a knife in between the flowers, though, so you'll always have it, along with the gun I insist you carry every day from now on."

"You need to be careful, Julia, very careful. All the time." Katie said. "I'm so scared for you! I'm so scared!"

"Some men only understand the power of a bullet," Aunt Lydia said. "Only the power of a bullet."

I nodded. Robert would be one of those men. And yet I hated the idea of a gun. I hated the idea of anyone, even any animal, getting hurt, and I wasn't sure I could shoot Robert. He was dangerous and sick, but shoot your ex-fiancé? Kill a person?

"We will persevere!" Aunt Lydia interjected, her voice strong. "We will win this fight, female against male, good against evil, estrogen against dick-headedness!"

"Or, we can just shoot them," Katie said, wiping her eyes. "Just shoot the fuckers."

I had never heard Katie use that language before. Neither had Aunt Lydia, and her hands stilled. Even Caroline looked like she was coming back from the dead.

We laughed. And laughed and laughed. Sometimes life is so lousy, so very, very bad, that all you can do is laugh.

And so we did.

Due to Caroline's little premonition, Stash was taking me out to target practice every other day.

I must say I got better and better. Perhaps the raging woman in me was emerging, or perhaps my raging fear of an imminent attack was simply helping me to focus.

Whichever. I was now a darn good shot.

Even Stash was impressed. "Honey, when you first started target practice I didn't think you could hit the broad side of a cow from six feet away." He put an arm around my shoulder and looked right down at me. His eyes twinkled. "Now I do."

❧ 25 ❧

The stars must have been shining just perfectly for a few minutes because I got orders from three other stores for my chocolate. I was now working almost 'round the clock. In deference to the knee-wobbling fear that Caroline's premonition had given me, I gave up my newspaper route. Reaching out to shove a newspaper into a box and having someone (Robert) reach out to strangle me had little appeal.

I woke early in the morning, did my chores around the farm with a gun strapped to my waist, prepared my chocolates, drove to Story Hour, came home, cared for Aunt Lydia, and then whipped up those chocolate desserts, truffles, brownies, penises, and breasts until the wee hours of the morning.

I paid a young high-schooler in town to drive the chocolate orders to Portland so I wouldn't have to be away from Aunt Lydia. She had good days and bad days. Sometimes very bad days. She complained that she was a burden, and I always assured her she wasn't.

Because that was—*is*—the truth. Aunt Lydia will never, ever be a burden to me. It is an honor to care for her. I told her that, and she knocked me on the head with a weak fist.

"Now you're getting all sentimental on me, but I love you, too. Just quit with all that crap."

Dean called me at least twice a day to chat, to laugh, to check up on Aunt Lydia and the kids and Katie and Stash and Caroline and me. But it was in the late evenings, usually after Stash and I got Aunt Lydia settled, that Dean and I really talked. In one way, our conversations were routine. We shared what we had done that day, but everything I said, everything he said, seemed to be charged with that electricity, that awareness, that oomph, that makes being together so much fun, so exciting. I did not tell him about Caroline's premonition, and I made the other women swear they wouldn't, either. I also had not told him about the dead cat, or stabbed chicken, or the letters that continued to arrive, now one a day.

He told me he missed my kisses and missed them so much he could barely make his opening statement in a trial the day before. He told me that he needed to hug me because nothing seemed right without one of my hugs. He told me that I was the first person he had been able to talk to in a long, long time.

I wasn't surprised by this. Although I could see how Dean Garrett would have many admirers, he was the lone-wolf sort.

I happened to like lone wolfs.

On weekends when he came out to Golden, we were together. He took me to restaurants, cooked me dinners at home, and invited Shawn and Carrie Lynn out with us for day trips. They were slowly but surely beginning to trust him, although Carrie Lynn didn't say much. He taught them how to ride horses and run a tractor. I taught them how to make chocolate.

We figured they would probably be cocoa farmers when they were older.

When I was with Dean I felt safe. When he was gone, that old fear came back, like hundreds of tiny little, freezing-cold knives running up and down my back. The police patrolled in front of our house on a regular basis, and I made sure I stuck to well-populated roads wherever I went. I kept a gun in the top drawer of my dresser, and I knew where Aunt Lydia had hidden the other ones. We had to lock all of them up because of the kids, but I had the keys with me all the time. Stash spent every night at our house to help Aunt Lydia.

I was on high alert, but living. Still living.

But sometimes the living have to deal with evil, and my day was coming.

A couple of weeks later, an exhausted-looking Stash took Aunt Lydia to the hospital. Her chemotherapy had made her ill and dehydrated, and she needed much more care than we could provide. Dr. Ray of Sunshine had ordered her in and, surprisingly, she agreed to do what he told her to do. "Dr. Ray of Sunshine is a demanding boy, a willful and stubborn boy," she said, her voice so weak I could barely hear it. "I'm only going because he says he misses me."

I bent down to hug and kiss her and tried not to cry.

"Wear your Protection Wreath," she whispered to me. "Don't take it off. The knife is imbedded on the right-hand side of the wreath, right by the orange bow. The orange is for courage."

I nodded my head, couldn't speak.

Stash and I had been up all night for many nights caring for Aunt Lydia, and I was so worried about her, I felt ill. There's something about watching someone you love more than life itself go through cancer treatment, dealing with your own Dread Disease, and wondering when a psychopath will walk through your door that makes one a little crazed.

It was my plan to finish my work on the farm, then head for Portland. Katie would watch Shawn and Carrie Lynn for the weekend. Scrambler and Dave would watch after the farm animals. Marie would take care of Alphy and the birds and, she reassured Aunt Lydia, she would spend time chatting with Melissa Lynn and the piglets.

Out of respect for Aunt Lydia I wore the beautiful Protection Wreath she had made me, then went out to the ladies in their little barns. They clucked around my feet. I had spent some extra time with Melissa Lynn and her piglets that morning, as Aunt Lydia had asked. I knew we would not be eating any of them for Christmas. We would eat a Nameless Pig, as Aunt Lydia liked to say.

I finished collecting the eggs and turned around to set the carton on a nearby shelf before cleaning up a little.

"Hello, Cannonball Butt."

The words sent icicles shooting through my body. My breath caught. Even the ladies went quiet.

And then, as if sensing my abject fear, they clucked and clucked as if they'd never clucked before and would never get the chance again so they had to get all their clucks out then.

I turned and faced Robert.

He was even better-looking than I remembered. Everyone had always been surprised when gorgeous Robert had introduced me as his girlfriend. What was a man who looked like Robert doing with me? I could hear them asking themselves.

Tall, fit, black hair, hard jaw, piercing, cold gray eyes. He was magazine-cover gorgeous. But when you looked closer, you saw an alarming combination of shallowness, vanity, and rage. It was amazing how I'd convinced myself in the beginning not to see it.

"Long time, no see, Possum." He picked up a chicken and broke its neck. The ladies didn't like this and clucked even louder.

I had forgotten my gun. The knowledge hit me like a hammer to the gut. In the hurry and worry of getting Aunt Lydia off, I had left it in my bedroom.

I backed up two paces as he took three steps toward me,

then stopped. I would not back down to this Monster-Creep again, I told myself. Not again. The cold spread to every little atom of my body.

"What? Can't talk?" He kicked a chicken aside, as if he were kicking a football, the violence of his action at odds with the pleasant smile on his face. "I thought you would greet your long-lost fiancé with a little more enthusiasm. A hug maybe? Or a kiss?"

I shuddered. "What are you doing here, Robert?"

He laughed, the sick laugh you often hear in horror flicks, a laugh that indicates the evil murderer has completely lost it. "Well, I came here to reclaim my fiancée. It's that simple. And now that I've found you, I think we'll go. I can't stand farm life. It's dirty. It smells. It's so low-class. I can see why you feel comfortable here. But it's not for me, which means it's not for you, either."

He was now about five feet away. "It's for me, Robert. And I'm not leaving."

"Sure you are, baby. You sure as hell are." He picked up another chicken, then dropped it on his swinging foot. The ladies were now officially flipping out. *Cluck, cluck, cluck!*

I wanted to kill him. I loved those chickens. I felt my own anger rising, the cold in my body receding at the sight of his cruelty to the chickens.

He smiled again, the smile spreading across his features. The eerie look in his eyes made the smile sickeningly scary. I stifled a sob.

"Did you honestly think that you could run away from me, you bitch?"

"Yes, I did." I started edging toward a shovel I knew was always hung on a rafter to my right.

Robert laughed. "I always knew you were stupid, Julia. You get that from your trailer-trash background. That damn slut of a mother of yours. But you're wrong. You can't escape. I found you, didn't I?"

"Get out of here, Robert. I don't want you here. I don't

want to see you again." The words were brave, but I cursed the way they wobbled their way out of my mouth. Panic does that to a person, though. Words wiggle wildly. I almost laughed at my clever alliteration, but as I could see I was soon going to have the shit beat out of me, the semi-hysterical laughter was lost somewhere in the muscles of my throat.

He lunged then, and I turned to run, but he caught hold of me, both hands encircling my throat, the Protective Wreath I'd sworn I'd wear falling to the ground. I grabbed his wrists and pulled, but he just squeezed my neck harder.

"Let go of my wrists, whore," he said, so pleasantly.

"No," I whispered. "Let go of me."

He squeezed again.

I could feel my eyes starting to bug, my air supply constricting even more. I dropped my hands.

He laughed then, cocked his head. The look in his eyes said to me, *I can kill you with my bare hands. And I'll enjoy doing it, too.*

"You cunt. You think that you can humiliate me the way you did? Walk out on our wedding day without any consequences? Walk out on the love we shared without getting a payback in return?" He smiled down at me, then bent his head. I turned my face at the last second, and he kissed my cheek.

As a punishment, he tightened his hands. I tried to kick him as hard as I could in the shins, but he saw it coming and kicked me back. He was wearing boots, so when I heard a crack in my own shin I wasn't surprised. When I put weight on that leg I had to slam my teeth together, the pain ricocheting right up my body as if a knife had sliced me in two.

"Don't ever do that again," he whispered. He kept one hand around my neck and with the other he ripped my shirt from top to bottom, the buttons flying off into the darkness of the barn.

He studied my boobs, heaving in a new pink lace bra I had bought—just in case I disrobed again in front of Dean. It was silly to be wearing that bra to the barn, but I had taken to wearing pretty bras. For the first time in my life I felt like celebrating my boobs, although not at that exact second. Between the excruciating pain in my shin and the pressure on my neck, I was not in a good place. Not good at all.

And then out came a knife, glinting like silver fire in Robert's hands. He released my neck, then pulled at the front of my bra, slitting it right open.

The watermelons fell out, and I instinctively wrapped my arms around my chest.

"Don't hide from me, Cannonball," he soothed, taking another step closer. I backed up until I was against the wall of the barn. He put the knife back into a holder, then shoved a knee into my crotch. I screamed in pain, but that didn't slow him down. He held my wrists behind my back with one hand. I struggled and he laughed, hitting me across the face with an open palm.

I saw those stars again, but it was not my good fortune to slide into unconsciousness.

"I have missed your breasts, baby," he said, taking one breast into his vile hand, kneading it with his fingers until I cried out. He laughed again, then bent down to my nipple and bit down on it. I instinctively struggled, tried to kick out at him, while tears streamed down my face as if I'd turned into a darn waterfall.

To show me he was in control he bit down until I froze, the pain wrenching.

With his teeth still chomped down on my nipple, he hissed, "We're gonna do it right here, you slut, right here in the barn where you live. Right here with all these damn chickens." He released my nipple and my hands, then grabbed my pants and yanked them down to my ankles.

I tried to push him, to turn away. "Get away from me, Robert! Get away from me! I hate you! God, I hate you!"

"You hate me?" he said between pants, then whacked me in the face with his palm again. It knocked me to the ground.

I tried to grab for my pants, but he was on me too quick. "Good. That will make for better sex. I like a woman who fights. You were always so pathetic before, so limp in bed, just like a doll."

I could tell the very thought of my fighting excited him, and if I had any doubt at all, his hard dick pressed against me confirmed it. I felt the bile rising in my throat as one of his hands slid down my stomach.

I fought then, knowing I had nothing to lose. I tried to kick him, tried to wriggle away, tried to hit him in the face, but he caught both of my wrists and held them high above my head. "You've lost weight, Julia." His ice-gray eyes stared into mine. I could feel his dick trying to force its way through my underwear. "For who, dammit? Are you cheating on me? Were you cheating on me back in Boston? You slut. You're just like your fucking mother."

He pushed against me again, and my whole body arched up. The chickens were clucking all around us, and Robert released one of my wrists to swat at one. Had I thought about it, I know I wouldn't have done what I did, but I didn't have time to think. I grabbed at the wreath, felt the knife, yanked it out, and drove it into Robert's side as hard as I could.

I was feeling so woozy from being hit on the side of my face that my strength was about nil. I could not have punctured him by more than an inch, but the shock whitened his face as he realized what I'd done. To my own shock, I twisted the knife as his hand raised to slap me, and he screamed in pain. I used his pain to my advantage, wriggling away and pulling the knife with me.

I kept that knife front and center as I yanked up my pants with one hand, my breath coming in short gasps. "Don't come near me, Robert," I panted. "Get away or I will kill you. I. Will. Kill. You."

He stumbled to his feet. His hand was soaked with blood, which dripped down his leg. He stared at his hand as if he'd never seen it before, then looked at me. I buttoned my pants and tried not to think about the fact that I was cornered in the barn.

Then suddenly he laughed, his face full of delight. A sick, twisted sort of delight. And as quick as lightning hits the ground, then gets sucked back up into the atmosphere, Robert lunged at me. The knife went flying out of my hand, and Robert was on top of me, his twisted face an inch from mine.

"God, I love this, Beaver Face. I love you fighting me. We're going to do this again and again." He ground his hips against mine. "I had no idea you had this kind of fire in you, no idea." He bent his head to kiss me, and it was that kiss that did it. I didn't want Robert to touch my lips. Kissing was too personal, too intimate. The only one I wanted kissing me on the mouth was Dean Garrett. Ever. Only Dean Garrett.

So I screamed. Screamed in fear and frustration and the utter despair that was welling up in my body. I knew no one was around to hear, but I screamed anyhow. Robert tried to cover my mouth, so I bit him, and he cracked me again on the face with his fist.

And then, as everything started going black, and this time I feared that I would pass out and would wake up naked and beat up, or wake up dead and in heaven, I saw Caroline standing above me. Shock made the scream die in my throat as she raised both hands up and then brought something down as hard as she could on Robert's head. Robert slumped onto my body. The last thing I remember is looking into Caroline's deep green, worried eyes, and I noted to myself that neither one of her eyes was twitching.

And then I let myself pass out.

What else is a girl to do?

I didn't get to sleep long. When I could pry an eye open again, I noticed that Caroline was dragging me out of the barn by my ankles, hay all the way up my shirt. I wanted to go back to sleep because my whole body was aching, but she saw my eyes open and she bent over me, her face panicked and white.

"Help me, Julia," she said, panting, sweating. "Help me get you out of here. I hit that bastard with a shovel, but he'll probably only be out for a few minutes. Please, Julia, please. Honey, get up. We have to get you to the hospital and call the police."

She yanked me by the shoulders, and I remember thinking that Caroline was such a great friend, and she looked so worried, that I would do as she said. That very second. But as soon as I stood up, I fell back down again because my shin felt like it had been split in two, and my head was spinning like a top and aching as if someone had stuck an ice pick in it, and my vagina felt broken, but she helped me up again.

When I was finally standing, swaying on my feet, I dared to look back into the barn, and I could see Robert lying flat on the ground. His head was moving, back and forth, like an angry bull, like he was trying to wake up, and that galvanized me like nothing else.

Leaning heavily on Caroline, I hopped out of the barn. This task was made even more difficult because I could see out of only one eye. I figured it was because the other was swollen shut and because my brain felt like it was on fire, but I didn't think about it much. Caroline shoved me into her car and slammed the door.

She locked the doors as soon as she was in, and we roared off, using her cell phone to call the police and an ambulance.

We met the ambulance in front of the general store, which had, of course, attracted a crowd of townspeople. My body was throbbing with pain, and everything looked fuzzy to me, but it was not so fuzzy that I couldn't see the townspeople's utter shock and horror when they looked at me slumped in Caroline's passenger seat. I tried to remember to keep my shirt pulled together. I heard several women start to cry.

Scrambler's face appeared before me, intense and furious.

"The man who did this is at Lydia's?" he asked Caroline, his voice still well-modulated, almost harmonious.

She nodded. "He's in the barn."

"Let's go and visit the man in Lydia's barn, shall we?" Scrambler said to the two other ranch hands who were with him.

The paramedics took one look at me, and one ran for the stretcher. Caroline and I were speeding toward the hospital within seconds. I figured that since I was in an ambulance and on my way to a hospital, it was now completely safe to pass out, at least for a while.

So I did.

When I awoke, a number of nurses and doctors were all peering down at me as if I were a specimen in a Petri dish doing something scientifically fascinating. Tubes were flying out of my arm, and an oxygen mask was over my face. I think I even had one up my vagina, but I sure wasn't going to look. Pain splintered through my head, my shin, and my breast.

And then the Dread Disease hit. My heart started to race like it was in a dead sprint. I couldn't breathe, and I became freezing-cold. The doctors and nurses jumped into action, and I prepared for my death as I heard a nurse say, "Her heart rate is escalating. It's at a hundred and seventy . . . eighty . . . ninety . . . two hundred . . ."

Two doctors ran out the door, then ran back in pushing a giant machine with those electroshock things they put on people's chests when they're having a heart attack. Four other people poured into the room, all looking at the machines, all shouting at each other, touching my chest, my face.

"She's cold and clammy . . . heart rate is two hundred . . . blood pressure is normal. . . ."

And then, suddenly, as usual, I could breathe again. The air poured down my lungs, I felt my body go limp, my legs stopped shaking, my hands started to sweat.

As I relaxed, I saw the doctors' and nurses' faces relax, too.

Finally, one young doctor with horn-rimmed glasses leaned over me. "How long have you had panic attacks, Miss Bennett?"

Panic attacks. That's what I had. Later that night, as I was watching Letterman, I started to laugh. I laughed again and again.

Panic attacks.

The nurses and the doctors had explained what they were. Every symptom they spoke of—racing heart, sweating palms, trembling, feeling like you're going insane, not being able to breathe—was something I had experienced.

For some people, panic attacks appear to be genetic. Sometimes women can trace them back to their mother and grandmother and great-grandmother, who might have complained about having "spells" where they would have to lie down. For others, panic attacks are caused by a prolapsed mitral valve or hormones or menopause. For still others—me included, apparently—they were caused by life.

Stressful, freaked-out, whacked-out, out-of-control, unhappy lives. It was the body's way of saying, "I've had it."

But, the doctors told me, patting my hands, smiling. I could get rid of them.

One of the nurses wiped the tears from my face.

"So I don't have some dreadful disease? I don't have cancer? I'm not dying?"

"No, no, no," said one of the nurses, an African American with the brightest white teeth I'd ever seen. "Except for the injuries that boyfriend of yours gave you, you are good to go."

Good to go.

I needed rest, they told me, and peace, and maybe a little sedative. I nodded at the sedative. "Bring me a couple," I told them. *Bring me a hundred*, my brain cried out. *Even a thousand.*

But a huge weight had suddenly been lifted from my shoulders. Not even my cracked shinbone could diminish my joy. I knew what had caused my panic attacks: Robert.

And Robert was now in jail, Oregon-style. Rich daddy would not be able to buy him out or buy any favors.

I was free.

❧ 26 ❧

Although I was free of Robert, I had a tiger of a different sort to deal with.

Caroline had called Dean in Portland right after I was admitted to the hospital and he came immediately. In fact, he arrived at the hospital so quickly I shuddered to think of how fast he had driven. I made a tired crack about this, my voice raw, and he told me a friend had flown him into town.

I nodded, closed the one eye that was not already swollen shut. I did not want Dean to see me like this, did not want to bring him into this ugly part of my life. I did not want him to feel sorry for me. In particular, I did not want him to be angry with me as I had not been open, in any of our many, many conversations, about Robert's continual harassment of me.

I wanted our relationship to be pure, good. Pure, honest goodness. Now, Dean could make the argument that a relationship that was "pure, good" would also involve honesty, and I would definitely have to concede that point.

He was kind and gentle when he saw me, hugging me close, his cheek on mine, our tears blending together as they ran down our faces.

That lasted for two days. But by the third day, Dean Garrett, my very own Paul Bunyan, had something to say. He paced in front of my hospital bed, and from where I lay, with my leg up, my stitches bandaged, my neck in a brace, he looked so, well, yummy, I could have eaten him. I just wished, so wished, that he wasn't angry.

Strong, lithe, commanding, tough-looking Dean Garrett strutting across the room, running his hands through his hair in agitation, was sex in motion. I wanted to grab him and hug him and never, ever stop hugging him.

I couldn't help smiling.

"Stop smiling, Julia," he said in a clipped voice. "I am so damn mad at you."

I tried to stop smiling. But there was so much to be grateful for. Robert had been arrested for assault. Here in Oregon, they don't screw around. Mommy and Daddy were flying in the lawyers, but no amount of hotshot lawyers could alter the fact that Robert's fingers were on the letters and the boxes where the dead cat and chicken had been.

No amount of hotshot lawyers could alter the fact that Caroline had seen him pummel my face.

And no amount of lawyers could explain away how my leg had been broken, my face busted, and my nipple damn near bitten off, especially since there were actually teeth marks on my skin. Though I knew they would try.

But currently, Robert was in jail, and I, unbelievably, was alive. Aunt Lydia was feeling much better, and she and Stash were taking a lunch break in the hospital's cafeteria when Dean arrived in my room.

"I know you're mad at me, Dean," I said. I also wanted to tell him that I wasn't wearing any panties under my hospital gown and that if my leg hadn't been up in a sling and I hadn't had bandages covering half my face, I would have felt downright sexy.

Dean Garrett could always set that vagina of mine on fire.

He stopped pacing and sat on the edge of my bed. I wished he would hold my hand, but he didn't.

"You should have told me."

I nodded. He was upset, and I felt really, really bad.

"You should have told me that you were getting the letters."

I nodded again, feeling worse.

"You should have told me about the chicken with a knife in its neck."

I nodded. Now I felt bad and scared.

"You should have told me that he mailed you a dead cat."

I nodded again, still scared. Still feeling bad.

"Why didn't you tell me?"

I took a deep breath, then told him the truth: That I didn't want him dragged into the messy part of my life. That I didn't want to taint what we had with my past. That our relationship was too new to burden it with the news of a psychotic ex-fiancé.

"Those excuses aren't good enough for me, Julia."

I closed my eyes, preparing myself. *Here it comes. Dean is going to walk out and have nothing more to do with me.* I felt a sense of loss that I had never before experienced.

"I would have protected you, Julia. I would have moved you to the city with me. I would have sent investigators out looking for him. I would have hunted him down myself. I would have kept this from happening."

I had emasculated Dean Garrett. I hadn't meant to, but I had.

"You didn't share with me what was really going on in your life. You didn't trust me, Julia."

"I did. I do. Please, Dean," I tried, knowing I was losing him.

He shook his head, kissed me on the forehead. But it wasn't the kiss of a lover, it was the kiss of a friend. A friend who forgave you, but wouldn't forget what you'd done.

I wanted to plead with him, beg him, but his expression—guarded, hurt, showing reined-in anger—told me it would be useless.

I looked into those cool blue eyes, eyes that had always warmed up when he'd looked at me before but were now cold and distant. I realized that I'd hurt him horribly. Dean Garrett was an old-fashioned kind of guy, the kind of guy that is almost now extinct. He wanted to protect home and hearth, and his woman in that home and hearth. I hadn't let him be the man.

As dated as that sounded, it was the truth. I hadn't leaned on him, hadn't asked him for help, hadn't been truthful. And it hurt him.

"Dean," I put my hand on his face, ran my thumb over his lips, tried to memorize how they felt. I summoned up the courage to tell him the truth. "I love you."

My words fell into silence. Then Dean turned and buried his face in his hands, his back to me.

I was going to say more, but Aunt Lydia and Stash burst into the room. "Turn on the TV!" Aunt Lydia boomed. "Katie called us. Quick, do it, Stash!"

Stash turned on the TV. Dean sat up straight, and I sighed. What on earth could possibly be on TV that I had to watch?

And then I saw America's most beloved talk-show host. She was wearing white and looked gorgeous, which was nothing new. What was new was that she was eating a box of chocolates. I sat up. The gold box with the little gold stars she was holding was one that I had created.

Amelia Zaphyl held up a chocolate cat. The camera took a close-up shot. The hostess laughed and took a bite. A look of pure heaven came over her features. "These are the best chocolates I have ever had in my life. I feel bad about eating a cat, but it is totally worth it, folks. Look at this one!"

Next she held up a tiny chocolate mouse, then a dog, then a monster. I had put the monster in the gold box of chocolates with the cat and dog and mouse just for fun.

"Folks, I've got more to show you," Amelia said, laughing. "Chocolates like this don't come around every day." Then she held up the chocolate penis and the chocolate boobs and the chocolate bottoms I had made. The censor sent a fuzzy ball over the front of them so the viewer couldn't quite make out what she was looking at, but the hostess explained it succinctly.

"Delicious," she said again. "This chocolate is better than an orgasm. I am not kidding. No, don't laugh. This chocolate is better than an orgasm. It is called 'Julia's Chocolates.' The woman who makes this chocolate is named Julia Bennett. She lives in a tiny town called Golden, in Oregon. She's got a paper route, and she works as a storyteller at the library, and in her spare time she makes chocolates that taste like orgasms. I am not kidding you, folks."

How she knew all this I didn't know, but I didn't think about it too long. On the Internet you can find out anything about anyone in seconds. Of course, why would me and my former paper route be on the Internet? Again, I didn't ponder it for too long. This moment would have been perfect if only Dean had held my hand and smiled at me.

"You gotta get some. I feel odd eating chocolate breasts, I will admit," she went on. "But they are fabulous breasts. Splendidly fabulous."

The show cut to a commercial, and there was silence in the room. I knew my mouth was hanging open. Aunt Lydia turned to me, shaking her bald head. Stash turned and smiled, his whole face lighting up. In Dean's eyes I saw a deep joy and pride and something else I wanted to see more of.

"Damn, Julia," Stash said, slapping both hands on his thighs in delight. "It looks like you're in the chocolate business!"

I was soon buried in orders for chocolate. All day, every day, except when I was napping off the effects of Robert's fists and teeth, I made chocolate. Aunt Lydia insisted on helping me. I offered her half a share in my company. She declined. I begged her. She declined. I insisted. She declined again.

So I made her my highest-paid, and only, employee.

We were quite a pair: Aunt Lydia, bald and fighting cancer, and me, with stitches on my cheek, a crutch under my arm, and my neck in a brace.

On the one hand, it sounds heartless to say that I employed a woman who was battling breast cancer with every single fiber of her frail body. On the other, helping me with the chocolate business, taking orders over the phone and credit card numbers, pouring chocolates into their little molds and wrapping them in little boxes kept Aunt Lydia's mind off her chemotherapy.

It kept my mind off of it, too, although Aunt Lydia's sweet little bald head was a constant reminder.

We were swamped with running a rapidly expanding business, and I had to do interviews over the phone with a vast array of newspapers, local and national, and even two TV national spots that picked me up after hearing about me on Amelia's show.

I put the TV spots off as long as I could because of the damage that Robert had done to my face, but within a week I was on the air.

I made for a good story. The press, of course, found out I had had the guts beat out of me by Robert Stanfield III. As his family was rich and spoiled, and I, as they found out, had come from much humbler beginnings, it was a great sell. Especially since I'd run off on my wedding day. In addition, I was trying to launch my tiny business from my aunt's home, an aunt who was fighting cancer and had giant pigs in her front yard and a bunch of flowering toilets. . . . Well, we were hot commodities.

Because of several story-hungry reporters, a lot of dirty laundry the Stanfield. family had been hiding came up.

When the family tried to deny that Robert had mangled my face and body, three of Robert's ex-girlfriends spoke of abuse, as did an array of women that his father and uncles and brothers had been involved with. To say the least, the family was utterly humiliated and quickly determined that it would be to their detriment to make me out as a psycho-slut, their usual attack against women who protested their beatings at the hands of male family members.

But the biggest surprise came with Caroline.

Caroline's name had been in the local paper because of her role in protecting me. A reporter looked it up for the fun of it and found out who Caroline really was, which made the story even juicier. Caroline, my friend and local pauper who sold her psychic readings and her vegetables and breads to survive and collected coupons like mad and bought used clothing, was none other than Caroline Harper Caruthers, only beloved daughter of Martin and Shirley Caruthers, owners of Caruthers Electronics.

The wealth of the Caruthers family, although very new-money, made Robert's family look like, well, trailer trash.

The press went berzerk when they found out that the Carutherses' billionaire daughter had shunned the high life and lived on almost nothing. Caroline flipped out at all the attention, wished us all well, told us she loved us, and then disappeared for two weeks to some island in the Pacific her family owned. She called every day.

All would have been wonderful except for Dean Garrett.

He saw me home from the hospital but didn't kiss me on the lips at all, even when he left and went back to Portland to a trial he had managed to put off when I was in the hospital. And his eyes had lost their warmth, and his smile had lost the secret sparkle he shared only with me, and our conversations were not charged with that special electricity anymore.

Things were not good. Not good at all.

When I was finally able to get up, I worked and worked, and tried not to think about Dean Garrett, tried not to think about how the phone was so very, very quiet. I thought I would give him some space. I thought I would pretend that he would come back, that he would forgive me.

But pretending didn't change anything, and I was miserable.

It had not been my intent to get involved with any man after Robert. But I had not planned on meeting Dean Garrett, either.

"You're gonna have to go after him," Aunt Lydia told me, as she very carefully filled boob molds with chocolate one afternoon. Although it was cool outside, and had snowed the day before, the sun was streaming through the windows, the firs swaying in the distance, the mountains almost purple.

"He's a man whose testosterone has backed up into his balls. He's hurt, baby. And mad because you didn't give him a chance to be the man he wanted to be around you. You didn't give him a chance to be a part of your real life. You weren't honest with him."

I nodded. Of course she was right.

"I know why you didn't tell him about the King Prick, Julia, and I understand. But he doesn't, not really. You have to tell him you want him, that you love him, that you need him. He's a fine man, honey. And if I could pick one man for you to spend the rest of your life with, I would choose him. He's the stars' winner."

I smiled. Alphy licked my hand, and I patted him. When I was younger, Aunt Lydia always said the stars in the sky were the only things that could pick the winner.

I hugged her, took off my apron, and headed to the bathroom. Within a half an hour, I had my bag packed, my hair washed, and I was hobbling to Portland.

Dean Garrett was so darn sophisticated I could only shake my head in wonderment as I looked around his loft in the middle of the Pearl District in Portland. I had read about "the Pearl." Upscale shops, upscale living, upscale lives.

I knew where he lived, and I had a key to get into his loft. He had given it to me once, telling me he wanted me to come and visit him in Portland.

"Any time, sweetheart," he told me. "Surprise me. I'd love to come home from work and find you there, I really would."

I was too shy, too unable to commit, so I had never done it. As I walked around his two-bedroom loft, I realized now how my never making any move to go to Dean, my making him come to me in Golden all the time, had probably hurt him, too.

And though I liked his loft, liked the modern lines, liked the openness and the view of the river and the city, it had a frigidity about it that I didn't like. I couldn't see Dean here.

Granted, he didn't have a lot of furniture, and the inside looked like a single heterosexual man was living here, which means it was plain and beige, but there was something fundamental about it that didn't appeal to me. I liked the country. The chickens and the pigs. The dewy sunrises and color-streaked sunsets. The space and the clean air and the mountain views. And I liked the peace.

This was fine to visit, but I couldn't see myself living in the city.

But, I told myself, I would, if Dean asked me to live in the city with him, I would do it.

I put the take-out Chinese food I had bought us in the fridge as I didn't know what time he would be returning home, then I flicked on a couple lights, turned the heat up, and lit a few candles. It was raining here in Portland, and for a while I watched the raindrops dripping down the glass. When I felt myself nodding off, I hobbled over to the bedroom, slipped off my clothes, pulled a lacy nightgown over my head, and went to sleep in Dean's bed.

The sound of Dean's keys unlocking the front door woke me up. By then the moon was shining through the window of his bedroom. I could have gotten up and greeted him, but I was too tired, so I sat up and ran my fingers through my hair and waited.

I heard the door shut and his briefcase drop to the floor. I knew he was probably now looking at the place settings I had set out, the box of chocolates in the middle of the table, the wine I had in an ice bucket. I started counting to five, knowing it would take about that long for him to get to the bedroom. By the time I got to three, Dean was walking in.

My first thought was that he looked awful. Even in the dim light I could see that he had lost weight. His face was gaunt. He looked absolutely exhausted as he leaned against the door frame, dark circles under his eyes.

I gripped the sheets and blanket with my hands, suddenly nervous. Suddenly insecure. But then my joy at seeing him again, of even being in the same room with Dean overcame me, and I smiled as my heart tripped and then thudded, in a happy "I love you so much" kind of way.

"Hi, Dean." Yes, what an inane thing to say.

He nodded at me, the corners of his mouth lifting just a bit. He was wearing a beige raincoat and a formal suit, and he looked so darn cute I wanted to eat him up.

"Julia."

We stared at each other for long seconds before I finally looked away. That vagina of mine was on fire again, but this time I was ready to let the good times roll.

"I've seen you on TV several times," he said.

I nodded. Yes, I had seen the interviews, too. Their makeup artists and hair people had gone to town, and I hadn't looked half bad except for my swollen and shut right eye and bruising on my cheek. I had become the unwitting poster child of abused women.

"I've also read the articles about you and Julia's Chocolates. Congratulations. Sounds like you've got yourself a great business."

I nodded again.

"Good for you. How's Lydia?"

I told him, then said, "Are you hungry? I brought dinner."

He smiled, but it was a sad smile. He took off his raincoat, tossed it on a chair, then came and sat down on the edge of the bed. "What are you doing here, Julia?"

How to start? What to say? I probably didn't want to say that my vagina was a hot, liquid mess because then he would think I just wanted him for sex. And I didn't want to say that I was crazy in love with him because that would sound too desperate. And I didn't want to say that I was just passing through because there's no way he would believe it.

I took a deep breath. "I wanted to see you."

He ran his hands over his face.

"I've missed you, Dean."

He nodded, as if he knew, then looked me square in the face. I swear that man had aged since I last saw him, and he looked so darn worn-out I just wanted to pull him right into bed with me and make him sleep for three days.

"I don't want the relationship that we have now anymore, Julia."

I could feel the blood draining from my face. Oh joy! Here I was, dressed in sexy lingerie, in Dean Garrett's bed, and I was being rejected.

"I need to know, Julia, what you want, why you're here."

What did I want? I wanted Dean. Every day.

"I can't be in limbo with you anymore, Julia. You've made absolutely sure that I don't get too close to you, that we never take our relationship to a serious level. I could understand it in the beginning. You'd had a horrible experience with Robert, and you were scared, and rightly so. But you've never trusted me, and I'm beginning to doubt you ever will." I saw him clench his jaw, a pulse throbbing in his temple. "I don't think you and I want the same things out of our relationship."

Fear knotted my stomach. "What . . . wh . . . what do you want?"

He shook his head, then stared at the ceiling, before piercing me again with those eyes. "You tell me first, Julia. And be honest. Lay it on the line, because that's all I want to deal with."

The moonlight slanted in on his face, and he had never looked so beautiful to me. Tough and yet gentle; strong, yet vulnerable. I almost choked on my own poetry, but it was so true.

"I want . . ." I stopped, tried to summon up my courage. Surely I had courage somewhere in my battered body?

He raised his eyebrows at me, wanting me to go on.

"I want you." There. I said it.

I thought he would smile, but he didn't. "You want me? For what? Friendship? You want me to be your boyfriend? You want us to be together, with no real commitment for twenty years, like Stash and Lydia?"

I bent my head and let my curls hide my face while I thought. Being in the hospital had given me so much time to think. Now that my greatest fear was fuming behind bars I felt like I could dream again. Live again. Have a future.

"Julia?" he prodded.

So Dean wanted the truth. The very truth. Then I would give it to him. "I want to get married. I want to have at least four children. I want to live in the country with a few of Melissa's Lynn's piglets and a bunch of chickens. I'd also like five lambs. I want to run my chocolate business. I want to go to Psychic Night each week. I want to laugh and sing and dance outside. I want to roll in the sand at the beach and make snow angels. I want to learn how to make decent cinnamon rolls and plant a giant garden. But, most of all, I want you, Dean. I really, really want you."

His face relaxed during my little speech. I held my hands together nice and tight so he wouldn't see them shake. He smiled a little smile again, but this time he actually looked somewhat happy.

"You didn't mention love. Don't you want love?"

Oh, God, did I! So much! "Yes, I want love. Your love in particular, Dean. Loving you has been the greatest thing I have ever done in my entire life. I love loving you." I spoke from the heart, and I could almost feel my heart still, waiting for his answer before it beat again.

And when he did speak, when he covered my hands with his and kissed me smack on the lips, long and slow, I heard all I wanted, or needed, to hear.

"I love you, Julia. I loved you from the first day I met you when you were covered in chicken shit, and I will love you my entire life. Always, always, always I will love you."

He bent to kiss me again, and it was the greatest kiss any man has ever given a woman, I am sure of it. We decided to make love all night, with breaks for dinner and, of course, chocolates.

❧ 27 ☙

Lara showed up at Aunt Lydia's house three weeks later. We ran out to greet her, our aprons dotted with melted chocolate and various colored icings we were using to make different colored nipples for boob chocolates, and gave her a huge hug.

We had to stop and gape at her outfit, which was a pure city look: black boots, black leather coat, a jade green halter type of shirt with long sleeves, and way cool jeans. She had let her hair grow and was wearing makeup beautifully applied. Yes, Lara Keene was a stunner.

And she had never looked so miserable.

Pale, and way too skinny, and tired—so tired.

"You're pale, and way too skinny," Aunt Lydia told her. "And you look tired. Don't you ever sleep in New York? Come on in. You need some chocolate."

We made small talk until the three of us were settled at Aunt Lydia's table with chocolates and wine. A couple of birds flew overhead, but we largely ignored them.

"New York was fabulous," Lara said, her voice quiet. "My art sold everywhere."

We nodded.

"New York itself is fabulous."

We nodded again.

"I loved living with my brother and his partner and meeting all their friends. They were fabulous."

We nodded again. I was about fabulous-ed out, though.

She made a choking sound in her throat, then massaged her neck.

"What?" Aunt Lydia and I said at the same time. Lara said something, but we couldn't catch it. Then she repeated herself.

"I said that I can't live without Jerry. I can't live."

Aunt Lydia and I leaned back in our chairs. Two birds who had refused to go back into their cages that morning chirped from the corner of the room.

"Well, then, what are you going to do?" Aunt Lydia asked. "If you're confused, summon the strength in your breasts, ask your estrogen for answers, demand that your femininity give you advice."

Lara nodded. "I thought I hated living here. I hated how small it was. I hated how I had to work all the time. How I was the church secretary and in charge of Sunday school and the choir and women's groups. I couldn't stand it anymore."

Sheesh. No wonder. I wouldn't be able to stand it, either. Being a minister's wife definitely had its dreary moments.

"I wanted to be me. I wanted to be an artist. I wanted freedom and success and an exciting life."

"And?" Aunt Lydia asked.

"I found that I can't have an exciting life without Jerry. I was so lonely in New York for him I thought my loneliness would eat me alive. I was so . . . empty, so dead. All these exciting things were happening to me, and all I wanted to do was tell him, because I knew he would be happy for me. All I thought about was Jerry, in fact. When I was painting, I thought of him. When I was out at dinner with my brother and his friends, I would think of Jerry. When I was at galleries or on the phone or even peeing I would think of Jerry. I couldn't sleep at night for more than three hours because I can't sleep without him. I was lonely in bed. I can't live without hearing his voice, without laughing with him, without planning a future with him."

Lara pushed her hair off her face. She had lost too much weight, she looked skeletal.

"I met so many men in New York, and they all made my skin crawl. All of them. What should I do? I love Jerry, I miss him, but I don't think he can forgive what I did." The last came out in a squeak as she buried her head in her hands. "I don't know what to do."

"Ah ha!" Aunt Lydia pointed both pointer fingers in the air. "This is the simplest answer to any problem I have ever heard."

"It is?" Lara snapped her head back up.

"It is?" I echoed. "But Lara doesn't like her life here in Golden, she doesn't like working in the church all the time and being a minister's wife. She doesn't like that she can't be herself. She wants to be an artist, she wants an exciting life. She loves Jerry and can't live without him, but she can't live with him here, either. How can she combine all of that and make it work?"

"You young women don't know how to feel your feminine juices any more," Aunt Lydia said, wiggling her fingers. "This culture, this fast and stupid culture, that judges people on their net worth not their *net character* has beat it right out of you."

"What should my feminine juices be saying to me?" Lara asked.

"Your feminine juices are saying this." Aunt Lydia took Lara's hands. "Grab the love."

"Grab the love?"

"Yes, dear." Aunt Lydia's face softened. "Grab the love. Hold on tight. Treasure it. Put that love you have for your husband first, arrange everything else around it, and all else will work out. Love must be cradled and nurtured and enjoyed and danced with. Never, ever, forget the love. It's why we want to live."

Lara nodded. She left five minutes later.

❧ Epilogue ❧

Six months later

Sometimes, somehow, real life works out. If only for a few months, a few weeks, a few days, a few moments, life is sweet.

And, that's how it became for me.

It looked like Aunt Lydia had conquered Roaring Radiation, Creepy Chemo, and Cancer. Stash insisted they have almost no engagement time, so the two were married in his barn. All the Psychic Night women were attendants, and everyone in town received an invitation. Lydia wore a bright purple dress and a red hat. Stash wore a tux. Shawn was the ring bearer, Carrie Lynn the flower girl.

When Jerry finished leading them in their vows, Stash cried, picked Aunt Lydia up, and swung her around. He kissed her, kissed her again, kissed her once more, and Jerry had to break those two up before things got R-rated up there.

Lara and Jerry were back together. Three months earlier, she had had an art show inside the church, and it had been jammed. As she had made something of herself in New York, the state paper did an article on the show, and a lot of people from Portland had come down for it. Every painting sold out. Jerry was the proudest-looking husband I have ever seen. She donated 10 percent of the sales to the church.

Lara had made other changes in their lives, which Jerry seemed perfectly happy to accept. During the day she worked on her art. She wore the clothes she wanted to wear and tossed out all her prissy sweaters. One evening a week, she ran choir practice. She made changes there, too. She taught the choir how to rock out. No more of these boring, depressing church hymns. No, Lara picked popular Christian music, recruited townspeople who knew how to play electric guitars and drums and violins and flutes, gave a few people with excellent throat pipes solos, and that church rocked every Sunday. They had to add another service.

The only person who grumbled was Linda Miller. She took her complaints to one women's group after another in the church, but no one listened to her. Jerry eventually heard about it, told Linda he didn't think the church was a good fit for her, and suggested she leave.

She was flabbergasted, shocked. More shocked when she told other people what that young uppity minister had told her and the only response she got from them was that they thought she should leave, too.

So Linda Miller left. And soon Lara heard from people at the church in another town what a pain in the ass Linda was and would Jerry and Lara take her back?

Lara had made her peace, and she was finally happy.

Katie lost about forty pounds and had never felt better. She was in love with Scrambler, and he with her. Despite what she'd said earlier about not needing to hear the words "I love you" from a man, she told me she loved hearing Scrambler say it. "It's like verbal sex to me, Julia."

Almost as exciting, Katie's book sold to a major publisher. One of her characters was a real-life abusive, alcoholic jerk who happened to say and do exactly what J.D. used to say and do and who just happened to get shot in the groin by the end of the book and lost both balls.

When the news trucks left and Golden returned to normal, Caroline returned from her family's island. She told me later that since our last Psychic Night meeting, before Robert had tried to rearrange my face, she had spent a lot of time in the yoga position with burning candles surrounding her, waiting to hear my cry of help. In the process, she had heard the cries for help from hundreds of other people, whose locations she couldn't ascertain, and whose misery almost sent her over the edge.

But finally my cry for help had penetrated. She told me the cry had been very distant, very faint, but she had recognized my voice and had raced to Aunt Lydia's house.

She had saved me from being raped, maybe killed.

As Chief Sandstrom was in charge of the criminal proceedings and had no intention of letting his prisoner off at all, justice proceeded quickly, and Robert became a guest of the Oregon State Prison system. I learned later he was a poor prisoner and roomed in an isolation cell for much of the time he was incarcerated.

Not even Mommy and Daddy could buy him out that time.

Dean, Stash, Aunt Lydia, Katie, Scrambler, Caroline, Lara, Jerry, and I ended up spending quite a bit of time with Martin and Shirley Caruthers when they came to visit Caroline after her island break. It was Martin and Shirley Caruthers who Caroline had seen on the cover of the magazine in the supermarket.

It was odd at first to be hanging around with people who landed on the covers of magazines, but we found the Carutherses to be lovely people who adored their daughter but couldn't figure her out. Both Martin and Shirley had grown up dirt-poor. They met in sixth grade and married when they were eighteen. They didn't have a dime. But Shirley understood computers, and Martin understood finance, and together they built a company.

They couldn't understand why their daughter chose a basically penniless life—a life they had worked hard to get away from. Still, they were crazy about her.

The Carutherses hung out in Golden for two weeks. Martin liked helping out Stash on the ranch, and Shirley and Caroline helped me and Aunt Lydia with the chocolates. I tried not to let Shirley read my mind, but one day she said to me, "Don't worry, Julia. I'm not trying to read your mind. I wouldn't invade your privacy like that."

Later, as we mixed ingredients for a batch of Chocolate Nut Bars, she said, "My gift is much easier to bear than Caroline's is, and my greatest hope is that one day she will be rid of hers. The way she knows that terrible things are going to happen, her inability to stop it, the way she feels people's anguish, has been horrible for her." Shirley swiped at her eye.

Aunt Lydia looked at Shirley, her eyes narrowed, then started muttering something about cursing away Caroline's "gift" to another universe. I knew what we would be doing at our next Psychic Night.

We all played poker together, but at the end of their vacation in Golden, the Carutherses both refused to play with either Aunt Lydia or Stash as those two always won. I asked Shirley why she just didn't read Stash's mind.

She looked aghast. "That would be cheating!"

Olivia Cutter took my place at Story Hour, with Roxy Bell as her enthusiastic helper.

At first, I heard, Olivia was stiff. But then Carrie Lynn and Shawn came to visit her every day during a school break, and for some weird reason that seemed to give her confidence. She was soon dressing up as a queen to read fairy tales, as a farmer to read farm stories, and she brought in firefighters and police officers to read firefighting and police stories. She also brought in other guest speakers, one of whom brought reptiles. A snake escaped and couldn't be located for a week.

Olivia finally found it near the romance novels.

The reptile man, who seemed to be sweet on her, according to Roxy Bell, was invited back on a monthly basis, the whole event having been very exciting.

Olivia was still very involved with Shawn and Carrie Lynn's lives, coming to their school musical performances, the Open House, and any and all dinners we invited her to. She always brought everyone a book as a gift. Aunt Lydia named a beautiful red bird that she bought at the pet shop "Olivia."

I adopted Shawn and Carrie Lynn, to their delight and mine. About fifty of us went to the courthouse together and then came home for a party. We tied ribbons around the necks of Alphy, Melissa Lynn, and all the piglets. We decided the chickens, now four hundred strong, looked just dandy without ribbons.

My chocolate business was a success. I ended up renting an older building, hired a bunch of people from town who knew more about running a business than I did, and we were off and running.

The chocolate business had an impact on the rest of the town, too. When we renovated the building, with money from Stash and Dean (which made them partners in the business), we built huge floor-to-ceiling glass windows so tourists could come and watch us make the chocolate, put it in the molds, view the conveyer belts, watch employees wrap the chocolates in the boxes, etc. Soon we had quite a good side business going. The tourists ate at the restaurants in town and spent the night to enjoy other attractions in the area.

As for me and Dean, our wedding is a week from Sunday. As in Aunt Lydia and Stash's wedding, Shawn is going to be the ring bearer at the wedding and Carrie Lynn the flower girl. Aunt Lydia is the matron of honor, and Caroline, Lara, and Katie are bridesmaids. Three friends of Dean's will also be in the wedding party, as will Stash.

Katie's older son, Luke, assured me that for this very special occasion he will wear his three very favorite layers of clothes and his three favorite pieces of underwear which he will show me that day. Logan whispered that he would make sure his Spiderman outfit would be extra special clean for my wedding. Haley decided she would branch out and buy new antennas for her head, this time in pink to match her new pink wedding dress, and Hannah, for once, is going to wear purple instead of black.

I am going to wear red—bright, bold, happy, freeing red. Aunt Lydia is making the wreath I will wear on my head, Caroline is making my jewelry, and Katie and Lara are in charge of the decorations in the church. Lara has promised to paint a picture of me and Dean on our wedding day.

I looked up from my desk in The Chocolate Business, as I called it, as Aunt Lydia burst in. Her hair was about an inch long. She was wearing a bright pink T-shirt that said "I Beat Cancer" on the front and "I Am Damn Happy To Be Alive" on the back. She had one for every day of the week in a different color. Her underwear matched her shirts, and she did not hesitate to show anyone her butt who asked to see the underwear. "I don't have time anymore to be worried about how my ass looks, thank God."

"Don't be late tonight, Julia," she said to me, raising her fists in the air. "All work and no play will make your vagina dry up and shrivel into nothing. You don't want that. We all need to keep moist and happy vaginas. Especially with your wedding vows coming up so quick. We must keep the soul of the woman in you healthy and hopeful."

I nodded sagely, not caring if my employees could hear her loud, booming voice. I adored Aunt Lydia, was grateful for every single second I had with that woman, and she could say anything she damn well pleased at any time, even if she insisted on shouting it over the intercom.

"Did you hear the name of our sacred Psychic Night?" she asked, setting a hip on my desk.

I had named two new chocolate boxes after her. Lydia's Chickens consisted of chocolates in the shapes of chickens, eggs, roosters, and wine bottles. Lydia's Life had chocolates in the shapes of pigs, a rainbow bridge with colored icing, toilets with flowers flowing from the top, and a bottle of vodka. They were huge hits.

"No, I haven't heard yet. What's the name of the Psychic Night tonight?"

"Loving Your Clitoris!" She did a little twirl. "It's Loving Your Clitoris Psychic Night. You won't want to be late!"

In this warm, funny, thoroughly candid novel, acclaimed author Cathy Lamb introduces an unforgettable heroine who's half the woman she used to be, and about to find herself for the first time . . .

Two years and 170 pounds ago, Stevie Barrett was wheeled into an operating room for surgery that most likely saved her life. Since that day, a new Stevie has emerged, one who walks without wheezing, plants a garden for self-therapy, and builds and paints fantastical wooden chairs. At thirty-five, Stevie is the one thing she never thought she'd be: thin.

But for everything that's changed, some things remain the same. Stevie's shyness refuses to melt away. She still can't look her neighbors' gorgeous great-nephew in the eye. The Portland law office where she works remains utterly dysfunctional, as does her family—the aunt, uncle, and cousins who took her in when she was a child. To top if off, her once supportive best friend clearly resents her weight loss.

By far the biggest challenge in Stevie's new life lies in figuring out how to define her new self. Collaborating with her cousins to plan her aunt and uncle's problematic fortieth anniversary party, Stevie starts to find some surprising answers—about who she is, who she wants to be, and how the old Stevie evolved in the first place. And with each revelation, she realizes the most important part of her transformation may not be what she's lost, but the courage and confidence she's gathering, day by day.

As achingly honest as it is witty, *Such A Pretty Face* is a richly insightful novel of one woman's search for love, family, and acceptance, of the pain we all carry—and the wonders that can happen when we let it go at last.

**Please turn the page for an exciting sneak peek of
Cathy Lamb's
SUCH A PRETTY FACE,
coming in August 2010!**

I know when it started.

It was June 14th, two days after my tenth birthday. An eerie red-gold haze enshrouded the moon. Frothing grey and black clouds drifted across it, as if they were trying to hide its evilness, but couldn't quite overpower the white light.

I noticed that moon as we sped toward the river, our car careening back and forth over the yellow lines as she chanted and I clung to my terrified sister.

The raindrops came down in drizzles, stopped, then pounded the top of the car, like millions of tiny black cannonballs had been released from the bag of the Devil himself.

"Mommy, stop!" I cried, as she barreled through two red lights.

But she couldn't hear me, not with the other voices clamoring in her head. She whispered, she raged, she yelled at her hallucinations. "Get out of here, Punk. This isn't about you. I'm not getting tied down to that chair again! You won't put your tentacles and ropes on me!"

I tried the other name. "Helen! Can you hear me, Helen?" She didn't respond, smashing her floppy yellow hand down on her head with both hands as we sped on down the highway.

I realized that the voices had won. It had been a long, soul-crushing battle, but I tried anyhow. There was nothing else left to do. "There's no chair! I'll tell Punk to leave and take his ropes and tentacles with him. I'll get him for you!"

"Punk is bad, he's chasing us with his red eyes and he won't let us go. I'll save you, kid!"

We veered again, left and right, back and forth, all over the road, barely missing a truck.

"I scared, Stevie, I scared," my sister whimpered, her little face tucked into my neck.

I was scared, too, so scared I felt like my brain was rattling in my head, my knees knocking together. "It's okay, Sunshine. Grandma and Grandpa will be here soon."

But I knew it wasn't going to be soon enough.

I knew that.

When we got to the middle of the bridge, she slammed on the brakes, the car fishtailed, and we crashed into the rail. She tried to yank us out of the car and Sunshine clutched me, screaming, as I gripped the seat, trying to save us both, my new charm bracelet cutting into my skin. When my hands lost their death grip, I grabbed the door handle, then the door.

Helen was strong, the voices made her stronger, and my fingers were pried away, one by one, Sunshine clinging to my waist. She dragged us to the rail as the angry clouds parted and that strange moon peeked out in the distance, the only witness to our dance with death.

She'd wrapped tin foil around the waist of her black dress and it ripped as we fought her, as we scratched and shrieked. She was wearing her best black heels and they tapped on the wood of the bridge, the black line up her nylons perfectly straight, which was so unusual, so surreal, it scared me more than anything else.

"Now you've made Command Center mad!" she yelled,

wrestling us over to the rail. "Don't destroy the communications!"

We pleaded, we tried to run, and she punched both of us in the face. "Shut up, kid! Shut up, trash heap!" She had never done that to us before and it stunned me into silence, into obedience, for one shattered moment. "They're spying on us! They can see everything!"

I felt dizzy and I wrapped my arms around Sunshine, who was gasping with fright and bleeding. Helen ripped us apart and I knew that what was left of my mother, if there was anything gentle and kind left in her, was way, way back, at the end of a labyrinth of tunnels in her troubled mind, crisscrossing sanity and insanity.

Her arms banded across my chest and my waist as another pelt of raindrops hit me, the wind lifting my skirt up. I didn't recognize the raw, terrified scream that tore from my throat as I squeezed her neck and bony shoulders with my arms, my tears mixing with the rain, her floppy yellow hat flying off into the wind.

"No, Mommy, don't," I begged. "Please, Mommy! Stop!"

"Leave us alone, Punk," she screamed to the moon. "You can't read my mind anymore. You're done. It's all done. Take Command Center with you down to hell."

She heaved my struggling body up on the rail and as my legs dangled over the side of the bridge, she briefly held me close, rocking me like a baby, and kissed me on the lips. I saw Sunshine fight to stand up, blood streaming from her head. She tugged on our mother's arms, kicked her shins. "I hate you! I hate you! Let go of Stevie! Let go of sister!"

Her words flew into the churning sky, swirled around the moon, and then they were gone, making no impact on my mother.

"I am saving you," Helen yelled at me, the stormy wind whipping her blonde hair around her face. "I am saving you from *them*." Then she dropped her head back and hollered, edgy and guttural. "Save yourself. Do not save *it*. Don't save that trash heap." She shoved me over the rail of the bridge, then yanked my hands from around her neck, our fingertips the last to touch before I tumbled and somersaulted into the rushing river.

It was freezing cold and pitch black, the water wrapping me up tight as I plunged to the bottom. My feet never hit and I paddled to the top, choking, sputtering, knowing Sunshine would soon join me.

I had to save her. I had to save Sunshine.

I fought against the water as the current swirled me away, waves splashing against my face, surrounding my body like a wet vice. I twisted in the river's grasp and saw Sunshine, her pink dress billowing out like a bell as she was thrown over the rail into the murkiness of the river. She screamed, high and thin, and it echoed under the bridge.

I swam, my arms pinwheeling as hard as I could toward her but I was panicking, gasping for breath, the water dragging me away, my black hair covering my face.

Between the shadows I saw my mother stand on the rail of the bridge, arms outstretched, head back. The red-gold haze parted and the moonlight illuminated my mother. I couldn't hear her, but I knew she was singing and I knew what song it was.

In some weird corner of my mind I noted her outfit again as she teetered on the rail. She was wearing her black cocktail dress, her best black heels, and her pearls. She got dressed up to kill us, I thought, as another wave swamped me. *She got dressed up to kill us.*

She curved her body, palms together over her head, then dove into the choppy water. I never saw her come up again. They did, however, find her best black heels later. Downriver.

I saw the pink dress but not for very long, as another current came, perhaps the sister current to mine, and swept Sunshine away. I heard her terror, I heard her sobbing my name, I hollered back at her, told her I was coming, promised I would be there, but in the inky darkness, fighting off the chill of the water and the swirling waves, I couldn't get to her.

I heard her death in the rigid silence as soon my ragged voice was the only one left in that tragic, shattered night.

Under that moon with the eerie red-gold haze and those frothing clouds, that's where it all began.

I started inhaling food the next day. Mountains of it.

It continued for over two decades.

And the song my mother was singing?

It was "Amazing Grace."

My mother, after throwing her two kids off a bridge, was singing "Amazing Grace."

GREAT BOOKS, GREAT SAVINGS!

When You Visit Our Website:
www.kensingtonbooks.com
You Can Save Money Off The Retail Price
Of Any Book You Purchase!

- All Your Favorite Kensington Authors
- New Releases & Timeless Classics
- Overnight Shipping Available
- eBooks Available For Many Titles
- All Major Credit Cards Accepted

Visit Us Today To Start Saving!
www.kensingtonbooks.com

All Orders Are Subject To Availability.
Shipping and Handling Charges Apply.
Offers and Prices Subject To Change Without Notice

More by Bestselling Author
Hannah Howell

__Highland Angel	978-1-4201-0864-4	$6.99US/$8.99CAN
__If He's Sinful	978-1-4201-0461-5	$6.99US/$8.99CAN
__Wild Conquest	978-1-4201-0464-6	$6.99US/$8.99CAN
__If He's Wicked	978-1-4201-0460-8	$6.99US/$8.49CAN
__My Lady Captor	978-0-8217-7430-4	$6.99US/$8.49CAN
__Highland Sinner	978-0-8217-8001-5	$6.99US/$8.49CAN
__Highland Captive	978-0-8217-8003-9	$6.99US/$8.49CAN
__Nature of the Beast	978-1-4201-0435-6	$6.99US/$8.49CAN
__Highland Fire	978-0-8217-7429-8	$6.99US/$8.49CAN
__Silver Flame	978-1-4201-0107-2	$6.99US/$8.49CAN
__Highland Wolf	978-0-8217-8000-8	$6.99US/$9.99CAN
__Highland Wedding	978-0-8217-8002-2	$4.99US/$6.99CAN
__Highland Destiny	978-1-4201-0259-8	$4.99US/$6.99CAN
__Only for You	978-0-8217-8151-7	$6.99US/$8.99CAN
__Highland Promise	978-1-4201-0261-1	$4.99US/$6.99CAN
__Highland Vow	978-1-4201-0260-4	$4.99US/$6.99CAN
__Highland Savage	978-0-8217-7999-6	$6.99US/$9.99CAN
__Beauty and the Beast	978-0-8217-8004-6	$4.99US/$6.99CAN
__Unconquered	978-0-8217-8088-6	$4.99US/$6.99CAN
__Highland Barbarian	978-0-8217-7998-9	$6.99US/$9.99CAN
__Highland Conqueror	978-0-8217-8148-7	$6.99US/$9.99CAN
__Conqueror's Kiss	978-0-8217-8005-3	$4.99US/$6.99CAN
__A Stockingful of Joy	978-1-4201-0018-1	$4.99US/$6.99CAN
__Highland Bride	978-0-8217-7995-8	$4.99US/$6.99CAN
__Highland Lover	978-0-8217-7759-6	$6.99US/$9.99CAN

Available Wherever Books Are Sold!

Check out our website at
http://www.kensingtonbooks.com

Romantic Suspense from
Lisa Jackson

See How She Dies	0-8217-7605-3	$6.99US/$9.99CAN
Final Scream	0-8217-7712-2	$7.99US/$10.99CAN
Wishes	0-8217-6309-1	$5.99US/$7.99CAN
Whispers	0-8217-7603-7	$6.99US/$9.99CAN
Twice Kissed	0-8217-6038-6	$5.99US/$7.99CAN
Unspoken	0-8217-6402-0	$6.50US/$8.50CAN
If She Only Knew	0-8217-6708-9	$6.50US/$8.50CAN
Hot Blooded	0-8217-6841-7	$6.99US/$9.99CAN
Cold Blooded	0-8217-6934-0	$6.99US/$9.99CAN
The Night Before	0-8217-6936-7	$6.99US/$9.99CAN
The Morning After	0-8217-7295-3	$6.99US/$9.99CAN
Deep Freeze	0-8217-7296-1	$7.99US/$10.99CAN
Fatal Burn	0-8217-7577-4	$7.99US/$10.99CAN
Shiver	0-8217-7578-2	$7.99US/$10.99CAN
Most Likely to Die	0-8217-7576-6	$7.99US/$10.99CAN
Absolute Fear	0-8217-7936-2	$7.99US/$9.49CAN
Almost Dead	0-8217-7579-0	$7.99US/$10.99CAN
Lost Souls	0-8217-7938-9	$7.99US/$10.99CAN
Left to Die	1-4201-0276-1	$7.99US/$10.99CAN
Wicked Game	1-4201-0338-5	$7.99US/$9.99CAN
Malice	0-8217-7940-0	$7.99US/$9.49CAN

Available Wherever Books Are Sold!
Visit our website at **www.kensingtonbooks.com**